SCOTT

The Cross

A V O N

AVON
A division of HarperCollins*Publishers*
77–85 Fulham Palace Road,
London W6 8JB

www.harpercollins.co.uk

A Paperback Original 2011
1

A catalogue record for this book is
available from the British Library

ISBN-13: 978-1-84756-213-5

Set in Minion by Palimpsest Book Production Limited,
Falkirk, Stirlingshire

Printed and bound in Great Britain

As ever, thanks to my intrepid and tireless editor at Avon, Keshini Naidoo, who luckily for me enjoys the blood and gore of a vampire story even more than I do . . .

Thanks also to Nathan Shallcross at Armed Combat and Tactics UK for expert coaching in some particularly effective and nasty fighting techniques with the European longsword. Learning how to whip an opponent's head off their shoulders with a four-foot blade is definitely the most fun I've ever had researching a novel.

Nearly thirty years of domination ensured that the hallowed traditions of the vampire race were all but eradicated under the rule of the Vampire Federation. Gone were the days when vampires were free to claim the blood of human victims at will, leaving their exsanguinated remains for the crows or turning them into vampires like themselves. Strict laws were laid down by Federation rulers and enforced by VIA, the Vampire Intelligence Agency, with agents like Alex Bishop licensed to hunt down and destroy vampires who flouted the rules.

It seemed as if the vampire way of life had changed forever. Until, that is, the uprising led by rebel vampire Gabriel Stone attempted to drive a stake into the very heart of its hated enemy the Federation. Only the chance intervention of a human, Joel Solomon, wielding an ancient and powerful anti-vampire weapon the legends call the Cross of Ardaich, prevented the complete annihilation of the Federation leaders and a resounding victory for the Traditionalist rebellion.

In the wake of the battle on the ramparts of Gabriel Stone's Romanian castle hideaway, the rebellion has been crushed, the Cross of Ardaich destroyed and the Federation left in tatters. Surviving Federation leaders like Supremo Olympia Angelopolis will declare a victory . . .

But not everyone within the Federation is so sure . . .

Prologue

The village of St Elowen
South-west Cornwall

Where two quiet lanes crossed, just a stone's throw from the edge of the village, the grey stone church had stood more or less unchanged since not long after Henry V had ascended to the throne of England. The glow from its leaded windows haloed out into the frosty November night. From behind its ancient iron-studded, ivy-framed door, the sound of singing drifted on the wind.

Just another Thursday evening's choir practice.

Although that night would be remembered quite differently by those villagers who would survive the events soon to become infamous as 'The St Elowen Massacre'.

Inside the church, Reverend Keith Perry beamed with pride as the harmonies of his fourteen singers soared up to the vaulted ceiling. What many of them lacked in vocal ability, they more than made up for with their enthusiasm. Rick Souter, the village butcher, was the loudest, with a deep baritone voice that was only a little rough and almost in tune. Then there was young Lucy Blakely, just seventeen, giving it all she had. The most naturally talented of them all was little Sam Drinkwater, who in a few weeks' time was set to audition for a place as boy soprano at King's College, Cambridge. Sam's parents, Liz and Brian, were there too, sharing a hymn book as they all belted out 'All Things Bright and Beautiful' to the strains of the electronic organ played by Mrs Hudson, the local music teacher.

The only face missing was that of Charlie Fitch, the plumber. Charlie was normally punctual, but his elderly mother had been quite ill lately; Perry prayed that nothing awful had happened.

That was when the church door banged behind them. A few heads turned to see the man standing at the entrance, watching them all. Mrs Hudson's fingers faltered on the organ keys. Reverend Perry's smile froze on his lips.

The drifter had been sighted on the edge of the village a few days before. The first concerned whispers had been exchanged in the shop and post office, and it hadn't been long before most of St Elowen's population of three hundred or so had heard the talk. The general consensus was that the drifter's presence was somewhat worrying, somewhat discomfiting; and everyone's hope was that it would be temporary. He was unusually tall and broad, perhaps thirty years old. Nobody knew his name, or where he'd come from, or where he was staying. His appearance suggested that he might have been living rough, travelling on foot from place to place like an aimless vagrant. His boots were caked in dirt and the military-style greatcoat he wore was rumpled and torn. But he was no new-age traveller, the villagers agreed. His face was as clean-shaven as a soldier's, and his scalp gleamed from the razor. There were no visible tattoos. No rings in his nose or ears.

Just that look that anyone who saw him found deeply disconcerting. Cold. Indifferent. Somehow not quite right. Somehow – this was the account that had reached Reverend Perry's ears – somehow not quite *human*.

4

Mrs Hudson stopped playing altogether. The voices of the choir fell away to silence as all eyes turned towards the stranger.

For a drawn-out moment, the man returned their gaze. Then, without taking his eyes off the assembly, he reached behind him and turned the heavy iron key. The door locked with a clunk that echoed around the silent church. The man drew the key out of the lock and dropped it into the pocket of that long greatcoat of his.

Little Sam Drinkwater took his mother's hand. Lucy Blakely's eyes were wide with worry as she glanced at the vicar.

Reverend Perry swallowed back his nervousness, forced the smile back onto his lips and walked up the centre aisle towards the man. 'Good evening,' he said as brightly as he could. 'Welcome to St Elowen's. It's always a pleasure to see—'

As the stranger slowly reached down and swept back the hem of his long coat, Reverend Perry's words died in his mouth. Around the man's waist was a broad leather belt. Dangling from the belt, at his left hip, was an enormous sword. Its basket hilt was lined with scarlet cloth. Its polished scabbard glinted in the church lights.

Reverend Perry was too shocked to utter a word more. The man said nothing either. In no hurry, he reached his right hand across his body. His fingers wrapped themselves around the sword's hilt and drew out the weapon with a metallic swishing sound. Its blade was long and straight and broad and had been crudely etched with strange symbols.

Reverend Perry gaped dumbly at the sight of the weapon in his church. He was only peripherally aware of the gasps and cries of horror that had started breaking out among the choir members.

The drifter smiled for the first time. But it was no ordinary smile. Reverend Perry almost fainted at the sight.

The man's teeth were sharp and pointed. Like the fangs of a monster.

And then, in a smooth and rapid motion that was over before anyone could react, the intruder swung the sword.

The chopping impact of the blade was drowned out by Mrs Hudson's scream. Keith Perry's severed head bounced up the aisle and came to a rest between the pews. And the choir exploded into screaming panic.

The drifter held the blade up lovingly in front of his face. He licked the running blood off the steel and swallowed. Began walking slowly up the aisle towards the terrified parishioners.

'The vestry door!' Lucy Blakely shrieked, pointing. Liz Drinkwater grabbed her son's arm tightly as she and her husband fled for the exit at the right of the altar. The others quickly followed, tripping over each other and their own feet in their desperation to get away. Rick Souter snatched up a heavy candlestick. With a scowl of rage he ran at the intruder and raised his makeshift weapon to strike.

The drifter swung the sword again. Rick Souter's amputated arm fell to the floor still clutching the candlestick. The blade whooshed down and back up, slitting the butcher from groin to chin so that his innards spilled across the flagstones even before he'd collapsed on his face.

The drifter crouched over the fallen body to dab his fingers into the pool of blood that was spreading rapidly over the church floor. With a look of passionate joy he smeared the blood over his lips, greedily sucked it from his fingers. Bubbles of it frothed out from the serrated gaps between his teeth and trickled down his chin and neck. Then he stood, raised his face to the vaulted ceiling and his laughter echoed through the whole church.

'You think you're safe in here? Think your *God* will protect you?'

The vestry door was bolted from the outside. Lucy Blakely and the Drinkwaters were desperately trying to force it open, but even as the other choir members joined them, they knew the door wouldn't give. Little Sam howled as his mother clutched him to her. Brian Drinkwater was looking around him in panic for some other way out.

But there wasn't one. They were all trapped in here with the monster.

Charlie Fitch parked his van outside the little church. As he walked briskly down the stone path leading to the door, his mind was still full of his hospital visit to his mother earlier that evening. Thank God she was okay and would be home again soon.

Then Charlie heard the sounds that froze the blood inside his veins. It wasn't the singing of his friends in the choir he could hear from inside the church, nor the playing of the organ. They were screaming.

Screaming in horror and terror. In agony.

He rattled the door handle. The door was locked. He scrambled up the mossy bank behind him so he could peer in through the leaded panes of the stained-glass window.

The sight he saw inside was one that would remain with him until his dying day. The church floor littered with corpses and severed body parts. Blood spattered across the altar, on the pews, on everything.

In the middle of the nightmare stood a man in a long coat. Blood was spattered across his face and his shaven head and the blade of the sword he was swinging wildly at the fleeing, screeching figure of Lucy Blakely. It was surreal. Charlie watched as the girl's head was separated from her shoulders by the gore-streaked blade. Then the madman turned to little Sam Drinkwater, who was kneeling by the bloody bodies of his parents, too frightened to scream.

It wasn't until he witnessed what the man did to the boy that Charlie was able to break out of his trance of horror and run. He ran until his heart was about to burst, fell to his knees and ripped his phone out of his pocket.

Nineteen minutes later, the police armed response unit broke in the church door and burst onto the scene of the devastation. The first man inside nearly dropped his weapon when he took in the carnage in front of him.

Nothing remained of the Reverend Keith Perry or his choir members. Nothing except the horrific gobbets of diced human flesh that were scattered across the entire inside of the church.

The killer was still there. He stood calmly at the altar with his back to the door, stripped naked, bloodied from head to foot. His sword lay across the altar in front of him, gore still dripping from its blade. In his powerful hands he held a blood-filled chalice over his head.

The squad leader yelled 'Armed police! Step away from the weapon!' The man ignored the command and the guns that were aimed at his back. Murmuring softly to himself, he slowly turned his face upwards and tipped the bloody contents of the chalice over his head, drinking and slurping greedily.

'*Who the fuck is this person?*' The squad leader hardly realised he'd spoken those words out loud.

Not until the man at the altar turned round to face him. And said: 'I am a vampire.'

Chapter One

Romania
Five nights later

Sometime in the dead of night, the whistling wind drove away the snow-clouds to unveil the stars. From among the shadows that the moonlight threw across the deep forested valley below, the towers of the ancient castle of Vâlcanul were a craggy silhouette against the distant mountain peaks. All was silent. All was still. A place of desolation and morbidity.

The inert body among the trees, half-covered in snow, was that of a man. His clothes were tattered and bloody. Snowflakes clung to his hair and his eyelashes. His face was deathly pale. He had no pulse. Soon, he might be food for the wolves and other wild things in the forest.

Except that the night creatures knew better than to approach.

Inside the motionless body of the man, something was stirring. Something was awakening, resurfacing from the depths of a sleep so infinitely profound that only a very few could ever return from it. Gradually, his senses began to reanimate. As consciousness returned, he became dimly aware of the softness of the snow under him, of the weight of his body resting on it. A finger twitched. His frosted eyelids fluttered and then opened briefly to a stab of pain from the bright moon and starlight above him. Slowly, he reopened them, and could see again. A long sigh whistled from his lips.

Memories flickered through his mind, weakly at first, gradually gaining strength and clarity. He recalled a name, and realised it was his own.

Joel Solomon.

Joel sat up slowly, snow falling away from his body, and gazed around him at the white-topped forest, at the craggy mountainside and the castle towers perched high above. The road running down through the valley was now invisible under a foot of fresh snow. A few steps from Joel, the wreck of a four-wheel-drive truck lay overturned and half-buried in a snowdrift. He blinked, staring at it. Had he been in a car accident? What had happened to him?

He looked down at the thin sweatshirt he was wearing, and saw it was torn and bloody. Whose blood was this? Some of the holes had been made by bullets, another by a knife slash. He ripped the shirt open; why wasn't he cold? The wounds in his flesh were livid and raw; why wasn't he dead?

The memories grew more vivid. He remembered being up on the castle battlements. A blinding blizzard. A man pointing a gun at him. The sound of the shot, the terrible impact of the bullet, the sensation of falling. Unconsciousness coming and going. Then, being carried. A woman's voice in his ear. Alex speaking softly to him as she cradled him in her arms: '*Don't try to speak.*'

And his own voice, weak and faint: '*Alex . . . I'm scared.*'

Then nothing.

Joel strained his eyes at the snowy landscape all around him. He could see no trace of her. Had she just gone, left him here like this, all alone?

Alex. He'd loved her. Or thought he had, until he'd realised who she really was. *What* she really was.

He touched his fingers to his neck. Felt the holes there, and the sticky congealed blood. The realisation was like another gunshot punching through his body.

She'd bitten him. Drunk from him. His life blood flowing into her, while her own filth flowed into his veins.

He'd become . . .

He'd become . . .

No. *No.*

Joel sprang to his feet. The scream burst out of him. It echoed across the snowy valley. Rolled around the mountains.

NOOOOOO!!!

He fell back into the snow. He arched his back and ground his eyes shut and pounded his fists on the ground and beat them against his head. There was no pain. He shoved his thumbs into his mouth, felt for his upper canine teeth and pressed hard against them. They didn't feel any different. Absurd. Insane. Maybe it was all a bad dream.

Except that it wasn't. He'd destroyed enough of these things to know they were real. For centuries, for millennia, they'd been there, these parasites, living off the blood of human beings.

And now he was one of them.

Joel sat there in the snow, hugging himself and rocking slowly back and forth. His mind was numb, choked with indistinct thoughts, paralysed with cloying horror. An infinite expanse of time seemed to drift by before he eventually turned his head slowly to look at the blood-spattered watch on his wrist and then up at the sky. The stars were fading as the first blood-red glimmers of light tinged the eastern horizon.

Dawn wasn't far away.

Many years before, when Joel had been just a child, his grandfather had told him what would happen to a vampire that was exposed to the rays of the sunrise. The primal instinct now flooding warnings through his mind, so alien to him and yet seeming to come from the very depths of his being, told him that his grandfather had been right.

Joel tried to imagine what it would feel like. First, the rising apprehension giving way to terror as the glow in the east grew more intense. Then the golden rim of the sun's disc would appear shimmering over the horizon and it would be as if a million hot needles were piercing his skin. Within seconds, the lethal radiation would be cooking him, boiling the blood inside his veins; the flesh blackening and peeling from his bones, falling away in brittle carbonised flakes that drifted off like cinders on the morning breeze as he screamed and screamed and watched himself disintegrate. When the torment was over, there would be nothing left but a crater in the snow to mark his final, irreversible destruction.

And he'd welcome it. His life was already gone, the world he'd known already lost to him. The future that lay ahead of him now was unthinkable, unendurable. Joel's eyes were fixed on the east as the red glow gradually bled across the sky.

Let it come.

Veins of gold began to spread through the crimson. The first light slowly creeping across the faces of the distant mountains.

Joel was afraid. And he was prepared to be even more afraid, and resolute in the face of terror, before the end. But the overwhelming horror that suddenly gripped him as the dawn approached was like a physical force, far beyond anything he could have imagined. Before he'd even realised what he was doing, he was on his feet and staggering away through the snow.

Behind him, the first glittering rays of sunlight peeped over the mountains. He felt it like a nuclear blast on his back. He screamed and ran harder, bolting through the trees like a wild animal instinctively impelled to survive at all cost, suddenly possessed with a speed and power that he'd never known in his thirty years of human life. All he knew was that he must find shadow. Must seek out darkness. The searing light was quickly gaining ground.

He looked up, shielding his eyes from the pain. The sunrise gleamed on the castle turrets and ramparts high above. The ancient fortress offered all kinds of dark spaces where he could hide away – but he knew that, even endowed with incredible physical strength as he was, he had no hope of scaling the mountainside and reaching it in time.

He was going to burn.

But there was a chance. The foot of the mountain was just thirty yards away; and as Joel ran he saw the dark recess in the rocks. *Let it be what it looks like*, he prayed. He slipped on an icy rock and went sprawling in the snow. A sunbeam cut between the naked trees and slashed across his outflung hand like a laser. The skin sizzled and he smelled burning. He screamed again. Scrambled to his feet and hurled himself towards the cave entrance.

The cave was deep and low. Bent double, crawling desperately on his knees, he wished like he'd never wished for anything before that the terrible light couldn't reach him there. The shaft tightened as it deepened, and it took all his strength to force his body through. Then, with a surge of relief that made him cry out, he realised it was opening up again, into a wide crooked fissure that ran diagonally upwards into the bowels of the mountain. A pitch-black sanctuary where the sun hadn't penetrated for a billion years.

Joel snuggled deep into the darkness. For a few moments, the fierce joy of survival burned intensely through him and he couldn't stop grinning. He'd done it. He was safe from the hateful sun. He'd survived. He'd won.

No, Joel, said another voice in his mind. *You lost. You failed miserably.*

He closed his eyes as his ecstasy suddenly gave way to revolted self-loathing. He'd had his chance to end it, right here, right now. But not even the steeliest resolve he could muster up stood the remotest chance against the vampire's all-conquering urge to survive. Not now, not ever. He was doomed to go on like this for the rest of eternity.

As the sun rose over the snowy forest and mountains and began its arc across the sky, Joel remained in the darkness of the cave, thinking of only one thing. He was going to return home and destroy the woman who had done this to him. Her and all her kind.

Send them all back to hell where they – and now he – belonged.

Chapter Two

Prague

Alex Bishop stood alone at the railing of the bridge, the wind in her hair. Beyond the river and all around her, the city lights were fading with the coming of the dawn. The rising sun glittered off cathedral domes and glassy high-rise towers and cast a diffused golden streak across the water. She could feel its warmth on her face. If it hadn't been for the last remaining Solazal photosensitivity neutraliser pill that she'd managed to retrieve from the castle before her escape from Romania, she'd hardly have been standing here to welcome the sunrise. As for any other vampire, it would have been a straight choice between frazzle and hide. Nobody ever voluntarily opted for the former.

She sighed to herself as she gazed out across the cityscape. So much had happened in the last few days that even her ultra-sharp vampire mind was reeling from it. None of it was good. All through the night she'd been making her way as best she could from the snowy wilds of Romania. A stolen farm truck had got her as far as a desolate country railway station, where she'd hitched a ride on a freight carriage. Now here she was in Prague, not quite halfway to where she wanted to be and hoping that her call to Utz McCarthy was going to pay off.

She didn't have to wait much longer before a black BMW SUV peeled off from the growing traffic over the bridge and pulled up a few yards from where she was standing. She stepped away from the railing to meet it. The driver was alone. His door opened. He climbed out and walked towards her, grey-haired, tall and lean, not quite smiling, not quite frowning, wearing a long raincoat that billowed in the wind.

At only eighty or so years of age Utz McCarthy was much younger than Alex, but he looked much older: compared to the twenty-nine years she'd spent as a human, he'd survived for over half a century before an unexpected encounter with a vampire had set him on a whole new course. Nowadays, he was a minor sectional official running the small and somewhat dingy Prague offices of the same organisation Alex belonged to: the global Vampire Federation. Part of Utz's job was facilitating the movements of VIA agents like Alex.

The last time they'd met face to face had been eighteen months earlier, when Harry Rumble, Alex's boss at the Vampire Intelligence Agency Headquarters in London, had sent her out this way on a mission to check out reports of rogue vampire activity in the Czech city of Brno. As it had turned out, it had been a false alarm. No Federation regs were being contravened, the local vampires were behaving themselves and not turning unauthorised victims; no arrests or Nosferol terminations had been necessary and all had been well.

Alex's job wasn't always so easy.

Utz looked distraught. 'Jesus, Alex, are you okay?' he blurted out. 'I can't believe what I've been hearing. An attack on the Federation grand assembly? A fucking helicopter *gunship*, taking out the whole conference centre? Tell me it's not true.'

'I was there,' Alex said coolly. 'It's true.'

'But how could this *happen*?'

'It happened because we broke one of the cardinal rules of warfare,' Alex said. 'Never underestimate your enemy. When a rogue vampire like Gabriel Stone decides to mount a rebellion against an enemy he perceives as a threat to everything he believes in, he does it on a major scale. It's a long story, Utz. The bottom line is that virtually the whole of the Federation top brass has been wiped out. Thanks to Stone's rebels and the moles he had working for him inside VIA, we just became a leaderless army.'

Utz gaped at her, visibly weakening at the knees. '*All* of them? The Supremos?'

She nodded. 'Goldmund, Korentayer, Hassan, Borowczyk, Mushkavanhu. Not to mention our illustrious former Federation second-in-command, the late and much-lamented Gaston Lerouge. Stone executed them all. With a guillotine.' She gave a dry smile. 'Some style, that Gabriel. You've got to hand it to him.'

'What about the Vampress?' Utz croaked. He was referring to Supremo Olympia Angelopolis, the grand Matriarch of the whole Federation. 'Surely not her as well?'

Alex shrugged. 'She might have got out. Things were kind of chaotic.' She didn't pretend to care any more than she did about Olympia's fate.

'This is unreal. You've got to be kidding me about this.'

She looked at him. 'You should know by now that I'm a very humourless person and I don't dick about making jokes. Especially when I've been shot at with Nosferol bullets, kidnapped and incarcerated in a damp cell in some middle-of-nowhere castle in Romania and then almost guillotined myself.'

And left behind the only man I've given a shit about in a

17

hundred and thirteen years, she wanted to add. Left him to fend for himself in the wilderness, more alone and more terrified than he could ever have imagined. Making that stark, brutal choice had ripped her guts out: either let Joel die in her arms of the terrible wounds he'd suffered in the battle with Stone's gang, or help him to survive, the only way she knew how.

Turning him had seemed the only option.

And now what? She knew he'd make it out of there. Of all the things vampires could do, survival was what they did best. He'd have sought out a dark place by now, to hole up in for the day. Come sundown, he'd begin his new existence – one he'd never forgive her for having inflicted on him. And then, sooner or later, more likely sooner, he'd come looking for her. The indelible connection between vampire and victim would lead him to her. When that day came, she'd have to account for what she'd done to him.

Alex quickly pressed that thought to the back of her mind. 'Got any Solazal?' she asked Utz. If she wanted to move around safely in daylight, she'd need more than just the twelve hours' worth of protection that one salvaged pill could offer.

Utz was still stunned from the news, leaning heavily on the bonnet of the car for support. He shook his head. 'Just what I need for myself,' he said distractedly. 'There's a shortage.'

Alex was well aware of that. Gabriel Stone's doing. In a lightning raid in Italy, his heavily-armed assault team had blown up the pharmaceutical plant where the Federation produced its special drugs. With a blast of high explosive, Stone's Traditionalist uprising had sent the vampire world halfway back to the sacred old ways of ducking and dodging the sun. It was anyone's guess how long it would be before

Solazal production went back to normal. As for Nosferol, the lethal anti-vampire poison that Federation agents used to destroy rogue members of their kind, the attack on the pharmaceutical plant had reduced stocks almost to zero.

'Have you reported back to Rumble yet?' Utz said, gathering himself.

'Rumble was with me in Romania, Utz. He isn't coming back. A certain vamp called Lillith was a little too handy with a bloody great sabre.' Poor Harry, Alex thought. He hadn't been all bad, even for a suit.

'How the hell did you get out of it?' Utz said.

'It was thanks to a human,' Alex replied after a beat.

'A what?'

'His name's Joel Solomon. He's a cop. Or was. If he hadn't turned up when he had, I'd have ended up as just another severed head in a basket. He got shot to pieces, but not before he'd managed to take out Stone's guards and most of his crew. As for Stone himself—' She shrugged. 'I don't know what happened to him.'

'A *human* did all this?'

'He had a little help. From the cross.'

Utz's eyebrows shot up. 'Come on. You don't mean—'

'That's right, Utz. *The* cross, the one nobody at VIA wanted to believe me about. The cross of Ardaich. Yes, it exists, and yes, it does what all the legends say it does.'

'I don't believe it.'

'You'd better.'

'Where is this thing now?'

She shrugged. 'Last time I saw it, it was flying over the battlements of Stone's castle. Something like a thousand-foot drop. Nothing but rocks below.'

'So it got smashed, right?'

'Probably.'

'What does that mean, "probably"?'

'It means I didn't actually see it get smashed, okay? Hard to believe anything could have survived that fall. That's the best I can tell you.'

'So it's gone . . . and we're safe. We *are* safe now, aren't we?'

'No more questions, all right?' she told him. 'I'm tired and I need a feed and I called you because I thought you could help me.'

'What are we going to do?'

Alex stared at him for a second. Then, quicker than he could react, she'd grabbed the pistol she'd known was in a shoulder holster under his jacket, flipped off the safety and aimed it square between Utz's eyeballs. It was a 9mm Beretta, not the big-bore stuff she personally favoured, but it would do the job. 'Utz, when I tell you something like "no more questions", I do mean it.'

'Hey. Watch out. That thing's loaded with Nosferol tips.'

She smiled. 'Of course it is. Standard field agent issue. All right, Utz, here's what we're going to do. I'm going back to base, to find out if there are any pieces left to pick up. If there aren't, it means Stone's beaten us. End of the line for the Federation, every vampire for herself from now on.'

'What about me?' Utz said in a small voice, squinting at the muzzle of the pistol.

Alex smiled sweetly. 'You're a VIA station chief, aren't you? Stealing hick farm trucks and stowing away on freight trains in the middle of the night isn't my style. While there's still some operational funds left in the coffers, you're going to get me on a nice, comfortable Federation jet to London with enough red juice on board to satisfy Count Dracula.'

Chapter Three

Dec Maddon swallowed hard and took another trembling, tiptoeing step down the darkened corridor. The big silver crucifix tightly clenched in his right hand glimmered dully in the near total blackness. The rasp of his breathing filled his ears. The frantic drumming of his heart made his throat flutter. He knew he was lost. Nobody would ever find him here.

Nobody except . . . *them*.

Something brushed his face, making him flinch violently and almost cry out in fear before he realised it was the silky touch of cobwebs hanging from the low ceiling. He clawed them away and moved on. Ahead of him, a solid rectangular patch of darkness stood out against the shadows. A doorway.

He reached out to push it open, his left hand a pale, ghostly thing in the darkness. The door creaked slowly open. Dec gripped the crucifix for all he was worth, took a deep breath and stepped through the doorway into the space beyond.

Immediately, and with a spike of shock, he knew he'd been here before. The stone pillars of the ancient cellar were dimly lit by the flickering orange flame of a wall-mounted torch. He took a trembling step across the uneven flagstones. Then another. He gulped. His mouth was dry. He thought

21

of the terrible scenes he'd witnessed the last time he'd been here – down here in the crypt beneath the vampire lair of Crowmoor Hall. He'd always known there were more of them, lurking down there, waiting for their moment to strike again.

His blood congealed in his veins as a sound echoed softly in the darkness. He froze, afraid to breathe.

Then he heard the sound again. A low cackle from the shadows.

And a dark shape detached itself from the pillar just steps away, and came towards him. As it stepped into the glow of the firelight, he saw it clearly. The hands reaching out for him. The predatory glint in the thing's eyes. The white fangs in its gaping mouth.

Dec stumbled back, raising the crucifix. 'Get back, vampire!' His yell came out as a choked whimper, barely audible.

The thing kept on coming. Dec screamed as he felt its hands clutching his arm.

It was shaking him.

Saying his name.

'*Dec. Dec. Wake up.*'

Dec snapped his eyes open with a gasp and jerked bolt upright in the bed, staring wild-eyed at the person standing over him. But it wasn't a vampire. It was his ma, still gently holding on to his arm. And he wasn't in the crypt at Crowmoor Hall, but at home in his bedroom in the suburban safety of Lavender Close, Wallingford.

'You were having a bad dream, son,' his ma said.

'Jesus,' Dec said, rubbing his eyes. He smiled weakly. 'I'm all right.'

'Oh, Dec, you didn't sleep in your *clothes*,' his ma groaned. 'Again? Is this what you are now, a slob?'

Dec glanced down at himself, and saw he had, shoes and all. He shrugged. 'Sorry, Ma.'

'I brought you some tea.' His ma motioned at the steaming drink she'd set down on his bedside table. She'd made it in his favourite mug, the Spiderman one.

Dec reached over and picked it up gratefully. 'Thanks, Ma.' He slurped at the steaming hot tea, the vividness of the nightmare still lingering in his mind. Glancing at his watch, he saw it was after eight.

'I see you've taken to wearing your cross again,' his ma said approvingly, pointing at the little gold crucifix that hung on a chain from his neck. She'd bought it for his confirmation, but it had lain forgotten in a drawer until very recently. Dec touched it and nodded as he slurped more tea.

His ma walked over to the window and jerked open the curtains, letting in the grey morning light. She peered out across Lavender Close, then tutted irritably. 'Look at that. They're back *again*.'

'Who's back again? Not the police, is it?'

She shook her head. 'Them bloody reporters. For next door.' She shook her head in disgust. 'They should leave folks alone, so they should. As if those poor Hawthornes haven't suffered enough.'

Dec made no reply. The nightmare of his dreams was gone now. Only the nightmare that was reality remained.

His ma turned away from the window and headed for the door. 'So are you getting up or are you going to lie there all day?' she said on her way out of the room. 'Your da needs you at the garage.' Dec's da was the boss of Maddon Auto Services in Wallingford, where Dec did a few hours' spanner-wielding each week.

'I'll be down in a minute,' Dec groaned, wincing at the idea of having to go into work today. When he heard his

23

mother's footsteps reach the bottom of the stairs, he fought the covers off him with his fists and feet, clambered out of bed and went to the window. The sight of the TV van and the reporter's car in the street outside, both parked outside the gate of Number 16 next door, filled him with anger.

Fuckers, he thought once more. For two days these pieces of shit had been flapping down on Lavender Close like flocks of vultures, picking at the dead.

Or, in this case, picking at what *might have happened* to the dead.

Dec could hear his ma and da talking downstairs. Like everyone else on the planet, it seemed they couldn't get their fill of yakking on about Kate Hawthorne. He cupped his ears and tried not to listen as the voices of his parents drifted up the stairs. It was unbearable. *Please, stop.*

The story had spread like bubonic plague through Wallingford and might have reached the outer galaxies by now, for all Dec knew. The news of the inexplicable, shockingly sudden demise of the teenager Kate Hawthorne from 16 Lavender Close had been awful enough; but the disappearance of her body, without a trace, from the hospital mortuary just hours after her death, had violently shaken the whole community. The speculation of the town gossips was savage and quick to venture where the media didn't dare: much more appealing than a gross administrative error was the popular theory that some deranged individual might have removed Kate's body from the morgue and was keeping it at an unknown location for his own indescribable necrophilic purposes. So many people had got carried away with that notion that the strange, somehow associated death of Bill Andrews, the Hawthornes' family doctor, had been largely glossed over to make room for it. Andrews had been found slumped on the cold tiles of the morgue floor, near to Kate's empty slab. Something had stopped the doctor's heart where he'd stood. A chance cardiac arrest? The shock at finding the dead girl gone? Or something else? Nobody knew.

Nobody but Dec.

Dec knew the truth of what had happened to Kate, and he was pretty sure it explained what had caused her doctor to drop dead of fright. It had almost done the same to him, when he'd met her walking in the grounds of the crumbling Oxfordshire mansion to which she'd been drawn from the morgue. It wasn't every day the dead girl from next door tried to seduce you in a see-through dress.

But his terrible knowledge was something Dec would admit to no one. Not to the reporters who'd come beating on the Maddons' front door after they'd found out that Dec and Kate had gone out together, albeit briefly, days before her death. Not to his parents, who'd ferociously warded the press hounds away from their son. And certainly not to the baffled cops who'd come to poke around and find out what Dec knew about her disappearance. Last time he'd tried telling the police about the vampires that were running amok in the Oxfordshire countryside, he'd been ridiculed and almost ended up in jail for his trouble.

In fact, Dec could barely even admit the truth to himself. And there was just one living soul in the world he could openly share it with: Detective Inspector Joel Solomon. Joel had been the only one who'd taken Dec seriously when he'd claimed to have witnessed a vampire ritual killing at Crowmoor Hall near Henley that terrible night. The only person who would have gone back there to investigate with him, when anyone else would have thought it was crazy.

And Joel was the only other person in the world who knew just why Kate Hawthorne had died so suddenly, and then apparently vanished. It had been Joel who had ended Kate's suffering, armed with the strange stone cross he'd refused to tell Dec too much about. A scene Dec wouldn't forget. It didn't matter that it had happened only two days ago. It wouldn't fade. Even if he lived to be a thousand and one it would stay burned into his mind, like a brand.

Joel hadn't just freed the girl – he'd saved Dec from the same fate after she'd enticed him with some power that had seemed almost hypnotic. Rendered him helpless with those sweet, sweet, terrible kisses. Dec felt the marks on his neck. They were healing well, but still painful to the touch and he'd taken to wearing a roll-neck jumper to hide them. If Joel hadn't stopped Kate when he had . . . Dec shuddered. He wondered where Joel was now. The last Dec had seen of him, he'd been heading for Romania to track the monsters who'd done this to Kate. There'd been no contact from him since. Dec had no idea where Joel was, or even if he was still alive.

Dec glanced back at his rumpled bed, and for a second all he wanted in the world was to clamber back into it, yank the covers right over him and stay in that little cocoon for the rest of his life.

He bit his lip. He wouldn't make the world any less insane by vegetating in his bed. But no way was he going into work, either. Feeling like he'd gone several rounds in one of the bare-knuckle boxing matches his da had told him about from his merchant navy days, he shuffled to the bathroom to pee and brush his teeth and beat his hair into some kind of order; then he sneaked down the stairs.

But it wasn't easy to sneak past old man Maddon.

'I need you today,' his da called from the kitchen doorway.

'I'm sick,' Dec said. Out of habit, he'd gone to grab the key to his old VW Golf from the stand in the hall when he remembered it was still in the repair shop after he'd crashed the damn thing getting away from Crowmoor Hall that night. He grabbed the key to his ma's Renault instead, knowing she wasn't working today. 'Got to go out,' he yelled as he ran to the front door.

'Thought you were sick, you wee skitter,' his da growled after him. But Dec was already out of the door and running to the yellow Clio. Before the reporters could collar him, he'd skidded down the drive, pulled a screeching K-turn in the street and gone speeding out of Lavender Close.

Roaring past the Hawthornes' house, Dec saw that the curtains were pulled tightly shut and felt a stab of desperate pity for Kate's folks – even if her mother hated him and looked down on his family. He'd have liked to have been able to tell the Hawthornes the truth, to offer them the sense of closure of at least knowing that their daughter was safe and in a better place now.

'Sure, Dec, that'll work,' he muttered to himself as he drove. He could just imagine the scene: the distraught parents looking up red-eyed as the grungy teenager from next door strode into their sitting room and announced: 'It's okay, Mrs Hawthorne. Kate was in trouble there for a while, because a vampire called Gabriel Stone made her into his wee play-mate. But then a pal of mine, Joel, set her free with this strange-looking cross that has the power to destroy vampires on sight. She'll be all right now, so she will.'

He sighed. Next thing, it would be the men in white coats coming to catch him with a big butterfly net and drag him off to a padded cell.

Dec headed aimlessly towards the centre of Wallingford. All around him were people going to their work, ferrying their kids to school, doing their shopping. Normal folks going about their normal lives, unaware of the things that were out there, lurking in the shadows by day, stalking their victims by night. Who would be next in line? It could be anybody, anywhere. Dec shuddered. It could be his own family – his ma, his da, Cormac. It could be anyone he knew. And these things would never stop.

'What are you gonna *do*?' He slammed the steering wheel with his fist. 'Gotta *do* something.' And then it came to him in a flash. He was going to devote his life to destroying these monsters. He was going to make it his mission.

Dec Maddon, vampire hunter. Mallet in hand, silver stakes and crosses glinting against the lining of his long black leather coat. Walking into a party, seeing the heads turning; being asked 'What line of work are you in, Dec?'; their faces as he coolly handed out his business card. He'd have an office, too. Like the ones in the old detective movies, with his name painted on the window. A busy phone on the desk. A wall safe filled with the tools of his trade.

'You big friggin' eejit. Dream on.' What was he going to do, turn up at the local college of further education to find out about NVQs in Vampire Hunting?

But he had to do something. Joel had, by going off to Romania armed with the cross to hunt down Gabriel Stone. Now it was Dec's turn to do what he could.

Five minutes later, Dec was pulling up in the car park outside Wallingford's public library and hammering up the stairs to the computer room. The rows of PCs looked antiquated and worn-out, but anything was preferable to using the laptop he shared with his elder brother. Cormac was uncomfortably expert at checking up on anything and everything Dec had been looking at online – and Dec could do without his sibling's considered opinions right now.

A couple of pretty girls looked up as Dec walked in. He brushed self-importantly past them. *Dec Maddon, Vampire*

28

Hunter. There was a terminal free in the back row, and he was thankful that it was right at the far end of the room where nobody could peer over his shoulder. He perched on the edge of the plastic seat, nudged the mouse on its pad and the screen flashed into life. Dec glanced left and right, then self-consciously keyed in the words 'proffesional vampire hunter'.

Did you mean: **professional vampire hunter**? the computer prompted him.

'All right, all right. Smart arse.' Dec clicked impatiently. The machine's outdated innards churned for a second, and then spat up a lot more stuff than Dec had been expecting. Scrolling through, he quickly realised that, unless he was going to check out a bunch of pulp novels or the old Hammer movie *Captain Kronos, Vampire Hunter* as reliable sources of erudite information on the pursuit of his future career, there was little of use to him here.

'Shite,' he said, and moved on.

'*A vampire hunter or slayer is a character in folklore and works of fiction, such as books, films and video games, who specialises in finding and destroying vampire and sometimes other supernatural creatures . . .*' Wikipedia informed him.

'This isn't a frigging video game. This is real, for fuck's sake,' Dec said a little too loudly. The two girls across the room looked up from their computer terminals and he heard a giggle. He flushed and clicked again. Next up came '*Semi-professional or professional vampire hunters played some part in the vampire beliefs of the Balkans, especially in Bulgarian, Serbian and Romany folk beliefs . . .*'

'Pish,' Dec said. Ancient folklore was one thing, but didn't anybody actually believe in this stuff any more?

'Crap.' Click, scroll.

'More crap.' Click.

Then Dec stopped and stared at the screen.

'Hmm,' he said.

THEY LURK AMONGST US.

Dec's eyes ran quickly across the couple of lines of text below the header: 'Errol Knightly is a professional paranormal investigator, historical scholar and vampire hunter based in west Wales. His new book, *They Lurk Amongst Us*, has shot up the bestseller charts and is being hailed as . . .'

Two thumbnail images were displayed alongside the header. One showed the glossy cover of Knightly's chunky hardback. The other showed the author as a slightly beefy guy with ruddy cheeks and thick sandy hair down past his ears, somewhat younger than Dec's da – maybe in his late thirties or early forties. He had a look of earnestness. A look that said 'You can trust me'.

'Hmm,' Dec said again. He rolled the mouse over the pad, landed the cursor on the web URL, www.theylurkamongstus. com, and clicked to enter the site.

Chapter Four

Romania

The mid-morning sun was bright over the mountains, gleaming down out of a pure blue sky across the fresh snows of the valleys. The only signs of movement on the landscape were the three skiers winding their way down the vast whiteness of the mountainside, slaloming through the pines, twisting to avoid jutting rocks. To those who were happily unaware of the half-buried local legends, the place seemed an unspoilt wilderness paradise. None of the three could have any idea that just a few miles off lay the deserted ruins of the ancient, accursed settlement that local people only whispered about. Only on very old maps did the name 'Vâlcanul' feature at all.

The three skiers glided to a halt at the bottom of the valley. Chloe Dempsey wiped the powder snow from her goggles, brushed her windblown blond curls away from her face and grinned back over her shoulder at her friends Lindsey and Rebecca.

'Had enough yet?' Rebecca called out.

'Not on your life,' Chloe said. 'I could go on all day.'

Lindsey's cheeks were flushed with cold and adrenalin. 'See?' she beamed. 'Didn't I tell you this place would be the best?'

Chloe smiled. 'You were right,' she admitted. It had been Lindsey who'd come up with the idea of a break from their studies at the University of Bedfordshire, flying out to Romania to take advantage of the year's unexpected early snows for three days of off-piste cross-country skiing. An adventure, she'd said. Lindsey's schemes usually ended up badly enough that Chloe had initially regretted letting her steer them so deep into the wilds, far away from any hostels and major towns. But there was no denying that Lindsey might actually have been right this time.

'Look at this place,' Lindsey said, gazing around her. 'Just look at it. Pisses all over St Moritz, I can tell you.'

'I'm sure you can,' Chloe said. It was all part of Lindsey's routine to take every possible opportunity to remind everyone around her that she came from a moneyed family and was, as a result, terribly familiar with all the in places. Chloe had stopped minding too much. Besides, having a rich college friend had its perks. Whether he even knew it or not, it was Lindsey's gazillionaire daddy who footed the rent for the luxury apartment the three of them shared. It beat living in cramped, dingy student digs. Being able to jet off for impromptu skiing vacations wasn't so terrible either.

'Hey, look,' Rebecca said, pointing upwards and shielding her eyes from the sun. Chloe turned to follow the line of her gloved finger through the pines. Funny – she hadn't noticed it before. Perched high up on a mountain crag above them, silhouetted against the blue sky, were the towers of an old castle. The snow lay thickly on the dark stone of its battlements.

'How old do you think it must be?' Rebecca said.

'Medieval times, I guess,' Chloe said. 'Maybe older. Wow.'

'You Yanks,' Lindsey snorted at her. 'Anything that's dated more than fifty years, you go all gooey about it.'

'We do have a little more history than that,' Chloe said.

'Huh.'

Rebecca made a face as she stared up at the castle. 'Makes me feel a bit shivery. Think anyone's up there, watching us?'

Lindsey laughed. 'Give us a break. It's just an old ruin.'

'I don't get such a good feeling about this place,' Rebecca said. 'I think something really bad happened here.'

'It's a *castle*, Beck. They used to have, like, wars and things. I'm sure a lot of pretty nasty shit happened here, a long, long time ago. That's why they call it *history*. As in, dead and gone? Come on, guys. I'm freezing my arse off standing here.'

Chloe stabbed her ski sticks in the snow and unzipped her backpack to take out her map. 'That's strange,' she said, studying it. 'The castle's not here.'

Lindsey snatched the map out of Chloe's fingers and gave it a cursory glance. 'Guess you're right. It isn't. Or else we've taken a totally wrong turn somewhere.'

Chloe shook her head. 'I know exactly where we are.'

'And I know exactly where I want to be,' Lindsey said. 'Somewhere else.'

'I agree,' Rebecca said. 'Let's move on. I don't like it here.'

They skied on down the valley, leaving sinuous, inter-twined trails behind them on the bright virgin snow. Chloe was the best skier and could have left the others far behind, but she hung back to keep a watch on the less experienced Rebecca. The valley skirted the base of the mountain, sloping steeply away from its rocky foot. The trees were thicker here, and the going was trickier. Chloe was slicing through the powder snow when Rebecca, fifteen yards ahead, gave a muffled yell and took a sudden tumble. With a big spray of snow she rolled flailing down the slope, toppled over a bluff, and disappeared from sight.

'Rebecca!' Chloe yelled, racing after her. There was no

reply. She glanced back over her shoulder. Lindsey was a long way behind, taking it easy over the terrain, and didn't seem to have noticed anything was wrong. Chloe made it to the edge of the bluff. Her heart was hammering and she was thinking about the long-range walkie-talkie in her backpack that she could use to call out the mountain rescue helicopter in an emergency. Her mind raced. Would they be able to find them? Would they make it out here while it was still daylight?

'Rebecca! Talk to me!' Chloe yelled as she tore at the quick-release mechanism of her ski boots, kicked the skis away and scrambled to the edge of the bluff.

She sagged with relief at the sound of Rebecca's voice calling up to her. Peering down, she saw her friend sprawled ten yards below, near a trickling stream that had melted a stony path through the snow. She'd narrowly avoided hitting a jutting outcrop of rocks at the base of the mountain. Her left ski had become detached and was sticking out of the snow halfway down the slope.

'I'm fine,' Rebecca called, struggling to her feet as Chloe scrambled down towards her. 'Must have snagged a root or something.' Putting weight on her left leg, she made a face and her knee seemed to give way under her. 'Ouch. Shit. My knee.'

'Sit on that rock and let me take a look.'

'Glad one of us has done all the first-aid courses,' Rebecca muttered as Chloe checked her over. The knee was grazed, but not swollen.

'That hurt?' Chloe asked, supporting Rebecca's ankle and gently flexing the leg.

'No . . . *ow*. Yes, a little.'

'You'll have a bruise like a rainbow,' Chloe told her, 'but I think you'll be okay. Could have been a lot worse.'

'I'm frozen,' Rebecca muttered, hugging her sides.

'Want some hot coffee? I think I have a bit left.'

'You're a lifesaver.'

Chloe fished the Thermos flask from her backpack, unscrewed the cap and poured out a steaming cupful. As she leant across to hand it to Rebecca, she knelt on something sharp and looked down to see what it was.

'That's a funny-looking thing,' she said, picking up the small, jagged object that had jabbed her leg. It wasn't anything like the other pebbles and small rocks scattered around the stream bed.

'What is it?' asked Rebecca through a mouthful of hot coffee.

Chloe showed her. 'Looks like a piece of something.'

'Pottery?'

'More like a stone carving.' Chloe turned the fragment over in her hands. It was the size of a walnut, made of some kind of pale, glittering rock. The faded markings on it looked like writing, but the language was one she'd never seen before.

'Here's another piece,' Rebecca said, reaching down between her feet and picking it up. 'It's got the same carvings on it. What do you suppose they mean?'

'No idea. My dad would probably know.'

'He's a historian, isn't he?'

'Museum curator,' Chloe said. 'Lives in Oxford now. You know what, I think I'm going to take these back to show him.' There were more pieces strewn across the stream bed, and yet more in the snow. She started gathering them up. 'Whatever this was, it must have got smashed on those big rocks. The bits are scattered all around here.'

Rebecca studied the fragment she'd found. 'They kind of look like ancient runes to me.'

Chloe found another, larger fragment in the snow. She dusted it off. Her little pile was growing quickly. 'Runes?'

'You know, ancient script. Spells. Maybe like some kind of talisman for warding off evil spirits.'

'Oh, come on. You don't believe in that stuff, do you?'

Rebecca shrugged. She pointed upwards at the looming mountain above them. 'You think maybe it fell from up there?'

Chloe looked up. Far above in the distance, she could just about make out the tips of the castle battlements.

'Something seriously creepy about that place,' Rebecca said darkly. 'Maybe that's what the talisman was put here for.'

'You don't know it's a talisman,' Chloe said.

'It's something, though, isn't it? And what was it doing here?'

'So *there* you are.' It was Lindsey's voice from the top of the slope. She stepped out of her skis and scrambled down the slope to join them. 'You two decide to hide from me for a secret coffee break?'

'Rebecca took a tumble down the slope,' Chloe told her. 'Hey, don't worry yourself though. She's fine.'

Lindsey pointed at Chloe's little heap of stone fragments, and frowned. 'Uh, Chloe, what are you actually *doing* with those?'

'They're bits of something,' Chloe said. 'We found them lying all around here.'

'How fascinating,' Lindsey said in a flat tone. 'Listen, I hate to spoil your fun, but we're really in the middle of nowhere here, guys. We need to move on.'

'Rebecca needs to rest a minute,' Chloe said.

'Moving on's okay by me,' Rebecca said, screwing the empty Thermos cup back onto the flask. 'I'm fine now.'

'You're sure?' Chloe asked her. Rebecca nodded and smiled. Chloe started stuffing the fragments into her backpack.

'I can't believe you're going to cart those bits of old stone all the way back home,' Lindsey said. 'It's ridiculous.'

For a second, Chloe almost felt like dumping them. Whatever kind of stone the fragments were made from, it was incredibly dense and she was worried about their combined weight on top of the rest of the stuff in her pack. But she couldn't bring herself to leave them behind. 'Lindsey, will you help me carry them? I really want Dad to see them.'

Lindsey stared. 'You've got to be kidding me. Why don't you go and grab a few bits of that castle while you're at it? Let's take the whole place home as a keepsake for Daddy.'

'Come on, Lindsey.'

'Why can't *she* carry some?' Lindsey demanded, pointing at Rebecca.

'I will,' Rebecca cut in.

'No,' Chloe said. 'Because she's hurt herself and I don't want her carrying extra weight.'

'Right then, Doctor Dempsey. So you want me to be your pack horse instead?'

'These could be worth something,' Chloe said. 'My dad'd be the first to tell you these kinds of relics can sell for a packet. Help me carry it, and I'll cut you in on whatever I make.'

Lindsey eyed her. 'Fifty–fifty.'

'Thirty–seventy.'

'Stick it.'

'Okay, fifty–fifty and I'll divide my share with Rebecca.'

'Let's just go, all right?' Rebecca said, glancing up at the castle.

'Deal.' Lindsey unzipped her pack and started stuffing in some of the stone fragments. 'Better be worth it.'

After a few minutes, the three students climbed back to the top of the slope, fastened their skis and took off down the valley.

The buzzard that had been observing them unseen from a high rocky perch watched the three tiny figures disappear down the hillside, then spread her broad wings and took to the air. She rode the thermals high over the mountain valley, making her unhurried way back to the nest lodged in the face of the cliff below the castle turrets.

Returning to the nest, the mother buzzard found her half-grown chicks still at work on the remains she'd scavenged from the castle battlements the previous day. There had been more than enough fresh meat for the taking up there, after she'd chased away the crows that had started the work of tearing it apart. She'd ripped away some large bloody chunks with her powerful beak, picked them up in her talons and carried them back to feed to the squawking fledglings.

Now a squabble was breaking out between two of the larger buzzard chicks, who were engaged in a tug-of-war over a choice hunk of meat. As they fought over it, a shiny object of very little importance to a buzzard fell with a dull thump to the bottom of the nest. The young raptors ignored it and went on squabbling until what was left of the severed human hand and wrist finally ripped in half and the argument was fairly settled.

The grimy, blood-spattered gold watch had landed on its face so that its engraved back-plate could be seen. And if a bird of prey could have read human language, the buzzards would have known the name of the man whose flesh was going to keep them sated for the next few days. The engraving read:

Jeremy P. Lonsdale

Chapter Five

As the sun eventually sank below the forest skyline and the lengthening shadows merged into the rising darkness, Joel emerged tentatively from the safety of his cave. He peered around him. It had been snowing heavily through the day, and the trail of his deep footprints leading to the mouth of the cave had been covered over. He felt the biting wind on his face but the rawness of the cold was something his senses registered only objectively. Like a machine. Like something that was alive but not alive. Something that was neither human nor animal.

The night sounds of the forest filled his ears and seemed to press in on him from all around as he scrambled down the rocky slope from the cave and set off through the trees. The fresh snow crunched bright and sharp under his feet. He could feel every microscopic ice particle through the soles of his boots, every rotted leaf, every fallen twig.

He trudged on, eyes front, jaw tight and fists clenched at his sides. Refusing to surrender to the tumult of thoughts that screamed in his head. Then, after a mile or so, he stopped. Sensing something. He turned slowly. From the darkness of the forest, glowing amber eyes were watching him. Another pair appeared, then another. Dark shapes gathering, alerted at his passage.

The wolf pack circled silently around him, cutting off the way ahead. His nostrils flared at their feral scent. He could hear the rasp of their hot breath and the low, rumbling growls from deep in their throats. Fifteen of them, maybe twenty. Their heads low, hackles raised, ears flat back. All watching, intent. Ready to attack, move in and rip their prey apart.

But something about this prey was different. As Joel stared back at the wolves, a ripple of unease seemed to pass through the pack. Growls turned to whimpers. The wolves backed off, then turned and melted away into the night.

Joel watched the predators retreat, and he was afraid. Not of the savage things that lurked in the dark. He *was* the dark. The night feared *him*. And that was more than he could bear.

He closed his mind and pressed grimly on. Leaping over fallen tree trunks, splashing through frozen streams and scrabbling up steep slopes, oblivious of the branches that slashed his face and the sharp rocks that gouged his hands.

An hour passed, then two, before his sharp sense of smell detected a new scent. A human scent. Woodsmoke.

From the top of a snow-covered rise he saw the speckle of lights through the trees in the distance. Even in darkness, he could make out the fine details of the little houses, and the old wooden church steeple that jutted above the forest.

He knew this place. It was the village he'd passed through on his way to Vâlcanul.

Joel hesitated for a long moment, unsure what to do. He could easily skirt around the edge of the village unnoticed – but he couldn't travel far, not in the state he was in. He badly needed to clean himself up and get hold of some new clothes. Someone would surely help him out. He still had some money left in his pocket – maybe enough for a cheap vehicle of some kind, to help him get back home.

He made his decision. The forest thinned out as he approached the village outskirts and the first of the old wooden houses. Snowflakes spiralled gently down in the soft glow from their windows. Their white roofs glimmered in the moonlight. The sides of the main street were piled with gritty slush where a snow-plough had cleared the way through. Joel's boots crunched over the icy ruts made by its tracks. He'd walked up this street before, only the day before – for him, a lifetime ago. The same hush of serenity hung over the place. It was just as he remembered it, like a forgotten throwback to a bygone era. Some things never changed.

While other things had changed forever.

Joel began to feel increasingly self-conscious as he made his way up the narrow, winding street. The feeling suddenly struck him that he did not belong here, any more than the wild wolves from the forest. His step faltered. He felt himself gripped by the overwhelming desire to turn and run, disappear back into the safety of the trees before anyone saw him.

It was in that moment of panicky indecision that Joel heard the sound from one of the nearby houses. The scrape of a latch, the creak of hinges. He turned to see a woman leaning out of a downstairs window and peering uncertainly through the darkness at him. She was in her fifties, with shoulder-length black hair showing strands of white, a patch-work shawl wrapped around her.

Joel realised he knew her. She was the teacher he'd met on his outward journey. The woman who'd tried so hard to dissuade him from travelling onwards to Vâlcanul, the place the villagers feared and hated so deeply that they wouldn't speak its name or even willingly acknowledge its existence. 'Then you will not come back,' she'd said when he'd insisted on finding the place. She'd been more right than she knew, he thought.

The frown on the woman's face melted into an expression of surprise and relief as she realised it was really him. 'You,' she called out in English. 'You have come back.'

Joel forced his face into a weak grin. He crossed the narrow street and stepped into the light from the window. 'It's me, all right,' he said without conviction.

The woman stared at his tattered, filthy clothes. On his outward journey, he'd been carrying a rucksack and a photographer's equipment case. Now he was empty-handed. The woman said, 'What happened to you?'

The wheels spun fast in Joel's brain. 'I never made it as far as Vâlcanul,' he lied. 'I got lost in the woods. Some hunters must have thought I was a deer or something.' He poked a couple of fingers through the holes in his clothes and shrugged. 'But I'm okay. They missed me.'

'You have blood on your clothes.'

'Oh, that? I know. It's not mine. I . . . er . . . I slipped and fell on a deer the hunters had killed.' He winced inwardly at how lame it sounded.

The woman clicked her tongue and shook her head. She shut the window and disappeared inside the house. Seconds later, the door opened and the woman waved at him to come inside. 'I have clothes to give you,' she said. 'And you must be cold. You want eat, no? Come.'

Joel hesitated.

'Come, come,' she insisted.

The house was small and warm and cosy, and smelled of freshly-cut firewood and chicory coffee. The wooden walls gleamed with centuries of varnish, the stone floors were covered in heavily-worked rugs. The woman smiled. 'We were not introduced before. My name is Cosmina.'

'It's good to meet you again, Cosmina. I'm Joel. Listen, I don't want to be any trouble . . .'

'No trouble,' she said. 'My son leave home last year. To study business in Bucharest, yes? He leave behind some of his things. You are the same size. No trouble.'

Joel reached into his pocket and brought out a handful of lei banknotes. Cosmina frowned at the money, then waved it away.

'Please,' he said. 'Then I'll be on my way.'

'Later. First you eat. Then we get clothes. Then you stay here and wait for the *autobuz* in the morning. Yes?'

'That's really not . . .' he began, then decided there was no use in arguing. A wave of heat slapped him in the face as she fussed him into a small kitchen at the top of the hall. Next to an antique cast-iron cooking range, a woodburner crackled, giving off a faint smell of smoke. A cat that had been curled up in a basket near the fire arched its back at the sight of Joel, spat ferociously and then scuttled into hiding under a tall oak dresser.

Cosmina seemed not to notice as she sat Joel down in a wooden chair at the kitchen table. As if nothing could please her more, she battered about for a few moments fetching down an earthenware plate the size of a wagon wheel from the dresser, some cutlery and a huge stone pitcher from a cupboard. Using an oven glove, she slid a large iron pot onto the hotplate of the range to warm up. It smelled like some kind of meat stew.

The kitchen door suddenly burst open and an old man walked in. Joel remembered him, too. Cosmina's father. He was about eighty, whiplash-thin and bent, with a mane of pure white hair and a face like saddle leather. Snow clung to his boots. In one wiry hand he clutched a walking stick; under the other arm he had a stack of freshly-cut logs that he dumped with a loud clang in a metal bin by the woodburner. There was a big bone-handled Bowie knife in a sheath

43

on his belt. He looked even more of a hard, mean old bastard than the rangy hunting dog that trotted into the room behind him.

Cosmina stared disapprovingly at the dog and rattled off a stream of Romanian to the old man as she stirred the bubbling stew. The old man pulled up a chair opposite Joel and said nothing. His eyes were deep-set, wrinkled and inscrutable, taking in every detail of Joel's appearance.

'I tell my father you become lost in forest,' Cosmina said, filling Joel's pitcher from a jug of what looked like home-brewed dark beer.

'That's right,' Joel replied, smiling at the old man. The old man didn't smile back. Staring fixedly at Joel from beside the table, the hunting dog bared its fangs and let out a long, menacing growl. Joel glanced down at it. Its tail curled between its legs and it retreated behind its master's chair. The old man's stare was just as fixed on Joel as his dog's.

'Please excuse Tascha,' Cosmina said, looking perplexed. 'She does not normally act this way with people.'

'Animals don't like me very much,' Joel said, as Cosmina ladled a mound of stew into Joel's plate and set it down in front of him. She stepped back and watched him expectantly. 'You eat now.'

'This looks lovely,' Joel muttered. He picked up his fork and spoon. His objective senses told him that the stew smelled delicious. He'd lost count of how long ago solid food had last passed his lips. Normally his mouth would have been watering so badly that wild horses couldn't have stopped him diving in and stuffing himself.

But some other sense, some internal voice that seemed to override all his lifelong instincts, was telling him that this food was worthless to him. No amount of it would satisfy his real hunger.

Joel's hand was shaking as his fork hovered over his plate. He swallowed. His mouth was dry. Cosmina was hanging on his every movement and expression. He speared a piece of meat, carried it up to his mouth and chewed it.

Cosmina looked suddenly crestfallen. 'Not good? You don't like?'

'No, no, it's delicious,' Joel protested, and tried to eat with enthusiasm. He felt both daughter and father's gazes on him in stereo as he ate. The dog was still snarling quietly from its hiding place.

The old man let out a loud snort. He leaned back in his chair, slipped the big knife out of its sheath and began nonchalantly picking out the grime from behind his finger-nails with the tip of its eight-inch blade. Cosmina scolded him angrily in Romanian. He appeared not to notice.

'I go to find clothes for you,' Cosmina said to Joel, and left the room.

Joel went on eating half-heartedly. The only sounds in the room were the ticking of an old clock on the wall and the low growls of the dog. The old man went on ignoring him. Having finished reaming out his nails, he now set about using the knife to scrape dirt from his fingers. Joel sneaked the occasional glance at him as he continued eating, and for a few blessed moments he felt almost normal in contrast to this strange, mad old bugger. He watched out of the corner of his eye as the old man pressed the edge of the blade against the pad of his thumb. Hard enough to split the flesh. A fat splot of blood dripped down on the table, then another. The old man looked at his cut thumb, then glanced at Joel.

Joel didn't feel the fork clatter out of his fingers and onto his plate. He was lost in a sudden trance as he stared, mesmerised, open-mouthed, at the blood ebbing out of the old man's thumb.

Instantly, a desperate battle was raging inside him.

No. It was too repellent. It was loathsome. Sickening.

And yet it wasn't. He could smell the blood. Taste it. Feel it flowing down his throat, warm and thick and filled with goodness. The desire, deeper and more feverishly intense than anything he'd ever felt in his life, threatened to blow away all resistance.

As suddenly as it had appeared, the startling red blood was hidden from Joel's view as the old man plucked a grimy handkerchief from his pocket and wrapped it around his thumb. Joel was shaken from his trance. He picked up his fork with a trembling hand. His breath came in gasps.

The old man hadn't taken his eyes off him the whole time. There was a sparkle in them that Joel couldn't figure.

Cosmina called from the stairway, 'I find clothes. You come get changed now.' Joel was grateful to make his escape from the kitchen. He climbed the creaky wooden stairs to where Cosmina was waiting for him on the landing, leaning against a massive hard-carved banister post with depictions of the moon and stars. 'My son's room,' she said, and motioned through an open doorway.

Joel looked inside the tiny, windowless bedroom. In one corner was a basic sink with a towel on a rail and a shaving mirror. Cosmina showed him the clothes she'd laid out on the narrow bed: a denim work shirt, a thick woollen pullover, fleece-lined jeans and a pair of socks fit for hardcore mountain-eering. Joel thanked her again, and tried once more to offer her some money. She shook her head vehemently, then left him alone to change. She shut the door behind her, and he heard her footsteps descending the stairs.

Joel quickly peeled off his dirty rags. He looked at himself in the mirror and saw that all trace of his wounds had completely disappeared. Was it his imagination, or were the muscles of his torso harder and more defined than he'd ever seen them? He splashed water over his chest, shoulders and arms and watched the filth and blood wash away down the sink.

Towelling himself dry, he could hear the old man downstairs jabbering agitatedly to his daughter. That crazy old bastard didn't like strangers in the house. Fine. He'd made his point. Joel wasn't planning on sticking around. Maybe someone in the village bar would know of a cheap car for sale, maybe an old 4x4 if the roads were bad. Then he'd be out of this place and nothing was ever going to bring him back.

He pulled on the socks and the jeans. The work shirt was a size too large, but better roomy than too tight. Joel was halfway through buttoning it up when footsteps came thundering up the stairs. The boards creaked outside the door.

Joel craned his head to listen, and heard whispers and fumbling. The lock clicked, and then the footsteps went thumping back down the stairs in a hurry. The sound of the front door being ripped open. Noises and voices from out in the street.

Joel rattled the door handle. The door didn't budge. Now he could hear shouting outside, more voices joining in. The cry of a woman.

Seconds later, the first clang of the church bell resonated through the still night air. Then again and again, ringing wildly, as if three strong men were hauling on its rope for all they were worth. Nearer to the house, the flat report of a shotgun boomed out once, twice, through the night air. The clamour of voices was getting steadily louder, and steadily closer. It sounded like half the village had suddenly emerged from their homes. They sounded scared, and they sounded angry as hell.

And now Joel could hear what the villagers were chanting amid the yells and panic.

Moroi! Moroi! Vârcolac!

He knew those words. They'd been written in the forgotten and decayed diary of a man who'd sacrificed his whole world, endured the ridicule and rejection of his own family, to fight the thing he'd hated most. Crazy Nick Solomon. Joel's grandfather.

The words were from the darkest corners of ancient Romanian folklore. They meant *Vampire*.

Chapter Six

It was way past time to get the hell out of there. Joel yanked on his boots and laced them up feverishly. He hammered at the door. It wouldn't give. He drew back his fist and punched at it. To his amazement his fist tore right through the solid wood. He felt no pain. Withdrawing his fist, he peered through the shattered hole and saw the stout length of rope that connected the handle on the outside to the carved banister post. He'd let them trap him in here as easily as he'd given himself away to that tricksy old man.

Bastard humans.

The thought had materialised consciously in his mind before he was able to catch it and drag it back. He wanted to vomit. But there was no time for self-pity. He lashed out again and felt the door buckle. Dust and splinters flew. Two more hits, and with alarming strength he'd torn the whole thing out of its frame and was trampling over it and racing down the stairs four at a time. He crashed through the front door.

Scores of villagers had gathered in the snowy street outside the house. More were running down the street from their homes. Young men and boys, old women, everyone who could be mustered was out in force as the alarm spread, many of them clutching whatever improvised weapons they could grab. Among the axes and shovels and scythes Joel saw a chainsaw and a crossbow, and at least a couple of double-barrelled shotguns.

Heading up the crowd was Cosmina's old father, dementedly waving his walking stick in one hand and the big Bowie knife in the other, whipping them all up to a frenzy with his screaming chant of '*Moroi! Vârcolac!*' Cosmina stood behind him, fearfully clutching his wiry arm. Beside her towered a bulky, heavily-bearded man with long black hair and hands like hams clenched around the hilt of some kind of ancient gypsy scimitar that he was swinging above his head as if about to decapitate a bullock with it.

Few things could spell a quicker end for a vampire than the sweep of a well-honed blade lifting their head from their shoulders. Joel knew that, all too well. He'd once been forced to do the very same thing to his own grandfather.

He tried to imagine what it would feel like, watching the blade come whooshing towards his throat. The parting of the flesh as the steel sliced cleanly through. Would it hurt? Would unconsciousness come instantly? Or would his senses remain alert as his severed head hit the ground and bounced and rolled out of the path of his falling body? For all that he craved for his torment to be over, the urge to run was like nothing he'd ever experienced before.

'There he is!' The shout needed no translation. Angry cries and gasps of horror. Fingers pointing. Faces turning to stare at him, eyes filled with fury and teeth bared. The wild old man waving the knife at him.

'Why do you hate me?' Joel wanted to yell at them. 'I've done you no harm. Just let me go. I won't come back here.'

For a few frozen moments, he hovered there on the doorstep of the house as the crowd, more than a hundred strong now, hung back. Then, at the same instant that the old man let out a roar of fury and led the charge towards the house, Joel bolted. With blinding speed he tore across the tiny front yard, vaulting the low wall into the neighbouring property.

The screaming mob came rushing after him. Joel sprinted harder, unleashing power from his heart and lungs and muscles that he'd never dreamed possible. A crossbow bolt cut whistling through the air towards him; he heard it coming and dipped his head, and it embedded itself with a juddering *thwack* in the wall of the house inches away.

Both barrels of a shotgun boomed out in rapid succession and a window smashed. Joel skidded around the side of the building, crashed through bushes, vaulted clear over the derelict body of an old car and leaped a six-foot fence as if it were nothing.

Suddenly, he was alone. He stopped, assessing his surroundings. He wasn't even out of breath. A narrow lane ran up between more houses, curving away out of sight between dilapidated wooden fences. He could hear the shouts of the mob approaching. 'Get him! Get the *Moroi*! Cut off his head!'

Joel took off up the lane, stumbling and slipping in the snow that had drifted up against the fence. Lights were coming on in windows all across the village. Up ahead, the lane opened out onto the main street through the village.

Joel burst out into the road and glanced all around him. More villagers were spilling out of their houses and massing together in a second hunting party just a hundred yards down the street. Nobody saw him as he kept down low in the shadows and ran like crazy over the ice-rutted road towards the edge of the village.

He desperately tried to recall the layout of the place. Where was the rundown old service station from which he'd managed to borrow a motorcycle and sidecar for his outward journey?

If he could find it again, maybe he could steal a car or truck before the mob caught up with him again. But then he remembered the Alsatian dog that had been chained up outside the garage. If it was still there, it would raise the alarm. Not wise.

He kept moving, constantly glancing back over his shoulder. Any moment now, he'd hear the yells and they'd be after him again, ready to beat him to the ground and stamp him into the dirt and dismember him, to chop him up into quivering pulp and torch whatever remained. Suddenly the full force of the realisation was hitting home. He truly understood now what it was that Alex Bishop had done to him. This was his destiny now: to be this abhorred, detested creature, spurned and condemned and hunted wherever he went. *This* was her parting gift to him.

As he dashed towards the village outskirts, he heard the chatter of a diesel engine and yellow headlights appeared around a bend. It was a battered old Nissan pickup truck with jacked suspension and snow chains that clanked and rattled against the road surface as it headed his way down the street. Joel ran straight towards it, waving his arms.

The pickup slowed, then slid to a juddering halt in the middle of the slippery road. Its roof and bonnet were thick with snow. Its wipers blinked away the white dusting on its windscreen.

Joel tore open the driver's door. The fat-gutted guy in his fifties, wearing a baseball cap and a quilted bodywarmer, was alone in the vehicle. Joel grabbed his chubby arm, hauled him violently out of the cab and spilled him tumbling across the snow.

'Sorry.' Joel threw himself behind the wheel, crunched the truck into gear and stamped on the gas. The vehicle slewed violently around in a circle, the snow chains biting deep and throwing up a spray of mud and grit and slush.

The crowd had spotted him. In his rearview mirror he could make out the hobbling figure of Cosmina's father leading them furiously down the street. At the old man's side, the big guy with the beard was waving his flashing scimitar as he ran. Joel floored the accelerator and the diesel roared. The snow chains flailed and crunched against the icy ruts in the road. For a frightening instant the crowd seemed to loom large in the mirror and then he was accelerating away and leaving them in his wake. The *ka-boom* of a shotgun, and his wing mirror disintegrated. Houses flashed by as he sped through the village outskirts.

Then the last house was behind him, and he was alone again. Just him and the snowy road ahead, and the mountains, and the wild forest creatures that knew to stay away from him.

Joel drove on, and wept.

Chapter Seven

London

Twelve hours' worth of Solazal protection had only just been enough to get Alex safely home. She'd been watching the clock intently for the last couple of hours of her long journey, teeth on edge. Half a day was about the longest any vampire could expect to get out of one of the photosensitivity neutralisers. When the effects eventually wore off, which they had a habit of doing very suddenly, the spectacular results had once or twice over the last twenty-five years been mistaken by non-vampires as the rare phenomenon of spontaneous human combustion. These days, unsuspecting passersby witnessing the fiery demise of a careless vampire might be convinced that they'd come close to being engulfed by some kind of half-hearted incendiary suicide bombing.

Either way, it didn't make for a very pleasant end for the vampire concerned. Alex was mightily relieved to see the sun sinking behind the London skyline as she finally made it to the door of her Canary Wharf apartment building and rode the lift to her penthouse.

Once inside, she grabbed a remote control from a table. At the touch of a button, thick blackout shutters whirred down to cover every one of the flat's many large windows, blocking out the sunset glow that was settling across the river, and plunging the whole apartment into pitch darkness.

Safe. She sighed. This was how vampires had lived once, before the Federation had come along and introduced the whole new modern era that had so incensed the champions of the old ways. Alex, who'd been turned back in 1897, remembered the old ways and the old days very well – and in her more reflective moments, she had to admit privately that she'd never felt fully comfortable with the idea of popping pills to help her walk about in daylight. Someone else had put it more eloquently than she could:

'*To cheat the sun, embrace the night. Living dangerously, living free. To hunt, to feed like a real vampire, honouring our sacred heritage and a culture that had reached its pinnacle when human beings were still dragging their knuckles in the dust and grunting like apes.*'

Those had been the words of the rebel vampire Gabriel Stone to her, just a couple of days earlier, when he'd been trying to recruit her to his crusade to bring down the heretical Federation forever. Alex had to confess they'd left a mark on her. She also had to confess she was beginning to run out of illusions when it came to the Federation that had employed her since its foundation in 1984.

Uncomfortable thoughts. 'Back to work,' she said to herself, and pressed another button on her remote, activating dim sidelights throughout the apartment. She fetched herself a glass of chilled blood from the kitchen – not quite the freshly-spilled article, but satisfying enough – then settled at her desk and fired up the laptop.

Vampires tended not to have a very active social life, so it wasn't a surprise when only two emails landed in Alex's inbox. The first was from Baxter Burnett. That *was* a surprise.

She didn't normally receive emails from movie stars. Baxter Burnett was currently raking in the millions, and getting slated by the critics in equal measure, for his role in the Hollywood schlock-horror, mega-budget *Berserker* franchise. Except that Baxter was no ordinary movie star: what his millions of adoring fans didn't know was that he was also a vampire. His little secret was the reason that he and Alex, in her official capacity as a VIA agent tasked with keeping vampires in line with Federation regs, had had some recent dealings. As she recalled, things hadn't ended too amicably.

She clicked on the email. The message was short, pithy and to the point:

Fuck you, Bishop!!!
Love, BB

'Thanks for that, Baxter,' she said, and then moved on to the other message. If anything, it was even less welcome than the first. Its sender, Ivo Donskoi, had been a Prussian army colonel back in the day, before he'd become responsible for hundreds of tortures and executions as part of the East German secret police; now he was personal assistant to none other than Olympia Angelopolis, the Vampress herself, at the Federation's main HQ in Brussels.

'What does *he* want?' Alex groaned aloud as she opened the email.

Agent McCarthy reports from our field station in Prague that you are now en route to London. Be advised that Supremo Angelopolis has returned to Federation Headquarters. You are hereby requested and required to provide your full written account of recent events *without delay* on your

return, to be sent directly and solely to this office.
Failure to comply will result in the strictest
penalties.

There was a lot to say in the report, and eleven o'clock had come and gone before Alex had finished typing it all up. The Vampress might not like everything that was in it, but she'd asked for a full account and that was what she'd get.

Alex emailed it back to Donskoi's office, then got up from the desk and went over to put on some Satie piano music that had been popular around the turn of the twentieth century. Ever since she'd become a vampire, Alex had tended not to keep up with musical trends too much, and she normally found the Satie relaxing. But as she reclined on the sofa with her eyes shut, trying to let the tension ease from her muscles, she knew she didn't feel safe here any more. As much as she loved the place, with its spacious rooms and views over the river, there was no way she could stay here. It was the first place Joel would come looking for her.

The phone rang, interrupting her thoughts. Alex flashed out an arm and grabbed it from the coffee table. She immediately recognised the crisp, efficient tones of Miss Queck, one of the admin staff at VIA's London office. 'Agent Bishop, your presence is required at base.'

'When?'

'Now.' Queck ended the call.

'Bitch,' Alex said. She looked at her watch. If she moved fast, she could be at the office just after midnight. She sighed, then flipped herself up, catlike, from the sofa, scooped another remote and Utz McCarthy's 9mm pistol from the side table and trotted up the polished aluminium spiral staircase that led to her bedroom. The floor-to-ceiling mirror at the far end of the room slid aside at the touch of a button on the remote. She strode through into the large hidden space beyond the glass.

The concealed weapons store was filled with racks of firearms of various shapes and sizes, mostly high-velocity semi-automatics compatible with the Nosferol-tipped rounds produced by the Federation munitions-manufacture division for its VIA personnel. Alex preferred something a little more potent than the standard issue: across one wall was the crowded work-bench where she prepared her own special handloaded cartridges for the massive .50 calibre Desert Eagle pistols she personally favoured for their unstoppable penetration and sheer knock-down power. Combined with the horrific effects of Nosferol on a vampire's system, it made the pistols the most formidable weapon in her, or anyone's, private arsenal.

Discarding Utz's comparatively feeble 9mm on the bench, she took one of the matching Desert Eagles from their wall rack, snatched up a loaded magazine and rammed it into the grip. She slipped on her well-worn calfskin shoulder holster, clipped the pistol snugly into place against her left side, and headed back into the bedroom, using the remote to close up the weapons store behind her.

She selected a long suede coat from her wardrobe, put it on and looked at herself in the mirror. Fashionable without being too distinctive. In her job, it was important to blend into the human crowd – and the coat hid the gun perfectly. Alex nodded to herself and trotted back down the spiral staircase. She grabbed her handbag and VIA ID from the table in the hallway.

Sixty seconds later she was riding the lift down to the neon-lit underground car park. Her sleek black Jaguar XKR fired up with a throaty blast that echoed through the concrete cavern. She reversed hard out of her parking space, hit the gas and her tyres squealed as she sped up the ramp and out onto the deserted night street.

She cut westwards across the city. The VIA offices were twenty minutes' drive with a human at the wheel. She'd be there much sooner.

Chapter Eight

Wallingford
Around midnight

Once the strip of light under his bedroom door had gone dark and he could hear the rhythmic snores of his da through the wall, Dec crept out of bed. He was fully dressed again, though this time he'd had no intention of falling asleep that way.

He paced across the dark bedroom and, as quietly as he could, unzipped the sports bag that contained his prized new acquisition. After his visit to the Wallingford public library earlier that day, he'd driven straight to the computer superstore on the edge of town and picked out a shiny new laptop.

Nigh on four hundred quid, courtesy of Barclaycard. He'd worry about the payments later. If his ma and da found out what he'd done, they'd give him hell. But you couldn't be a modern-day pro vampire hunter without your own state-of-the-art computer, and he was proud of his new piece of kit: the very first item – and by no means the last – in the inventory of Dec Maddon & Associates, Vampire Hunters Ltd. He didn't know who the associates were going to be yet, but it had a good ring to it.

The second vital piece of equipment he'd acquired was the fifteen-year-old Audi parked outside in Lavender Close. On his return from the library that day, Dec had – with some difficulty – managed to persuade his da to loan him one of the knackered old runarounds the mechanics used at Maddon Auto Services until his VW Golf was back on the road. The Audi rattled like a tin can full of marbles and smoked like a factory stack, but it was wheels. Couldn't hunt vampires without wheels.

Dec lifted the laptop out of his bag, laid it softly on his bed and pulled up a stool to sit on. He plugged in a pair of earphones before turning on the machine, angling the screen away from the door so its glow wouldn't be seen from outside. Where the ancient library computers had struggled to download anything bigger than a few bytes, the fancy new machine zipped online with incredible speed. Dec googled up the URL for Errol Knightly's website, www.theylurkamongstus. com, and clicked.

The screen momentarily blacked out, plunging the bedroom into darkness; then out of the blackness a pair of sinister red eyes materialised, staring at him. Dec swallowed, uncomfortably reminded of his nightmare.

Beneath the eyes, an animated line of script appeared in crimson font. Dec's earphones filled with creepy, chilling music and a deep voice narrating the lines as they appeared in turn before dissolving away into a gleaming red pool.

THEY LURK . . .
THEY WAIT . . .
THEY WANT *YOUR* BLOOD . . .
AND THEY'LL COME FOR YOU . . .
TONIGHT

Dec's jaw dropped open. He shuddered.

Then a hand landed on his shoulder and he almost fell off his stool. He whirled round, ready to let out a scream of terror.

He'd been so transfixed by the website that he hadn't noticed his brother creep into the room. He tore off the earphones and flipped on his bedside lamp. '*Christ*, Cormac!' he hissed furiously.

'What's this?' Cormac demanded, pointing at the screen.

'Shush. Keep your frigging voice down.'

'Where did you get this computer? What are you doing?'

'Fuck off,' Dec rasped at him, shutting the lid of the laptop. 'Leave me alone.'

'Still going on about fuckin' *vampires*, Dec? Is that why you've started wearing that cross again?'

'They exist. They're out there. And I've got to do something about them, so I have. Or else . . .'

'Or else what?'

'You don't want to know,' Dec said darkly, a quaver to his voice.

'Catch yourself on, bro.' Cormac jerked his chin at the curtained window, in the direction of the house next door. 'Listen. I'm just as gutted about that poor wee girl as you are. But friggin' *vampires* . . .?' He shook his head. 'You keep goin' on about this stuff and Ma and Da are going to have your scrawny wee arse put away in the loony bin, so they are. Look at the state of you – big dark rings around your eyes like a friggin' panda.'

Dec pointed a warning finger at him. 'You've got no idea what's happening, Cormac. None of you have.' He snatched up the laptop and started bundling it back into his sports bag.

'Where'd you get the dosh for that thing, anyway?'

'None of your business,' Dec muttered, slinging the bag over his shoulder and heading for the door.

Cormac stared after him. 'Fuck d'you think you're off to this time of night, wee man?'

'Keep out of it, all right? I fucking *mean* it, Cormac.'

'Right. Right. Steady, bro,' Cormac said, backing off.

Dec tugged open the bedroom door and listened for a moment to the steady snores coming from his parents' room. Satisfied that they were safely asleep, he padded down the stairs, let himself silently out of the back door and carried the sports bag to the Audi. He was watching his parents' bedroom window as he started the rattly motor. No lights came on. He drove off.

On the edge of Wallingford was a quiet lane with a layby where truckers sometimes parked up overnight. The layby was empty. Dec pulled into it and killed the Audi's engine.

He was definitely going to need a proper office. He didn't think the credit card company would stump up for that though. Better start doing the lottery, and hope he'd more luck with it than his folks did. He slid across into the passenger seat, unzipped the sports bag and laid his laptop across his knees. Thankful that he'd paid that bit extra for mobile internet connection, he went back into Errol Knightly's vampire hunter website. The inside of the car flickered with the glow from the screen as he clicked from page to page of the site.

'Have you been feeling unwell?' one section asked in bold capitals. 'Lethargic? Not quite yourself? Having strange dreams? IF YOU THINK YOU MAY BE THE VICTIM OF A VAMPIRE, PERHAPS YOU ARE. Click here to find out how WE CAN HELP YOU or to order one of our special vampire protection kits. All major debit and credit cards accepted.'

'This is so cool,' Dec said out loud. Clicking open another page, he came across the video segments that he'd been unable to access on the public library computer. When he saw that one of them consisted of a recent satellite news channel interview with the man himself, he went straight to it and maximised the image to full size on the screen.

Errol Knightly was seated in a plush TV studio armchair across a low table from the pretty, rather elfin blonde interviewer. For effect, a lit candlestick stood on the table, next to a glossy hardback copy of Knightly's bestseller *They Lurk Amongst Us*.

The star of the show was dressed all in black, with a large silver cross on a chain around his neck. He looked completely at ease and was flashing warm smiles at the interviewer.

'Your book has been out a month and is quickly becoming one of the year's literary phenon . . . phenomena,' the pretty blonde said, glancing at her script, 'with worldwide sales of over thirty thousand copies a day. How would you explain its appeal to so many people?'

Knightly's smile grew even broader at the mention of his sales figures. 'Because it's all true,' he replied without hesitation. 'Vampires exist. They're out there. And in our hearts, millions of us know it.'

'Fuck, *yes*,' Dec breathed, watching intently.

The pretty blonde looked about to move on to her next question, but Knightly graciously overrode her, producing a piece of paper from his black jacket.

'This,' he said, flourishing it, 'is just one of thousands of letters my office receives, from ordinary people whose lives have been touched by these monsters. This lady – we'll call her "Mrs Evans" – wrote to me to tell me of the sudden, tragic disappearance of her husband John, after forty years of happy marriage. Mr Evans went out for a walk with the dog one night. The dog came home, alone and in terror. John Evans hasn't been seen again. Except,' Knightly added darkly, 'I'm sure he *has* been seen, by the innocent victims whose blood he has since feasted on.'

The blonde seemed to balk at his assertion. 'You believe he—'

'Became a vampire. Yes. I know he did. My extensive research indicates that, of the thousands of people who disappear mysteriously every year, a significant proportion end up as members of this unspeakable race we call the Undead.'

'A significant proportion? How many people are we talking about?'

Knightly made an expansive gesture. 'Of course, it would be foolish, and completely unscientific, to try to put a figure on it. The fact is that nobody knows. Potentially, I would estimate that it could be anything up to fifty per cent.'

'Fifty per cent!' Dec echoed, awestruck.

Knightly paused, his expression serious and earnest. 'The historical records on this date back many centuries, you know. This is nothing new. It's been happening all along, right in our midst, from ancient times until the present. Look at the Highgate Vampire, for example. From 1967 to 1983, this creature terrorised London, claiming young women and drinking their blood. This is proven fact, not fiction. And many hundreds of other cases like it have never been explained, until now.' Knightly grabbed the book off the table and held it up for the camera.

Not taking his eyes off the screen, Dec touched the marks on his neck.

The pretty interviewer forced a smile. 'Absolutely fascinating, Errol. I'm sure, though, that many viewers will still find this . . . well, a little hard to believe. What would you say to people at home who feel these stories of vampires are just a bit far-fetched?'

'Wankers,' Dec muttered – and then realised that, until just a couple of days ago, he would been one of the disbelieving wankers himself.

But Knightly retained his composure with polished cool. Replacing the book on the table, he leaned back in his seat and chuckled. 'Everyone's entitled to their personal view,' he said, 'if it helps to keep them in their comfort zone. I only hope and pray for their sakes – indeed, for their very *souls* – that they never find out the hard way that they were wrong. The good news is – and it is good news, believe me – that there are ways we can protect ourselves from these abominations, and help rid the world of the scourge of vampirism forever.'

'In your book, you claim to have personally killed vampires,' the interviewer said, making little attempt to hide her scepticism. 'How many would you say you've killed?'

Dec scowled at her.

Knightly fingered the crucifix around his neck and looked grimly brave. '*Destroyed*, Kelly. We should remember that these things are already dead.' He paused. 'The actual number isn't something I'd choose to dwell on.'

'Fucking *thousands* of the bastards, I'll bet,' Dec muttered, blown away with excitement. What a discovery this Knightly was. If only Joel could have been here to watch this with him.

The interviewer shifted a little in her seat. 'Lastly, Errol, I'm sure viewers would be interested to know what's next for you?'

'That's a very interesting question, Kelly. In fact, I'm already working on my next book, *Planet Vampire*. But at the moment what I'm really excited about is something one of my contacts in Romania sent me only yesterday.' Knightly paused a beat, then went on, half-addressing the camera. 'I now have in my possession conclusive video evidence, not only that the Undead lurk amongst us, but that government departments know about them and, in fact, may have known about them for a long time.'

The interviewer looked stunned.

So did Dec.

'The Romania video clearly shows recent footage of some kind of special agent or operative,' Knightly continued, 'sent on a mission to destroy a vampire. This person, whoever she is, was obviously equipped with some kind of special weapon that I believe has been secretly developed for just this purpose.' He made a fist. 'It's my belief that our rulers are all too aware of this problem, and for that reason have created a secret department called the "Federation".'

'The Federation?'

'That's correct, Kelly. So much is clear from the footage. But the powers-that-be have been working hard to maintain public ignorance. It's a conspiracy, and I intend to blow the lid right off. I have technicians working on the video clip as we speak. Within days it will be on my website for the world to see.' Knightly turned to fully face the camera. 'They-lurk-amongst-us-dot-com. You heard it here first.'

The video clip ended.

'I *have* to talk to this guy.' Dec clicked on the 'contact' tab on the site, and a page flashed up with a form to fill in and email. Typing clumsily by the dim overhead light, his fingers tripping over each other in his haste, he spilled out as much as he could: Kate's unexplained disappearance from the morgue; her reappearance as a vampire; how she'd tried to turn him, and would have, if it hadn't been for the cross wielded against her; the way she'd been reduced to cinders by its powers.

Lastly, Dec expressed his desire to become a vampire hunter. 'If you can help me,' he finished, 'PLESE get in touch with me.'

He re-read his message a dozen times. It was messy, full of repetitions, and there was just too much stuff whirling around in his head to be able to get it all down. But the gist was there. If Knightly agreed to meet and talk, Dec would have the opportunity to tell him everything. He took a deep breath, then hit 'send' and launched his message into the ether.

It was done.

He was on his way.

Chapter Nine

London

Just after midnight, Alex screeched the Jaguar to a halt in the parking lot of the imposing steel and glass building. Using her special night pass, she let herself in the main entrance, under the granite nameplate that said SCHUESSLER & SCHUESSLER LTD, and crossed the empty foyer to the lift. The bottom three floors were the domain of the large legal firm whose senior partners had no idea of the real nature of the company, Keiller Vyse Investments, that occupied the upper two levels. By definition, the world headquarters of VIA, the Federation's Vampire Intelligence Agency, needed to keep itself strictly secret.

After passing through the security doors, Alex was greeted by the unsmiling, austere presence of Miss Queck in the reception area. Going through the routine retinal security scan, she felt – as she always did, but even more so tonight – that Queck was secretly dying to squeeze the trigger of the Nosferol-loaded pistol that was concealed beneath her desk in case of emergencies. A mean one, that Queck.

Walking inside the open-plan office space of the VIA nerve centre, Alex could almost taste the fear that hung so thickly in the air. Nervous faces turned from their computer terminals and wall-mounted screens. Utz McCarthy would have been quick to notify his superiors that Harry Rumble hadn't made it back from Romania. These kinds of things spread pretty fast.

At the far end of the upper floor was a row of doors. The first led through to Alex's own office; as she went to open it, she noticed the half-open door marked CHIEF OF OPERATIONS and walked inside with a twinge of sadness. Rumble's cluttered desk hadn't been cleared. Alex gazed at his empty chair, the leather of its seat worn to a polish by countless hours spent at his desk running VIA's worldwide activities. Mounted on the wall above the desk was the crystal plaque engraved with the three principal laws of the Vampire Federation:

1. **A vampire must never harm a human**
2. **A vampire must never turn a human**
3. **A vampire must never love a human**

'Yeah, and I know someone who's broken all three,' Alex murmured under her breath. If her superiors ever found out what she'd done, they'd waste no time. The rules were strict, and Alex knew all too well from her own experience how rigorously enforced they were. Somewhere inside the Federation main database, locked down under a mass of access codes, were the official statistics on exactly how many vampires had taken the one-way trip from the Federal detention centre to the infamous execution block. There, transgressors against Federation law were strapped in a titanium chair and given the lethal injection of Nosferol that exploded their blood vessels and ripped their bodies virtually inside out. VIA agents sometimes indulged in a little black humour about the place: *Termination Row: where we make Undead things deader.*

Alex had known the risk. And taken her chances willingly. If that made her a heretic, then so be it. She wondered where Joel was at that moment. It was hard to keep him out of her thoughts.

As she left Rumble's office, Alex saw Jen Minto, Harry's secretary, rushing over to talk to her. Her short blond hair was a mess and her face looked drawn. If she'd been a human, there would have been tears in her eyes. Alex had often suspected that Minto's affections for Harry ran deeper than she'd admit.

'Tell me it isn't true,' Minto said in a tight voice.

Alex shook her head. 'I'm sorry, Jen. Harry's not coming back.'

Minto's shoulders sagged and she put her hand over her face. 'Was it quick?' she murmured.

'He never saw it coming,' Alex said. It was no lie. For an instant she was reliving the scene again in her mind: the rapid whoosh of the sabre blade coming up behind him faster than Rumble could react, slicing horizontally through flesh and bone. The glint of animal triumph in Lillith's eyes. The innocent surprise on Harry's face as his head toppled to the floor and rolled towards Alex's feet.

'And Xavier Garrett?' Minto asked urgently. 'He was one of them?'

'He was Stone's inside guy all along,' Alex told her.

'Working right alongside Harry,' Minto muttered in disgust. 'The lousy bastard. To think we trusted him, all these years.'

Alex was about to reply when she heard a familiar voice and turned to see the tall, dark-haired figure of Cornelius Kelby, one of the VIA senior managerial officers, striding rapidly over in their direction. His tie was crooked, and like everyone else in the place he looked tired, strained and unfed.

73

'So the rumours were right,' Kelby said. 'You made it. I'm so glad, Alex.' He gave her a weary pat on the shoulder. 'We've been waiting for you. We all have so many questions.'

'It's all in the report I emailed to Supremo Angelopolis earlier tonight,' Alex said. 'Eyes only. Special orders.'

'Wow. Must be a hell of a report.'

'Who's in charge around here now?' Alex asked.

'I am,' Kelby said. 'I think.' He took her elbow, guiding her away from the office doors and back down the corridor. 'Come on. It's just about to start.'

'What's just about to start?'

'Emergency conference. We're hooked up live to Brussels. The Vampress wants you to be a part of it.'

'Me?'

'You and she are the only survivors. Could be a big promotion in it for you, Alex.'

She gave a grim laugh. 'I wouldn't bet on it.'

As they headed towards the conference room, Kelby dug in his pocket and came out with a tube of Solazal pills. 'In case you were getting low,' he said, handing them to her. Alex took them gratefully.

Kelby showed her into the conference room. It was only the third or fourth time she'd ever been inside the place – lowly field agents were seldom granted the privilege of attending high-level meetings. There were a lot of empty seats at the long conference table, vacated by the members of the London VIA office who'd perished in Gabriel Stone's recent helicopter attack.

The same sense of doom Alex had felt among the office staff hung over the remnants of the VIA top brass. She recognised most of the faces: there was Doug Slade, looking scruffier and more dissolute than ever. Despite his appearance, he was one of the most important vampires in the

Federation, overseeing the Pharmaceutical Division's global distribution of Solazal and Vambloc. Ironically, it had been the destruction of the Federation's pharma plant in Italy that had kept him too busy to attend the ill-fated conference in Brussels. Other officials around the table included Nathaniel Creasy, Jarvis Jackson and the stern-looking, monocled Petronella Scragg, one of the directors of the Federation Treasury.

Another face Alex recognised, to her surprise, was that of Cecil Gibson. The gingery, rodent-like vampire was a field agent like her, somewhat further down the ranks and not too popular among the VIA personnel. Their paths had crossed a few times over the years. What he lacked in imagination and dynamism, he made up for with his plodding, by-the-book methodology and a particularly cloying way of brown-nosing his superiors. He'd just returned from a diplomatic mission to Athens, evidently managing to sit out the whole recent crisis in the safety of a hotel room.

Alex gave him a polite nod and wondered what an agent of his status could possibly be doing at this meeting. As Kelby showed her to a chair and sat down beside her, she hoped this wouldn't take long. Her relationship with bureaucracy was about as healthy as that of a vampire with a speeding Nosferol bullet.

At the head of the room, overlooking the end of the long table, was a large flatscreen monitor. All eyes were turned expectantly towards it. Moments later, it flashed into life and Alex found herself faced, in pin-sharp high-definition, with the impressive white-robed, iron-haired figure she'd last seen fleeing from Gabriel Stone's castle in Romania.

Olympia Angelopolis was regally poised on a large red velvet throne, deep in the safety of her Brussels HQ. Flanking her in the background, a pair of machine-gun-wielding vampire goons wore the crisp black uniforms of the Federal Armed National Guard, with the F.A.N.G. emblem on the breast pocket.

Everyone but Alex greeted their Supremo with enthusiastic applause. Olympia's steely face melted for an instant. As the applause faded, she wiped away an imaginary tear.

'My friends,' she began. 'Once again I must ask you all to offer a few moments' silence in remembrance of those dear colleagues recently taken from us by the forces of evil.' She bowed her head and closed her eyes. Everyone around the conference table immediately followed her example. After a beat, Alex impatiently did the same.

Only a few seconds passed before Olympia raised her head and gave a little cough to announce the silence was over. 'By now I am sure that every Federation vampire is familiar with the terrible details of recent events,' she said. 'It was a horrendous moment for us all. I am not ashamed to admit that even I' – the Supremo clapped a manicured hand to her bosom – 'was frightened. Only my deep faith in the unshakable strength of the Federation sustained me through those hours.'

Alex smiled at the memory of the panic-stricken Olympia desperately trying to bribe her way out of trouble at any price as she and the helpless Supremos were being led away at swordpoint by their captors.

'But we cannot afford to dwell on the past,' Olympia went on firmly. 'Let us now look to the future, to rebuilding our Federation into the veritable New World Order for our kind that it is destined to become.' She paused, drawing breath as if the power of her own words had stunned even her into silence. A few awed murmurs rippled up and down the table. Alex's lips remained tight.

'We may have sustained some minor damage,' Olympia

continued, 'but we are more resilient than our enemies suppose. Such contingencies, unthinkable as they may be, were foreseen from the very foundation of our organisation. I assure you, my friends, everything is under control.'

'That's the same line she spun us in Brussels,' Alex whispered to Kelby, leaning close to his ear, 'a couple of minutes before Stone's helicopter blew the shit out of the place.'

The whisper might have been a fraction too loud. Petronella Scragg swivelled her long neck in Alex's direction and gave her an icy stare. Olympia glowered momentarily from the screen, and then went on, waving a magnanimous hand in the direction of Doug Slade. 'As we all know, our pharmaceutical plant in Italy was also destroyed by these cowardly terrorists. But thanks to the tireless efforts of Mr Slade, whom I am now promoting to the position of Director of Pharmaceuticals, the production of Solazal and Vambloc is expected to reach normal operating levels very shortly.'

'One of our technicians came up with a new formula that halves the time it takes to complete the Solazal creation process,' Slade explained laconically. 'As for the new plant in Andorra, we have construction teams working night and day.'

Olympia smiled benevolently. 'Excellent.'

'But stocks are still dangerously low,' Slade went on. 'My department's drafted a memo to all registered Federation members, recommending that everyone needs to ration their consumption and limit activities to after dark whenever possible. Of course, that means some vampires with day jobs may have to take time off work. Not much we can do about that, I'm afraid.'

'The Federal Treasury is looking into reserving a special fund to compensate loss of income,' Petronella Scragg said importantly.

'Synergy,' Olympia sighed, and linked her hands together. 'Friends, this is what makes our Federation so special, so indomitable. We truly are a *family*.'

Everybody applauded again, except Alex, who was leaning back in her chair with her arms crossed.

'The immediate threat is gone,' Olympia said, motioning for silence. 'Gabriel Stone and his followers have been defeated. But we must not be complacent. Moving forward, a major part of our reconstruction is to ensure that this never happens again. I therefore propose the creation of a special new task force, whose purpose will be to compile intelligence records on every single vampire suspected of having been linked, however loosely, to this rebellion. The task force will have unlimited powers of arrest and surveillance – putting cameras in their homes, if necessary – as a means of cleaning up any pockets of terrorist insurgents that may remain. Only by digging up the roots can we ensure that the weed never regrows.'

She turned to Alex. 'Agent Bishop, apart from myself you are the sole survivor of the tragic recent events in Romania – making you the most senior VIA operative with direct experience of dealing with these Traditionalist rebels. For that reason, I am appointing you in charge of the new task force, with the rank of commander.'

All eyes turned towards Alex. Not everyone was smiling. Kelby nudged her elbow and flashed her a wink, as if to say, 'See? Told you so.'

Alex said nothing.

'In the wake of the annihilation of Gabriel Stone and his band of criminals, other misguided vampires may seek to follow in his footsteps. Your job from now on will be to make any renewed attack on the Federation an utter impossibility. To assist you in this role, I propose appointing Agent Gibson as your lieutenant.'

Alex fired a glance at Gibson across the table. Gibson must have seen her expression, as the broad smile at the news of his promotion quickly dropped off his face.

'Do you accept this enormous responsibility we are entrusting you with?'

Alex maintained steady eye contact with the Vampress. 'Before we go any further,' she said, 'I think it would be a mistake to assume that Gabriel Stone has been "annihilated".'

Shocked silence reverberated around the table.

Olympia frowned darkly. 'But in your report you state . . .'

'My report states simply that I saw Stone and his second-in-command, Lillith, go over the castle battlements,' Alex said. 'It's true, they'd taken a bad hit from the cross, especially Stone himself. But annihilated? I wouldn't assume that they didn't survive. Which means they still could be out there – and I don't think Stone would give up his plans to bring down what's left of us. I met him. I talked to him, face to face, and I can tell you that no vampire was ever more dedicated to their cause than him.'

She gazed steadily at each vampire around the table in turn. 'And there's something more. Supremo Angelopolis knows about it, because I included it in my report. But I wanted to make sure everyone here is aware of it.' She gave a dry smile. 'Just in case any information got accidentally overlooked.'

Olympia's expression had hardened into granite. She raised a warning eyebrow. 'That will be enough for now, *Commander* Bishop.'

'They need to know,' Alex said.

'Need to know what, Alex?' Kelby asked, frowning.

'We all talk about Gabriel Stone's rebellion,' Alex said, 'as if the whole thing had been his idea. It wasn't. He was working for someone else. The uprising against the Federation was just the first step in a much greater plan, and that plan wasn't devised by ordinary vampires.'

Olympia's face loomed large onscreen as she stepped closer to her webcam with a look of thunder. 'I am *warning* you, Commander.'

'Gabriel Stone's superiors, and the masterminds behind this whole thing, are the Übervampyr,' Alex said.

The words seemed to suck all the air out of the room. There was a long, bewildered silence.

Nathaniel Creasy gasped. 'But they don't . . . really . . .'

'. . . exist?' Jarvis Jackson finished uncertainly.

'The Über-*what*?' Gibson said, looking confused.

Olympia slammed her fist on her desk, making the webcam shake. 'Hearsay!' she shouted. 'You foolish child. Stone was just playing games with you, in order to frighten you. You will *not* believe these dangerous lies, nor will I allow you to promulgate them among your colleagues. Did you even *see* any of these alleged superiors of his?'

'No,' Alex said. 'You know I didn't. You were there in Romania.'

The Supremo's face was quickly darkening to a shade of deep crimson. 'Of course you didn't,' she screeched, the power of her voice overloading the monitor's speakers. 'Because the Übervampyr are a figment of myth and folklore. Hocus-pocus and bogeyman tales from an age of superstition that has thankfully long since been abandoned in our modern, enlightened era.'

'Like the myth of the cross of Ardaich?' Alex said.

'The cross that is now destroyed,' Olympia spat. 'It has been consigned to history where it belongs. As if it had never existed.'

'If it had never existed,' Alex replied, 'your head would be in a basket about now, alongside the heads of the other

80

Supremos Stone guillotined on the battlements. Or have you forgotten already?'

'Enough!' Olympia shrieked. 'One more word from you, Bishop, and I will have you incarcerated and terminated as a traitor to the Federation.'

'Ma'am,' Kelby protested, getting to his feet. 'With all due respect, Alex Bishop is no traitor. I believe she's proved that enough times.'

Olympia glowered from the screen. She raised a finger. 'This discussion is over,' she seethed. 'What you have heard today is not to leave this room. On pain of extermination. Is that absolutely clear to every single one of you?'

A rapid round of nods and 'Yes, Ma'am's around the table. Several of the vampires rose from their seats, looking disapprovingly at Alex.

'And as for you, Bishop,' Olympia said, 'you are hereby demoted back to your former rank of field agent.'

Kelby rolled his eyes. *Here we go again*, his expression said.

'I can't be demoted,' Alex said, 'because I never accepted the position in the first place. I won't have anything to do with putting spy cameras in the homes of Federation members. It isn't right.'

'Silence!' Olympia shrieked even more loudly. 'Count yourself lucky that I do not – for now – sanction your immediate termination.' She turned to Gibson. 'Commander Gibson, you are henceforth placed in charge of the special task force.'

Gibson's face lit up.

Olympia clapped her hands sharply. 'This conference is now officially concluded.'

The screen went dark.

Chapter Ten

Cell 282, Blackheath High Security Prison
North York Moor, 15 miles south of Middlesbrough
1.09 a.m.

The only sounds Denny Morgan could hear as he lay in his bunk that night were the soft, rhythmic snores coming from Pete Tulleth in the bunk beneath him, and the tramp of the guards' footsteps patrolling the corridors on the other side of the thick steel door. The cell was pitch black, except for the little barred square of dim moonlight from the single window.

Denny was still and his eyes were shut, but he was wide awake and his mind consumed by a state of furious brooding, unable to shut out the thoughts that had occupied him over the last few days.

Denny Morgan was a guy who knew what he liked: and he liked things always the same. Back when he'd been a free man, it had always been the same beer drunk with the same mates in the same pub, with the same tracks playing on the jukebox; the same Tandoori chicken dish from the same Indian take-away every Wednesday night; the same steak and chips on a Friday. That had always been his way, deriving comfort from routine, invariably bristling with resistance to change of any kind. So much so that, when his wife Mandy had come home one day with the long blond hair she'd had since the age of eighteen unexpectedly, shockingly cropped and dyed black, Denny had – quite justifiably, as far as he was concerned – beaten her to death with an empty beer bottle: Newcastle Brown Ale, his favourite.

Denny's preference for a steady routine had adapted itself well to the prison life he'd now been living for eight years; and for the last two of those years, he'd shared cell 282 with a pair of other inmates he got along well with. Pete Tulleth was given to unbelievably malodorous bouts of flatulence, though he made up for it with his inexhaustible supply of jokes. Kev Doyle was a sombre and pensive man, didn't say too much, but you could trust him with anything. Both of them steady, dependable blokes. For the last couple of years, Denny had been pretty content with the way things were.

Until the recent arrival of the cell's fourth occupant had changed everything.

As infuriating and unacceptable as Denny considered it, it wasn't just the violation of the established regime in cell 282 that he objected to most vehemently – it was the fact that, as both Pete and Kev concurred, this new guy whose presence had been imposed on them was a real fucking weirdo.

Denny opened his eyes and rolled his head to the left across the thin pillow. Eight feet away on the other side of the cell, the new guy was lying completely still on the opposite top bunk, with his HM Prison Service regulation bedclothes draped over him from head to toe, so all that could be seen was his silhouette in the dim moonlight. Denny could make out the shape of his hands crossed diagonally across his chest, palms flat over his shoulders.

The mad bastard had been lying like that all day. Never seemed to move. He didn't speak, didn't get up to take a piss, didn't snore, barely even seemed to be breathing. It was like sharing a cell with a fucking reanimated corpse.

All that the other inmates of Blackheath knew about the new occupant of cell 282 was what they'd gleaned from the papers and the TV in the rec room, which was a fair amount. His murderous sword attack on the little parish church in Cornwall had been so widely reported by a scandalised British media that even the guys banged up in solitary confinement knew about it. Many of the inmates who were committed Christians, especially those who'd turned to religion in prison as a way of dealing with their past sins, were angry about the new guy. This 'Ash', this self-proclaimed 'vampire', with his fucked-up filed teeth and his strange ways, was neither liked nor trusted.

Denny Morgan was no Christian, but he was no less pissed off with the new arrival, and even more irate with the prison governors for having picked this, of all cells, to dump him in. *Why did they have to put him in with us?* he thought angrily to himself, glowering hard at the opposite bunk as if he could project his rage by telepathy. The shape under the covers didn't flicker. Denny whispered it out loud: 'Why did they have to put you in with us, eh, you fucking fucker?'

Nothing. The body on the opposite bunk remained deathly still.

What kind of a stupid name was 'Ash', anyway?

'Fucking shithead weirdo,' Denny muttered. 'Vampire my arse.' And closed his eyes again.

After a few minutes, his brooding indignation finally started to give way to sleepiness. His body relaxed into the bunk's mattress, and his breathing fell into a soft and shallow rhythm. The corners of his mouth twitched as he slept. In his dreams, he was walking into his garage back home, slowly pulling back the tarpaulin to reveal the glittering chrome mag wheels and gleaming candy-red paintwork of the Dodge Viper underneath. His, all his. He was running his hands over the contours of its cool, smooth, waxed body. The key was in his pocket. Just him and this beauty and the open road. He could almost hear the growling note of the tuned V8 . . .

Denny's eyes snapped open and a chill gripped his heart as he turned his head to stare again at the opposite bunk.

It was empty.

It was empty, because Ash had risen. In the pale square of moonlight from the window, Denny saw the tall, powerfully-built figure cross the narrow cell towards him and his heart began to flutter. He propped himself up on one elbow. 'Oy! what you up to?' he demanded in a hoarse whisper that had more of a quaver to it than he wanted to hear.

Ash stopped at the side of the bunk and cocked his head curiously, peering up at where Denny lay. He bared his sharpened teeth in a crooked smile.

The pair of prison guards patrolling the corridor were the first to respond to the unearthly, high-pitched screams emanating from cell 282. Their footsteps reverberated off the hard floors and bare white walls as they sprinted to the door with their extendable batons drawn and ready for action. The terrible screaming continued from inside the cell. One of the guards wrenched the ring of keys from his belt clip. The other turned on the external light switch beside the riveted steel door, flipped open the viewing hatch cover and tried to peer through.

'Oh, my Christ,' he groaned. The glass was smeared opaque with thick, bright blood. 'Hurry.' As his colleague frantically twisted the key in the lock, the screams were rising to a tortured wail of terror and agony that neither of the guards had ever heard before, not with over thirty-five years' prison service experience between them. Bursting inside the cell, clutching their batons, they recoiled at the scene in front of them.

'Oh, Jesus. No.'

The cell was rank with the hot stink of death. It looked as though it had been hosed down with blood. The floor swimming in it; the walls running; the crisp white HM Prison Service bed linen soaked and dripping with red.

In the spreading pool on the floor lay the broken corpses of Tulleth and Doyle. Tulleth's head was twisted almost 180 degrees on his neck. He had no chin or lower teeth, because his jawbone had been torn out by the roots. Doyle's brains were exposed, like grey-white cauliflower, through the shattered mess of his skull.

Denny Morgan was still alive, though only for a few seconds more. He was thrashing like a landed fish and screaming his lungs out, dark blood pumping and spraying everywhere. Most of his face had been pummelled beyond recognition. Both eyes gouged from their sockets.

From the centre of the cell, the fourth inmate of 282, the prisoner known as Ash, turned to gaze impassively at the guards. He looked as if he'd dived into a lake of blood, as if all he wanted in the world was to bathe and swim in it, smear it all over his body and feel its warm taste trickling down his throat. He regarded them for a moment with an expression of detachment, then quietly turned his attention to the thing he was clutching in his hand.

For a few moments, the guards could do nothing but gape dumbly at the scene – then one of them let out a yell of repulsion as he realised that the livid object trailing from Ash's bloody fist, long and red and gleaming and quivering as if still alive, was the tongue that he'd ripped from Denny Morgan's throat, along with most of his trachea and oesophagus.

As both men stared, Ash raised the meaty fistful to his mouth and ripped into it with his teeth. He sighed and smiled with pleasure, gobbets and veins dangling from his lips. Blood flowed down his neck, down his chest, splashing down into bright crimson pools on the floor that reflected the white neon striplights.

One of the guards tore the radio from his belt and found his voice. 'Situation on Level 2. Get everybody up here *now*!'

Chapter Eleven

Siberia

Deep in the icebound heart of the Russian province of Krasnoyarsk Krai, where the continuous winter blast kept temperatures well below minus forty Celsius, the barren wilderness of frozen lakes and tundra and snowy mountains stretched for a million square miles. Soon the polar night would descend, lasting from December through January, and the mining communities of Norilsk, the nearest human settlement and one of the coldest and most polluted cities on the planet, would see no sun at all for six long, dark weeks, temperatures plummeting towards minus sixty.

Out in the frozen wastes beyond the nickel mines, virtually nothing lived except for the polar bears and the few other wild animals that had evolved to withstand the harsh environment.

Or nothing, at any rate, that was known to the few humans who ever ventured there. When travellers vanished, as they fairly often did, it was generally assumed that they must have succumbed to the murderous cold, stumbled into a whiteout and frozen to death, or lost their way and slipped into a ravine.

Sometimes, that assumption was correct. Sometimes not.

Because other creatures lived here, too, unseen,

underground. Creatures that had spent a very long time, and put a great deal of effort into, concealing their existence from the rest of the world.

For much of history they'd been down there, hidden from human eyes. At a time when Northern Asia had belonged to the Empire of the Huns, the creatures had already long since made it their home. A thousand years later, when Siberia had been conquered and occupied by the Mongol hordes, the hidden networks of tunnels and caverns deep beneath the ice had already been greatly expanded. Their occupants emerged to hunt only under cover of darkness, while it was safe for them to move. When they did, there were no witnesses. Nothing left behind that could have alerted anyone to their presence.

There had always been enough for them to feed on. Many nomadic tribes had wandered across the region through the ages, staying a while before being displaced by another: the Yakuts, the Uyghurs, and other Turkic peoples whose camps and villages made easy targets during the night when the humans were at their most vulnerable. The blood of countless victims had allowed the creatures to thrive and quietly go on building their lair under the ice, where the feeble Siberian sun never penetrated and night and day were all one. Now and then, they'd allow a human to turn, and gradually amassed a contingent of humanoid vampires: inferior, bastard beings that the creatures despised and treated with contempt, but allowed to live among them as their servants and occasionally released into the world.

But reclusion was not the natural state of such an aggressively predatory race. It had never been their intention to remain permanently hidden in their lair: their leaders had long, long pored over their plans to broaden the extent of their realm – to extend it very far indeed.

They were in no hurry. When the time was right, they would strike. And the planet would change forever.

In the meantime with the passing of the centuries, the underground domain had grown into the vast subterranean citadel that now stretched nearly twelve square miles from east to west and plunged down further into the earth than the nickel mines of Norilsk.

It was inside one of those icy chambers, hundreds of yards beneath the surface, that three unusual visitors had come to the end of a long and difficult journey east. Only in these exceptional circumstances had they been allowed to enter the hallowed inner chambers of the citadel.

Two of the visitors were conscious and on their feet. Their names were Lillith and Zachary. They were vampires. Zachary was a huge figure, towering over Lillith. Many centuries earlier, in his native Abyssinia, he'd been a hunter famed for killing lions armed with only a spear. The lion-skin loincloth was a distant memory. Over a black silk shirt, he wore a tangerine-coloured suit that shimmered in the light of the ice walls.

Across the other side of the chamber stood Lillith, a raven-haired beauty in a red leather jumpsuit. Hanging from a belt around her slender waist, she still wore the empty steel scabbard of the sabre she'd lost back in Romania, before their trek eastwards. The shoulder of her jumpsuit was ripped from when their helicopter had come down in a blizzard, and her memory was fresh with the four days of hiding from the sun as they'd made their painful way a thousand miles across the deserts of ice. Finally, at the secret entrance to the underground citadel, they'd been met by the vampire servants who'd escorted them down here and told them to wait.

Lying inert on his back on a smooth, icy slab between Lillith and Zachary was the body of their leader, the vampire that Lillith called brother: Gabriel Stone. He was tall, slender and dark, and even in his state of deep unconsciousness he managed to look elegant and composed.

'Is he going to make it?' Zachary asked in his deep bass rumble, peering down worriedly at the still body. He'd asked that question so many times on the journey from Romania, carrying Gabriel's limp form on his shoulder, that Lillith had stopped replying. She stepped to her brother's side and ran her fingers down his cold cheek.

'Come back to me, Gabriel,' she murmured. She'd been there with him on the battlements when he'd been exposed to the force of the weapon the human Joel Solomon had carried into the castle. She remembered the way Gabriel had shielded her body with his, absorbing the lethal energy before they'd both hurled themselves over the edge of the battlements and gone tumbling down hundreds of yards to the rocks below.

Vampires could take a few knocks. Leaping from the top of a cliff had its risks but, as long as they didn't smash themselves too irreparably, it was nothing they couldn't survive. One thing they couldn't take, though, was the devastating effect of the cross of Ardaich. Of all the ancient myths and legends within vampire folklore, that cross was the most dreaded, the darkest, its name the most quietly whispered. And it was also the most mysterious. Its origins, and the source of its power, had remained an enigma since the time the humans called the Dark Ages.

'So badly hurt,' she murmured, stroking Gabriel's motionless arm.

'If he doesn't make it,' Zachary said, 'what are we going to do? I mean, we've followed him since . . .' He frowned as he tried to put a figure on the years their band had been together. 'Without him, we're lost.'

'He'll make it,' Lillith said. 'He has to. *They*'ll help, surely they will.'

'I sure hope you're right.' Zachary thought for a moment. 'Those trips Gabriel made sometimes . . . all he'd say was that he was going east . . . days at a time. He was coming here, wasn't he? They know him?'

Lillith nodded. 'He's been in contact with them a long time, learned many things from them. Once, years ago, he brought me here. That's why I know some of their language.'

'Just what are *they*, Lillith?'

'I once asked Gabriel the same question. He told me it was better I didn't know.' She paused. 'Our kind call them the Übervampyr. Many of us don't believe they really exist.'

As the two of them stood there over Gabriel, strange forms became visible through the thick, rippled walls that had been sculpted in the ice. The figures were tall. Hooded and robed. Watching them.

'They're here,' Lillith said. 'Now listen, Zachary. These Übers aren't like us. They're not . . . *humanoid*.'

'I ain't either,' Zachary said, not understanding.

Lillith shook her head. 'You *were* human once, remember. They never were. Just be ready for what you're about to see. And be careful. Don't look them in the eye. It offends them.'

A portal opened in the icy wall, and several of the tall, strange figures entered the chamber. One drew close. Towering several inches above Zachary's head, over seven feet in height, it reached up with its clawed, long-fingered hands and drew back the hood of its robe to reveal its face. The skull was tapered and bald, the ears long and pointed. Its skin was the colour of a washed-out winter sky, and so translucently thin that thousands of dark veins could be seen under its wrinkled surface.

Only a thing this hideous could have made Zachary turn pale and back off a step.

Lillith found it hard to tell the Übervampyr apart from their strange, horrible facial features – but she knew from his robes that this was one of the Masters that Gabriel had told her about.

When he spoke, his voice made Zachary back off another step. The ancient language was rasping and guttural. 'My name is Master Xenrai-Ÿazh.'

'That is one *ugly* mother,' Zachary muttered.

Lillith shot him a furious glare, then turned to address the Übervampyr, bowing her head and avoiding eye contact. 'It's an honour, Master. Gabriel has often spoken of you.'

'I have known Gabriel a very long time,' the Master said. 'In our language we call him *Krajzok*: "the young one".'

'I'm afraid for him. He's been very badly hurt. The cross—'

The Master raised his long, thin hand, silencing her. 'Yes. Our servants have already informed us of what happened. Of course, you fear for Gabriel. But you must leave him now. He is to be taken from here.'

'What's he say?' Zachary asked, keeping his eyes low.

Lillith ignored him. 'Taken where?' she asked, frowning.

'To the heart of the citadel,' the Master said, 'to a place where none of your kind may normally enter.'

'Are you going to help him? We brought him here in the hope that you could save him.'

'We have the means to restore him. The cross's power was not fully expended on him.'

'Then you *have* to make him better.'

The Master was quiet for a moment. 'It is not so simple. The Grand Council is convening.'

Lillith didn't want to show her irritation, but it was hard

94

to disguise. 'Gabriel is slipping away and all you can do is hold a meeting?'

'It is about Gabriel that we must talk,' he said. 'Only once the Council has made its decision can we act.'

'I don't understand. What decision?'

'Gabriel is to be placed on trial. If found innocent, he will be spared. If guilty, then according to our custom, he will be executed. I am sorry.'

Lillith was unable to avoid staring straight into the Master's dark, inscrutable eyes. 'Guilty of *what*?' she demanded. 'How can this be? What trial?'

The Übervampyr made no reply. At a wave of his clawed hand, six vampire servants marched into the chamber. Four of them lifted up the ice slab on which Gabriel lay. The other two drew long, curved swords from their belts and pointed them at Lillith and Zachary.

'Something tells me this ain't going too well,' Zachary rumbled.

The Master motioned to the four slab-bearers. 'To the Hall of Judgement,' he ordered.

Chapter Twelve

Romania

The sleet had given way to a mist of icy drizzle that blanketed the hills and forests as Joel drove the stolen pickup truck through the night. With every mile that passed, he kept glancing at the sinking fuel gauge. The only thing that terrified him more than being stranded in the middle of nowhere, lost, penniless and alone, was the horror of being caught in the open by the rising sun. He kept thinking he could see the first red glow of dawn on the dark eastern horizon.

'Relax,' he muttered out loud over the beat of the windscreen wipers. 'You've got hours yet. Everything's fine.'

Yeah, he thought bitterly. *You're a vampire now, and everything's just fucking fine.*

After the endless empty roads, a sweeping stretch of lights in the distance told him he was approaching a town. He was suddenly gripped with terror at the thought of entering such a dangerous alien environment. Humans would be everywhere. But he fought the urge to shy away from the town, and gripped the steering wheel tightly as he joined the thickening flow of night-time traffic. He was growing dizzy with hunger. He needed to eat. No, not to eat. To *feed*. The thought made him feel sick.

Driving by the illuminated windows of an all-night supermarket on the edge of town, Joel swerved into the little car park next to it and pulled up in the shadows. There was only a smattering of other vehicles in the car park, and he figured that some of those must belong to the staff.

As he watched from the dark interior of the truck, a woman came out of the supermarket carrying a shopping basket and started heading across the car park towards an old Peugeot estate, picking her way between the puddles that reflected the neon light from the windows.

Joel didn't need the shop lights to see his target with incredible clarity. She was short and plump, dark-haired, in her late forties or so. Under her raincoat she was wearing a nurse's uniform; he guessed she must be picking up some provisions on her way home after a late shift at some local hospital.

Joel could smell her blood. Hot and thick and dark, pulsing through her veins. The intensity of his senses was frightening.

Though not as frightening as the thing that was happening inside his mouth. His teeth didn't feel right. He ground them together, pressed his thumb-tips against his canines and gasped in shock at how elongated and sharp they suddenly felt. Something was taking control of him.

The woman kept walking across the car park. A few more steps and she'd have reached her Peugeot.

Joel opened his door with a trembling hand and stepped out. In the cold night air the scent of her blood was even thicker and more intoxicating.

He shuddered.

Fight it. Fight it.

He could smell something else, too. The pungent odour of the packet of raw meat in the woman's shopping basket.

98

She turned to stare at him, curiosity turning quickly to alarm as he stumbled up to her in the darkness.

'Please,' he said, aware that she couldn't understand him. 'I don't want to hurt you . . . I just need . . .' Then, with a speed and strength that astonished him even more than it did the frightened woman, he shot out his arm and tore the shopping basket from her hand. Its contents spilled out: two plastic milk containers, a block of processed cheese, a box of eggs that cracked and broke on the concrete; and a plastic-wrapped oblong package that Joel stared at for a split second before scooping up off the ground.

The woman screamed at him in Romanian as he turned and ran back to the truck. Its engine roared into life and he took off out of the car park.

A couple of miles down the road, Joel couldn't stand it any more. Pulling over to the side, he ripped open the package on his lap. The sharp tang of animal offal made his nostrils flare. Raw livers. He sank his teeth into them and felt the dead flesh rip. Cold, congealed blood and watery fluid ran across his tongue and down his throat, spilled down his chin onto his trousers. He bit deeper, devouring the meat with a ferocious passion that his sense of disgust couldn't deter.

Before he knew it, he'd wolfed down the entire contents of the pack. He let the empty polystyrene tray fall to his feet, coughing and spluttering through the awful cold, congealed blood that coated the inside of his mouth. An intense surge of self-loathing made him want to put his head through the windscreen. He pounded the steering wheel and moaned and cursed until he'd exhausted himself; then, finally settling down, he numbly put the truck back into gear and drove on.

Hours passed, and Joel was frantic with worry about running out of night by the time he found the stream of lorries heading for the seaport. He followed the heavy freight vehicles through tall gates. Nobody stopped him.

He abandoned the pickup truck in a dark corner of the docks, between two enormous steel containers. His agility, as he sneaked through the shadows, stunned him. He was like a cat, rapidly learning to make use of his new powers of stealth and physical poise. The raw livers seemed to have given him enough energy to keep moving for now, but the hunger still gnawed deep inside and some terrible instinct told him that he couldn't survive on a diet of animal flesh.

Fine. Then he'd starve. The other option was just too awful to contemplate.

Joel ducked around the corner of a crumbling building and crouched behind a stationary fork-lift truck as he heard steps approaching. He saw a cigarette glow in the dark. The shapes of two men ambling through the dockyards, a hundred yards away. They were talking in low voices, sharing some anecdote that made one of them laugh. As they came nearer, Joel's acute hearing picked up words of English, and he strained to listen to what they were saying. Once he'd caught enough to realise they were part of a British crew on board a freight vessel setting sail for the Port of Southampton that same night, he slipped out from his hiding place and followed them.

The sailors never once sensed what was pacing along behind them. They cut a path between dockyard buildings, past mounds of scrap and stacks of crates, giant coils of chain and cabling. Finally, they emerged onto a quay and Joel caught sight of the vessel they were heading for.

The container ship was a hulking black mass, the gently swelling tide slapping and sucking at her sides, rocking her almost imperceptibly on her moorings. Light streamed from an open hatch. The two sailors climbed up the gangway and disappeared inside.

Cautiously, glancing left and right, Joel followed. Nobody saw him as he slipped on board and started looking for a place to hide.

Chapter Thirteen

Siberia

The thousand-year-old ice cavern had a domed ceiling higher than that of the Sistine Chapel in Rome. Like the glittering white pillars that stretched up to it from the mirror-smooth floor, it was adorned with ornate carvings depicting venerated mythic scenes from the ancient Über culture. Solemnly gathered at one side of the great Hall of Judgement were the Council members for the prosecution; on the other side were the representatives for the defence, far fewer in number. Seated high above them, his ceremonial robes draped majestically across the wings of his gleaming ice throne and surveying the assembly with a cold eye, was the venerable Elder Xakaveôk, the Grand Judge. To his left, still unconscious on his stone slab that was now encased within a cage of razor-sharp icicles, lay the accused, Gabriel Stone.

Master Tarcz-kôi, the speaker for the prosecution, was in mid flow and the great hall resonated to the rasp of his voice as he hurled charges against the humanoid vampire whose presence in their midst was so distasteful to many of the assembly.

'The traitorous tendencies of the accused are established fact, and have been for an age,' he insisted yet again. 'Long has he harboured an unhealthy interest in the vile culture of the humans; long has he immersed himself in the study of their degenerate history, their primitive and unspeakable so-called art and music. Are we to permit him to continually dishonour us in this way?'

Master Xenrai-Ÿazh got to his feet and raised a claw for permission to address the court. 'With respect to Master Tarcz-kôi, as the accused is one of our most valued envoys, sent into the human world to carry out tasks at our behest, I regard it as only correct that he be granted a degree of freedom in order to integrate into their society. May I remind my learned friend that this is why we created these creatures in the first place? While we ourselves could neither adapt to, nor exist in, the human world, Gabriel and his kind have made it possible for our culture to thrive, albeit in attenuated form, at the heart of human civilisation these many centuries past. To this end, the accused is no mere student of their history. Has he not personally lived it?'

'No matter,' Tarcz-kôi said with a dismissive wave. 'He cannot be trusted.'

Master Xenrai shook his head. 'I would suggest that my learned friend's antagonism towards the accused appears more a matter of subjective bias than of reasoned debate. Our Hall of Judgement is no arena for illogical opinion-mongering.'

'Do not attempt to cloud this discussion,' Tarcz-kôi insisted angrily, his ears angling back and specks of foam appearing at the corners of his mandibles. 'The charge remains one of the utmost severity. Why did he keep the rediscovery of the *Zcrokczak* a secret from us? We maintain that he intended to use this fearful weapon against this citadel. Against us. We, who nurtured him, who gave him his powers and his immortality. We misguidedly entrusted him with the task of aiding our plans, beginning with the overthrow of the scourge of the Federation. He has failed us, and in doing so has provided ample evidence that our faith in his ability was grievously misplaced. Of course, if the Council had listened to *me* . . .' he added archly, pausing to cast a long, sweeping, severe glare at the rest of the assembly before going on. Drawing himself up to his full height, he pointed a claw at the accused in his ice cage. 'The gathering for the prosecution therefore calls for immediate sanctions against this traitor. I call for an immediate execution.'

'Whatever's happening in there, it isn't good,' Lillith said to Zachary in a low voice. The blades of the vampire guards were still pointed at their throats.

'Guys,' Zachary rumbled at the guards. 'How about you lower those things before someone gets hurt? 'Cause it ain't gonna be me.' When the guards' faces remained blank, he said to Lillith, 'I don't think these assholes understand what we're saying.'

'Either that, or they're well trained.'

Zachary smiled. 'Say, you remember that time, way back, in . . . where was it again?'

'It was in Istanbul,' Lillith said. She'd been thinking the same thing.

'Worked then,' Zachary said.

'Those were humans.'

'Still.'

She nodded. 'On three, then. One . . . two . . .'

'Three.' Zachary's massive arm shot out and his fist closed on the tip of the sword blade nearest him. Before the surprised guard could do anything about it, he'd used the leverage to swing the blade up in the air and push back hard to spin the guard round on his feet while arcing the weapon over the top of his head. Lillith did the same, and their mirror-image movements synchronised perfectly. Up and over; then step in fast and bring the blades round on themselves in a scissoring action that slammed the guards violently together, twisted their sword hilts out of their hands and forced them hard against the ice wall with the sharp steel edges against their throats.

'Still works pretty good,' Zachary said. 'Now let's go get Gabriel.'

Lillith's guard yelped in fright at she pressed the sword blade just hard enough into his neck to split the skin and let out a stream of dark vampire blood. 'One more sound and I'll take off your head,' she said in the old Über language. When he looked even more frightened, she smiled. 'Understood that all right, didn't you? The Hall of Judgement. Lead the way.'

'Holy shit,' Zachary said as they ran through the underground passages, prodding the vampire guards ahead of them with the points of their own swords. 'Look at this place. How long have these things been down here?'

'Since long before our time,' Lillith said. Her guard was slacking his pace. She jabbed the sword into him. 'Move.'

As far as the eye could see and beyond, great tunnels and smooth-walled caves had been carved out of solid ice and rock. As they rounded a corner and emerged onto a high galleried walkway, they looked down and saw a vast space stretching out below them, larger than a human cathedral. From its ceiling, not smoothly arched like that of the tunnels, hung clusters of huge icicles. Hundreds, thousands of them, like great gleaming stalactites. Long glassy tubes, many of them filled with a bright red substance that seemed to ooze and pulse down their twisting lengths, connected the tips of the icicles to rows of carved-ice vats that were mounted on platforms the length of the chamber. The tubes were constantly drip-filling the vats with blood that they were somehow carrying away from the icicles.

On the ground, scores of workers, no taller than children and draped from head to toe in rough hooded habits like those of medieval monks, were attending to the fuller vats by siphoning the blood into smaller ice containers, loading them onto trolleys and transporting them back and forth, back and forth. As the vampires watched from above, one of the small figures paused to peer up at them, drawing back its hood for an instant: a glimpse of its shrivelled, wizened features, lidless eyes and brutish jaw, and then it pulled down the hood and carried on about its tasks.

'Those little critters are even uglier than the uglies,' Zachary rumbled.

Lillith was about to move on when a movement from one of the giant icicles caught her eye. Something *inside* – they were hollow, she now realised. Whatever it was that wriggled and squirmed sluggishly, trapped behind the thick, semi-opaque conical ice walls, was hard to make out. Then the distinct shape of a human hand appeared, pressed flat against the inside of one of the icicles, and she finally understood their purpose.

'Storage,' she said to Zachary. 'Humans on ice. They keep them here, and they harvest them.'

Zachary stared. 'Even *we're* not that mean.'

'Keep moving,' Lillith said, prodding her guard onwards.

The first shrill cry of alarm came from a passage to the side as they ran by. It quickly raised more.

'Shit,' Lillith said. 'Quickly.' They pressed on, herding their captives ahead of them at a sprint that few humans could have kept pace with. But in seconds, they were being pursued by a crowd of vampire guards led by two fast-moving Übervampyr in plain robes. The ice-light glittered off drawn blades.

'Faster,' Lillith yelled. The two guards in front of them were stumbling in their panic, slowing them down, and the crowd was gaining on them.

'Keep going,' Zachary yelled. He turned and launched his powerful body upwards in a tremendous leap, lashing out with his sword at the tunnel ceiling. The ice was as hard as concrete, and Zachary's blade impacted against it with such force that the steel shattered.

A huge blue fissure appeared with a rippling, grinding crack. The ice ceiling gave way in an avalanche of crystalline boulders that filled the tunnel and blocked their pursuers' path. Zachary let out a whoop, threw away his broken sword and ran after Lillith.

The vampire guards stopped within sight of a grand sculpted entrance flanked by grotesque Übervampyr statues.

'The Hall of Judgement,' Lillith said.

More guards blocked the doorway. Seeing the intruders coming, they stepped forward and raised a warning hand, making the harsh rasping sounds of the old Über language. Zachary knocked one of them flying with a backhander that would have broken the neck of an ox. Lillith doubled up another with a kick to the stomach, then caught another in the face with the pommel of her sword as Zachary crashed open the tall ice doors to the Hall of Judgement.

'What is this outrage?' screeched the Judge, rising in his throne as Lillith and Zachary marched inside the echoing courtroom. He wagged his long clawed finger at the intruders. 'Your kind have no place in the Hall of Judgement. Guards!'

Lillith quickly laid down her sword and dropped to one knee in the aisle of the Hall. 'Please forgive the manner of our entry,' she said in the old language. 'But since when was justice meted out without hearing the testimony of witnesses?'

The prosecutor Tarcz-kôi snorted in disgust. 'We have no truck with the ways of human law.'

'I beg you, please listen to me before you pass judgement on my brother,' Lillith said, getting to her feet. Zachary stood at her shoulder with his arms folded and his brows heavy, shooting warning glances in all directions.

'He is a traitor,' Tarcz-kôi said flatly. 'Only a traitor would have kept secret from us the rediscovery of such a weapon of power.'

Lillith took a deep breath and spoke loudly to the whole assembly. 'If Gabriel's only crime was to fail to tell you that our enemies had recovered the cross, it's only because he didn't want to cause alarm. He had his plan, and he believed in it. Now the cross is destroyed. We may not yet have won this war against the Federation, but the greatest risk to all of us has been averted. What we have now is an open road to victory. I beg this court to repay Gabriel's loyalty to you by giving him a second chance. We won't fail this time.'

'Besides,' Zachary said, 'you fuckers harm Gabriel, there's gonna be a lot of dead uglies in this place.' One or two of the Übervampyr assembly frowned to hear his strange language, but to Lillith's relief, none of them understood him.

For a long moment, the Hall of Judgement was filled with murmurs and whispers. Master Xenrai nodded at Lillith and his features distorted into what she took to be a smile. The look on the face of the prosecutor was unmistakably one of hatred.

The Judge tapped a claw against his throne to signal silence. 'Enough. Let us cast the vote. All those in favour of executing the vampire Gabriel Stone, known to us as Krajzok, stand and be counted.'

Lillith and Zachary watched tensely as, one by one, many of the Übervampyr got to their feet. Lillith counted ten of them: half of the assembly. She trembled as an eleventh seemed about to rise as well, sealing Gabriel's fate. Zachary put his big hand on her shoulder. 'We won't let them do this,' he whispered in her ear.

The eleventh juror hesitated, then relaxed back in his seat.

The Judge tapped his claw again. 'As we see, the Council is divided.' Lillith searched his hideous face, but all she could see in his eyes was cold impassivity.

'According to our ancient custom,' the Judge went on, 'the final decision is now mine to make.'

A long silence in the hall. Zachary's grip tightened on Lillith's shoulder.

'My decision is that Gabriel Stone be taken from this court to the Chamber of Whispers,' the Judge said, 'where justice will be carried out. This pronouncement is final, and the trial now ended. Take him away.'

Instantly, four guards appeared from a side entrance, opened the cage that encased Gabriel and carried him out on his slab. The Council members all began filing towards the exit.

Lillith turned to Master Xenrai in alarm, but couldn't read his expression. 'What's happening?' she asked desperately as he approached her and Zachary. 'They're going to execute him, aren't they?'

Almost tenderly, the Master laid his long hand on her arm. 'No,' he said softly. 'The Chamber of Whispers is our room of healing. The Judge's pronouncement is that Gabriel be given the second chance that you desire. Congratulations. You have saved your brother.'

Chapter Fourteen

Alex was at VIA Headquarters before nine the next morning, wading through the backlog that had amassed in her absence. In the wake of the heavy casualties inflicted by Gabriel Stone's uprising, she now found that her workload had taken a sudden 300 per cent leap thanks to a mountain of ongoing investigation files inherited from deceased VIA agents. It looked like she was going to be tethered to the desk for a while.

The file currently open in front of her had come from the vacated desk of agent Rakesh Mundhra, one of her colleagues taken down in the gun battle with Gabriel Stone's gang on board the *Anica*, the Romanian cargo ship now docked in London that Stone had used to smuggle himself and his cronies into the country. Alex felt a jab of sadness at the memory of Rakesh. So much had happened in the short time since the incident that it seemed like months ago. Pushing her regrets to one side, she went on scanning quickly through his notes.

The case Mundhra had been investigating was that of a highly publicised massacre that had taken place a few days earlier in a quiet little parish church in a place called St Elowen,

Cornwall. It was the first Alex had heard of it – but then, she'd had other matters on her plate. It seemed that the church choir, composed of singers from the village community, had been engaged in their regular weekly practice when an intruder had entered the church armed with a sword. After slaughtering fifteen people including the vicar, a young boy and his parents, a teenage girl and the local butcher, the killer had made no attempt to escape. When the police firearms response unit had arrived some time later, they'd found him drinking the blood of the victims. Pouring it over his body. And proclaiming himself to be a vampire.

'Interesting,' Alex said to herself.

She read on. The killer, a drifter who had first been sighted apparently living rough near the village a few days before, had been arrested and locked up in a maximum security prison awaiting trial. The media had gone wild in the wake of the 'St Elowen Massacre' and predictably it had been the vampire angle that generated the most sensation: VAMPIRE IN CORNWALL; DRACULA SWORD MANIAC; FEAST OF BLOOD were just some of the typically asinine headlines the humans had come up with.

Mundhra's initial feeling had been that the attacker might be a Federation-registered vampire running amok. These things occasionally happened, as Alex knew only too well – though seldom so publicly – and one of the daily duties of VIA field agents was to check each and every possible report of rogue vampire activity. More often than not, the case turned out to be a hoax, a false alarm or just another stupid psychopathic human inflicting atrocities against his own kind. When it wasn't, agents like Alex were called to step in.

She spent a few minutes online, checking out the development of the St Elowen Massacre news story over the days

112

since Mundhra's final report. The killer called himself 'Ash', refusing to give any other name. Detectives were still trying to establish his real identity, starving the howling media hounds of any really juicy tidbits of information about his past or background – and the fact that he couldn't be finger-printed, due to apparently having mutilated his own fingertips at some stage with a razor blade, didn't help matters either. He was around thirty years of age, and it seemed he'd lived off the grid long enough for any official trace of him to have disappeared. His sharpened teeth were the subject of a lot of appalled fascination; it appeared he'd done the job himself with a file. *A set of pointy gnashers doth not a vampire make,* Alex thought to herself. The murder weapon itself had been a cheap reproduction of a Scottish basket-hilted broadsword, crudely inscribed with weird markings that the tabloids were proclaiming 'satanic'.

The latest on Ash was that he'd murdered and partially dismembered three of his prison inmates, apparently in order to drink and anoint himself with their blood. Seemed like old habits died hard. Ash was now in solitary confinement and several heads had rolled within the prison service admin-istration for having placed such a crazed murderer in a shared cell. The press were either morbidly lapping it up or screaming for justice system reforms, depending on which paper you read.

Alex searched out some related articles. Shortly before his prison cell stunt, the self-styled 'vampire' had been taken under heavily-armed police escort to the first court hearing prior to the start of his trial. There were pictures of him being marched from a prison van to the back of the court, amid the usual angry scenes: a tall, muscular figure, hooded to hide his face from the photographers swarming to get a shot of him.

And right there was a dead giveaway that Mundhra would've spotted, if he'd been around long enough to get the chance.

'Daylight,' Alex said to herself. No fizz, no pop, no inexplicable spontaneous human combustion when they marched the killer out into the morning sun. At that point he'd been well past the twelve hours' worth of protection that Solazal could have offered. Not easy to smuggle any of the stuff into a high-security prison, and anything he'd had on him at the time of arrest would have been confiscated and analysed.

'You're no vampire, Mr Ash-whoever-you-are,' she muttered. It was just as she'd suspected. Nutjobs like this guy were strictly a human problem, not hers. She reached for a stamp. *Bang.* Case closed. 'Bye, bye, Ash. Enjoy your stay in prison. Watch it in the showers.'

The next file in the heap was one that had come straight to her. When she opened it, she saw the reason why.

'Oh, Baxter,' she groaned. 'What have you done now?'

It wasn't so long ago that Alex had been tasked by Harry Rumble to go and have a gentle chat with the movie star and secret vampire, Baxter Burnett, about the latest hot role he'd been gunning for: the part of Jake Gyllenhaal's wayward, feckless younger brother in the upcoming Universal production *Firestorm*. The part was perfect for Baxter, and it was set to propel him into the A-list. VIA had just one issue with it: in all the years since his first breakout hit, *Down and Dirty*, Baxter had very noticeably not aged a day; now here he was, playing yet another fresh-faced thirty-year-old. CGI effects couldn't account for his eternally youthful appearance. The movie magazines and the nerds online were beginning to talk about it. It was the kind of attention that VIA didn't want.

So, under orders, Alex had leaned on him. Just a little.

Persuading him not to take the part had involved sticking a cocked .44 Magnum loaded with Nosferol tips in his face. At the time, she'd thought he'd got the message.

Now it looked like she'd been wrong.

The top page of the case file was a printout from the website of *The Hollywood Reporter*. 'BURNETT SIGNS UP FOR *FIRESTORM*', proclaimed the headline.

'This is the most demanding role I've ever taken on,' the star was quoted as saying, next to a photo of him beaming at the camera with a blonde on each arm, 'but I was born to play this guy. I can't wait to work with Jake and Stephen. I'm their biggest fan. I'm just so jazzed about this!'

And the rumoured twelve-million-dollar paycheque couldn't have been much of a disincentive either, Alex thought. Now she understood what his email to her had been about. She sighed. 'Baxter,' she groaned again. 'You're a very silly boy.'

It got worse. Clicking into the official Baxter Burnett website to check any latest news, Alex noticed that the star's blog had had more than a dozen updates in the last few days.

It was the one titled 'FUCK VIA!' that drew her eye.

'Come and get me, dipshits,' it said. 'You think you're so fucking powerful. What do you think you can do?'

And a few lines lower down:

'Ha ha! Agent Bishop, you can stick your gun up your ass. You can't fucking touch me, and you know it.'

The rants went on and on. Alex scanned down them to the bottom, where Baxter's fans had posted hundreds of comments in response. 'WTF????' asked one bemused poster. 'What is Baxter on about? Is he nuts?'

'Baxter is not nuts,' said another. 'His new part in *Firestorm* is emotionally very intense. As a method performer of the highest integrity, what you're seeing here is Baxter psyching himself up for the role of his career.'

'What's VIA?' asked another. 'Sounds like some kinda government department? I looked it up but can't find it. Is Baxter under investigation for something?? Worried.'

'Shit,' Alex said. 'Not good.' Suddenly, the rest of her caseload would have to wait. She was going to have to deal with this fast, before this idiot splashed the Federation across the whole human media.

Chapter Fifteen

Oxford

A cold, thin morning drizzle was falling over the city centre as Chloe Dempsey got off the Oxford Park and Ride bus, pulled her coat collar up around her ears and set off at a brisk walk towards the museum where her father worked. In the duffel bag over her shoulder were the broken stone fragments she'd found, each piece carefully bundled up in tissue and bubble-wrap.

As the church-like façade of the Oxford University Museum of Natural History on South Parks Road came into view, Chloe smiled to herself. One of the benefits of having taken the plunge and come to study in England was that she could zap down the motorway to see her dad as often as she wanted. She treasured the chance to catch up on the lost years every bit as much as he did. He was a little fatter now, a little greyer, possibly a little scattier, but still the same old dad she'd loved and missed. The quirk that had most exasperated her mom was the thing that most endeared him to Chloe – the way he could just lose himself in his work, passionately absorbed for hours on end. Sometimes Chloe thought that if nobody ever disturbed him, dear old Dad could sit staring at some historic relic until he died of hunger.

The inevitable divorce had come when Chloe had been fourteen. It still hurt her, the way her mother had treated him back then. The kindly, gentle New Jersey academic had never been quite ambitious enough for his wife; dusty, half-forgotten books held infinitely more appeal for Professor Emeritus Matt Dempsey than aspiring to membership of the country club.

That was where Chloe's mother had first met Bernie Silberman, the millionaire cosmetic dentist. Within six months she'd packed her bags, moved out of the cluttered, rambling old family home and traded the life of a professor's wife for the glamour of Bernie's high-society circles and the house in the Hamptons, dragging the reluctant teenage Chloe with her.

The sudden split had plunged Matt Dempsey into a bout of depression that had cost him his job and, if he'd carried on drinking the way he had been in those days, almost his life. It was his passion for history, the thing that had driven his ex-wife so crazy, that had saved him. When Chloe was sixteen, her father had cleaned himself up and taken the radical step of emigrating to England and settling in Oxford. With his academic record he'd had no problem in getting a job as curator at the prestigious Pitt Rivers Museum, the home of one of Britain's most extensive and valuable collections of antiquities from across the world.

Chloe had detested living with her mom and Bernie, and it would have been easy for her to slip into a disaffected teen rebel rut – not that either of them would have noticed. Instead, she'd poured her angst and frustration into her school work, excelling in academic subjects but especially at sports. When she'd announced that she'd gained a place at the University of Bedfordshire in England to take a degree in Sports Studies, her mother – whose life now orbited solely around her teeth, her tan, her wardrobe and her golfing buddies – had barely batted a Botoxed eyelid.

Entering the Natural History Museum, Chloe took the familiar path across the ground floor to the Pitt Rivers entrance on the far wall. Walking into the small, cluttered, somewhat musty museum was like stepping back into the past. Chloe skirted around the display cabinets filled with ancient model ships and the giant carved totem pole and headed towards the workshops and staff section. Her father could usually be found at his desk, utterly absorbed in some old artifact. Today it was a sheaf of yellowed documents in a forgotten language Chloe wasn't even going to try to identify. As ever, the small office was a crazy clutter, papers everywhere, bookshelves threatening to split from the sheer weight of the volumes stuffed into and piled on top of them, more books piled on chairs, on the floor.

'Hi, Dad.'

'It's great to see you again.' Matt Dempsey rose up quickly to hug her, then started clearing a space for her to sit down. 'When did you get back from Romania?'

'Just last night.'

'I was about to make a coffee. Want one?'

'From your third-century BC percolator? Love one.'

'How's the course?' he asked as he fiddled with the battered machine.

'Loving it. Did I tell you – I'm starting training for next year's national inter-college pentathlon championships?'

'Ah, the noble pentathlon, sport of the mythological Jason, lauded by Aristotle. The magnificent discus of Perseus. The venerable art of wrestling.' Matt paused. 'Though that sounds a little rough, I have to say. Are you sure—'

She laughed. 'Things have moved on a little since Ancient Greece, Dad. They dropped the wrestling, discus and javelin centuries ago. Nowadays we do cross-country running, swimming, horse-riding, fencing and shooting.'

Matt's face fell. 'They let you handle firearms?'

'Just an air pistol.'

'Honey, why did it have to be *guns*? Guns never did any good in this world. History tells us that.'

Chloe sighed. 'If you saw it, you'd see it's just a competition target pistol. Nothing too dangerous, I promise. Unless you happen to be a flimsy paper target. Then you're in *real* trouble, especially when I'm on the other end. I'll show it to you sometime.'

'I just don't want you getting hurt.'

'Don't sweat it, Dad.'

He handed her a coffee. 'Anyway. Sounds like you're having a great time. No regrets, then.'

'About coming over here to study? Not a shred of a regret. And I get to come here and see you, don't I?'

Matt smiled. 'Have you heard from your mother recently?'

'Not since the last facelift.'

He grimaced. 'Heavens. How many is that now?'

'Put it this way, I think Bernie started making secret calls to his accountant. She keeps on like this, she'll bankrupt the sonofabitch. Couldn't happen to a nicer guy.' Chloe started unzipping her bag. 'Listen, Dad, I actually came over here specially to bring you something I found in Romania. Here it is. It's kind of in pieces, but I think you'll find it interesting.'

Her father was already carefully unwrapping the fragments. He cleared a space on the desk, angled a bright lamp and examined them closely as Chloe quickly described how she'd stumbled over them at the foot of the mountain. 'What they are,' she said, 'I have no idea.'

Matt started arranging the stone pieces into different

patterns on his desk. 'Well, they obviously all belong to the same object. Fascinating. It's old, that's for sure. Very old.'

'I figured, if anyone could make sense of it, it'd be you.'

'I don't know about that. It'll take me some time to put it all together properly. But I'd hazard a guess that this is a cross of some kind. Look at this fragment here. See how the crosspiece seems to join up with part of an outer circle? Typical of the Celtic style.' He jumped up suddenly and went over to one of the crammed bookcases, gazed along a row of spines and plucked out a book. Chloe smiled as she watched him flicking eagerly through the pages. *Hooked already*, she thought.

'Like this one,' he said, turning the book round so she could see the drawing.

Chloe nodded. 'Beautiful.' She pointed at the pieces on the desk, running her fingertip along the faded inscriptions. 'What about these markings? Rebecca thought they were some kind of ancient runes.'

'Ancient carvings of a sort, certainly. Strictly speaking, all known examples of so-called "Celtic" runes were in fact either Scandinavian or Germanic in origin, so whether . . .' His voice trailed off and he paused with a frown, stroking the cool, smooth, creamy stone with his fingertips. 'As for the material it's made from – it's like nothing I've ever encountered before. A type of quartz, perhaps? Moonstone, maybe. No, moonstone doesn't have these tiny coloured flecks. It's something else.'

'Well, it's yours now, so you can take all the time you need.'

'Really? Are you sure?'

'I told you,' she smiled. 'I brought it back for you.'

'That was very thoughtful of you,' he said, looking touched. Before he could start getting all emotional on her, Chloe knocked back the last of her coffee and stood up.

'I have a lecture after lunch. Should just make it if I hit the road now.'

'I'm sorry to see you leave so soon.'

'The hectic life of the ambitious young student,' she laughed.

'What are you doing the day after tomorrow? I could make us dinner, that meatball thing you like. You could stay overnight and drive back in the morning. Unless you have an early lecture.'

'That'd be great. I'm going to be on my own anyway. Rebecca and Lindsey are going to some crappy gig.'

He beamed at her. 'Then it's a date.'

When she was gone, Matt Dempsey went over to his desk and spent the next hour piecing the strange stone fragments together. He'd been right – the object that gradually formed on his desk was a Celtic cross, probably the oldest example he'd ever seen. Thankfully it seemed as though Chloe had managed to find all the pieces. Their broken edges were sharp and fresh, not worn smooth with the passage of time, telling him that the cross had only very recently been damaged.

What a terrible shame, he thought. To have survived so long, only to be broken like that. Chloe had said she'd found it at the foot of a cliff, far below the battlements of an old abandoned castle: maybe it had fallen from there. Or been dropped. Matt was fully aware that, even today, there were self-appointed treasure hunters still ransacking every corner of Europe for items of historic value. This one had evidently – and perhaps literally – slipped through their fingers.

Matt rooted through a box of odd bits in the corner of the office until he found what he was looking for, some lengths of thin wire. With great care, he wrapped the wire around the reconstructed cross and twisted its ends together to form a cage-like casing that would hold the pieces firmly in place. Once it was reassembled, he used a digital caliper gauge to note its exact dimensions, and then spent another half hour making a careful, detailed sketch.

The more he studied the cross, the more fascinated he became. Nothing quite like it had ever come his way before. Those markings: what could they mean? He prided himself on his knowledge of ancient languages, but this defeated him. 'Damn,' he muttered, scanning his bookshelves. He could think of a couple of titles that might conceivably help him puzzle this mystery out, but they were at home.

He thought guiltily about the Etruscan vase restoration project that was going on across the hall, and of the arrangements for the party of Japanese historians who were arriving tomorrow. But his capable assistant Mrs Clark had all that under control, didn't she? It was nothing he couldn't leave until the morning, was it? Matt hesitated.

It was no use. He simply had to know more. He picked up the phone and told Janet Clark he was going home early. Then, after carefully packing the wired-together cross into a box of shredded paper along with the sketch he'd made of it, he hurried off to catch the bus.

Chapter Sixteen

The morning was crisp and bright as Dec sped westwards
in the Audi banger, but it wasn't the sunshine that was putting
a broad grin on his face as he drove. Glancing at the shiny
new laptop on the passenger seat next to him, he instinctively
reached out and patted it like a faithful dog.

The reply from Errol Knightly had arrived just after seven
o'clock that morning.

> Hello Dec,
>   Thank you so much for your fascinating
> message. I certainly would like to meet up with you
> to discuss these enormously important matters. I've
> just returned from my national book-signing tour
> and am now back at my home, Bal Mawr Manor,
> in west Wales. Why don't you come and see me
> a.s.a.p.? We have a lot to talk about.
>   Yours, Errol T. Knightly

Dec had jumped straight into his banger and burned rubber
– inasmuch as the Audi *could* burn rubber – all the way out
of Wallingford. Four hours later, and just about as far west
as you could get before dropping into the sea, he saw the
first sign for Newgale, Pembrokeshire, and his heart began

to thump all over again at the prospect of meeting up with a real vampire hunter.

Him and Errol Knightly. What a team they were going to make. Dec was so excited about it that when the radio news came on, with one of its top items the growing concern over the apparent disappearance of MP Jeremy Lonsdale, he was too lost in his thoughts to even notice.

It wasn't much longer before he arrived at Bal Mawr Manor, nestled among the rolling hills of the wild Pembrokeshire coastline. As he goaded the protesting Audi up a long hill, the glittering sea to his left, his first sighting of the place was the spectacle of four tall towers, circled by clouds of seabirds and silhouetted against the sun; beyond them was the greyly glittering Irish sea.

'Looks like a frigging castle,' he muttered to himself. The Audi managed to drag itself over the crest of the hill and the building came more fully into view. Dec let out a low whistle. The manor house was an arresting sight, perched on the cliffside overlooking an immense sweep of white beach. The nearest neighbours were farms dotted here and there against the green hills. A scattering of buildings in the far distance was all that remotely resembled a town anywhere within sight.

Dec drank it all in with a sense of awe as he approached the tall gates of the manor and found himself on a thickly tree-lined private road that stretched on for ages. Just as he was beginning to think he'd taken a wrong turning, the trees opened up and the road ended abruptly at a barrier. Beyond it was a ten-foot drop to a wide expanse of water that Dec realised with amazement was a moat surrounding the entire manor house.

On one of the barrier's high pillars was a small black box that he knew from movies to be an intercom system.

He wound down his window, pressed a button, and a moment later a crackling voice from the speaker asked him who he was. Dec stammered out his name.

For a minute, nothing happened; Dec sat in the car gazing at the incredible dwelling across the water. The place was at least five times bigger than the whole of Lavender Close put together. What he'd at first taken to be ivy growing up the manor's walls was actually a climbing sprawl of thorn bushes. Black shapes in the still waters of the moat were the half-submerged blades of two huge paddle wheels. Above the water, the massive closed wooden gate wasn't a door, but a drawbridge, held up by enormous iron chains. Either side of it were gleaming metal crosses three yards high.

A sudden wave of self-doubt washed over Dec as he sat there, bewildered by the spectacle. What was a poor stupid kid like him doing, thinking he could get involved with something on this scale?

But then, just as the impulse gripped him to turn the car around and head for home, the drawbridge began to descend over the moat, lowered on its chains by some hidden mechanism behind the walls to reveal a huge stone archway and the courtyard beyond.

Dec gaped. The drawbridge touched down. The barrier rose. The crackling voice on the intercom informed him that he could enter. Dec swallowed hard and drove the Audi over the moat and into Bal Mawr. As he pulled up inside the courtyard, the drawbridge was already closing behind him.

Dec got out of the car. The same thorny growth covered all the walls. In one corner, a long carport housed a cherry-red Porsche 959 and a big dark blue Bentley. The Bentley had a puddle of oil under its sump.

An iron-studded door flew open and a big, beefy figure that Dec instantly recognised as Errol Knightly came striding confidently out to meet him. The Man Himself extended his hand warmly. 'It's a delight to meet you, my boy.'

'I'm almost eighteen,' Dec said as his hand was crushed in Knightly's grip.

'Of course. Come in, come in. Welcome to my humble abode. Sorry to have kept you waiting. The drawbridge is a little slow, but entirely necessary. As I'm sure you're aware, the creatures of the night daren't cross running water. I have the moat blessed by the local priest every Tuesday and those paddle wheels are activated from dusk till dawn to keep the current flowing. Can't be too careful.' Knightly pointed up at the walls. 'See those thorns? Specially imported from Transylvania. Vampires can't abide the sight of them.'

Dec couldn't find much to say as Knightly led him inside the biggest hallway he'd ever seen. It made the entrance of Gabriel Stone's mansion, Crowmoor Hall, look like a hovel. Huge iron candlesticks around the walls gave the place a medieval air. Dec's nostrils twitched at a strange, sharp odour. Knightly noticed his expression, and boomed with laughter. 'We burn incense in every room, twenty-four hours a day. For cleansing and protection. Vampires loathe the smell.'

Can't say I blame them, Dec thought, trying not to breathe the stinging smoke as he followed Knightly through a doorway.

'As you can see,' Knightly said, 'we're well protected here. I only leave the place when absolutely necessary.'

'That'd be when you go off on your travels to hunt down vampires? All over the world, like?' Dec asked eagerly.

'Yes, yes, to go off and hunt vampires.' Knightly smiled broadly. 'Let's talk in the library. I'll have Griffin bring us refreshments.'

Dec gaped in wonder as they entered a gigantic wood-panelled room with bookcases twenty feet high.

'Sherry?' Knightly asked.

Dec had never tasted sherry. 'Um, got a beer?'

Knightly frowned, then smiled. 'Beer it is.' He tugged at an ornate sash that hung down the wall. Instants later a wizened, stooped little man who could have been any age between sixty and a hundred appeared in the doorway.

'Griffin, this young gentleman would like a pitcher of whatever finest ale we have in stock. Just the usual for me.'

'Right then,' Griffin said. The crackling voice hadn't been the fault of the intercom.

'Griffin is my faithful manservant,' Knightly boomed, clapping Dec on the back. 'He's been with my family for many years. Griffin, this intrepid young fellow wishes to join us in our crusade against the Undead.'

'Aye,' Griffin crackled sullenly, and shuffled off.

'Now,' Knightly said, rubbing his hands. 'To business.'

Chapter Seventeen

Siberia

A mile beneath the frozen wastes, far beyond the reach of the pale sun, Gabriel Stone stood at the window of his small quarters adjoining the Chamber of Whispers, wearing a long velvet tunic that brushed the ice floor. He was deep in contemplation as he gazed out at the crystalline sculptures of one of the citadel's many subterranean gardens. Cut into the towering domed ice ceiling high above was the ornately-carved, ice-shuttered oval window that the Übervampyr Masters called the Ecliptic Portal. The thousand-year-old astronomical device allowed the dwellers in the citadel to gauge the path of the sun, using dully polished mirrors to reflect only the tiniest degree of sunlight, unharmful to vampire eyes, thus telling them when it was safe to venture to the surface.

The sound of his chamber door opening disturbed him from his thoughts, and he looked round to see Lillith crossing the room towards him with a happy smile. She threw her arms around him. 'You're back, brother. I can hardly believe you're on your feet again so soon.'

Gabriel smiled and stroked her raven hair. 'The Masters are custodians of many secrets and much wisdom,' he told her. 'Thanks to their powers, I feel my strength quite restored.'

'Zachary's going to be so happy. He was worried about you. We both were.'

'Master Xenrai tells me that I have much to be grateful to you both for,' Gabriel said. 'You saved me. I won't forget.'

'You did the same for me,' Lillith said. 'Now you need to rest a while. We have to be sure that you're fully recovered before we make our next move.'

He shook his head. 'Celerity is of the utmost importance in this situation. Now that our mission is renewed, I intend to see it through. There will be no one to stop us this time.' He pointed out of the window at the dim glow of the Ecliptic Portal. 'It is still light out there. As soon as darkness falls, we can leave.'

'Gabriel, we have none of the human money. It'll be hard to travel without it.'

'Our friends here are not without resources, sister. The gold and diamonds we can carry with us, irresistible as they are to the humans, will see us a long way. As for hard currency itself, we still have millions in our Swiss bank account that our dear, departed and rather hapless ghoul, Jeremy Lonsdale, kindly donated to our cause. The moment we reach our destination, we can liberate all the funds we require.'

'What destination did you have in mind?'

'We will journey to England,' he told her.

She raised an eyebrow. 'Back to England? Are you sure that's wise? It's not long since we had to flee from there.'

'Our mission takes priority, Lillith. If we want to strike back at the heart of the Federation, we must crack the hard nut that is VIA. In order to be close to our enemy, we will establish our base in the former home of our beloved ex-ghoul.'

132

'Lonsdale's estate in Surrey,' Lillith said, her doubt giving way to a smile of pleasure. 'The Ridings. Nice. I like it.'

'The last place our enemies would look for us,' he said. 'As for the human police, we have little to fear from such benighted halfwits.'

'We have little to fear from *anything*,' Lillith said. 'Now that the cross is gone.'

Gabriel said nothing in reply, and for a few moments the two of them stood in silence gazing out of the window.

'Gabriel, what is that thing?' Lillith asked, pointing across the subterranean garden, beyond the ring of sculptures, at an enormous cylindrical tower that rose up high towards the ceiling.

'The Masters have long been astronomers,' he told her. 'That is their form of what the humans would call a telescope. This garden, with its portal above, is what the Masters use as their observatory. Look, sister – you see the mechanisms that allow the segments of ice to be slid apart, allowing a full view of the night sky? They have a passion for viewing the stars and planets of this galaxy and the countless others that surround it.'

She frowned. 'I love the night too. But the stars? What can be so fascinating about those tiny pricks of light?'

'There is much you do not know, sister.' Gabriel moved away from the window and began to pace the length of the chamber, looking pensively at his feet.

'Something wrong, Gabriel? You seem very serious all of a sudden.'

'It's nothing,' he replied.

'I know you better than anyone. I can see something is troubling you.'

He seemed unwilling to say; then sighed and came out with it. 'Since I awoke, I've been aware of . . . I find it hard

133

to explain. Little more than a sensation, but one that fills me with unease.'

'A sensation of what?'

He stopped pacing and fixed her with a piercing look. 'It has become part of me now,' he said. 'The cross. As if somehow it were burned into my soul.'

'Gabriel, you *know* you don't have a soul. What are you talking about?'

'I can only tell you what I feel. I feel it with a growing certainty.'

She laughed nervously. 'Gabriel, you're scaring me. Come, now. You've been very ill. That *thing* almost destroyed you. It's like nothing we've ever encountered before. But these feelings will pass. The cross is broken, gone. Its powers are lost, and it'll never harm us again.'

He stared at her for a moment longer, then slowly shook his head. 'I fear you are wrong, Lillith. It is the cross's presence I can sense. It was broken, but now it has been remade.'

'Gabriel—'

'Please don't ask me how I know this. But there is no doubt in my mind. We have not seen the end of this cross.'

Chapter Eighteen

Bal Mawr Manor

Errol Knightly listened intently as Dec told him everything he knew. He started from the beginning, with the account of how he and Kate Hawthorne, the girl next door, had argued while out for a drive; how she'd run off and got a lift in a Rolls with some rich guy, and gone with him to this party at a manor house called Crowmoor Hall.

'You might have heard of the place, like?'

'Certainly I have. It's where they found all those bodies recently,' Knightly said, perched on the edge of his leather armchair, already into his third top-up of sherry and heading for a fourth. 'It was on the news. Henley-on-Thames, isn't it?'

'What they won't tell you on the news is that it was a nest of frigging vampires,' Dec said darkly. He went on to describe how, after following Kate and her party hosts down to a strange crypt underneath the house, he'd witnessed the ritual slaughter of another girl. How they'd hung her from chains by her ankles, and then this black-haired vampire bitch with a sword had slashed her throat open, how the bastards had all stood there taking a shower in her blood. 'You should have seen it. You should have been there.'

Knightly had turned very pale by this point in Dec's story.

Soon after that, Dec continued, Kate had started going funny. The doctor hadn't been able to understand the illness that had struck her after her return from the party. Nobody would have wanted to hear Dec's story. 'But I was right.'

Knightly made a lunge for that fourth top-up. 'She *bit* you. A vampire actually *fed* on you?'

Dec nodded and showed him the faint marks on his neck. 'But like I said in my email, it wasn't enough to turn me. My mate Joel reckons she didn't have the powers, like Gabriel Stone did.'

Knightly's eyes were popping. 'And this Joel fellow . . . he's . . .'

'The one who destroyed her.'

'With . . .'

'With this weird-looking cross.'

'I see.' Knightly paused. 'Er, weird how, exactly?'

Dec pointed at the shiny crucifix Knightly was wearing around his neck. 'It wasn't like that. Or this one.' He pulled out his own to show him. 'It had a ring around the top bit.'

'You mean a Celtic cross?' Knightly said, fingering his crucifix.

'That's right. And it was made of stone. About this size.' Dec held his hands eighteen inches apart.

'So they *do* work,' Knightly sighed in immense relief.

'What?'

'I meant Celtic crosses,' Knightly said, collecting himself.

'Why wouldn't they? Are they not as holy as other crosses, or something?'

'Well, you see, Declan, some scholars have maintained—'

'It's Dec,' Dec said. 'Anyway, it worked pretty frigging well as far as I could see.'

'Tell me about Joel. Where is he now?'

'He went after them. To Romania, like. I haven't seen him since.'

Knightly drained the last of his sherry and looked wistfully at the bottle. 'And what about this Gabriel Stone?'

'He's the leader. Of the vampires, I mean.'

'And you've actually *seen* him? I mean,' he added carefully, 'seen him in a way that would make it clear that he really was a vampire?'

Dec nodded without hesitation. 'I saw his fangs and everything. I told you. He was there in the crypt. Then after that, he was the one who turned Kate.' He clenched his fists. 'I hope Joel's destroyed the bastard. If he hasn't, I will. And that's why I'm here, Mr Knightly.'

Knightly looked at his feet and said nothing.

'I know what you're thinking,' Dec pleaded. 'You're the big leagues. The real deal. I'm nothing compared to you. But I can't do this by myself. I'm just a kid, really. I'm all alone. I can't talk to me ma and da about this. Me brother thinks I'm a nutcase. The police . . . forget it. For all I know, Joel's not coming back. You're all I've got. The only person who understands. You've really *done* these things. Mr Knightly, you've got to help me.'

Knightly sat quietly for a long time, deep in thought. 'Normally, of course, I would have to charge for my services.'

'I don't have much money,' Dec blurted out. 'But I've thought about that. I'm a mechanic, so I am. Well, trainee, like, but I could fix that Bentley of yours. That's a nasty oil leak. I'll valet the Porsche, too. I'll clean your windows. Skim the moat. I'll do anyth—'

Knightly raised his hand, cutting him off. 'None of that will be necessary. In fact, under the circumstances, I would be willing to pay *you*, if you'd agree to let me include this incredible material in my next book. I'm already working on it. But I don't have *anything* like the kind of stuff—' Knightly broke off suddenly. He was sweating. 'How does a hundred pounds sound?'

Dec frowned. 'You don't understand, Mr Knightly. I want you to help me catch them. Like you said, they dwell amongst us.'

'It's "lurk". They *lurk* amongst us.'

'Dwell, lurk, whatever. I want to rid the world of them. All of them. I want you to learn me everything you know. I want to become a vampire hunter just like you. I want—'

Knightly's face flushed. He stood up and walked to one of the library's tall windows, gazing out to sea and thinking hard.

'If you aren't going to help me,' Dec said in a pained voice, 'I'll have to find someone else.' He thought for a moment, then added more brightly, 'Maybe I could join up with that Federation. You know, the one you talked about on TV. Maybe they'd take me on?'

'Fact is, Dec, I don't know any more about them than you do. I've no idea how you could contact them, or who they are. That video clip isn't much to go on.'

Dec's shoulders drooped. He slumped deep in his chair with a look of defeated resignation. 'Then it looks like I came all this way for nothing, so it does.'

Knightly sighed heavily, and turned away from the window to face him. 'Where are your family? Who else knows you're here?'

'Me ma and da and brother Cormac are home in Wallingford. I didn't tell them where I was going.'

'What about work? College? Is anyone expecting you back tomorrow?'

Dec shook his head. 'I work for me da. I can call him and make an excuse. I do it all the time. He's used to it.'

Knightly let out another big sigh. 'Very well. I'll help you.

You can stay here for a while. I'll teach you everything I know. I'll train you in the use of anti-vampire weaponry. I'll even give you one of my advanced vampire detection kits – worth £49.99. You can be my apprentice.'

Suddenly glowing with joy, Dec jumped out of his armchair. 'Cool!'

'On the strict understanding that every evening, after your training's over, you'll sit with me and help me get every detail of this down on paper. I mean everything. The house. The vampires themselves, what they looked like, how they talked, how they dressed, exactly what they did.'

'No problem. I remember it all.'

'And all about this cross. This library has books centuries old, filled with illustrations of ancient crosses. We'll go through them systematically, until we find one that's similar to yours. We'll make drawings of it. You'll tell me precisely what happened when your friend pointed it at Kate. Every last shred of detail.'

Dec's face fell. 'I can remember that too. I could never forget it.'

'It's a deal, then?'

'Deal,' Dec agreed.

Knightly grabbed his wallet and peeled off two fifty-pound notes. 'Here's the money.'

Dec hesitated, embarrassed, then thought of the credit card payments for the new laptop and took the cash.

'Good. Now, I need to make a phone call,' Knightly said, looking at his watch. 'Griffin will show you to the guest quarters.' He walked over to the sash and gave it a yank to summon his manservant.

As the bent old man led Dec away from the library, Knightly waited until they were gone, then ripped a mobile phone from his waistcoat pocket and feverishly dialled his agent's number in London.

'Harley, it's me,' he said breathlessly. 'Listen, you won't believe what's just happened. You know the *thing* I told you about . . .?'

'Your little, ah, problem?' the agent's voice said dryly.

'My writer's block.'

'Or basic lack of material,' Harley said. 'Other than that phoney video footage some nutter sent you from Romania. Maybe if you'd ever *done* any of the things you've written about, instead of just putting on this dismal Van Helsing act for your readers. It would help even more if you actually believed in vampires.'

'I *do* believe in them,' Knightly exploded, deeply hurt. 'Just because I've never had actual, you know, first-hand experience of them . . .' He flapped his arm impatiently, as if the inconvenient truth was an irritating mosquito he could swat away. 'Anyway, never mind all that. I've just come across enough material for three more bloody books. Five more, if we pad it out a bit.'

'So you won't have to refund that hundred grand advance-on-signature payment,' Harley said. 'That's welcome news.'

'And you'll get to keep your commission.'

'Even better. What is this new material?'

'Pure gold. I'll tell you all about it over a champagne lunch next week,' Knightly said. 'You're going to love it. The publishers are going to love it even more.'

Chapter Nineteen

London

It was just before midday by the time Alex arrived at the Ritz off Piccadilly and walked up to the desk.

'Hailey Adams,' she said to the receptionist, charming but authoritative, flashing her VIA ID too quickly for the woman to scrutinise it. 'Starburst Pictures. I'm here to see Mr Burnett. The Trafalgar Suite, right?' It was only fifty–fifty, she thought as the receptionist checked the register, that Baxter hadn't left his regular London hideaway and headed back home to the States. Life as one of the beautiful people.

The receptionist smiled. 'Trafalgar Suite, that's right.'

Alex used the stairs. Lifts were too slow. Arriving at the door to the suite, she pushed straight through with a splintering of wood.

The lavish rooms were just as she remembered them. Except . . . no Baxter. The only sign of him was the Armani jacket carelessly thrown over the back of one of the Louis XI settees and the laptop sitting open on a marble-topped coffee table. Alex strode across the Persian rug and peered at the screen-saver, a handsome close-up of Baxter's face, a still shot from one of his *Berserker* movies – Alex couldn't remember which. Still, it was definitely his computer.

With a flick of the keys, the screen-saver vanished to reveal Baxter's opened email program. The last message to have come in was clocked at 10.38 that morning. Its heading was 'Let's have lunch'.

The name of the sender, Piers Bullivant, was one Alex recognised. A cinema fan right from the days of silent movies, she'd been there for the heyday of Keaton, Chaplin, the Marx Brothers, all the greats, and must have seen a hundred thousand films since. She rarely missed an issue of *Movie Mad* magazine, and Piers Bullivant was one of their long-standing writers. Alex had read enough of his articles to know that Bullivant was a savage and vitriolic critic of anything to do with the commercial movie industry, Hollywood in general, and vulgar, untalented and overpaid stars like Baxter Burnett in particular.

Let's have lunch? It seemed just a little unusual, Alex thought to herself, that Baxter should be in friendly email correspondence with the critic who, more than anyone, seemed to delight in every opportunity to hack and bludgeon him to death with the pen. But then, looking at the message more closely, she saw something even odder. Bullivant's reply read:

Dear Gwendolyn – Lovely to hear from you again. Yes, I agree, it would be great to meet up. How about lunch today, my place?

Below, Bullivant gave his address in Wimbledon. Seeing that the email had been replied to, Alex clicked into the sent messages folder. The reply from GwendolynCooper@hotmail. com had been posted at 11.46, just a few minutes before she'd got here.

Hi Piers,
It's a date. See you at 12.30. I'll bring a bottle.
Gwendolyn xxx

'Shit,' Alex muttered as Baxter's ploy began to dawn on her. She scrolled up and found six more messages from 'Gwendolyn' to Bullivant. Attached to the first message was a picture that most definitely wasn't of Baxter Burnett. The blonde was maybe nineteen or twenty. Low-cut blouse, painted-on jeans, heavy eye-shadow, glossy lipstick, provocative pout, the works. Apparently, she was a final-year media student at London University and a huge fan of Piers's work, passionate about getting into film journalism; and did he know of any openings coming up at *Movie Mad*? She'd just love to meet and talk.

'Come on, Bullivant,' Alex snorted. 'Even a human can't be this easily taken in.'

But, seemingly, a human could. It hadn't taken much wooing from Baxter before the critic had gulped down the bait.

'Bugger,' Alex said, looking at her watch. Baxter must have left just a few minutes ago, but he still had a pretty good headstart on her. She'd little more than quarter of an hour to cut across town to Wimbledon, if she wanted to interrupt the romantic lunch date before it went too badly for Piers Bullivant.

Seconds later, Alex was tearing out of the smashed door of the Trafalgar Suite and running for the stairs.

Chapter Twenty

Wimbledon

A giant poster of Jean-Luc Godard frowned sardonically down from the wall over Piers Bullivant's desk in the cramped study of what he liked to call his *bijou residence*. Tapping on his keyboard and pausing every few words to titter to himself, the critic was just putting the finishing touch to his latest torpedo attack.

> *On the strength of its director and most of its cast,* Firestorm *has the potential to be a passable little thriller, by Hollywood standards at least. However, even before the cameras shoot a single frame, this movie is doomed by a fatal, irredeemable flaw. And the name of that flaw is Baxter Burnett. Never in the history of cinema has an actor been so guaranteed to destroy single-handedly any production in which he takes part . . .*

When he'd finished tinkering with it, Piers read the piece back out loud and gave a satisfied cackle. He looked at his watch, wishing it was a twenty-four-carat Rolex Oyster like the one that bastard Baxter Burnett had been flaunting in his last TV interview. But, Piers quickly consoled himself, was it not he, and not the hated Burnett, who was about to be visited by the super-hot Gwendolyn Cooper? Was it not he who . . .

12.26. She'd be here any minute. Piers shot out of his desk chair and hurried into the tiny living room of his flat. He put on some mood music, lit a scented candle, tore open a bottle of wine, set two glasses on the table, polished his thick spectacles with the hem of his short-sleeved shirt, adjusted his tie in the mirror, took a breath spray out of his pocket and gave it a couple of squirts. He smiled and felt in his other pocket, touching his fingers against the packets of condoms in there and wondering if two would be enough.

Piers's heart leaped as the doorbell rang. After a last-minute armpit sniff-check, he raced to the door and flung it open with a beaming smile on his face. 'Come in, Gwe—'

That was as far as he got before Baxter Burnett grabbed him by the tie and almost ripped his head off as he hurled him backwards into the room. Piers triple-somersaulted into the sofa and overturned it, sprawling across the rug. Baxter slammed the door shut and marched inside the flat. He was wearing a heavy black cowhide motorcycle jacket, leather jeans and boots. In his hand was a torn-out page from *Movie Mad*.

Squirming on the floor, Piers recognised it as last month's review of Baxter's star vehicle, *Berserker 6*.

Baxter stood over him. 'Pleasure to meet you at last, asshole. Hey, nice fucking place you got here, toilet licker. Couldn't swing a mouse in it, but hey, you won't be needing it much longer. Now, something I wanted to ask you about what you wrote.'

Piers stared up at him and could only whimper.

Baxter held the torn-out page out in front of him and stabbed the text of the article with his finger. 'Says here, now let's see . . . "the Parisian café scene is one of the most risible pieces of cinema ever committed to celluloid, featuring a Burnett performance so wooden that one might have mistaken him for part of the pine café furniture". Oh, yeah?' Baxter shook the paper furiously. 'And what about this bit – "The twist that follows is so insultingly contrived that the smallest infant could see it coming from thirty miles away. This is a film that should never have been allowed to escape from pre-production . . ."' Baxter lashed out with his foot, and Piers doubled up in agony. 'All right, scum sucker, let's talk about the twist. Tell me what you know, dumbass. Spit it out.'

Piers opened his mouth, but all that emerged was a string of bloody mucus.

'Oh, the great critic's at a loss for fucking words. You know what? I don't think you even saw this movie. You know how I know that, inchworm? Because that part was in the fucking *trailer*' – Baxter kicked again, harder, and Piers screamed – 'and it never even made it to the final fucking cut. So you just gave yourself away, you big dicksmoking phoney.' Baxter crumpled up the sheet and smiled. 'And now you're gonna die.'

Piers Bullivant's bladder let go at the precise moment that Baxter opened his mouth wide and the fangs came out.

The Jaguar's dashboard clock read 12.37 as Alex skidded to a halt outside Piers Bullivant's apartment building. She sprinted to the entrance. Pounded up the stairs, and crashed through Bullivant's door.

Whoops. Too late.

Among the blood-soaked wreckage of the tiny living room, the movie star was crouched on the floor, bent low over the twitching, but very obviously lifeless, body of his critic, gnawing and sucking at the ripped flesh of his throat.

Baxter looked up as Alex appeared in the doorway. The blood that slicked his chin was running down his throat and soaking into his shirt.

'Hi there, Agent Bishop,' he said, bright red foam bubbling at the corners of his mouth.

Alex popped the retaining strap of her shoulder holster and drew the pistol. 'Don't do anything silly, Baxter. You know what I've got here, don't you?'

'Nosferol bullets,' Baxter sneered. 'Right. As if your goddamn Feds won't pump me full of that shit anyway.'

'What's got into you, Baxter?'

'Fuck you!' Baxter sprang to his feet, seized the over-turned sofa and hurled it across the room. Alex ducked out of the way, but the sofa hammered into the wall next to her and bounced back at an angle, knocking the gun out her hand before landing with a crash on a side table. A pair of wine glasses and a lit candlestick tumbled across the carpet. Flames quickly caught a hold on the bottom of one of Bullivant's flowery curtains, but there wasn't much Alex could do about that right now. She grabbed the pistol from the floor as Baxter leaped across the room and through a doorway into the tiny kitchenette. There was a smashing of glass.

Chasing after him, Alex got there just in time to see him dropping the eight yards to the ground and sprinting frantically away through the little gardens at the back of the apartment building. She raised the Desert Eagle and felt the light trigger break against the pad of her fingertip. The blast of the gunshot punching against her eardrums. The hard recoil back into her palms being absorbed through her elbows. The fat .50 calibre shell casing spat from the pistol's maw as the breech opened and closed faster than even a vampire eye could see. Masonry dust erupted from the wall of the neighbouring building as Baxter darted around the corner and out of sight. Alex vaulted out of the window after him and hit the ground running for all she was worth towards the spot where Baxter had disappeared.

She heard the roar of the engine a fraction of a second before the blazing headlight and raked-out chrome front forks of the Indian V-twin motorcycle bore down on her from around the corner. Baxter's fists were tight on the handlebars and his hate-filled face glared at her from between the clocks. She dived aside just in time to avoid being run down. The bike thundered past and kept on going.

Alex scrambled to one knee and let off three more pounding shots from the Desert Eagle. The Indian's back light exploded and its rear wheel stepped out of line as the fat tyre burst apart. Baxter sawed wildly at the handlebars, but couldn't prevent the machine from toppling over and sliding across the pavement with a grinding of steel on stone, showering sparks. The movie star tumbled to the ground but was quickly back up on his feet. A glance over his shoulder at Alex already coming after him with the gun, and he was off like a madman down the street.

It was a quiet residential area, only a few terrified passersby and a smattering of traffic. Public gun battles weren't strictly part of VIA's low-profile policy, but then allowing a celebrity vampire to run amok wasn't exactly on the agenda either. Alex raised the pistol again and was about to fire at the fleeing figure of Baxter Burnett when she realised that the set of open wrought-iron gates he'd just sprinted past was the entrance to a school and that there was a crowd of kids gathered just inside them. Some of the older ones, girls and boys of up to about twelve or thirteen, had ignored the frantic shouts of their teachers to get inside, and had come running towards the street at the sound of the gunshots.

Alex lowered the gun, not daring to risk a shot. Killing humans wasn't on the cards for her.

A couple of yards from the crowd of schoolkids, Baxter's run faltered. He turned to look at them. Suddenly they were all pointing at him, eyes were opening wide and mouths were dropping open. There was a shout of 'It's Baxter Burnett!' Those who could tear their gaze from their cinema idol stared delightedly at Alex. Not a camera or crew anywhere in sight, but they obviously thought they were in the middle of a film shoot, complete with blank-firing movie weapons.

'He isn't Baxter Burnett,' Alex called out to the kids. 'He's just a lookalike. Get away from him.'

But before anyone could react, Baxter reached out and grabbed the nearest of the crowd, a girl of about twelve with masses of golden curls and a look of bedazzlement that very quickly turned to terror as he dragged her roughly across the pavement and wrenched a handful of her hair to one side to expose her little neck. 'I'll bite her,' he yelled at Alex. 'I'll turn her.'

Alex hesitated. The kids were screaming. The teachers had run back inside the building.

'Put the gun down, Agent Bishop,' Baxter shouted.

Alex tossed the Desert Eagle to the ground. 'Now you let go of the child.'

'Back off!'

Alex retreated a step. 'This isn't going to look too good in *The Hollywood Reporter*,' she said. The little girl in Baxter's grip was howling. Most of her friends had run in fright back towards the school buildings. Others hovered uncertainly, rigid with terror.

'Like I care,' Baxter screamed. 'I'm sick of being told what to do all the time! I'm not going to take it any more, not from you, not from the goddamn fascists you work for!'

'There's nowhere you can run that they won't track you down,' Alex said.

'Oh yeah? I heard the rumours. I'm not the only one that's joining the Trads.'

'There are no Trads left, Baxter. We wiped them out.' There wasn't much conviction in Alex's voice as she said it.

'Bullshit. I'm going to find them, I'm going to join them, and I'm going to come back and kick your Federal ass.' Spotting a car coming down the street, Baxter dragged the little girl to the kerbside and out into the road, blocking its way. Baxter hauled the child around with him to the driver's side, wrenched open the door and with his free hand hauled the elderly woman driver out from behind the wheel, sending her spinning to the opposite kerb.

Alex could do nothing. Baxter dumped the child on the road, then hit the gas and took off with a maniacal laugh.

Alex scooped up her gun and launched herself at the back of the car as it accelerated away. Her fingers raked smooth metal, but she had no purchase and went sprawling to the ground as the car sped into the distance.

The twelve-year-old girl was still crying hysterically at the roadside. Alex went over to her and quickly checked her for scratches or bites. Nothing. She trotted over to the old woman Baxter had pulled out of the car. Minor grazing, a couple of nasty bruises.

'I'm with the police,' Alex told her. 'My unit's on its way. They'll look after you.' The wail of sirens had been within vampire earshot for the last few seconds. The teachers had reported the gunshots, she guessed, and someone must have called the fire brigade too. A dark column of smoke was rising from Piers Bullivant's nearby apartment building.

As Alex helped the old lady to her feet, suddenly feeling hungry and trying not to think about the human blood flowing within easy range, the first police car came screeching into view at the top of the street.

Alex wasn't worried about getting away from the cops. But explaining to her Federation superiors that Baxter Burnett had now officially gone rogue, evaded her and was on the loose . . .

That part might not be quite so simple.

Chapter Twenty-One

Oxford

For the last three years, Matt Dempsey's home had been a rambling three-storey Victorian terraced house in a quiet street in North Oxford, fifteen minutes' bus ride from the city centre. The place was much too big for a solitary academic, but over the years he'd nonetheless managed to fill it with stuff his ex-wife would have called junk. In many cases, Matt secretly admitted that she'd have been right – the collection of antique brass lamps jostling for space on the mantelpiece of his downstairs study, for instance – but he prized them just as highly as the fourteenth-century Chinese statuettes on his bookshelf, the rare Mayan pottery in the display cabinet and the Italian medieval-period lute that hung on the wall behind his battered desk.

At this moment, though, they were the last things on his mind as he struggled to figure out the strange markings that ran around the circumference of the stone cross's outer ring and along its pitted crosspieces.

It took him a while to root out the books he needed: the most useful of the cracked, musty leather-bound volumes were Crosman's 1822 *Lexicon of Ancient Tongues* and Kerensky's 1906 edition of *Lost Runic Symbols of the Early Dark Ages*, both long since out of print and very difficult to come by. Matt pored over them so intently and for so long – flicking through the yellowed pages, filling a pad with detailed notes and scribbles and furious crossings-out, one false start after another and a pile of crumpled paper mounting up at his feet – that he lost all sense of place and time.

Finally, after what could have been three hours or thirty, he found himself staring with bleary eyes at what he reckoned was the closest possible translation of the markings on the cross.

Bizarre. Had he got it right? Some of the inscriptions that hadn't been destroyed by the ravages of time still eluded him, and not even the scholarly erudition of A.P. Kerensky could shed light on them. But there it was, as best he could figure it out:

He who wields this cross of power shall gain protection from the dark revenants of Deamhan, drinkers and plunderers of the life of Man. May the Divine Virtue of Our Lord descend upon thee and hold thee safe.

Matt studied the smooth, creamy-white stone of the cross and wondered how old it must be. There could be no question of sending it off for testing through the normal Pitt Rivers Museum channels – that could take weeks. But what about his pal Fred Lancaster? Stiff from being bent over the desk for so long, Matt hobbled over to the phone and looked up his number at the Oxford University Department of Geology.

'Fred? Matt Dempsey here.'

'Matt, old boy. How long has it been?'

'Listen, I need a favour. Wondered if I could run by the lab with something interesting that's come my way?'

Chapter Twenty-Two

Southampton docks

The voyage seemed to have gone on forever. After the incessant, monotonous rumbling of the ship's diesels and the echoing boom of its motion through the sea finally died away, Joel hesitated a while in the half-empty freight container deep in the bowels of the hold where he'd found a place to stow away. The faint glow of his watch dial, radiating the stored energy of the only sunlight he could bear to be exposed to, told him that it was after one in the morning. He held back another half hour, then, frightened that the ship might suddenly set off again and carry him off to some unknown destination, he crept out of the hold and made his way undetected to deck level.

In the middle of the night the Port of Southampton was a blaze of frenetic industry. Dock workers swarmed this way and that like ants under the glare of the lights that streaked across the water, while giant cranes reared high overhead like dinosaurs, carrying out the endless cycle of loading and unloading cargo onto the decks of the hulking ships moored against the harbour walls. Joel was able to sneak away through the vast facility without anyone challenging him. By the time he'd made it out to the streets of Southampton his energy was all but sapped and he had to stop frequently to lean against a wall. He was already fearfully counting the hours until sunrise. This awful nightly race against the clock was going to be the centre of his whole existence now, for the rest of eternity. Would there never be a way out for him?

Passing the pitted brickwork mouth of an alleyway that was cluttered with old metal bins and crates of empty bottles, he heard the dull *thump-thump-thump* of a nightclub in full swing and moved on hurriedly to avoid any chance of getting caught up in a crowd. Some drunks loitering about in the street ignored him as he went by.

A few yards further on, Joel heard something that made him stop in his tracks. Even as he whipped around at the sound of the woman's cry of distress, he was falling instinctively back on his police inspector's training. His eyes darted across to the nightclub doorway and picked out the figures of a burly man in a leather jacket and a woman who was staggering away from him. As Joel watched, the big guy pursued her aggressively across the street, slurring loudly, 'I'll smack your teeth out, you fucking bitch!'

There were no club bouncers anywhere to be seen, nobody except the drunks Joel had passed by, who were all propped against the wall or slouched on the pavement, smoking and grinning inanely and obviously disinclined to intervene in the situation. The woman couldn't run properly in her high heels, and in just a few steps the man caught up with her, grabbed her arm and slapped her hard across the face. She screamed and lost her footing, her legs kicking out, one shoe tumbling into the gutter.

Still clutching her arm, the big guy started dragging her roughly towards the dark entrance to the alleyway. She screamed again as he swung his arm around and hurled her crashing into the row of bins. A stack of crates collapsed and empty bottles rolled across the alley floor as the woman struggled to get to her feet.

The big guy swayed up to her and started undoing his belt and fumbling for his flies. He was so focused on his wriggling victim and on what he was about to do that not even a noisy human coming up behind him would have drawn his attention.

Joel tapped him lightly on the shoulder. Up close, the guy was as broad as a bear and a good three inches taller than him. The big man turned round and snarled at Joel. 'Fuck off.'

'Police,' Joel said, and for just an instant it was like stepping back into the lost world of his past. But the illusion didn't last long. He reached out an arm and grabbed a fistful of the guy's lank brown hair.

Even in Joel's state of extreme hunger and weakness, fifteen stone of muscle and lard felt like no weight at all as he lifted him clear off his feet with one hand. The guy kicked and thrashed in mid-air, yelled in pain and rage and clapped his hands to his head, trying to prise Joel's fingers away. Joel drew back his fist and punched him in the midriff. He went flying as if he'd caught a cannonball in the stomach. The impact against the alley wall drove a grunt of air from his lungs. He bounced, hit the ground hard and lay still.

The woman staggered to her feet. Scrabbling for her lost shoe, she stared up at Joel with big, frightened eyes. 'You're not the cops,' she said uncertainly. 'No way.'

'Are you all right, miss?' Joel asked her, and she nodded. He tossed away the big fistful of hair that had come away from the guy's scalp, roots and all, and pointed down at the slumped heap on the ground. 'Who is he?'

'Dunno. Just some guy who wouldn't take no for an answer.'

'Okay. You'd better get out of here,' Joel said.

She hesitated a second, then stepped into her shoe. 'You take care, now,' Joel called after her as she scurried away up the street, leaving him alone with her attacker. The guy was slowly coming round now, groaning and trying to gather himself up. Joel grabbed the collar of his jacket and dragged him a little deeper into the shadowy alley. He glanced back at the street. The drunks were out of sight. Nobody was around.

This is it, he thought. *You have to do this. You won't survive otherwise.* He could feel the teeth grown long and sharp behind his lips, just as they had before. Except it wasn't like before. This time, it felt right. This time, he was going in for the bite. The dark instinct that was surging up from some unknown place deep inside him commanded him to surrender, and it was a force he couldn't deny any longer. Joel yanked the guy's collar down, exposing a few inches of thick neck. The scent of human blood made him quiver with anticipation.

Joel opened his mouth and felt his upper lip roll back from the long vampire fangs. The big guy's eyes opened wide in terror as the sight jolted him fully awake. He let out a strangled whimper and tried to crawl away. Joel held him tight.

But then he looked into the liquid, pleading, pitiful eyes of the helpless human, and he stopped.

No. He couldn't bring himself to do such a thing.

Joel let the man go. He sat heavily on the ground as he watched the human scramble desperately to his feet and stagger blindly away up the alley.

The guy didn't get very far before a shape lunged out of the shadows and caught him with a hard, fast blow to the neck that knocked him cold.

The shape stepped over the unconscious body and clumped towards Joel in heavy boots that echoed in the alley.

'Who are you?' Joel called out. It was the shape of a man – but Joel already knew he was no man. As the figure came closer, Joel could see him more clearly. He was short, stockily built and, to judge from the grizzled beard that hung halfway down his chest, he looked about sixty in human years. A long Viking-like grey plait of hair was draped down one shoulder of the chunky Aran sweater he was wearing.

As Joel stared, the figure spoke in a deep, rumbling voice. 'That wasnae such a clever idea, laddie.'

'Who *are* you?' Joel said again.

'Once you've hooked your wee fish, you dinnae let him go. Not until you've done the necessary.'

Joel blinked. 'I . . . I couldn't—'

'No room for pity, laddie. Pity won't get you very far. Something tells me ye're a bit new to this vampire lark, aye?' The thick grey beard broke into a grin. 'The name's Tommy. Tommy McGregor. Luckily for you, I've been around a while longer. Now let's get this thing done properly and get oot of here before someone comes.'

Speechless, Joel watched Tommy one-handedly drag the unconscious body of the human across the alley and prop it up against the wall. 'Big bugger, this one,' the grizzled vampire muttered. 'Like a damn sack o' spuds.'

Joel turned his face away and closed his eyes as Tommy lunged towards the human's throat. The sounds of sucking and slurping made him feel queasy. When Tommy finally pulled away, letting out a loud belch and wiping his mouth with his sleeve, Joel risked a glance and saw that his beard was slick and dripping with blood.

'Dear me. Looks like I've landed on a real newbie, all right,' Tommy said, grinning at his expression. 'So where'd you spring up from, eh?'

'I . . . I just came off a ship,' Joel stammered. 'I don't know exactly where from.'

Tommy clicked his tongue. 'We really are a wee bit confused, aren't we? Have you got a name, or do you not remember that either?'

'My name's Joel.'

'Well, Joel, if ye dinnae mind my telling you, you've got a bit of learning to do.' Tommy reached into a pouch on his belt, and with a flourish he produced a syringe. He used his teeth to pluck away the cork on the end of the needle, then stabbed it to the hilt into the bloody neck of his still-unconscious victim and pushed the plunger all the way home.

'There we go,' he grunted with satisfaction as he yanked the needle out and stuck the cork back on. 'When yer man wakes up in the morning, sick as a dog wi' a few bruises and these wee holes in his neck, he'll just think he was too pissed to stand up straight and had an argument wi' something sharp. See how it's done? In the old times, we wouldnae have gone to all this trouble. Nowadays, we've got to stay in line. Or else,' he added darkly.

'What the hell is that stuff?'

Tommy dropped the syringe back in his belt pouch and zipped it up. 'Oh, it's probably got some fancy chemistry name, but the Feds call it Vambloc. Pretty nifty stuff it is too. Stops the humes from turning, erases their short-term memory and heals them up fast to boot. No' the worst idea the Feds have had. Still gottae hate the bastards, though.'

'Feds?' Joel asked, frowning.

'Aye, Feds. They make the rules. And ye dinnae want them catching you, believe me. They've got their own way of dealing with illegals like you.'

'Illegals?'

'Listen, laddie, instead o' just repeating everything I say

like some kind o' moron, why don't ye come and have a wee snifter yourself?' Tommy pointed down at the inert human, then at Joel. 'Ye look like ye need it. Don't be shy. I dinnae mind sharing.'

'I . . . I can't . . .'

Tommy roared with laughter. 'Takes me back, laddie. Takes me right back to my first time. Tell ye what. Hold on.' He snatched up one of the empty beer bottles that were lying around the alleyway. Then, crouching down to grab the human's limp wrist, he nipped open a vein with his teeth and a small fountain of blood jetted out. Tommy caught it with the bottle, which quickly started filling with the dark, viscous juice.

'He's going to bleed to death,' Joel said.

Tommy shook his head. 'Vambloc hasnae kicked in yet, is all. Yer man'll soon clot up right as rain. I wouldnae worry about the fucker. If I were you, I'd be more worried about myself.' Letting the bleeding arm flop to the ground, he stood up and offered Joel the bottle.

'What if I don't? What if I just starve myself?'

'You cannae die,' Tommy said. 'You're already deid, ye silly arse.' His grin gave way to a grimace. 'But if ye dinnae like the idea of being a vampire, ye'll not be very happy aboot becoming a *wraith*: a poor, miserable withered ghost of a thing that's neither vampire nor human. A fate worse than undeath, believe me. Forget about it, laddie. Take the plunge. Drink up.'

Joel grasped the bottle that Tommy was holding out to him. He raised it hesitantly. The blood looked almost black inside. It clung thickly to the glass, and he could feel its warmth against his hand.

'This is disgusting,' he muttered.

But it wasn't. It was luscious and nourishing. The elixir

of eternal life. Scarlet ambrosia. Joel suddenly wanted it more than anything in the world. He pressed the neck of the bottle to his lips and began to drink greedily. He gasped at the sensation of energy flowing into him, like nothing he'd ever experienced before.

Tommy watched approvingly. 'Hard to describe the buzz, isn't it?' he laughed. 'There's nothing like that first time. I envy ye, laddie. Now let's make ourselves scarce before someone comes.'

Chapter Twenty-Three

The Ridings, near Guildford

Adjoining the seven-bedroom, eight-bathroom, twelve-and-a-half-million-pound mansion, with its five acres of sweeping grounds comprising tennis courts, indoor pool, gazebo, stables and helicopter pad, was a comfortable little former coach-house that for the last six years had been the home of the middle-aged couple employed by the cabinet minister Jeremy Lonsdale to look after the place when he wasn't around. Which, as the great man could more often be found enjoying the bachelor lifestyle at his Kensington apartment or lounging around his Tuscan villa than at his English country pile, was most of the time.

Sharon and Geoffrey Hopley had spent that evening by the woodburner in the cosy sitting room of the coach-house, discussing the problem of their missing employer. As the days passed and the anxiously-expected phone call never came, they'd been growing increasingly worried. The visit from the police had only deepened their anxiety. Had something awful happened to Mr Lonsdale? And – more to the point, since Sharon and Geoffrey were much more attached to Castor and Pollux, Lonsdale's pair of great Danes, than they were to the man himself – what would happen to their jobs and their home if he never returned?

Another subject of discussion that evening, over mugs of Horlicks before bed, had been the unexpected delivery earlier in the day. The Fed-Ex drivers who'd unloaded the three large boxes had almost broken the hydraulic lift of their truck with the weight of them.

The typed instructions attached to the delivery note had been strict and clear: the items were to be stored in the mansion's basement under lock and key, and on no account was anyone except Mr Lonsdale to open them or tamper with them in any way.

Two of the boxes were about the same size, about six feet long. The third was closer to seven, much wider, and weighed almost twice as much. Getting them down into the basement had been a grunting, straining, gut-busting endeavour. In the end, they'd had to lower them in with ropes via the disused Victorian-era coal chute, and when it was done, Geoffrey was talking about suing Fed-Ex for the pain in his back.

Tucked up in bed sometime after midnight, Sharon rolled over and nudged her husband on the shoulder. 'Psst. Psst. Are you awake?'

'No,' he grunted in the dark.

'I can't sleep. I was thinking—'

Geoffrey propped himself up against the pillow and rubbed his eyes. 'What is it now?' he moaned. 'Christ, my back.'

'Maybe we should tell the police. About that delivery. I mean, maybe it could, you know, help them find Mr Lonsdale, maybe.'

Geoffrey was wide awake now. 'It's just something he must have ordered before he went off,' he said irritably. 'You saw the instructions. He won't be very happy when he comes back and finds that we've opened his private mail.'

'Those things aren't just any old mail. And he's not coming back, and you know it.'

'I wish you wouldn't say that.'

A silence; then Sharon said, 'Those boxes could be coffins, you know.'

Geoffrey reached out and clicked on the bedside light, turned to stare at his wife in bewilderment. 'Coffins! What the hell makes you think they're coffins?'

She shrugged. 'Something creepy about them, if you ask me. Why, what do *you* think's in them?'

'Crates of wine, perhaps, or antique furniture. Or artwork? Mr Lonsdale collects artwork, as you know.'

'Too heavy for artwork. And if it was wine the boxes would be marked "fragile". No markings on them at all. Don't you find that a bit odd?'

'I don't know, Sharon, and I don't care. Can we please get back to sleep now? Honestly.' Geoffrey turned the light back out and buried his head in his pillow.

For the next few minutes, the only sound in the dark bedroom was the gentle rasp of Geoffrey's snores. Sharon felt herself getting drowsy. Maybe Geoffrey was right, was her last thought as sleep came down like a curtain.

Then, in their kennel outside, Castor and Pollux suddenly began to bark furiously.

Sharon sat bolt upright in the bed. 'Geoffrey!' she whispered. 'Listen!'

'For God's sake, it's probably just a fox,' he muttered.

As suddenly as it had begun, the chorus of barking ended in a high-pitched whimper. Sharon tore the covers off her and scurried to the window. She could see nothing outside. 'Someone must be out there.'

Geoffrey nodded, suddenly alert and panic-stricken. 'I'll get the shotgun.' There had been burglaries in the area recently, and he'd taken to keeping the old side-by-side behind the door. Sharon clung to his arm as they crept downstairs and ventured out into the cold night air.

'Who's there?' Geoffrey yelled in a quavering voice, sighting the shotgun down his torch beam as he swept it left and right at the barns, the gazebo, the helicopter hangar. No reply. A low-lying freezing mist drifted around the house, making them shiver.

'Who's there?' Geoffrey repeated. 'Whoever you are, I have a gun.'

As they passed the kennels, the torch beam landed on the cowering shapes of Castor and Pollux. The two dogs were pressed against the wire mesh as far away from the house as they could get, their tails between their legs, quivering and whining with subdued fear.

'Look at them, Geoffrey. What the—'

'Never mind the dogs. Look at *this*,' Geoffrey whispered hoarsely, shining the torch on the coal shute trapdoor that led down to the cellar. It was open. The concrete cellar floor was covered with scattered pieces of ripped cardboard and splintered wood. All three crates had been smashed apart.

'Someone's broken into them,' Sharon gasped, gripping her husband's arm. 'Oh my God. We have to call the police.'

Geoffrey stared at the debris a moment longer. 'Wait a minute. It looks like . . . no, it can't be.'

'Can't be what?' she asked him in terror.

'Those crates haven't been broken into. They've been broken *out* of. They're burst open from the inside.'

The two of them hurried breathlessly back to the coach-house to dial 999. As they did so, a figure stepped out of the mist.

Sharon let out a shriek. It was the figure of a man – tall and dark, in a long leather coat that hung elegantly from his slim body. Even in their shaking panic, the couple could see that this was no ordinary intruder. There was something distinguished, somehow almost princely, in his bearing as he stepped towards them. The leather coat was unbuttoned despite the cold, his white silk shirt casually open at the neck. 'Good evening,' he said with a smile.

'Who are you?' Geoffrey demanded.

The intruder just kept smiling. Out of the freezing fog behind him appeared two more figures. The woman had the wild black hair of a gypsy and was clad in tight, gleaming red leather. The other was the towering shape of the biggest, broadest man Lonsdale's caretakers had ever seen. The three figures advanced, all smiling and exchanging knowing glances.

'Don't come another step,' Geoffrey quavered, brandishing the shotgun. 'Stay back, I tell you. This gun is loaded. I'll shoot. Sharon, run inside and call the police, quick.'

'There's really no need for violence,' said the elegant man in the long coat.

'I mean it,' Geoffrey said. 'Not another step. I don't want to hurt anyone. But I will, if you make me.'

'I doubt that very much.' The man came on another step, still smiling.

Geoffrey Hopley made a terrorised gurgling sound from his throat, gripped the twelve-bore tightly and closed his eyes and jerked the trigger. The crash of the gunshot shattered the night and the darkness was lit up by its white muzzle flash as he discharged one barrel straight into the man's chest at close range.

Then he opened his eyes, ears ringing from the shot, and his knees almost buckled under him as he saw the man still standing there.

The man tutted, fingered the tattered, bloodied hole in

his silk shirt, and shook his head disapprovingly at Geoffrey. 'I had always found the English to be such a hospitable and welcoming people,' he said sadly. 'How things change.'

Geoffrey was about to fire off the second cartridge when the enormous black man stepped forward, snatched the gun from his hands and bent its barrels into a U-shape as easily as if it had been a stick of liquorice.

Sharon had begun to gibber.

'Allow me to introduce myself,' said the wearer of the ruined silk shirt. 'My name is Stone. Gabriel Stone.'

Chapter Twenty-Four

Southampton

Tommy led Joel back to a sooty red-brick building in a narrow little empty street some way from the docks. At the bottom of a flight of steps, he clinked open a triple-padlocked door and ushered Joel inside. The place was a basement, windowless and bare brick but clean and well maintained, filled with organised clutter. Glancing around him, Joel took another swig from his bottle. Despite his disgust at the thought of it, he could feel his strength growing with every sip. It was all he could do to resist gulping the whole lot down.

'Unless ye're planning on starting to juice properly for yerself, I'd be sparing with that,' Tommy warned. 'Here, take a seat.'

Joel sat on the chair Tommy pulled out for him. Hating himself for the lust he felt for the stuff, he slipped the blood bottle back into his pocket and resolved to leave it there for a long time.

'What do you do?' Joel asked. Vampire small-talk. It felt absurd, surreal.

'Buy and sell stuff,' Tommy replied. 'Bit o' this, bit o' that.'

'So . . . how long have you been . . .?'

'A vampire?' Tommy chuckled. 'Don't be coy, laddie. Eternity's a long time to spend ducking and diving from the truth. A long, long time, is the answer to yer question.'

'How did you become one?'

Tommy slumped on a worn armchair and kicked his boots out in front of him. 'Now, see, that's not something ye should ask too freely, son. Some vampires find it rude. But I dinnae mind telling ye. Ever heard o' the Baobhan sith?'

'The white women of the Highlands,' Joel said, and Tommy seemed taken aback. 'I read about them somewhere,' Joel explained. He was being deliberately vague, because the place he'd read about them was in his vampire hunter grandfather's diary.

If he could see me now, Joel thought. He'd have been so proud to see his grandson become the thing they both hated most in all the world.

'The white women, aye,' Tommy said pensively. 'Then ye'll ken that they were a Celtic vampire warrior tribe back in what the humes call the Dark Ages. They were like Amazons, except with teeth. Their prey was young laddies, that they'd mesmerise with their beautiful singing. One of those young laddies was my only son, Stuart. It was in the year 1301, around the time Willie Wallace was stirring it up wi' the English. Cold winter it was. One night Stuart was out with his bow, hunting in the forest. That's when they took him. When I went off searching for him, they took me and all.' Tommy sighed. 'Long time ago.'

Joel's mind was boggling. Over seven hundred years that Tommy had been living this life. Or *un*life, or whatever it was. 'What happened to Stuart?' he managed to ask.

'Destroyed,' Tommy muttered. 'By the hunters.'

'Vampire hunters?'

'Aye. They caught him in the daytime. Put ma wee boy

in a cage and dragged him oot intae the sun. Fuckers.' Tommy spat.

'I'm sorry,' Joel heard himself say, and he frowned. He'd travelled home intent on destroying every vampire who crossed his path. Now here he was, sitting with one of them, drinking blood with him, genuinely grateful for what he'd done for him and sympathising with him for the loss of his vampire son.

'Every one of us has a story tae tell,' Tommy said. 'So what's yours?'

'A woman did it to me. A woman I thought I loved. She kind of held back from me that she was a vampire.'

Tommy nodded thoughtfully. 'And ye resent her for it, don't ye?'

Joel said nothing.

'Normal enough. Nothing tae be ashamed of. It happens tae all of us who've been forced to turn, against their will. But time passes, and a strange thing happens. Ye begin tae see the advantages. Then, when some more time passes, ye begin tae like it.'

Joel had no answer to that. Another question was pressing on his mind. 'This woman who turned me,' he said. 'She told me she worked for the Vampire Federation,' he said. 'Some kind of agent.'

Tommy's bushy eyebrows raised an inch. 'An agent? She was taking one hell of a risk turning a human. Goes against Federation rules.'

'We're talking about a federation . . . of vampires?' Joel said. 'I want to know more about it. Tell me everything.'

Tommy sighed. 'It's no' the same world any more, laddie. The humes are a damn sight more organised and technologically advanced than they were back in my day. So, modern times, new ways. Back in '84, it was – that's *1984* – when

171

the Supremos first got together and announced that things had tae change if vampires wanted tae avoid getting noticed. Maybe they were right. Maybe we'd all have been exterminated now, otherwise. Who knows? Whatever the case, it caught on fast. Before we knew it, it'd become this huge big organisation, laying doon the way it was going tae be from now on. No more turning humes willy-nilly, for a start. Strictly forbidden, on pain of termination. Execution,' he explained. 'By Nosferol. Anti-vampire nerve toxin. Not nice.'

'And they'll do the same to the victims they've turned?' Joel said, thinking of what Tommy had said earlier about illegals.

'Unless the Feds decide tae enlist them, then aye, 'fraid so. The way they see it, they've got tae keep the whole thing locked doon tight. Too many humes out there would love tae become like us, see. There's a lot of money in it. There had tae be a disincentive.'

'I can't believe humans *want* to become vampires,' Joel said, aghast.

'Come on, laddie. Think of it. Eternal life, unlimited power.'

'And all you have to do is drink people's blood every night,' Joel said bitterly.

'Well, maybe there's a lot of humes that wouldnae find that too high a price to pay, morally speaking. Not when ye weigh up the advantages. And thanks tae the Federation, even after they're turned they can go on pretty much like before, making their money and swanking aboot in their fast cars. Except they never die.'

'But the sunlight,' Joel said, puzzled. 'How can they go on like before, if—'

'Like I said, laddie, times change. The Supremos declared that the more we integrated intae their society, the safer

172

we'd be. Vambloc isnae the only wee pill they forced us tae use.' He stood up and clumped over to a sideboard, yanked open a drawer and took out a little tube about the size of a packet of mints. He tossed it to Joel.

'Solazal?' Joel said, reading the label.

'Dinnae ask me how the fuckin' stuff works. Some fancy chemistry bollocks. But it enables vampires tae walk aboot in daylight.'

So that was how Alex had been able to fool him, Joel thought. 'It really works?' he asked in amazement.

Tommy nodded. 'Imagine the first poor fucker they tested it on, though, eh? Must've been shitting himself. Aye, it works, all right. Try one and see for yerself. Take the whole tube, if ye want. Take half a dozen – keep ye going for a while. I've got plenty. Hardly touch the stuff, except tae go shopping once in a while or visit the bank. Gives me heartburn, tell the truth.'

Joel examined the tube carefully, studying the fine print on the label. It looked for all the world like a normal pharmaceutical product. 'This is amazing. I can't believe how organised these people are . . . I mean, vampires,' he corrected himself.

'It's global, laddie. Offices in just aboot every major city. But Europe's where it all started, back in '84. The main headquarters is in Brussels. The Supremos run the whole kit and caboodle from there. They make the rules, and VIA enforce them. That's V – I – A; stands for Vampire Intelligence Agency. Investigative division and police force, all rolled intae one. Now, as far as I ken, VIA's based up in London. Where exactly, I couldnae tell ye. Top drawer stuff. They wouldnae trust the rank and file vampires wi' information like that.'

'You don't sound very fond of them,' Joel said.

'I willnae say too much,' Tommy said. 'Let's just say there's a lot of us who'd scrap the whole fucking bureaucratic shower o' them if ye gave us half a chance. They force us tae register and use their bloody drugs, then they keep hiking the price on us.' Tommy paused. 'And there's those that do more than just grumble about the Feds. There're rebels. Rumour has it that some vampires started an uprising.'

'Gabriel Stone,' Joel said. 'I think he's one of them.'

'You seem to ken more aboot it than me. Anyway, the Federation Gestapo have been around asking questions. Trying to find oot if I've been involved in any of it. Hassling me over why I hadn't been getting more o' their drugs. I'm not the only one who's been questioned. But VIA's job is tae keep these things quiet. They never tell us the truth.'

'So are you one of the rebels?' Joel asked.

Tommy roared with laughter. 'Me? Forget it, pal – I keep well out of all that shite. I just want tae get on with things, nice and quiet in my own wee corner, like I've always done.'

'I want to find the London headquarters,' Joel said.

'Why? Tae surrender yerself?'

'I have some business with somebody there.'

Tommy smiled, understanding. 'Right, aye. The agent lassie who turned ye.'

'Her name's Alex Bishop. The last time I saw her was a few days ago in Romania. But I'm certain she's come back to Britain, that she's back in London. I don't know how I know that, but I do.'

Tommy nodded. 'Vampires and the victims they turn have a kind o' bond between them. Telepathic, or something, I suppose it is. Some have it stronger than others. Depends on the vampire that did the turning. See, we get more powerful as we get older.'

Joel remembered how Kate Hawthorne, cornered in a flat in Wallingford before he'd destroyed her, had been able to guide him to Gabriel Stone's castle in Romania. It had seemed bizarre at the time. Now he understood. 'You think maybe I could use that bond to find her in London? How does it work? If I concentrate really hard, I might—'

Tommy smiled and shook his head. 'It's no' quite that simple, laddie. Besides, even if ye did find yer lassie and get tae the VIA Headquarters, from the rumours I've heard, ye wouldnae get past the front door before ye got zapped with Nosferol. Ye don't want to find oot what it can do. Trust me on that.'

Chapter Twenty-Five

Just after 4 a.m., and the black Rolls Royce Phantom was streaking through the lanes of rural Kent at over a hundred and twenty miles an hour. A relaxed Gabriel Stone was at the wheel, idly listening to a Mendelssohn string quartet as he hurtled the big car through the night. Beside him in the luxurious passenger seat, Lillith was pouring more of the 1993 Dom Pérignon champagne into a crystal flute.

Zachary lounged stretched out in the back, a bottle in one giant fist and a full glass in the other. 'One thing you gotta say about Lonsdale – that human-ass motherfucker certainly liked to do things in style.'

Gabriel's hands tightened a little on the wheel in disapproval of Zachary's language, but he said nothing.

'What a fun evening this has turned out to be,' Lillith said, glancing over her shoulder at the bundle of antique sabres, rapiers and broadswords propped up against the back seat next to Zachary. She could still taste the blood from the social call they'd just made to the secluded house a few miles from Rochester. It had been easy enough to find the antiquities collector via an auction catalogue.

'All in the line of duty,' Gabriel said.

'This mission is becoming more and more fun,' Lillith laughed. 'I feel quite refreshed, and it's so nice to be properly armed again. Come on, brother,' she said, passing the brimming champagne glass to Gabriel, 'step on it. We barely seem to be moving. What's wrong with you? I miss my Lotus,' she added with a sigh.

Gabriel put his foot down as he quaffed the champagne, and the car surged forward. 'That's more like it,' Lillith said, pouring him another glass.

As the car sped along with uncanny smoothness, flashing blue lights appeared in the rearview mirror.

'Looks like we got some company, guys,' Zachary rumbled from the back seat.

For a while, Gabriel amused himself speeding along the lanes, skidding round icy bends and leaving the police car floundering in his wake as Lillith and Zachary craned their necks to look back and laugh at the antics of the humans. When the game began to bore him, he slowed the Rolls to a crawl, letting the police car catch up, and then pulled up alongside the grassy verge on a lonely stretch of wooded country road.

The police car's tyres crunched to a halt on the road a few yards behind them. Its doors opened and two officers climbed out, shining torches at the Rolls. One cop rapped on Gabriel's window while his younger colleague stood officiously by with his arms folded.

'Oh, boy,' Zachary muttered into his champagne, his shoulders quaking with mirth.

'Shush,' Lillith giggled, bright-eyed. 'Try to look nervous.'

Gabriel calmly whirred down his window. 'Can I be of some assistance to you, orifice? That is to say, officer.'

'Do you realise that you're driving without registration plates, sir?'

'Certainly,' Gabriel told him. 'I refuse to be reduced to a number.'

The older cop narrowed his eyes. 'Have you been drinking, sir?'

'Why yes,' Gabriel told him. 'We all have, in copious quantity. Would you care for a glass? There's plenty for everyone.'

Zachary fished another bottle out of the icebox to show them.

'Any idea how fast you were driving back there, sir?'

'I believe we peaked at just over a hundred and thirty?' Gabriel said. 'I could have gone faster, but the roads are a little slippery tonight.'

'See your licence, please,' the older one snapped. His officious-looking colleague was having a hard time taking his eyes off Lillith.

'I'm afraid you have me there, officer,' Gabriel said with a smile. 'I never quite got around to taking the driving test.'

The officer stared at him. 'Name?'

'The name is Schreck. Maxwell Schreck.'

Meanwhile, the younger cop had managed to tear his gaze away from the beauty in the passenger seat and was shining his torch beam around the rest of the car's interior. The light glinted off the steel blades in the back. 'What are those?' he asked, pointing.

'I believe those are technically known as *swords*,' Gabriel explained slowly and patiently.

'They belong to you?'

'Well, until this evening, they were the property of a collector chap who lives a few miles from here. He, ah, well, you might say he has loaned them to us. Indefinitely.'

'We may want to verify that, Mr Schh— uh, sir,' the older officer said.

'You could try calling him,' Lillith purred from the passenger seat. 'But I think the poor man's feeling a little drained right now.'

179

The younger officer was beginning to lose his cool. 'You do realise it's illegal to carry those weapons in public?'

Gabriel made a gesture of mock amazement. 'Speeding, consumption of a little wine, driving without a licence or registration, unauthorised transportation of a few inoffensive swords: my list of crimes grows with each passing moment, it seems. Tell me, officer, is *anything* still legal in this strange, frightened little nation in subjugation? It was great once. I remember those days well, and cannot for the life of me imagine what has become of them.'

The cops were both doing their best not to look flustered. It wasn't a convincing act. 'Step out of the vehicle, sir.'

'Happy to.' As Gabriel opened the door and climbed out, Lillith couldn't hold back her fits of giggles any longer and was rocking back and forth in her seat. Glowering at her, the older officer asked, 'Something amusing you, madam?'

'It will,' she said. 'Just wait and see.'

The officer turned the glower on Gabriel. 'How much would you say you've had to drink tonight, sir?'

'Oh, three, perhaps four,' Gabriel said.

'Glasses?'

'Bottles. A very good vintage, too.'

'You *are* aware of the drink-driving limit?'

'Why yes, officer. That's why I was drinking. I consider it my civic duty. You see, I read that three out of ten accidents are caused by drunken drivers. In which case, should you not be more concerned about the seventy per cent of sober drivers who are the true culprits behind the carnage on our roads?'

'Sir, I think you're in a good deal of trouble,' the officer said, producing a breathalyser.

'Not nearly as much as you are,' Lillith muttered.

'Don't you want to know what else I had to drink tonight?' Gabriel asked him.

'Four bottles of champagne not enough for us, then? Blow into this, please.'

'The champagne was merely the chaser. Before that, I drank . . .' Gabriel turned to Lillith. 'How much would you say we drank tonight, sister?'

'Hard to tell exactly,' Lillith said. 'He was a biggish guy.'

'She's right – he *was* a large fellow,' Gabriel said. 'Not quite as substantial as my friend Zachary here, but fairly hefty nonetheless. Say seven of your standard British pints? Divided three ways, I calculate that would come to approximately 2.333 pints each. As I note from your rather blank expressions that neither you nor your colleague has the wits to fully grasp my meaning, let it be clear that I am, in fact, referring to his blood.'

'. . . You've been drinking blood,' the older cop said numbly.

'Well done. Correct. And I will soon be drinking more.'

'And whose blood do you think you'll be drinking, *sir*?' smirked the officious-looking one.

Gabriel smiled at them both. 'Care to hazard a guess? Either of you?'

The officers looked at each other in bewilderment. Just for a second, because in the next, Gabriel reached out and grabbed the older one by the shoulder, jerked him off his feet and sank his fangs deep into the man's neck.

The tortured, burbling, hysterical screaming began. Lillith and Zachary stepped casually out of the Rolls as the other human tried to make a run for it back to his patrol car. He was less than halfway there when Zachary knocked him to the ground, took one ankle in his large fist and dragged the struggling, wailing human over to the verge.

'Ladies first,' Zachary said, holding him down with one hand and motioning politely to Lillith. 'Careful, Lil. This one's a kicker.'

'Such a gentleman, Zach.' Lillith's eyes twinkled with anticipation as she knocked back the last drop of champagne from her glass, fell on the human, shoved his head back and ripped into his throat with her teeth. She laughed for joy as she felt the warm pleasure jetting out of his severed artery onto her parted lips. She drank, swallowed, laughed again and drank some more, until she was breathless and heady with it – then wiped her mouth, leaving a red smear across her perfect cheek.

'Blood and champagne,' she gasped in ecstasy. 'Does it for me every time. But darling, I'm being selfish.' Jerking the human upright, she held the champagne glass under his torn throat, watched as the spray of luscious red juice quickly filled it to the brim, and gave it to Zachary to knock back in a single gulp.

'Always tastes better from crystal,' he rumbled, smacking his lips. 'Why is that, you think?'

Gabriel had finished with his human. As he approached, leaving the exsanguinated corpse by the roadside, Lillith handed him the refilled glass. Gabriel sipped from it, then passed it back to her.

'To victory,' she smiled, raising it in a toast.

'To eternity,' Gabriel said.

Chapter Twenty-Six

Oxford

Joel had caught the early train from Southampton, using the money that Tommy had lent him. In his pocket were six tubes of Solazal pills, and he could still taste the one he'd taken earlier. So far, the stuff seemed to be working: the pale morning sun seemed to have no effect.

At moments he almost felt normal again. And yet, walking through the crowds at Oxford station, it was bewildering to think that all these people around him had no idea what he really was, what he'd become. Even more bewildering to realise that, in such a short time since wakening up on that snowy Romanian mountainside, he'd already grown used to hiding himself away from the humans. Being openly among them now seemed alien to him.

As he scanned the faces of the people around him, Joel wondered if any of them were vampires like him – Federation vampires able to walk about in daylight. Would some recognition instinct kick in if he encountered one?

Heading out of the station building and towards the taxi rank outside, he passed a woman with a small spaniel on a leash. It suddenly transformed from a placid little creature to a furiously-snapping piranha fish on legs the instant he came within five yards of it.

'Quiet, Bethany,' the woman scolded, aghast at her dog's behaviour. 'What's got into you?'

'Dogs don't like me,' Joel explained with a weak smile, and walked on. Still dazed, he took a cab westwards through the city to his home district of Jericho. As they drove, the radio news was reporting the disappearance of a police patrol car and two officers in Kent the night before, but the reception was crackly and Joel caught little of it before the driver skipped impatiently to a loud music station. Ten minutes later the taxi pulled up outside the row of Georgian red-brick terraced houses in Walton Well Road. Joel paid the driver and got out, slamming the door so hard that it made the whole car rattle.

'Hey, steady on, mate,' the taxi driver said, scowling at him.

'Sorry,' Joel mumbled, and turned to climb the steps to the front door of his ground-floor flat. The door had been boarded up. He remembered the fight he'd had with Gabriel Stone's ghoulish manservant, Seymour Finch. Finch had burst through the glass panel as if it had been nothing. Yet he wasn't a vampire. What other powers could a vampire transmit to a human to give them such extraordinary strength?

Joel's dark thoughts were interrupted as the ruddy face of Mrs Dowling from next door appeared over the fence. 'Inspector Solomon? We've been worried about you. Maurice fixed up the door for you. We didn't know where you'd gone. Anyone could have just walked in.'

'Thanks, Mrs Dowling. I had to go away. I'm back now.'

'Your kitchen's completely wrecked. We thought of calling the police, but . . . well, seeing as you *are* the police . . .'

'Just redecorating,' he reassured her. 'Nothing to worry about. Thanks for thinking of it, though.'

'Is everything all right?' she asked, peering at him curiously. 'You seem . . . I don't know.'

'I haven't been quite myself the last couple of days,' Joel said.

'You don't look ill, or anything. Just different, somehow.'

Joel left her to figure it out and went inside. The wreckage of the kitchen had been tidied up a little – Maurice again, he supposed. He went over to the phone, checked his calls and messages and found that someone had been calling him repeatedly from a mobile whose number he didn't recognise. The messages, on the other hand, were from someone whose voice he knew right away.

Sam Carter was Joel's longtime friend, as well as his superior at Thames Valley Police. He'd always been a man of few words, and his phone messages were true to form.

'Need to talk. Give me a call right now.'

Chapter Twenty-Seven

The Ridings

One part of the late Jeremy Lonsdale's mansion that the pale morning sun couldn't reach was the vaulted, windowless wine cellar that ran almost the entire length of the house. It was filled with the kind of collection of fine vintages that only a multi-millionaire with a taste for the good life could have put together.

Now, though, the cellar had been put to another use. Back in business and on a mission to finish what he'd started, Gabriel Stone had designated the place the nerve-centre of his renewed rebellion against the Federation. The heavy oak wine racks had been shoved aside to make room for the long table they'd brought down from Lonsdale's plush dining room. Its gleaming surface was crisscrossed with a spaghetti of wires connecting the politician's desktop computer to a bank of extra monitors.

'Man, I don't know why you think I can do this,' Zachary groaned from where he sat hunched massively over the computer keyboard, tapping the odd key more or less randomly and scratching his head. 'I mean, this ain't nothing I've done before. Setting up email accounts and shit was always Anton's job.'

'Zachary darling, you know Anton's not with us any more,' Lillith said nonchalantly, honing the edge of her new heavy cavalry dragoon's sabre with a whetstone, a cloth and a bottle of gun oil at her elbow. 'Someone else has to do it.'

'Yeah, but why me? I ain't a morning kind of guy, you know?'

'Because we're busy,' she said, closing one eye and peering down the curve of the sword blade. 'Aren't we, Gabriel?'

Gabriel had been standing at the far end of the cellar, head bowed in meditation. He turned and looked coldly at Zachary. 'You know how to operate one of those small communication devices the humans carry around with them, do you not?'

'A mobile phone,' Lillith put in. 'Zach's a dab hand with one.'

Zachary shrugged his huge shoulders. 'Sure. But this—'

'Then you will soon learn to penetrate the mysteries of the technological Tower of Babel that our food source call the interweb, in order to re-establish communications with our network of associates. Surely the principle is similar.'

'They call it the inter*net*,' Zachary corrected him.

'There. Already it becomes evident that you are far ahead of either myself or Lillith in these matters. Now get on with it.' Gabriel walked over to the table and slid a piece of paper across it towards Zachary. 'With these electronic mail addresses you will be able to rally round the faithful. Send out the word of my survival, of our renewed mission. Summon them all here. Rolando, Petroc, Elspeth, Yuri and the others. And Kali, of course.'

'Oh, yes, let's not forget Kali,' Lillith muttered under her breath.

Gabriel turned to her with a frown. 'I believe my disapproving sister had been allocated the task of drafting a letter?'

Lillith looked up from her blade-sharpening. '"Dear Prime Minister, regret to inform you that due to personal reasons, blah blah blah, compelled to resign my position forthwith, will be taking a trip around the world and will not be contactable, etc., etc., yours sincerely, Jeremy Lonsdale." What am I, your secretary now? Get Kali to write it when she gets here, as you seem to value her so much.'

Gabriel was about to reply sharply when the cellar door creaked slowly open and a balding head appeared through the gap, followed by a slouching, stooped form. Lillith snatched up her sabre, then relaxed. 'Oh, it's only the ghoul.'

Already the few drops of vampire blood, tapped from an opened vein and forced down the human's throat, had worked a dramatic physical change on him. Geoffrey Hopley skulked across the cellar like a beaten dog, clutching a large tray on which were three steaming mugs and a folded newspaper. He laid it down reverently on the table.

Gabriel stared. 'What is this, ghoul?'

'Your tea, master,' Geoffrey croaked.

'*Tea?*'

'Mr Lonsdale always took a cup of tea with the morning paper. Perhaps master would care for a biscuit?'

Gabriel peered with revulsion at the tray. '*Biscuit?* Certainly not. And what makes you think we would be interested in consuming this vile liquid of yours? Not to mention,' he added, swatting away the newspaper, 'reading the infantile and usually mendacious drivel that the humans call news.'

'Can't get the staff these days,' Lillith murmured, returning to her sword-sharpening.

'Mr Lonsdale liked to k-k-keep up with what was h-happening in the world,' stammered the ghoul.

'As if the human race had the remotest notion of what is really happening in the world,' Gabriel snorted. 'You're wasting our time. Get back to your hole until we find further use for you.' He grabbed the newspaper and hurled it violently at the cowering ghoul. 'Do you hear me? Leave us, cur!'

Geoffrey picked up the tray and bowed and scraped his way backwards out of the cellar.

'I told you those two would be useless, Gabriel,' Lillith said with a smile when the door had banged shut. 'We should have just drained them dry and been done with it.'

'Damn them both. Too late now. Ghoul blood is undrinkable.' Gabriel stooped to snatch up the fallen newspapers and tossed them on the table. 'Zachary, are you making any progress?' he snapped.

'Give me time,' Zachary muttered, tapping more keys. 'I'll get it.'

Lillith casually reached down for the crumpled newspaper, peeled away the front and back pages and used them to test the edge of her blade. The steel sliced cleanly through the paper like a razor; the two halves fluttered to the floor. 'Not perfect,' she said, giving the blade a few more strokes from her hone before peeling off another sheet. She was about to cut it when she stopped and let out a loud shuddering gasp. Her sword fell with a clang to the tiled floor as she twisted away from the newspaper in horror.

'Lil?' Zachary said, alarmed. 'You okay?'

'What is it, sister?' Gabriel cried.

Lillith pressed a hand to her chest, catching her breath, and pointed at the newspaper without looking. 'I can't bear to see it. I never wanted to see that thing again.'

Gabriel strode over and snatched up the paper. His eyes searched the rumpled page, then narrowed with a blaze of anger and fear as his gaze landed on the small, crisp colour image in the bottom left-hand corner.

An image of a cross. A Celtic cross, one whose appearance

190

was terrifyingly familiar, its shattered fragments pieced together and held in place with wire. Who had done this?

The headline of the small article was: *HISTORY PROFESSOR'S DISCOVERY IS OUT OF THIS WORLD.*

'"Oxford University boffins are baffled,"' Gabriel read aloud, '"by the discovery of an ancient artifact in the mountains of Romania. Chloe Dempsey, 19, a pentathlete and student at the University of Bedfordshire, came across the mysterious object while on a skiing trip with friends and brought it to the UK to show to her father, Professor Matt Dempsey, 56, a curator at Oxford's Pitt Rivers Museum . . ." I will not read it all. Suffice to say that my fears were correct. The cross of Ardaich has been found.'

Chapter Twenty-Eight

Bal Mawr Manor

When Dec awoke it was to find himself staring upwards at the canopy of the four-poster bed. For a moment he couldn't remember where he was – but as he struggled out from under the satin bedcover and dragged himself sleepily over to the window to peer at the incoming surf crashing on the rocks, it all came back to him like something out of an incredible dream and he punched a fist in the air.

He was learning how to be a vampire hunter! YES!

But it wasn't going to be easy. Knightly hadn't been kidding when he'd said he wanted to know everything. The two of them had sat up until long after midnight, writing up notes on everything Dec could tell him about his first-hand vampire experiences and poring over old books searching for anything that resembled Joel Solomon's strange cross. By the time Knightly had eventually let him stagger off up to bed, Dec's mind had been buzzing so intensely that he couldn't sleep. Leafing through a bedside copy of *They Lurk Amongst Us* hadn't helped, either. Dec had never been much of a reader, but Knightly's accounts of his vampire-destroying exploits made his heart thump. It hadn't been until sometime after three that Dec had finally dozed off into a fitful sleep that was filled with flickering shadows and sinister looming figures.

He hauled on his jeans, took a pee in the biggest bathroom he'd ever seen, and wandered downstairs. After losing his way three times he eventually made his way to the breakfast room, where he found Knightly looking comparatively bright-eyed and heartily polishing off the remains of a plate of fried eggs and sausages.

'Ah, there you are. Sit down. Help yourself to coffee. Thought you'd never show up.'

'I got lost,' Dec said, pouring coffee into a fine china cup that he was terrified to touch in case it broke.

'Easily done, in this big old pile,' Knightly said through a mouthful of sausage. 'After breakfast I'll give you the tour.'

Which he duly did, proudly showing Dec through a seemingly endless procession of rooms and passageways. Bal Mawr was a veritable anti-vampire fortress. Everywhere Dec looked were hanging crucifixes, wreaths of garlic, bunches of hawthorn. On the outside of every door, a large iron cross had been securely screwed to the wood, bearing the words *'Vampyre, You May Not Enter Here'* in bold gothic engraving; and on its inside each door had two tall mirrors flanking it left and right, angled a few degrees inwards. 'So you can tell immediately whether anyone coming into the room has a reflection,' Knightly explained to a quizzical Dec. 'Though it's highly unlikely that any vampire could penetrate so far through my defences. Still, when dealing with the Undead one can't be too careful. They're a tricksy lot, you know, Declan.'

And on and on the manor went, room after room, filled with all manner of paraphernalia. Everywhere they went was the same pungent smell of sandalwood incense. In Knightly's grand salon Dec paused to admire a display of silver-bladed daggers and carved wooden stakes whose points had been rubbed with essence of garlic. 'These are really for show,' Knightly admitted. 'Most of the real weaponry is in the armoury room.'

'What does the holy water do?' Dec asked, pointing at the labelled bottles of the stuff on a sideboard.

'It dissolves them,' Knightly said. 'They just fizz away.'

'Kind of like those aspirins you put in water?'

'Exactly like that.'

'Now, this here's the bollocks, so it is,' Dec said, picking up a huge antique pistol from a table and weighing it admiringly in his hand.

'A Napoleonic infantry trooper's flintlock sidearm,' Knightly told him. 'I like to keep it handy, just in case. Careful, it's loaded. It fires a .75 calibre ball made of pure silver.'

'That'll do the job,' Dec said, aiming the heavy pistol towards the window at a distant ship tracking across the horizon, imagining that it was full of vampires.

'Only if you hit them right in the heart,' Knightly said, 'which requires a very exact aim. And you only get one shot, Declan. That's why a true vampire hunter needs to be proficient with the full range of weaponry at his disposal.'

Dec replaced the gun on the table and peered at a small gilt-framed photo that hung over the fireplace. It showed an attractive, pleasantly plump woman with sandy hair and laughter on her face, sitting on a beach. 'Who's that?' he asked.

Knightly gazed at the picture, smiled sadly and hesitated before replying, 'Someone I used to know.'

Dec thought it better not to pry. He pointed at a massive wooden sea chest whose lid was fastened by a padlock. 'And what's in there?'

'Oh, that's *money*,' Knightly said, as nonchalantly as he

could; but he was unable to hide the glitter that suddenly came into his eye, replacing the wistful look of a moment earlier. 'Cash. Lots and lots of it. You might call it my fighting fund against the forces of evil.'

They walked on through the house. Beyond the gleaming double doors of the library, a winding passage led to a circular hallway dominated by a full-size armoured knight mounted dramatically astride a rearing war-horse. From the knight's gauntlet hung a morning star mace – a length of stout iron chain attached to a heavy spiked ball that looked to Dec as if it could crush a car if swung hard enough. He ran his hand down the horse's glass-fibre foreleg.

'One of my more illustrious ancestors,' Knightly said, waving up at the shining warrior. 'You're looking at Sir Eustace Knightly, killed at the Battle of Tewkesbury in 1471. If you look, you can see the hole in the breastplate where the fatal arrow hit him. But aside from his military exploits, he was the very first of our family to wage a private war against the legions of the Undead.'

'You mean he was a vampire hunter too?'

Knightly nodded. 'Very much so. Of course, back then they had other names for them. The very first mention of the word "vampire" in our family records wasn't until my great-grandfather's day. Each generation of Knightlys has passed its knowledge down to the next.'

'Like you will to your son one day,' Dec said brightly.

Knightly looked away, and was momentarily quiet as he continued up the passage.

'I was reading your book,' Dec said, sensing that he'd accidentally touched some sensitive spot and should change the subject. 'It's awesome.'

'Very kind of you to say so, Declan.'

'So, like, how many does it come to altogether? I mean,

how many have you kill— destroyed? I know you didn't want to tell that daft interviewer, but you can tell me, so you can.'

Knightly shrugged modestly. 'Oh, you know, it's very hard to say—'

'Go on, tell me,' Dec urged him. 'Fifty?'

'Hmmm . . .'

'A hundred? A *thousand*?'

'Let's have a nice cup of tea,' Knightly said.

Chapter Twenty-Nine

The Wheatsheaf pub, central Oxford

'Where the hell've you been?' were the first words out of Sam Carter's mouth as his broad, boxy frame filled the doorway and his bulk creaked the old floorboards of the pub bar.

Sitting at a corner table with an untouched beer in front of him, Joel shrugged. 'Just out and about,' he said. 'What else is there for a guy to do when he's on suspension?'

'That's what I wanted to talk to you about,' Carter said. 'Hang on.' Carter never just walked anywhere. He charged over to the bar like a buffalo and came tramping back a moment later, foam from a pint of bitter spilling generously down his fingers. He banged the glass down on the table, then parked his wide bulk into a chair opposite Joel. 'You not drinking?' he asked, glancing at Joel's beer.

'Not thirsty,' Joel said. He'd taken a swig of Tommy's blood bottle in the pub toilets on arrival.

Carter squinted at him closely. 'What's different about you? Can't put my finger on it. You been working out or something?'

Joel shrugged and didn't reply.

'You must have seen the news?'

'Not really.'

'You should. A lot of things have been happening. Stone's place out near Henley, Crowmoor Hall? You were right, Joel. More fucking corpses tucked away than Rose Hill cemetery. I've never seen anything like it, and neither had Jack Brier. Thirty years as a forensic pathologist and the poor sod was being sick all over his shoes when we started pulling them out of there. Fucking body parts heaped up in piles. Little baby skeletons with their arms and legs pulled off. Jesus Christ. It was terrible. Brier's department has had to draft in extra staff from all over the place to start the work of sifting through all the body parts and skeletal remains to try to identify some of the victims. Brier reckons a few of them might have been homeless people, runaways and the like.'

Carter slurped his beer. 'Fucking *babies*,' he muttered, shaking his head in disgust. 'Can you believe it?' Collecting himself, he went on, 'And now we're launching a major manhunt for Gabriel Stone and the other sickos he hangs out with. One of them's already turned up dead. Some kids found him floating down the Isis with a .45 slug in him. Can't trace him on any records, but an officer recognised him as Seymour Finch. Stone's butler, or whatever the hell he was. The one you beat up. I mean, *allegedly* beat up.'

That had been the primary reason for Joel's suspension from duty. 'I did beat him up,' Joel admitted. 'And shot him, and drowned him too,' he could have added, but didn't.

'Anyway, the official theory is that Finch might have been about to dob Stone in, and so he put a bullet in him.'

Joel shrugged. 'Maybe. Nasty character.'

'With friends in high places,' Carter said in a lower voice. 'Friends like our illustrious cabinet minister Jeremy Lonsdale. Someone else we're very keen to have a little chat with. Keep this under your hat, Joel. All the press have been told is that an MP is helping with the inquiry. Truth is, Lonsdale's vanished. Nobody knows where the bastard is.'

'Try Romania,' Joel wanted to say. He remembered now. The familiar face of the man with the gun on Gabriel Stone's castle battlements. Stone had called him Lonsdale. But Joel wasn't about to mention any of that to Carter.

'Anyway,' Carter said. 'Let me cut to the chase. The reason I wanted to talk to you is that the old man wants you back.'

The old man Carter was talking about was their mutual boss, Chief Superintendent Lester Page, who had personally signed Joel's suspension from duty just days before.

Joel smiled bitterly. 'He does, does he?'

Carter nodded. 'You're to be fully reinstated. I watched him tear up the suspension papers myself. He wants you to head up a new team that'll be committed to this, twenty-four-seven, until we get Stone and . . .' Carter shot a glance back over his bulky shoulder at the other lunchtime drinkers in the pub '. . . and you-know-who. Lonsdale,' he added in a hoarse whisper, in case Joel hadn't twigged. 'Bastard's got to pop up somewhere. Can't just vanish into thin air.' Carter took another slurp of beer, peering at Joel over the top of his glass. 'One thing, though, Joel . . .'

'What?' Though Joel had a pretty good idea what was coming.

'This is a fresh start for you, yeah? You don't want to fuck this up. So no mention of the v-word. Get what I'm saying?'

'I'm over it now,' Joel said. 'I don't believe in v— I mean, I don't believe in that stuff any more. Don't know what got into me. Maybe I just let that kid Dec Maddon freak me out with his crap.'

'I'm pleased to hear it,' Carter said, beaming. 'Looks like Dec Maddon's come to his senses, too. Some officers went round to his folks' place in Wallingford, to go back over his original statement. Now he's saying he's not so sure he saw anything like that at all. Just a good old straightforward brutal, bloody murder.' He paused. 'So you want the job, then?'

'I want the job,' Joel said. 'I want to catch Gabriel Stone and every one of his . . .' He'd been about to say the v-word. He caught himself just in time. 'Everyone that's linked to him.'

Carter nodded briskly and drained the last of his beer. 'Excellent. Welcome back, then.'

'So when do I start?' Joel asked.

Carter glanced at his watch. 'I'm heading right back to St Aldates station this minute. You want to string along?'

Chapter Thirty

The Ridings

Lillith and Zachary sat in silence in the wine cellar as Gabriel paced furiously up and down, deep in thought.

'What do we do?' Lillith said eventually.

'It's simple,' Gabriel told her. 'We must take it back. We have to retrieve it. Such a weapon is perfect for us. Our enemies will be annihilated at a stroke. Then, once victorious, we will ensure that the cross is destroyed once and for all.'

'Brother, you surely can't have forgotten that we can't go near it?'

Gabriel nodded. 'Indeed. The sword is double-edged, so to speak. Which is why we need to enlist a human to carry out the task.'

'Not another ghoul,' Lillith groaned. 'Look at the two specimens we have with us here. And remember what happened with Lonsdale.' She spat out the name. 'We took him in, we gave him everything he could have asked for, and he betrayed us.'

'The motherfucker *was* a politician,' Zachary said, gazing closely at the computer screen and clicking the keyboard as he spoke. His big fingers were getting more accustomed to the keys. 'You can't trust those guys.'

Gabriel shook his head. 'No. No ghouls this time. This must be done properly. And evidently, the right candidate for this particular task will require a certain set of virtues. Leave that to me.' He paused, rubbing his eyes to clear away the mental picture of the cross that was still haunting him. 'In the meantime, we have another, very grave, problem. The Federation have agents combing the human media constantly. They only have to find this article, and they will know the location of the weapon.'

Lillith blanched. 'What if they already have? They went after it before; they can do it again.'

Gabriel pursed his lips. 'I believe we have the advantage in this situation. The Federation have no reason to be looking for the cross. However, it is only a *very* narrow advantage. We must act quickly to ensure we get to it first. Zachary, you are interrupting my train of thought with your incessant tapping. Pray leave the computer alone for now.'

'I was going into their news sites to see if there was more on the cross story,' Zachary rumbled.

'Is there?'

'I don't know,' Zachary said, still peering hard at the screen. 'I'm looking at something else. The kind of guy you'd be looking for – I guess he'd have to be the meanest hard-assedest motherfucking killer that ever walked the earth? For a human, I mean.'

'A man of little scruple, certainly,' Gabriel said. 'A man of physical strength and brutality. And one who is open to the sort of persuasion that we are in a position to offer.'

'What I thought. Then I think I might have found just the guy we need,' Zachary said, pointing at the screen as he heaved his bulk out of his chair. 'Take a look at this.'

With the air of a person forced against all principles of good taste to come into contact with something very

204

unsavoury indeed, Gabriel sat down at the computer. The online BBC news archive article Zachary had found was a few days old. Its headline was PRISON REFORM CALL IN WAKE OF VAMPIRE MANIAC SLAUGHTER.

Gabriel read the whole piece twice over, then sat back in his chair with a slowly spreading smile. 'Zachary,' he said thoughtfully, 'I think you may very well have made an interesting discovery. Now, listen. There is not a moment to lose.'

Chapter Thirty-One

Oxford

The operations room deep inside the St Aldates police building was one Joel had been inside many times before, but never as a task force commander overseeing an entire team of his own. They were a mixed bunch of male and female CID officers, some of whom Joel had worked with in the past. He was just glad that his old friend Superintendent Page was nowhere to be seen.

Sam Carter perched his bulk on the corner of a desk and bustled through the introductions. 'This is Inspector Solomon, for those of you who don't know him already. Inspector: Sneddon; Jenkins; Lloyd; Hardstaff; Cushley; Braddock; Myles. Okay?'

'Got it,' Joel said, memorising their names and faces more quickly than he'd have imagined possible. When the murmurs of 'Afternoon, sir' had died away, Joel pointed at DC Cushley. She was about thirty, blond-haired, the most alert-looking of the team with quick blue eyes. 'Cushley, tell me what we've got on Stone.'

Outwardly, he projected an impression of calm efficiency, focused on the job and completely in his element; exactly the same Joel Solomon that those who knew him would have remembered from all the previous times they'd worked together. But it was an impression he was having to fight to keep up. The humans' voices were beginning to echo in his ears, blurring into one, and the room swirled around him as his incredibly keen sense of smell threatened to take over completely. The scent of their warm blood, pulsing tantalisingly through veins and arteries . . . gallons of it, lakes of it and all within such easy grasp, there for the taking . . . it was intoxicating. He wanted to gasp. He wanted to run out of the room. But he fought it, maintaining his expression of thoughtful concentration and trying not to let his eyes linger on Cushley's throat as she spoke.

'Good deal less than we ought to, sir,' Cushley said. 'It's like no Gabriel Stone ever existed. No birth records, no National Insurance number, nothing. No vehicles registered to him either. The plates on the McLaren F1 taken from Crowmoor Hall turned out to be false. And we can't trace where it was bought.'

Joel had already checked them before his trip to Romania. 'Any luck digging up the property deeds?'

Cushley shook her head. 'Our guy seems pretty adept at not leaving a paper trail. Crowmoor Hall's bills were always paid in cash, we think by Stone's employee, Seymour Finch.'

'Now resident in the police morgue,' Carter said. 'Anyone been down there lately and seen the size of his hands, by the way? Buggering things are enormous. Hardly human, even.'

'Another blank there,' Cushley said. 'Finch is as much of a mystery as his former boss. Forensic analysis of the bullet dug out of him shows up an unusual rifling pattern, suggesting it was fired from an old wartime Webley .45 revolver. No sign of the weapon so far.'

That's because I disposed of it so carefully, Joel thought.

'Okay, let's move on. What about the Jeremy Lonsdale connection? Anyone?'

'Lonsdale hasn't surfaced yet, Inspector,' volunteered the tall, greying CID detective called Hardstaff. 'I've been working on tracking the movements of his private jet, and we have a record of a flight from Surrey to Brussels five days ago. That's the last we have on it. After that, it just disappears, along with the pilot and crew.'

Brussels? Joel wondered.

'Who the hell flew it out of there?' Carter demanded. 'I thought we were working on that.'

'We are. There's nothing,' Hardstaff said. 'Nobody knows where it went.'

'Inspector, there's one other thing,' said Myles, a female DS Joel had worked with on a drugs case a few months before. 'The day after Lonsdale's plane landed in Belgium, there was a major incident at a conference venue outside Brussels. The anti-terrorist boys are going through the place as we speak. Right now, there's no obvious connection to our case, but we're following up every lead we can.'

'Good. What about Lonsdale's homes?'

'Country pile just outside Guildford, pad in Kensington and a villa in Tuscany,' said Braddock, sliding on a pair of glasses and checking a file. 'We've talked to all his domestic staff . . . let me see . . . a Mr and Mrs Hopley are the live-in housekeepers at his estate, The Ridings. Officers visited them at the same time as Italian police sent people out to his Tuscan place. Nobody's heard a peep; same goes for his office personnel in Whitehall. The only thing they all say is that he didn't seem to be himself over the last little while. As if he'd been worried about something – he never said what. He'd been taking days off work, missing appointments, going off places without telling anyone. All very out of character, seemingly. But nobody's heard from him, and we've checked all the phone records and emails. Zilch to go on there.'

'You ask me, sir, a crashed jet's going to turn up somewhere and none of this will be connected to the Stone case at all,' said Sneddon, short and round with a mottled complexion that spoke of imminent heart failure. 'I think we're chasing down a blind alley. So Lonsdale has a few dodgy friends. You show me a politician who doesn't.'

'So basically,' Carter said, shifting his weight uncomfortably on the desk to face Joel, 'we have bugger all with knobs on. But hopefully, now that you're here, we can crack on and make some badly-needed progress. The old man's baying for blood.'

Joel stared at him. *Don't say that word, Sam. Just don't say it to me again.*

Chapter Thirty-Two

Blackheath prison
Solitary confinement block

Just under two yards wide and three yards long, the cold concrete floor of the cell was awash with sweat and the bare block walls echoed with the snorts and grunts as the prisoner called Ash pumped out his eightieth press-up in the dim light, wearing only his prison-issue boxer shorts. The muscles of his triceps and forearms were tighter and harder than steel cables. The points of his sharpened teeth ground against each other with the effort, while his eyes remained blank, unfocused.

He had no way to measure time, except for the routine of his meals and his daily muck-out. He knew that it was night. And he knew – had known for the last several minutes – that something unusual was happening inside the prison.

He knew it by the muffled noises he could faintly make out, coming from beyond the thick walls and steel door of his cell. Noises that, as they seemed to grow closer and louder and more intense with every passing moment, sounded like all hell breaking loose.

Ash paused for the merest fraction of a beat as another

terrible muted wailing scream, followed by another resounding crash, sounded from somewhere in the bowels of the prison. The corner of his mouth gave a twitch, and he went on pumping out more press-ups. Let them riot. Let war wage outside, let the whole world blast itself apart in a rain of hellfire and destruction. None of it was of any concern to him. When it was over, and he walked out of here into the ruins of a devastated planet, nothing would have changed for him. He would remain Ash. Doing what he did. And nobody would ever be able to stop him.

His muscles pumped faster, pain screaming through him, sweat running off his back and down his arms to his clenched fists and the pool on the concrete floor. He reached a hundred and kept on going. He was a human piston. No, not human. Other. Better. He was—

The door of his cell suddenly buckled with a shriek of rending metal. Not much could startle Ash, but as the door was ripped away from its hinges and slammed down on the cell floor, he had to stop what he was doing and look around.

Framed in the rectangle of smoky, flickering white-orange light where the door had been stood three figures. The man on the left was so massive that he seemed to fill the corridor. A curved Arab scimitar was thrust crossways through his belt. He was clutching something in his fist that Ash couldn't make out. The figure on the right was lithe and curvaceous – the shape of a woman, her one-piece outfit tight and smooth, the light shining through her wild hair and glittering off the steel scabbard that dangled from her waist.

The figure in the middle was that of another man, not enormous or musclebound like his male companion, and he had no weapon. Ash's concept of elegance was considerably limited, but that would have been the word he'd have used to describe the way the man held himself. There was

212

something about him – something about all three of them, in fact – some strange and mesmerising energy that Ash had never sensed before.

Ash slowly got to his feet, not taking his wary gaze from the three figures. The sweat was already cooling on his skin as cold air streamed in from the corridor. His nostrils flared at the smell of smoke. From somewhere outside his cell he could hear the soft crackle of fire.

It was the elegant figure in the middle who spoke first. 'You would be the man named Ash?'

Ash said nothing. He nodded once, imperceptibly.

'My name is Stone. Gabriel Stone. These are my associates, Lillith and Zachary. We have come for you.'

Ash remained silent; he cocked his head a little to the side, watching them intently.

'There will be time for explanations later,' Gabriel told him. 'Zachary, escort our friend from his chamber.'

Zachary ducked his head to clear the cell doorway. Stepping inside, he tossed away the thing he'd been clutching in his fist. Ash looked down at it. A human arm, ripped off at the elbow. Still wearing the shirt sleeve of the man it had been torn from. The sleeve was the colour of a prison guard's uniform.

Two vertical frown lines appeared on Ash's brow.

Zachary towered over him by a good four inches, and where Ash's muscles were tight and sleek like a leopard's, the huge man was built more like a Kodiak bear. Gripping him by the shoulder, Zachary propelled him towards the door. Ash disliked anyone touching him, but his protest was quickly cut short as he took in the scene of carnage and destruction outside his cell. The twisted, broken, slashed and dismembered corpses of eight prison guards littered the floor. The familiar stink of death mingled with the acrid smell of smoke. He

213

could hear the groans of the dying echoing down the corridor. Flames and black smoke surged from an electrical box that trailed sword-slashed wires. The security cameras lining the corridor were dead, sightless.

'What, you think we were gonna dig a tunnel into your cell, asshole?' Zachary said. 'Like a bunch of motherfucking rats? No way. We came straight in the front door.'

'Golden Boy better be worth the trouble,' Lillith said as they headed back through the maze of corridors, Gabriel silently leading the way, Zachary bringing up the rear steering the human ahead of him. She held up her sword hand. 'Look at this. I broke a damned nail.'

As they pressed on, they could feel the walls shaking with the roar and the stamping of the thousands of prisoners teeming behind locked doors, clamouring wildly to get out. Ash had stopped trying to shake off the big man's grip. All he could do was stare as they kept moving. The last time he'd seen these corridors, the way had been barred by thick metal doors that took a ring of keys to pass through. Now, the way was open and the doors hung twisted and limp on their hinges. Every few yards they stepped over another pool of blood, another dead guard. Rounding a corner, they came across one who was still alive and dragging himself pitifully along the floor by a mutilated hand. Lillith tutted, drew her sabre and buried its blade deep into the man's back. She dabbed a fingertip against the bloody steel and licked it. 'Want some?' she asked teasingly, turning to Ash. 'I mean, you *do* imbibe, don't you?'

'Save it for later, sister,' Gabriel snapped at her.

'Who *are* you people?' Ash said.

'It speaks,' Lillith said. 'Well, that's something.'

As they passed through a smashed doorway, the narrow block-built corridor opened up into a high, open space that blazed with bright neon light. Metal walkways and stairways lined the walls. The roar of the prisoners echoed deafeningly from three tiered rows of communal cells, a waving, yearning forest of arms stretching outward through the bars. When they saw the group approaching and the bewildered-looking Ash with them, the prisoners erupted into a wild cheer.

'We ought to let them all out,' Lillith shouted over the din, amping up the already enormous volume of noise with a flourish of her bloody sabre and a beaming smile to her audience. 'A mass breakout of thieves and murderers. Something to spice this dreary old island up a lit—'

Her words and the cheering of the prisoners were drowned out by the sudden blaring whoop of a siren.

'Shit,' Zachary mouthed, and he drew the scimitar out of his belt, still keeping a tight grip on Ash. Gabriel looked across to see a barred door flying open and nine prison guards swarming through towards them. It seemed that the survivors of the vampires' inward journey through Blackheath had regrouped and broken out their anti-riot equipment. Their terrified faces peered over the tops of their shields. Four of the nine men were clutching rubber bullet guns. Without waiting for a command, one let off his weapon with a booming thump.

The heavy cylindrical composite-plastic missile crossed the distance between the guards and the vampires at several hundred feet per second. Just a blur to the human eye, but to a vampire's senses it might as well have been a gently-thrown beach ball. Lillith slashed out with her sabre and cut the rubber bullet in half before it could reach its target.

The other three panicking guards let rip with their weapons in quick succession. Zachary easily deflected the second bullet with the blade of his scimitar, sending it bouncing away harmlessly across the floor. Gabriel reached out and simply snatched the third and fourth out of the air with his hands, like catching apples falling from a tree. He tossed them over his shoulders, clicked his fingers and said, 'Kill them.'

Lillith and Zachary charged. The fight was brief, bloody and brutally uneven. The roar of the prisoners rose to a frenzied howl as the two vampires' blades chopped and hacked. An ear flew. A hand. Lillith decapitated one guard with a single stroke. Zachary sliced another almost in half from shoulder to hip. In moments, nine men had been reduced to a pile of body parts lying scattered in a huge pool of blood.

'More will be on their way,' Gabriel said over the whoop of the alarm. 'Let's go.'

Before squadrons of armed police and half the British Army could descend on the place, the vampires had retraced their bloody steps back through the rest of the prison and burst out into the misty night. Ash ran hard to keep up as they sprinted to the perimeter fence and climbed out through the hole that Zachary had slashed in the wire earlier.

When Ash sucked in the cold night air, then laid eyes on the helicopter that was waiting for them on the tarmac beyond the fence, the rush of exhilaration at his newfound freedom made him want to shout in triumph. Lillith chuckled at his expression. 'Don't count your chickens just yet, Golden Boy. You don't know what's in store.'

Before the human could reply, Zachary had shoved him through a cargo hatch in the fuselage and slammed it shut. The three vampires piled into the cockpit. Gabriel calmly took the controls, and in seconds the rotors were building up speed.

'Hey, Gabriel, have you got a licence to fly this thing?' Lillith yelled over the screech of the turbine as the helicopter lifted off the ground, dipped its nose and accelerated aggressively skywards. Looking down, they could all see the ocean of flashing blue lights illuminating the North Yorkshire hills and hear the sirens as dozens of emergency response vehicles sped towards the prison. But by then, the chopper was already just a rapidly shrinking red twinkle among the stars.

Chapter Thirty-Three

Oxford

Hours after the rest of the team, exhausted by a long, fruit-less day of chasing up dead-end leads and blind alleys, had packed it in and gone home to their beds, Joel was still in the office. The last one to leave had been Cushley. Joel hadn't been unaware of the way the female detective kept glancing at him across the office, the lowered eyelashes and the frequent darting of her fingers to touch her hair whenever they were talking alone. Even worse was the way she'd undone the top button of her blouse in the stifling heat of the room, making him blush and look away, stammering and blinking as terrible unwanted visions sprang out of his fevered imagi-nation. It had been a huge relief when she'd finally left him alone and he no longer had to deal with the scent of her hot, fresh blood so close by, or the provocative pulse of her heartbeat pounding in his ears.

It was after 1 a.m. by the time Joel eventually wrenched himself away from his desk and left the building, feeling bitterly frustrated at making so little progress after so many hours' work and mentally drained by the effort to appear normal in front of his colleagues. Just another normal cop chasing after just another bunch of normal criminals.

In truth, Joel hardly knew where to begin. His head was whirling with confusion as he walked home through the quiet night streets.

He was desperately worried, too. The blood bottle Tommy had given him was emptying fast. The drop in its level seemed to be accelerating as he became more and more accustomed to the taste, no longer taking furtive little sips purely for the sake of survival, but beginning to crave great gulps of the stuff – all that remained in the bottle, and much more besides. The part of his mind that recoiled and protested in disgust at the idea seemed to be weakening by the minute, and it frightened him deeply that the old Joel, the human Joel, might be slipping away from him.

Was it?

Not yet, he reasoned with himself – or else he wouldn't be frozen with terror and horror at the inevitable prospect of having to refill his precious bottle when the last drop was finally used up. No, the old Joel was still alive somewhere inside him, still clinging resiliently on. But for how much longer?

With no need to sleep, he mooched restlessly about his flat. The more he worked himself up into a frenzy, the stronger the impulse became to grab the bottle from his pocket and feel the wonderful, dizzying, restorative energy of the blood feeding into his system. The constant internal struggle depressed him even more.

But this was no time for weakness or self-pity. If he chose to starve himself of blood and face the horrible fate Tommy had described, then whatever time he had left had to be devoted to his quest. If his resolve weakened, and he damned himself forever by taking some poor innocent as a victim, he could at least commit himself for all eternity to hunting down and ridding the world of this scourge. He'd annihilate all of them.

Joel thought of Tommy and felt a strange pang of guilt. Could he slaughter him so easily, just like that? Tommy, who'd given him sympathy and kindness when he'd been at his most vulnerable; Tommy, who attacked human beings and drank their blood. The moral compass was swinging all over the place. What was right? What was wrong?

And Alex Bishop. What about her? Could he destroy a woman he'd felt so close to? The idea made him shudder.

He balled his fists.

Joel, Alex is dead. She was dead long before you were born. She's not a woman, she's not a person. She's a thing, a terrible thing, a monstrosity. Just like you.

Then she did have to be destroyed, and he had to be strong.

Alex. She was never far from his thoughts. He closed his eyes and saw her face vividly in his mind, her image so clear that it was almost as though he could speak to her and she'd hear him and reply. He suddenly felt oddly separate from himself, drifting, falling into a dreamlike state . . .

Alex, he called out to her. *Why? How could you have done this to me?*

But she didn't reply. He stretched out harder with his feelings, yearning to touch her. *Where are you?*

Still no reply. And yet, he could almost sense her presence, uncannily close, somehow even tangible. She *was* close. 'Alex is in London,' he heard himself say out loud, in a voice that was almost trancelike. The sound of it startled him out of his half-dreaming state and he opened his eyes. He remembered what Tommy had told him about the strange, psychic, almost telepathic bond that existed between a vampire and its victim.

'Alex is back in London,' he repeated, more loudly. Only a wild impulse, but it felt right. He believed it.

Joel grabbed his jacket, burst out of the flat and broke into a fast run that didn't slacken until he'd raced all the way back through Jericho and the city centre to the bus station at Gloucester Green, from where Oxford Tube coaches ran all through the night to London. Boarding the near-empty 03.10 to Marble Arch, he sat in the back, as far away from people as he could get, and sat with his eyes half-closed, fingering the bottle in his pocket as the bus hummed and vibrated its way down the M40 towards London.

The night had become hard and starry by the time he stepped off at Marble Arch. Walking briskly, avoiding people and trying to stay calm, he flagged down a black cab and gave the driver Alex's address in Canary Wharf. It seemed like so long ago since he'd turned up at her place, begging for her help, thinking he'd found an ally he could trust.

As the taxi cut across the city, the volume of traffic even at four in the morning made Joel feel acutely aware of the hick Oxfordshire cop he was. Finally, snarled up in a queue at a red light, he couldn't stand it any more. He flicked a banknote at the driver and flung open the door to make the rest of the journey on foot.

He ran and ran, faster and faster, miles passing under his pounding feet. His energy seemed limitless as he sprinted through the streets, leaping over parked cars, feeling the exhilaration of the night. *My time*, he thought, and instantly felt ashamed. He covered the last few miles to Canary Wharf at a more sedate pace. Eventually, the twinkling river and Alex's apartment building came into view.

To Joel's amazement, his motorbike was still there, exactly where he'd parked it, apparently unmolested by thieves or vandals. He patted the seat of the Suzuki Hayabusa. The sleek supersports machine, which had once excited and frightened him so much with its speed and power, seemed to belong to a different life. The glass frontage of the apartment building towered up into the night sky, reflecting the stars and the lights on the water. Joel ran his eye up and across, trying to calculate which of its many windows were Alex's; then he pushed through the revolving door into the reception area and walked up to the desk.

The attendant looked up sleepily. 'Miss Bishop? Hold on, please.' Joel waited as he clicked his keyboard a few times. 'I'm sorry. I'm afraid it seems that Miss Bishop has moved out.'

'Did she leave a forwarding address?' Joel flashed out his police warrant card. The attendant eyed it, then checked on his screen again and shook his head. 'No, sir, I'm sorry, I can't help you.'

Joel looked flatly at him for a minute, then thanked him and walked back out through the revolving door. 'Shit,' he muttered, back outside. Was this some ruse Alex had set up, anticipating that he'd be bound to come looking for her?

He looked again at the front of the dark building. Yes, he was sure now which had been Alex's windows. Like most of the others, they were in darkness. No sign of movement behind them, but he still wanted to try. He moved cautiously away from the doorway, out of view of the reception desk. Cameras watched from every angle. He slipped into the shadows at the very foot of the building, and looked straight up at the towering expanse of steel and glass.

The old Joel would have hesitated much longer before making a crazy decision like this. And the old Joel, skilled climber though he'd been, wouldn't have been remotely capable of scaling the sheer building. The new Joel went up it like a spider, hand over fist, the wind tearing at his hair as he climbed higher and higher. He reached the jutting concrete lip of the first-floor balconies, pulled himself easily over, and moved upwards and onwards. A light came on; he ducked out of sight as a woman in a nightdress padded across her luxury bedroom. He waited until she'd disappeared into a bathroom, then climbed on. In less than a minute, he was peering through the dark window into Alex's apartment.

Whoever had designed the security for the building hadn't reckoned on an assault by a semi-suicidal, super-strong burglar coming in the hard way: when Joel cracked the thick reinforced glass with his fist it yielded like an eggshell without setting off any alarms. He reached through the jagged hole, undid the latch and let himself in.

He saw immediately that the receptionist hadn't been lying. Alex had moved out, and judging by the marks that the furniture had compressed into the thick carpeting, the place hadn't been vacated for very long. He spent almost thirty minutes combing the empty rooms for even the smallest trace of her, but the place had been stripped bare. She could be anywhere in London – and that was if his feeling was even right.

Joel heaved a sigh. What next? A sudden wave of despondency made him feel like staying here for a while. A long while. He didn't want to have to go back to work when day came. He didn't want to have to think, or breathe, or exist. He sank down to the bare carpet, curled up in darkness and prayed for the world to go away and leave him alone forever.

Lying there, he could feel the pressure against his thigh of the near-empty blood bottle in his pocket. And something else. An intense, gnawing, biting, electrifying, jangling, unbearable sensation building up inside him, working its way gradually through every part of his body from the marrow of his spine to the tips of his fingers.

The hunger was getting worse.

Chapter Thirty-Four

The Ridings

The two ghouls were waiting nervously as the chopper touched down on the helipad at The Ridings.

'Master,' Geoffrey Hopley croaked, scurrying beneath the spinning rotors to welcome Gabriel, 'some friends of yours have arrived.'

Gabriel batted him aside. 'Yes, yes, they were expected. Away with you, now. Lillith, Zachary, bring the human inside and prepare him. I will join you shortly.'

'Gabriel!' cried a chorus of familiar voices as he strode inside the hallway of the manor house. He turned, spread his arms in pleasure and greeted each of his trusted old allies in turn. Moustachioed Victor, silver-haired Yuri, the blond and handsome Rolando, the short, swarthy Petroc, fat Albrecht in the fedora hat and the shaven-headed Elspeth had all been part of the Trad assault team that had so effectively destroyed the Federation's pharmaceutical plant in the Italian Alps. Tiberius, tall and muscular with an air of nobility, had been Gabriel's comrade during his brief, and in retrospect ill-judged, stint with the Roman Praetorian Guard and they'd remained in contact ever since.

As for Kali, resplendent in the same exotic silks and jewels

Gabriel remembered so well, seeing her again evoked many delicious memories from years past.

'Gabriel, sweet, how long has it been?' she asked, beaming, her diamond-studded gold bangles jinking as she tenderly stroked his face. 'You haven't changed a bit,' she added, and they laughed. It was an old joke among vampires.

'And you, my dear, are as magnificent as ever,' Gabriel said, caressing her slender arm with real affection. The dusky, willowy, black-haired Asian she-vampire was, if anything, even more devastatingly beautiful than Lillith. The passionate liaison between her and Gabriel, which had lasted on and off for three centuries, had threatened for a time to cause a jealous rift between him and his sister and was a subject never discussed.

'You have found a fine new home for yourself, I see,' Tiberius grinned. 'We should have expected no less from a vampire of such taste.'

'Can't say I think much of your ghouls, though,' Elspeth said with a sniff. 'The male one is slow-witted and the female one smells.'

Gabriel dismissed it with a wave. 'Merely a temporary arrangement. More adequate replacements will be appointed soon.'

'But tell us,' said Yuri, looking concerned. 'You are well? We heard you had been badly injured. Is it true about the cross?'

'I am afraid it is true,' Gabriel said. 'And it grieves me to tell you of the loss of many of our comrades, including Anton and Anastasia. But all is not lost, as you will see. I have devised a plan that will presently turn the tide back in our favour. Ah, my friends, it gives me such pleasure to be reunited with you all, and to see our numbers replenished again.'

'More than you think, Gabriel. You have a surprise visitor waiting for you in the library.' Yuri opened a door, and a tanned, square-jawed vampire with a dazzling white smile and a rhinestone shirt came swaggering into the hallway.

'Who is he?' Gabriel said, his smile dropping, scrutinising the stranger with a look of faint distaste.

'His name's Baxter Burnett,' Victor said. 'He's a film star, Gabriel.'

'The name is familiar. But what is he doing here?'

'Our spy at VIA in London put him in touch with us,' said Rolando. 'He wants to join the cause.'

'Fuckin' A,' Baxter spat. 'I'm sick of being bossed around by a bunch of goddamn fascists tellin' me what to do. Heard about you guys, think you're doin' a great thing here, figured I oughtta hook up with you. Rolando here set up the RV. So here I am, m'man, ready to join the cause, just like he said. Baxter Burnett, *à votre service*.' He held out his hand.

Gabriel ignored the hand. 'I am *not* your man,' he said.

The pearly smile widened even more. 'Hey, if it's security you're worried about, no sweat. The guys here blindfolded me on the way over, so, abso-goddamn-lutely no idea where this little hideout of yours is. Not that I'd breathe a word to a soul. Say, you like movies, Gabe?'

'You may address me as Mr Stone. I regret to say I have not had the pleasure of seeing one of yours.' Gabriel paused, staring at him with some disgust. The California tan alone told Gabriel all he needed to know: the vulgar cretin hadn't yet realised that his obvious heavy reliance on the Federation's Solazal was something the Traditionalist revolution aimed to sweep away completely; and with it the freedom that too many vampires had enjoyed for too long to betray their sacred traditions and pursue such degenerate human activities as, for instance, film acting.

Gabriel was formulating the most crushing way to put this to Baxter, when a thought came to him and he changed tack. Laying a hand on Baxter's shoulder, he led him off to the side, leaving the others to chatter among themselves. 'The motion picture industry must surely be a fascinating world,' he said in a suddenly far friendlier tone.

'Sure is that,' Baxter said proudly.

'Tell me, Baxter – I *may* call you Baxter? – I suppose that performers of your stellar calibre must be very handsomely remunerated. Paid,' he added in response to the blank stare.

Baxter gave a modest shrug. 'If you call eighty million bucks in the bank well paid, I guess, then yeah. Not to mention real estate and a whole bunch of other investments, man.'

'Wonderful, wonderful. Such wealth must allow you to enjoy the very best in material comforts. A fine home, no doubt . . . as well as your own personal aircraft, perhaps?'

'Citation Bravo,' Baxter replied, delighted to be asked about his pride and joy. 'She's small, only an eight-seater, but she's got everything, Gabe. I use her all the time. She's sitting at Heathrow right now, waiting to take me back to sunny LA.'

Gabriel smiled. 'Please forgive my rudeness earlier, Baxter, and do call me Gabriel. Welcome to our little family.' He turned to the others. 'Now you must all come and meet our new acquisition.'

Gabriel led his growing little army of vampires outside into the grounds behind the house. Beyond the gazebo, the moonlight shone brightly down over the moss-covered ruins of what had once been a small Cistercian abbey.

'Twelfth century,' Gabriel murmured, running his hand down the craggy remains of a stone column.

'Glory days for us, Gabriel,' Kali smiled, and touched

his arm. Across the other side of the ruins, Lillith shot her a furiously hostile look that Gabriel pretended not to notice as he walked over to where Lillith and Zachary were standing guarding the human. Ash was utterly still and silent, studying his moonlit surroundings with a watchful eye. They'd dressed him in the black silk kimono that Gabriel had selected for him earlier.

'We haven't told him yet,' Lillith said to Gabriel. 'Thought we'd leave that bit to you.'

'Human, you have been chosen,' Gabriel said to Ash, his raised voice throwing a faint echo among the stone ruins. 'You have seen something of our prowess tonight. You must know that we are not ordinary mortals like yourself. However, in order that you fully comprehend your situation, and to dispel any doubts that may still linger in your mind, allow me to make a further demonstration. Lillith, your sabre, please.'

Lillith drew it and passed it to him hilt-first. Without a word, Gabriel walked over to where Baxter Burnett stood next to the others and, before the actor could react, thrust the sword violently through his stomach; then wrenched it out again and tossed it back to Lillith.

'Ohhh, that hurt like *fuck*,' Baxter groaned, bending double with his hands to his belly, as the other vampires broke into a chorus of laughter. 'That was a hell of a mean trick, Gabe.'

'Now tell me, human,' Gabriel said, turning back to Ash. 'Have you any notion at all of who we are?'

'Vampires,' Ash said softly. 'That's what you are.'

More laughter.

'That is one of the many names by which we have been known throughout the history of your race,' Gabriel said. 'We have walked this earth for centuries, for millennia, feasting on the blood of humans. Long has your abject species lived in dread of us. And yet, I sense little of that fear in you. I know of your fascination with our kind. Tell me, human, what is your greatest desire?'

Ash kneeled down in front of him. 'I want to be like you. I want to be a vampire. I want it more than anything.'

'Seems like everybody these days wants to be one of us,' Kali chuckled.

'Get up, get up,' Gabriel said testily. 'Who can blame a hapless, enfeebled mortal for aspiring to a state of total perfection? It is as I thought. We, and we alone in this world, can grant you this wish, and grant it we will. You shall have power, you shall have immortality, and wealth and comforts beyond your wildest imaginings. But this privilege is not bestowed unconditionally. You must earn it by completing a task for us. Succeed, and you have my solemn word of honour as a noble vampire that you will be inducted into our circle: *turned*, as you humans put it. But fail, and you will die the most terrible death any man has ever endured.'

'I'll do anything,' Ash said, his whole body quivering with excitement. 'Name it. I won't let you down, I swear.'

Gabriel smiled. 'Good. Very good. But before I can send you on your mission, I must be satisfied that you are equal to the task. Now, I understand you have a certain ability with the blade?'

'I like killing people with swords,' Ash said.

'We approve. A weapon of distinction, belonging to a more chivalrous age.' Gabriel moved across to where a red velvet drape lay across a flat section of the ruined wall. He whisked away the drape to reveal a long, broad sword in a battered brown leather scabbard. 'I have selected this for you,' he told Ash. 'I believe it an apt choice.'

The corner of Ash's mouth twitched. He walked over to where the sword lay, and at Gabriel's nod he tentatively picked it up and slid the scabbard off the heavy, broad, engraved blade. Its double edges were still razor sharp, drawing a bead of blood from the finger he caressed along them. Standing the weapon on its tip, the heavy steel pommel reached almost to his chest.

He'd missed his cheap reproduction sword extremely while in prison. Not any more. This was the real thing, and he could tell it had been used to kill: moonlight shone on the patches of dark staining on the blade that blood could leave if the steel wasn't cleaned soon afterwards.

Ash was in love. He swished the sword a couple of times, testing its weight and balance.

'I thought it would appeal to you,' Gabriel said, pleased by his rapt expression. 'This is an eighteenth-century German executioner's sword. The inscription reads "*Wenn ich das Richtschwerdt wohle Gott gnad der armen Seele, 1709*". Roughly translated, "On whom I use this sword of justice God give grace to his poor soul".' Gabriel smiled. 'I have no time for human superstitions. But God or no God, this will serve its purpose admirably.'

Lillith was getting impatient, slashing at the weeds with her sabre. 'Get on with it, brother. We're all waiting.'

'You want me to fight,' Ash said.

'Single combat,' Lillith purred. 'With me.'

'And may the best man win,' Kali said. Lillith ignored her.

Baxter Burnett, fully recovered now from being run through and only slightly humiliated, let out a snort. 'A human against a vampire? Give me a break. You've gotta be kidding, Gabe.'

'He's right,' Lillith said to Ash as she cut the air with a couple more vicious practice slashes. 'You don't stand a chance, bloodbag.'

Ash hefted the executioner's sword, spat on the ground

and he and Lillith approached one another in the middle of the moonlit ruins as the rest of the vampires crowded around at a safe distance.

'Slice him and dice him, Lillith,' Elspeth called out, and licked her lips. 'We all fancy a feed.'

'Take off her head, Ash,' Kali joked, drawing a jewelled finger across her throat. She flashed an alluring smile at Gabriel that Lillith noticed, and gave Kali a warning snarl.

'*En garde*,' Gabriel said. The fight had formally begun.

Chapter Thirty-Five

The two opponents circled each other. Lillith was quick and agile on her feet, the tip of her blade flicking up, down, left, right, keeping Ash guessing where her first attack would strike. He clutched the executioner's sword tightly with his right hand just behind the guard and his left on the pommel, his feet wide apart, knees bent, watching her every move. He'd seen what she could do.

But then, he thought, she hadn't seen what *he* could do. With all the explosive power he could summon up, he drew the sword back over his shoulder and slashed the blade ferociously downwards at her head.

Lillith saw the strike coming a mile away. Skipping lightly back out of its path, she immediately closed in again with a yell of aggression and a lunge-thrust to the chest that Ash had to move fast to block.

The bright clash of steel on steel echoed off the stone ruins as the fight began to step up in pace. The speed and power of Lillith's attack was terrifying. Wildly parrying strike after strike, Ash knew that if she kept him on the defensive she would control the fight. With an angry scream he rushed her, sweeping his heavy blade in a wide scything motion that made her retreat back a few dancing paces. The vampire spectators broke their ring to let them through.

But Ash didn't have the offensive for long. Seeing her eyes fix suddenly on his chest, he drew up his blade ready to block a centre thrust to his torso. By the time he realised she'd tricked him into opening up his outside line of defence, he'd already felt the impact to his right forearm and she was skipping away out of range with a grunt of triumph, blood flicking from the tip of her sabre. He looked down and saw the bleeding razor-straight gash in the right sleeve of his kimono.

'Yum yum!' she sang to Ash. 'A taste of what's to come.'

Nothing showed in Ash's eyes. He felt no pain. This was the fight of his life. Not that he feared death particularly. What he feared most was losing an opportunity that he'd dreamed of, night and day, for years. A one-in-a-trillion chance that had never been more than a fantasy. But now it was real, and he wasn't about to let it pass him by.

Lillith moved in again, feinted right, caught him off balance, cut around his defences and stabbed left. He gasped as he felt the cold steel puncture his left side, the cold air on opened flesh, and his knees weakened momentarily. Now she came in for the kill, raising the sabre high and bringing it down in a vicious cut aimed at slicing his skull clean down the middle . . .

. . . If it had found its mark. At the very last instant Ash threw up his blade to intercept hers with a double-handed block that had every shred of straining muscle and sinew in his body behind it. The two swords met just inches above the crown of his skull. One forged-steel razor edge crashing violently against the other, thousands of foot pounds of energy concentrated into a few microns of metal.

Too much for the slender curved blade of Lillith's sabre. The brute chopping force of the executioner's sword cleaved right through it, shattering it into fragments. She staggered back, her grip on the broken sword loosening just a fraction of a second long enough for Ash to recover his attack, leap forward with a shout of fury and hammer the heavy pommel of his weapon into her chest.

The vampires let out a collective gasp. All except Gabriel, who only raised an eyebrow.

The savage blow knocked Lillith onto her back. The broken sabre twisted out of her fingers and slid across the floor. Before she could writhe back up to her feet, Ash was standing astride her with the point of his sword pressing down hard against her throat. He looked across at Gabriel. 'I'll take her head off,' he said calmly.

And now, finally, after all these centuries of absolute confidence in her superiority as a vampire, here was a human who could best her. Lillith let out a strangled cry of rage and grasped the blade with both hands, trying to wrench it away from her – but Ash's grip was iron and his determination to win was absolute.

Gabriel raised a hand. 'Enough,' he called out.

Ash instantly stepped away. Lillith gathered herself up, quivering in defeat, touching her fingers to her bleeding throat and avoiding the stares of the other vampires as she slunk away to the shadowy far side of the ruins. Even Kali was looking at her with sympathy.

'Holy fucking shit, did you see that?' Baxter Burnett whispered, unable to take his eyes off Ash.

Zachary went over to Lillith, put his arm around her shoulders and spoke softly to her. For a few moments she seemed subdued, as close to tears as it was possible for a vampire to be. Then with a sudden snarl she broke away from Zachary and charged at Ash, fangs extended.

This time, if Gabriel hadn't been there to intercept her, she would have torn the human's heart out where he stood and sprayed his blood across the flagstones. 'Nobody does that to me,' she hissed. 'Nobody!'

'Accept your defeat graciously, sister,' he said, gripping her arm tightly. His tone was gentle and there was a half-smile on his lips, but the hardness of his eyes was enough to make her back down.

'You have passed the test,' Gabriel said to Ash. 'This weapon is now yours to wield as you carry out your mission. Obey my orders to the letter and return victorious, and we *will* fulfil our promise to you.'

Ash slipped the sword back in its scabbard. 'Whatever you want me to do, name it. It's done.'

Chapter Thirty-Six

Oxford
The following evening

Night had already fallen by the time Chloe arrived at her father's place with a bottle of his favourite Bordeaux to celebrate the fact that his discovery was making the news.

'You mean *your* discovery, honey,' Matt Dempsey said, uncorking the bottle in the kitchen and setting it aside to breathe. The smell of tomato and basil and minced steak and garlic was filling the whole downstairs, and his apron was covered with cooking splashes.

'I still can't believe it's from outer space, Dad,' Chloe said, crossing the hallway to peer in through the open study door. The cross was in its new home, a glass tank perched on his desk.

'Neither could Fred, at first. You should have seen his face, honey. He ran it through the spectroscope three times.'

'So the spectroscope gives you . . .'

'A complete mineralogical analysis of the material,' Matt said. 'And it certainly looks like we're right. Whatever kind of rock your cross is made from, it didn't come from this planet.'

'Amazing. So where'd it come from?'

Matt chuckled and shook his head. 'It's still early days. It'll take a lot more verification before anything can be officially confirmed. That means showing our findings to a bunch of people. So for starters, I'm taking it to London next week to show it to some of the guys at the Royal Astronomical Society.'

'Exciting times.'

'A little too exciting,' Matt said. 'I kind of wish I hadn't let Fred talk me into calling the media in on it so soon. I hate seeing my name splashed all over the papers.'

'You can't be a recluse forever, Dad.'

'Hey, I am not a recluse.'

The discussion carried them through until they were sitting down to a plate of Matt's home-cooked meatballs with rice, which Chloe knew was the only dish he could produce.

'The thing is, of course,' Matt said as he poured the wine, 'the lump of rock could have been here for tens of thousands, even millions of years, almost certainly after a prehistoric meteor shower, before it just happened to be picked up. Its finder probably just liked the look of it. Maybe he was the stonemason who sculpted it into a cross. In short, its extraterrestrial origin can't be anything other than pure coincidence.'

'That's a relief. I thought you were going to tell me that it landed here like that.'

Matt laughed. 'Now that *would* be something, wouldn't it? Sorry to disappoint you. It wasn't sculpted into that shape until the fifth century or so. But, you know, it would still have been a highly unusual find, even if it had been any ordinary bit of rock.' He reached into his back pocket and pulled out the folded sketch he'd made of the cross. 'I've arrived at a rough translation of the inscriptions. Wrote it down here to show you. Makes interesting reading.'

Chloe laid down her knife and fork, unfolded the paper, and read his translation out loud. '"He who wields this cross of power shall gain protection from the dark revenants of Deamhan, drinkers and plunderers of the life of Man. May the Divine Virtue of our Lord descend upon thee and hold thee safe."'

She looked up. 'Whoa. Freaky. Who are the revenants of Deamhan?'

'Deamhan sounds like . . .?'

She wrinkled her nose. 'Demon?'

'You got it. Ancient Gaelic for Auld Nick himself. Aka, the Devil. For whatever reason, this particular cross must have been regarded as a special sort of talisman to ward off evil spirits.'

'*Drinkers* of human life? Like, vampires?' She chuckled.

Her father shrugged. 'Those were deeply superstitious times, Chloe. Our scientific age has rightly taught us to disregard a lot of things, but certain phenomena must have seemed very real to the folks of that era. They looked to the early Christian church for protection, just as their pagan ancestors had looked to their gods and idols. One religion growing out of the previous one.'

'Well, here's to our strange and wonderful cross,' she said, raising her glass.

'To the cross.' They clinked.

When the meatballs were finished, Matt disappeared into the kitchen to prepare dessert and turned on some loud opera music. 'What are we having?' Chloe yelled through the door over the din.

'Ice cream,' he called back. 'Chocolate, your favourite.'

Leaving her father to potter about and sing along tune-lessly with the opera, Chloe ran up to the first floor to use the bathroom. As an afterthought, she trotted up the winding stairs to the spare loft bedroom she slept in when she was visiting. From up here, right at the top of the house, you couldn't hear the operatic din from downstairs. Chloe walked over to the bed and unzipped the bag she'd dumped on the duvet. Inside was the air pistol she'd wanted to show her dad, to alleviate his concerns about her shooting.

She removed the long, futuristic-looking pistol from its pouch. With its plastic anatomical grip and counter-balance, bright blue anodised aluminium body and electronic trigger attachment, the thing was more like a fantasy toy or a ray gun out of *Star Trek* than any sort of threatening firearm. He'd soon see that there was nothing to be concerned about. She twirled it around her finger and started heading back down the stairs to rejoin him.

As he opened the kitchen cupboard and fetched out a couple of bowls, Matt Dempsey was feeling more contented than he had in years, and without touching more than a glass or two of wine. It was just so good to be able to spend time like this with his daughter, and he was so proud to see her doing well and pursuing what she—

The dreamy smile fell from his face as a loud crash came from behind him. At first he thought a shelf had come down.

It hadn't.

He stared, petrified, as a man came smashing through the back door into the kitchen. A man with a shaven head. A long, dirty coat. And, in his gloved fist, a massive sword whose blade he was using to chop and slice his way through the remains of the door.

Matt barely had time to yell 'Who are you?' before the man strode into the house, grabbed him tightly around the neck and slammed him with incredible strength against the wall.

'Where is it?' His voice was a hissing rasp and his breath

stank like rotten meat. Matt gaped in horror at the man's teeth. Sharpened to points. Like fangs. Like the teeth of a monster.

'Where is what? I don't know what you're—'

The terrible mouth opened again to rasp at him. 'The cross. Where is the cross?'

Matt had read once that you should never confront a home invader. Let them have what they wanted. Even if it was an artifact of inestimable historic value. Even if you had no possible understanding of why they should want to take it from you. Just let them have it, so they'd leave you alone.

He thought of his daughter. Pointed towards the study door. 'There. In the glass case on the desk. Take it and go!'

An iron fist closed around his collar. Still clutching the enormous sword, the man dragged Matt bodily out of the kitchen and across the hallway to the study door, kicking it open with a violent crash. The jagged smile widened as he spotted the glass case on the desk with the cross inside. He hurled Matt to the floor, knocking the wind out of him. Raised the sword to the height of his left shoulder and sliced the broad blade diagonally down to shatter the glass case into a million spinning shards. Reaching greedily inside, he grabbed the cross and thrust it into the pocket of his coat.

Then turned back towards Matt and raised the sword again.

'You have what you wanted,' Matt gasped, tasting blood on his lips. 'Now go. For the love of God, go and leave us in peace!'

The man bared his teeth.

Matt realised he was smiling.

'Us?' the man said.

Chapter Thirty-Seven

Chloe had reached the first-floor landing on her way downstairs by the time she heard the horrible scream from below and her heart stopped and her legs turned to jelly.

DAD??!!

The cry died soundlessly on her lips as she heard it again. A terrible, tortured wail of agony cut short by a sickening butcher-shop crunch of tempered steel slicing through flesh and bone. Every muscle in Chloe's body tightened like a bowstring. She couldn't speak, couldn't breathe. She swayed on her feet. It wasn't happening. Wasn't—

She barely even felt herself stagger down the rest of the stairs. She looked in through the open study door . . . and saw her father lying there on the rug.

Or what remained of him. Bloodied, torn, twitching, dying. The horrible gashed slice that had almost severed his upper torso diagonally from the rest of him. The study wall, the fireplace, the floor, all were sprayed in livid spatters of blood.

And the man standing over her father's body. The huge sword in his fist streaked with red, the long broad blade dripping with it. For an instant, all she could do was stare. Her gaze dropped to the cross protruding from his coat pocket, then back up to meet his eyes as he slowly turned to look at her and bared his teeth. Chloe stood paralysed with terror.

The man bent and reached out a bloody fist. He grasped her father by the tatters of his shirt collar and hauled him up like a bundle of dead meat. Drew him close, and then, with a suddenness and ferocity that seemed unreal, he opened wide his jagged mouth and sank his teeth into his neck. Ripping. Sucking. Gnawing and slobbering and gargling in his blood.

That was when the shriek finally burst from Chloe's lips. The man instantly released his grip on her father, and the body slumped down to hit the floor with a wet crunch. Blood bubbled crimson between the man's bared teeth as he snarled at her.

Then he snatched up the huge, gory sword and charged.

For a millisecond, Chloe stood rooted and staring at the maniac coming at her with the swinging blade. All at once, her senses suddenly came rushing back and she bolted for the stairs. Still clutching the empty air pistol she leaped up towards the first landing. The sword blade whooshed in the narrow stairwell and crashed into the wall just inches behind her, bringing down a white shower of plaster dust. Chloe raced desperately on. She reached the first landing and made it to the bathroom door just ahead of him. She rushed inside and slammed the door behind her. The door was solid oak, like all the doors in the old house, with a proper iron lock and a large key. She fumbled for it with shaking fingers, twisted it, felt the mechanism slide home with a clunk.

Safe, for a short moment. Something crashed into the door with enormous force from the other side. Chloe saw the oak bend and the dust explode from the joints around the frame. She swallowed and stared around her, fighting back the panic and the horror and the grief that made her want to scream. It was only a small, simple bathroom. The only window was a narrow rectangle above the sink. Outside the window, gently waving, silhouetted in a dark blur in the amber glow of the street light outside, was the gnarled old tree that her father refused to have taken down even though its roots were working their way into the drains.

Another massive crash at the door, the thud of tempered steel chopping through wood. Plaster dust and white flakes of paint rained down onto the bathroom tiles. A ripping sound as the killer twisted and wrenched the broad tip of the blade out of the door for another swing. He was going to hack his way through to her, and it wasn't going to take him long.

Chloe stared at the little window and tried to marshal her thoughts. Was she slim enough to wriggle through, or would she be trapped halfway through with her legs kicking help-lessly inside the room, waiting to be sliced off by the maniac's sword?

She gaped at the empty air pistol in her hand. As a weapon, it was hopelessly ineffective. It threw its tiny lead pellet, smaller than a grape seed, with barely enough energy to penetrate anything more resistant than a floppy card target ten yards away. But it was all she had. She dug feverishly in her jeans pocket, and among the small change and crumpled till receipts her fingers closed on the small, hard shape of a pellet. One or two always got lost in the folds of the cloth, to remain there for weeks or end up rattling around inside the drum of the washing machine. She took it out and held it between trembling fingertips.

Bang. The sword buried itself in the door. Splinters flew. The tip of the bright blade poked through the wood for an instant, then withdrew for another attack. It wouldn't hold him back much longer.

Chloe checked the pistol's CO_2 tank. Still a good charge

of gas. Her fingers were shaking so badly she could barely open the tiny breech and slide the pellet into place.

I'm going to die.

She fluttered the pistol's bolt shut.

The sword chopped through the wood again with a rending crack as the planks split apart.

Chloe raised the pistol and stood braced with her back to the sink. She slid off the safety catch. Hovered her fingertip over the sensitive electronic trigger, frightened of releasing the shot too soon. It was the only one she'd have a chance to fire before he got to her.

With a roar, the madman was through the door, kicking the remains of the planking to pieces with a heavy boot and charging into the bathroom. He seemed to tower up to the ceiling. His eyes were rolling white in a spattered mask of her father's blood. Both fists clenched the handle of the sword. He was on her before she could react. The sword flashed up and then came hissing down.

Chloe sidestepped the strike by an inch and the blade crashed into the rim of the sink, shattering the ceramic bowl in half. For an instant, carried forward by the momentum of the brutal blow, the man was off balance. Chloe staggered away from him, raised the pistol again and touched off the trigger without time to aim.

The recoilless spit of the air gun was lost in the sound of the man's scream, and she knew she'd hit him where she wanted. He reeled backwards. The sword spun out of his fingers and fell among the debris of the sink as he clapped both hands to his left eye.

Chloe hurled the pistol in his face and frantically clambered up onto the edge of the bathtub. She punched open the window and launched herself towards the gap with a fervent prayer that she'd make it all the way through. She kicked and scrabbled and gasped with pain as part of the window catch dug into her flesh. Her fingers reached out into the cold darkness and touched damp wood. A branch: her fist closed on it. She used it to haul herself bodily through the narrow window, and then her knees were hitting the hard edge of the outside sill and her legs were dropping as all her weight hung from her hands. The branch was slippery. It tore out of her grip and she cried out as she fell.

A raking, whipping, tearing slide down through the cold bare branches, an instant of falling free, and she was on the ground with a hard thump, rolling dazedly on her back for an instant and whimpering in pain before she gathered her wits.

If anything was broken, it didn't matter as long as she could run. She sprang to her feet and took off without looking back up at the window. In the moonless night she could barely see where she was going as she raced across her father's back garden and half-vaulted, half-tumbled over the fence and into the little lane that led towards the main street.

She kept on running, blinded by pain and terror, screaming her lungs raw. Objects lost their meaning. She no longer knew where she was. Bright lights dazzled her. A loud blaring wail filled her ears.

Then the screech of tyres on the road, and Chloe knew nothing more.

Chapter Thirty-Eight

Chloe blinked. The white light of her strange surroundings were blurred at first, then slowly came into focus so that she could make out the figure that was standing over her, looking down. As the woman's features became clearer, Chloe could see the benevolent, sad smile on her face.

'Rest yourself, dear,' the nurse said as Chloe tried to sit up in the hospital bed. 'You've had a nasty shock.'

Chloe let her head sink back down into the pillow and gazed around her at the small private room she was in. Her mind was still a jumble as consciousness took its time returning. She thought of the last time she'd been in hospital, when she was thirteen and had been thrown from her friend's pony. She remembered her father coming to see her, standing at her bedside, his face pale with worry, clutching her hand tightly.

Dad . . .

The more recent memories began to return to her, and the tears rolled uncontrollably down her cheeks. Along with them came the pain. She glanced at her bandaged arm and remembered the lacerating branches of the tree that had broken her fall from her father's bathroom window.

'Where's my dad?' she asked the nurse. Her voice sounded thick and croaky. 'He's dead, isn't he?'

'Shhh. You need to take it easy.'

'Isn't he? Tell me.'

The nurse approached the bedside with a small plastic beaker of something. 'Drink this, love. It'll help.'

'What is it?' Chloe murmured.

'Something to relax you.'

Chloe didn't have the strength to resist. She accepted the sedative, and closed her eyes as its effects quickly began to wash over her, bringing merciful relief from the tormenting images she couldn't shut out of her mind.

When she awoke again, the kindly nurse was gone, but Chloe wasn't alone in the room. The two smartly-dressed visitors were watching her, as if they'd been there for a long time waiting for her to regain consciousness. The woman was sitting in a chair, the man standing at the foot of the bed. They were both in plain clothes, but even in her hazy state of mind she knew right away what they were from their body language and expressions.

The woman introduced herself first. She was Detective Sergeant Keenan of Thames Valley Police. Her eyes were soft and her brow deeply furrowed with care; Chloe could tell this was a duty she'd performed many times before. Breaking the news of sudden violent death to bereaved relatives required the right touch, even if she was only confirming what Chloe already knew in her heart. She started to cry again.

'Your father's neighbours saw you running from the house,' Keenan said softly when Chloe's tears had subsided a little. 'They called the police. I'm afraid nothing could have been done to help him.'

Keenan's colleague, Inspector Williams, lacked the soft touch. He said nothing, but his eyes were cold.

Chloe wiped away the tears with the tissue Keenan had

given her. 'Why would anyone harm my dad?' she sniffed. 'He was the kindest, most gentle person in the world.'

'Chloe, we will catch the man who did this.'

'The cross,' Chloe said, suddenly remembering. 'He came for the cross. He took it.'

Keenan shook her head. 'What cross?'

Chloe tried to explain, but it was hard to get it all out clearly and her words kept tripping and faltering. Then it hit her. 'Oh, God. If I hadn't brought it back for him. It was my fault.'

'We can talk about that later,' Williams cut in brusquely. 'Do you recognise this person?' He reached over the bed to show Chloe a glossy printed photograph that looked official, like a prison mug-shot.

Chloe squinted at it, then closed her eyes with a shudder. 'It's him. That's the man who killed my dad.'

'We know who the perpetrator is, Miss Dempsey. He calls himself a vampire. His real name is Ash. At least, we think it is.'

Chloe was finding it hard to breathe. Her heart was racing. 'You can't see it in the picture,' she whispered hoarsely, 'but his teeth are . . .'

'We know that too,' Williams said. 'It's believed he filed them himself. Part of his fantasy.'

Chloe grimaced. 'He really believes that he's . . . that he's a *vampire*? What kind of sick maniac is this? And how come you know so much about him? You said his name is Ash. Is that a first name, a second name? Ash what?'

Williams shrugged. 'That we don't know.'

'Wait a minute,' Chloe said, frowning. 'It was on the news. I remember now. You *had* this guy. You let him escape.'

'It's not quite that simple,' Williams said.

'Every available officer is assigned to this case,' Keenan

251

reassured her. 'We're launching a nationwide manhunt and poster campaign. He won't get far.'

Chloe pointed at the photo. 'Draw an eye patch on that, and he'll be easier to recognise.'

The officers exchanged glances. Williams's severe look became grimmer. 'Miss Dempsey, that brings us to an important matter we need to discuss with you: that is, the weapon found at the scene.'

'The sword? He had a sword. Like a two-handed medieval thing.' She couldn't bear to picture it in her mind, but she couldn't stop herself seeing it over and over again.

Williams shook his head. 'I was referring to the discharged firearm that our officers recovered from the bathroom, along with traces of blood and something called aqueous humour. That's eye fluid, to you and me. But it's not your father's, and it certainly isn't yours.'

'The air pistol is mine,' Chloe whispered. 'The blood and stuff belongs to the man who killed my father. You can test his DNA with it. Help you catch him.'

'What we needed to ascertain—'

'Yes, all right, I shot him in the eye, if that's what you want to know.'

Williams looked heavily at her. 'You understand anything you say will become part of the official statement, Miss Dempsey. You admit that you deliberately aimed and discharged the firearm into a man's eye?'

'It's an air pistol,' Chloe said, bristling at his tone. 'Six foot pounds of energy doesn't penetrate many parts of the human anatomy. I had to defend myself the best way I could. So, yes, damn right I shot him in the eye, and I just wish I could have got to the bastard a minute earlier. I'd have shot out the other eye, too, and then I might have saved my dad.' Her rage melted as suddenly as it had flared up, and she burst out crying again.

Keenan took her hand. 'Shhh. There.'

Williams remained stony-faced. 'It's my duty to advise you that you could be facing serious charges here, miss. Malicious wounding, premeditated use of a weapon . . .'

Chloe stared at him through a curtain of burning tears. 'My dad's been murdered and this is all you can talk to me about?' she interrupted him. 'What's more important to you guys, the murdering loony running free or innocent people trying to defend themselves?'

'This is not America, Miss Dempsey.'

'Are you *arresting* me? I want a lawyer here, right now.'

'Calm down,' Keenan said. 'Nobody is accusing you of anything.'

Although Chloe couldn't have sworn to it, she was sure she heard Williams mutter a quiet *'yet'* under his breath. But before anyone could say more, the door flew open and the nurse walked into the room, accompanied by a furious Indian doctor who led the officers out of the room and shut the door. The argument in the corridor outside was angry but brief. Williams reappeared momentarily in the doorway to say, 'Miss Dempsey, we'll be back to talk to you in the morning.'

Then he was gone, and Chloe was alone again for a long time. She cried non-stop for most of the next hour. Then, gradually, her rage and frustration and grief and shock all seemed to crystallise together into a sense of hard intent. 'To hell with this,' she said out loud, and punched away the bedclothes. Her mind was lucid now, her heartbeat calm.

Out in the corridor five minutes later, the nurse saw her heading for the stairs, fully dressed, and came running after her. 'Chloe, what are you doing? You can't leave. You should be in bed.'

'I'm fine,' Chloe said. 'And when those cops come back

in the morning, you can tell them that if they can't find this so-called vampire of theirs, then I will.'

It was just luck that Chloe kept her purse in the pocket of her jeans and hadn't left it behind at her father's house with her mobile and the rest of her stuff. She counted her change as she headed for the solitary taxicab waiting outside the hospital.

'Take me as far as this will go,' she said, giving the driver a handful of coins. She didn't care where she ended up. All she wanted was to escape from this place.

The taxi was into the city centre by the time the meter had eaten up all her money. It was after two, and the streets were emptying of people. A strong icy wind was gusting up Queen Street and whistling around Carfax Tower as she wandered aimlessly through the centre. Among the turmoil of her thoughts was the horrible weight of knowing that she was going to have to break the news to her mom. At a public phone in Cornmarket she made a collect call to the States, got through to Bernie's number and stood there waiting, shivering, shielding the receiver with cupped hands against the roar of the wind and watching McDonald's litter tumble across the street, until eventually someone picked up and she heard the breathless voice of Marguerita, the housekeeper. The Silbermans had gone off on their yacht, she informed Chloe – the Caymans, this time, she thought – and wouldn't be contactable until their return. Was there a message?

Chloe just hung up and walked away, trudging on and on with her head bowed and her father's face in her mind. Knowing she'd never see it again for real, or hear his voice. The wind felt raw on her wet cheeks. Her throat tightened as she thought about the man who had taken him from her.

Ash. Ash the vampire. What kind of a man called himself a vampire?

For an instant, the thought lingered. *A vampire killed my father.* Chloe let the scene replay in her mind and she saw those pointed teeth, red with blood. She shivered, not just from the cold. Then caught herself – an inward slap on the cheek. *Don't be ridiculous. There are no vampires.* There were only frightened people who believed in them. And mentally deluded people who wanted to believe they were one of them. Little wonder, she thought bitterly as she passed a bus stop and paused to glance under the street light at a poster advertising the latest movie release, *Sucker* – it seemed that everywhere you looked, you were assailed with media hype tirelessly drumming the message that vampires were cool, sexy, glamorous. Maybe in every crowd that walked out of the cinema, happily sated on movie blood and sex and make-believe pain, there was that one guy: the guy who'd been sitting alone in the back row, not there for the fun and the popcorn, but who took the whole thing very seriously, very personally, who bought into the image heavily enough to want to draw power from what he saw on the screen; to take that power and use it to project himself onto the world the way he desperately wanted to appear. Lonely people. Sad people, unfulfilled lives caught up in the wheels of a heartless world that promised everything but only took, took, took from them. People wanting more, wanting freedom, wanting immortality, wanting to be someone whose footsteps shook the earth. Craving it so badly, maybe, that the line between dreams and reality started to blur and fade out.

Yesterday, Chloe might have sympathised. Not any more, not if it meant innocent people suffering to pay the price of some psycho's delusions. Her fists were so tight in her pockets that her nails pierced the flesh of her palms. She wanted to cry, but she was empty now.

She'd walked the length of Cornmarket without realising it. As she neared the end of the street, the illuminated window display of a large bookstore shone out onto the pavement. She stopped and saw her reflection in the window glass, shoulders hunched, face pale and pinched with cold. Her eye ran across the displays of books on the other side of the glass, and she snorted. Look at this – more vampires. You couldn't get away from the damn things.

THEY LURK AMONGST US, shouted the stacked hardbacks in the window. They do, Chloe thought – but who are they?

Among the carefully-arranged books were glossy posters extolling the author, some guy Chloe had never heard of called Errol Knightly. That couldn't be a real name, could it? She peered more closely to read about him. It seemed he was the real deal, a pro vampire hunter with a glittering record of ridding the world of the scourge of the Undead. Read all about it for only £12.99. Chloe tossed her head and walked on.

But then, fifty yards down the street, her pace slowed.

How many of them must there be out there, these deluded souls who'd come to believe in their own vampiric powers? What if there was a whole weird subculture of screwed-up freaks truly convinced they belonged to a race of the Undead? Wouldn't they hang out together? A fantasy shared was a fantasy compounded. Maybe they congregated in certain places, like bats in caves. Drank tomato juice together and wore gothic fashion gear in vampire nightclubs. Had vampire conversations together on vampire internet forums. Mostly innocuous, of course; but wouldn't even the tiny minority of dark, dangerous ones – the ones who took their fantasy a step further, men like Ash – be just a little bit drawn to the edges of that subculture, feeding the delusion?

And, Chloe thought to herself, wouldn't a guy calling himself a vampire hunter know where to find those kinds of people?

She doubled back to the bookstore window and stood there with her nose to the glass staring at Knightly's face on the poster for a long time. She nodded to herself. In its own perverse, bizarre way, it seemed to make absolute sense.

She was still thinking about it on the long walk all the way back to the Park and Ride car park. And as she curled up, spent and cold and weak, to sleep on the back seat of her little Fiat, she knew what it was she had to do when morning came. She was going to contact this Errol Knightly. And then she was going to go and talk to him about catching vampires.

Chapter Thirty-Nine

'Can I have a word?' Carter asked as Joel wandered into St Aldates police station just before eleven the following morning. Joel was too dulled from hunger to ask what it was about, but he nonetheless noticed the stern note of authority in his friend's voice.

Once in the privacy of his office, Carter shut the door, turned to him and shook his head. 'Maybe I wasn't clear, but I thought you were back on the job now.'

'I am,' Joel said weakly.

'So where've you been the last thirty-six hours?'

Joel sat heavily in a chair. What could he tell him? That after a despairing night curled up on the floor of an empty London apartment he'd paced the streets of the city for endless hours, trying to ignore the terrible hunger pains that were getting worse by the hour? Could he tell him about the homeless man down by the Thames embankment that he'd stalked? How he'd very nearly given in to the almost over-whelming urge to attack him and drink his blood? That if it wasn't for the fact he knew it was futile, all he wanted to do was put a shotgun to his own forehead?

'I was chasing up a potential lead for the Stone case,' he said, rubbing his eyes. 'Turned out to be nothing.'

'Pull it together, Joel, you don't look good.' Carter

glanced at his watch and winced. 'Fuck. Listen, I need a progress report from you but you'll have to fill me in on the way. We had a right nasty murder up in North Oxford last night.'

Carter was acting testy and distracted as the car took them across the city and listened to Joel's weary report on just how little progress was being made on the Stone/Lonsdale case. It didn't take long to bring Carter up to date, and by the time they'd reached the crime scene in Frenchay Road and waded through the cordons of police tape, Joel had pretty much run dry of things to say. Carter wasn't happy. Following him inside the house, where the forensics team led by Jack Brier were still combing for evidence, Joel's nostrils twitched at the scent that hung in the air. Blood had been spilled here. A lot of blood.

'Should have seen this place yesterday,' Jack Brier said cheerfully. 'I've seen some butcher's yards in my time, but this was something else.'

Joel was already visualising it with a clarity that took his breath away. He could see blood pooled lusciously across the floor, almost taste the glistening red rivulets that trickled down the walls. He could hear the big round fat red velvety drips of it sploshing down from the mantelpiece. For a moment he was swimming through an ocean of it, warm and smooth as melted chocolate, laughing deliriously as he gulped down swallow after swallow . . .

'. . . Matt Dempsey,' Carter's voice said, breaking in on his daydream, and Joel realised he'd been talking to him. 'History guy, American, museum curator. Looks like an aggravated burglary, but we're still not sure what's been taken, if anything. Some dusty old relic that's probably worth a couple of bob on eBay or down the local flea market. Dempsey's daughter was here when it happened. Poor kid saw everything. She's in the JR being treated for shock. Williams and Keenan have been to talk to her.'

Even in his dulled state of mind, Joel remembered all too well his past encounters with Inspector Murdo Williams. 'Williams hasn't been put on this, has he? The guy's a total spoon.'

'You think I should have given it to you?' Carter said.

Joel ignored the dig. 'Any idea who did it?'

'How're we doing on those DNA results, Jack?' Carter boomed.

'Have something for you tickety-boo,' Brier called back jovially from across the room.

'Better have,' Carter said. 'Though from the daughter's description of the guy and what the bastard did here,' he said in a lower tone, turning to Joel, 'we all know who the money's on. The fucking bastard vampire.'

Joel's eyes opened wide. 'The what?'

'Not the kind you were so obsessed with lately,' Carter said. 'This loony just *thinks* he's a vampire. Even filed his teeth to look like fangs.' He shook his head quizzically at Joel's expression. 'Headline news, St Elowen massacre, jail-breaks, maniac sword killer on the loose, nationwide manhunt – none of that ringing any bells? Guess you haven't been watching the telly.'

'No.'

'What have you been doing?'

Joel shrugged.

Carter put a hand on his shoulder. 'I wouldn't ask, but you really do look like shit. Maybe you should go home. What's that bottle you keep fiddling with?'

Joel hadn't even been aware he'd been clutching it. It was completely empty now. 'It's nothing,' he said, tucking it back in his pocket.

'Jesus, that looked like fucking *blood* all crusted around the neck of it,' Carter said with a grimace.

'It's a sports drink,' Joel said. 'High protein stuff. Keeps me energised.'

'Well it ain't working, mate.'

'There's nothing wrong with me,' Joel protested.

'Got to be frank, Joel. I wouldn't have stuck my neck out for the old man to bring you back on the job if I'd thought you weren't up to it.'

'I'll be fine,' Joel said.

Carter wasn't any more convinced than Joel was himself about that. 'All right, listen. Go home. Take the rest of the day off. I'll cover for you when I get back to the nick. But tomorrow I want you back at work looking and acting like the Joel Solomon I used to know before you started getting all weird on me. Got it?'

The driver of the unmarked police car seemed a little bemused when Joel got him to drop him off at a little butcher's shop on Walton Road, half a mile from his flat. Black pudding was made of blood, Joel figured, so maybe it would help the hunger. He was chewing on a mouthful of it as he walked the rest of the way home. He didn't feel any better yet.

Halfway up the street, his phone rang. He swallowed down the revolting mouthful, answered the phone and heard an excited voice that he recognised immediately. 'Dec?'

'Joel! I've been shitting meself worrying about you. Are you okay?'

'I'm back,' was all Joel could reply.

'Did you get them? The vampires?'

'I got some.'

'What about that Stone?'

'I got shot before I could get him. I think he might have escaped.'

262

'You got *shot*? Jesus.'

'Just winged me,' Joel said. 'Nothing major.'

'Listen, Joel, this is frigging amazing and you're never going to believe me, but I've got some news,' Dec gabbled. 'I'm teamed up with this guy, a vampire hunter. A proper pro, he is. You should see this place. I told him all about you, about the cross and stuff. You should come out here and join up with us.'

Joel groaned inwardly. He'd told the kid to stay away from all this. 'What vampire hunter?'

'Errol Knightly's his name. Written a book about them, too. The stuff he says in it, Joel, blow your mind. I can't put the frigging thing down, so I can't. It's called—'

Joel had already pulled out his police-issue BlackBerry, tossed the remains of the black pudding in the nearest litter bin, and was running an online search. 'Got it. *They Lurk Amongst Us*,' he finished for Dec, scrolling quickly through the site as he walked.

'That's it. That's the one.'

'Come on, Dec. Open your eyes. You don't really think this guy Knightly—'

But Dec was too carried away to listen. 'If we could team up, with you and the cross and all, and then start recruiting more guys, we could have a whole frigging vampire hunter *army*. Just think, Joel. The Federation might even get to hear about us, and want to join forces, like. That'd be just so cool. Think how many of the fuckers we could put away. And Errol said that—'

Joel was just about to interrupt him by saying, 'I don't have the cross any more, and I don't know where it is' when something else he'd caught from Dec's high-speed babble made him stop. 'Hold on. Backtrack. What did you just say about the Federation? What Federation?'

'Errol's got this video footage from Romania. There's this group called the Federation that go round destroying vampires with some kind of special gun. They have these agents, highly trained. Errol reckons it's a black ops branch of the CIA, or MI5, you know, like *Spooks*? Or maybe it's some kind of military special forces team that nobody's ever heard of. I told you this was frigging amazing, didn't I?'

As Dec was babbling on, Joel had found the TV interview on Knightly's website. 'You've actually seen this footage?'

'It's awesome!' Dec burst out. 'Errol's just about to upload it to the site, any time now. There's this woman agent who works for the Federation. She's a stunner, so she is, with this great big frigging hand cannon that must be one of their secret weapons. She's not scared or anything. She's cool. You see her shoot this vampire, and he just frigging *explodes*, man—'

Joel was gripping the phone so tightly that the plastic casing was beginning to crack. 'Are you at Knightly's place right now? Give me the address. I'm on my way.'

Chapter Forty

London

VIA personnel needed only a brief glimpse of the look of thunder on Alex's face to know to get out of her way as she marched towards her office. She hadn't been back to HQ since Baxter Burnett had given her the slip and promptly vanished. Working from the hotel room that was her base until she could find another suitable apartment to rent, she'd spent countless hours on the phone, using up every trick and every contact she could think of to find out where he'd gone. Nothing. There was no point in just scouring the streets. He was gone, and now the only option left open to her was to admit failure. There would be no way to make this look good on the official report she'd now have to write up.

Alex reached her office door, wrenched it open sullenly, slammed it shut behind her and was about to hang up her coat and bag when she stopped in her tracks.

Cecil Gibson was lounging behind the desk with his feet up on a stack of her paperwork. His close-set eyes seemed to glitter as he saw her walk in.

'You're in my chair, Gibson,' she said.

Gibson clicked his tongue disapprovingly. 'I know that fool Harry Rumble cut you an awful lot of slack, but let me tell you this, honey bunny. Your days of insubordination are over. You answer to me now.'

'All right, then get the fuck out of my chair, *sir*. That do you? I'm busy.'

But far from flying into the indignant rage she'd secretly wanted to provoke, Gibson just smiled knowingly. Something was up.

'Maybe you didn't hear me,' she said suspiciously. 'I have work to do.'

He shook his head. 'You don't have time for that right now. You need to be getting ready.'

Hmm. Something definitely *was* up. 'Ready for what?' she asked.

'Ready for your visitors,' Gibson said. 'You're in the deepest shit imaginable, Bishop. They've been waiting for you upstairs.'

'Who's been waiting for me upstairs?'

'You'll see.' Gibson glanced at his watch. Right on cue, there was a loud hammering on the door, and Gibson sprang out from behind the desk to answer it.

The little stoat must have called upstairs the second Queck admitted her through security, Alex thought. Her mind raced to understand what this was about. If it was some kind of disciplinary hearing, it could surely only be about one thing. Could the VIA top brass already know about Baxter Burnett going rogue on her? Had his little escapade outside the school made it onto YouTube already? She could see the headlines: '*BAD BOY BURNETT ON RAMPAGE!*' '*MOVIE STAR IN CHILD ATTACK HORROR!*'

Gibson flung open the door with a dramatic flourish that looked like he'd been practising it in the mirror. Alex blinked as her visitors came striding into the office. Leading the way, nose in the air and robes trailing behind her, was Supremo

Olympia Angelopolis. At her side strutted the figure of her PA, Ivo Donskoi: grizzled hair cropped military-style, small, narrow-chested, dark suit, a laptop under his arm. Four F.A.N.G. guards marched in behind them, shut the door and stood either side of it with their high-capacity assault weapons cocked and locked.

Alex was speechless. Gibson just had time to throw her a quick smirk before he went scurrying towards the Vampress. 'Ma'am, it's a great honour to welcome you in person to our—'

'Quiet,' Olympia commanded with a snap of her fingers. 'I haven't cancelled some very important meetings and come all this way to bandy words on ceremony. Ivo, if you please.'

Without a word, Ivo Donskoi shoved the paperwork on Alex's desk to one side, set the laptop down on the desk and flipped it open. As the screen flashed into life, Alex found herself staring at the garish graphics of a website she'd never seen before.

'Do you know what this is?' the Vampress demanded. 'No, I didn't think you did.'

'"They Lurk Amongst Us"?' Alex said, peering at the screen. 'Errol Knightly – bestselling author, vampire hunter. Uh-huh. Right.' She looked up at the Supremo. 'Come on. We've seen these types plenty of times before. It's obvious this guy's just a showman.'

Olympia's lips tightened. 'And it seems you've become the star of his little show, my dear.'

'You're going to have to explain what this is about,' Alex said.

Donskoi cut in. 'Ten days ago, your superior Harry Rumble sent you on a mission to investigate possible rogue vampire activity in our eastern Europe sector. Correct? We want to know what happened.'

'It was in the Carpathian mountains,' Alex said, even more baffled. 'Out in the middle of nowhere. The VIA mainframe had flagged up a blog where some bunch of amateur wannabe vampire hunters were talking about going into this little rundown cottage in the woods where local rumour said there was a vampire. It was almost certainly going to be just another false alarm, but we decided to check it out. In the end, it turned out to be for real. It was one of the first signs that Gabriel Stone's rebellion was about to kick off. I think the vampire was one of his Trad followers.'

'And you dealt with the situation?'

'Yes, I did. This was all in my report at the time. Why are we going back over it?'

Olympia smiled. 'Let's go through it again.'

Alex shrugged and went on. 'Okay. The situation was messy. By the time I got there, the humans were already in trouble. Three of them, young guys in their twenties. The target took two of the humans down before I terminated him.'

'And you followed the proper procedure?'

'To the letter of the Fed regs. I injected the two dead humans with Nosferol to make sure they stayed that way, and gave the survivor a shot of Vambloc to kill his short-term memory. Then as an extra security measure I took out the whole place with an incendiary device. The report was logged with Harry Rumble and everything was gone through in the debriefing. I can't understand what the problem is.'

'Let me show you the problem, Agent Bishop,' Donskoi said.

Locked in an office in another part of the VIA Headquarters, someone was furtively taking out a very unauthorised mobile phone and dialling a number that nobody else within the organisation could ever know about.

'It's me,' the vampire whispered urgently, glancing at the door furtively, fearful that someone outside could be listening. 'Have you got it?'

'Yes,' said Gabriel Stone's voice on the other end of the line. He sounded tense. 'We have it. The plan is in motion.'

'There's been an unexpected development,' the vampire whispered. 'Angelopolis is here. She flew in unannounced from Brussels yesterday. It was all kept hush-hush, but she's in some kind of meeting with Bishop. The two of them are right here in the building.'

'My man is on his way as we speak,' Gabriel said.

'Tell him to get here fast. Angelopolis *and* Bishop – we can get them both if we hurry.'

Chapter Forty-One

Donskoi reached down to the laptop and clicked to another page of the same website: www.theylurkamongstus.com. In the centre of the screen, a video clip began to download.

Alex's gaze flicked sideways to the block of text that accompanied it.

STOP PRESS! Latest news from the front lines in the war against the Undead. For all you people out there who know the truth, and for all you doubting cynics who are about to be silenced . . . Errol Knightly is proud to present a sneak preview of the most sensational video evidence ever seen that VAMPIRES EXIST. Warning: what you are about to see is real, and not suitable for viewers of a sensitive disposition. Of the group of vampire hunters who captured this incredible footage in Romania, only one escaped with his life. Our technicians are hard at work cleaning up the rest of the footage and we guarantee that when you see the complete video, there will be no more excuses, no more doubters
. . . . YOU WILL BELIEVE.

'What?' Alex said. Nobody else spoke. She could feel their eyes on her as the video clip finished loading and the images began to play on the screen. Only then did she understand.

'Oh, shit,' she said.

'You might say that,' Gibson sneered.

The picture was grainy and indistinct, but Alex recognised the setting immediately as the dank, stinking basement of the semi-derelict cottage deep in the Romanian countryside where her mission had taken her. The greenish-hued images unfolded, jerkily but unmistakably, to a muffled, distorted soundtrack of wild screaming. The first human going down, writhing in a dark pool on the cellar floor; a blurred flash of brick wall; a snatched glimpse of the red-smeared face of the vampire, opening his mouth – just for a split second, the money-shot glimpse of his fangs, gleaming white in the murky shadows of the basement – before he grabbed the second human and ripped his throat out.

Alex had seen enough horror movies to know what a fake vampire looked like on a screen. This one didn't look fake. He looked every bit as real as he had face to face.

'But where was the camera?' she muttered. 'There *was* no camera. I'd have seen it.'

Gibson smirked. 'Maybe you have some other explanation as to why we're seeing this?'

'Silence,' Olympia said.

Now the hidden lens turned round to point in the opposite direction, and Alex's mouth hung open as she saw herself onscreen, walking down the cellar steps. She was wearing the tight-fitting black combat kit she'd used for the job, carrying the Desert Eagle in its tactical holster. Her features were a little grainy but clearly recognisable.

'What an entrance,' Donskoi said. 'Joan Crawford would have envied it.'

Alex couldn't speak. She heard herself on the video clip

saying 'Surprise!' Saw her hand go to her holster and draw the pistol.

Then, just about audible over the speakers:

'Federation scum. Your time is over.' The vampire's voice.

The next few seconds of footage left no doubt as to what was happening in the cellar. The flash and boom of the gunshot. The scream of the vampire, falling into the shadows, the Nosferol already ravaging his body. The camera gave a violent wobble and seemed to turn away in horror.

It was then that Alex realised how the footage had been filmed. The surviving human had had some kind of miniature spy camera attached to him, turning whichever way he turned, seeing what he saw. It could have been anything, a badge, a button on his jacket.

Alex suddenly felt very cold and shaky. The worst was yet to come. She remembered what the human had said to her next, when he'd seen the way she'd destroyed the vampire with a single bullet to the chest:

'How did you—'

And her reply, just before she'd injected him: 'It takes a vampire to destroy a vampire properly.'

Immediately afterwards, she'd pumped her syringe-load of Vambloc under his ear, erasing his memory of everything that had just happened. Her comment to him had been no more than a throwaway line, intended for dramatic effect and meant to be instantly forgotten. Just a way to liven up a routine chore she'd been carrying out for decades.

But captured on digital audio, an admission like that to a human was a Federal crime that meant a one-way trip to Termination Row.

And Olympia had heard it loud and clear, Alex thought. This was it, then. Her fate was sealed.

But just as it reached the crucial moment, the footage cut

273

off abruptly. In its place was a line of text that promised: 'TO BE CONTINUED . . .'

Alex let out a long inward sigh of relief.

'A fine day's work that was, Agent Bishop,' said Olympia.

'How could I have known?' Alex started to protest.

'What happened to the human?' Donskoi asked.

'I carried him out of there, pumped full of Vambloc.'

'With the camera intact,' Gibson put in. 'That's one memory you didn't erase.'

'Why didn't you dispose of him?' Olympia demanded. 'If you had destroyed the body, you would have destroyed the video evidence.'

'My job is to terminate rogue vampires, not to kill humans. I thought that was just slightly against Federation laws?'

'Your job,' Olympia snapped, 'is to protect and uphold the Federation. At all cost, vampire *or* human. The Federation laws are the code we expect our common vampire citizenry to abide by. For the sake of the greater good, however, those of us granted the appropriate authority may sometimes have to bend the rules in a considered fashion. I would have thought that you, as a senior agent, would have understood that.' She paused, visibly seething. 'Evidently not. And now, thanks to you, the humans know about us. *They know about the Federation.* The very thing we have most sought to avoid since its foundation. Concealment is, has always been, the whole purpose of its existence.'

'Did you speak to the human, Agent Bishop?' asked Donskoi, looking at her with the penetrating eye of a hardened interrogator. 'Is there anything we should know about – anything you might have revealed that will be shown in the next instalment this Knightly posts on his website?'

Alex stared at Donskoi. Did he know the truth, or was he just cleverly trying to lure her into incriminating herself?

She swallowed. 'Nothing,' she lied. 'I did the job I was trained and ordered to do, and I got out of there. That's it.'

'This Errol Knightly is gaining a great deal of publicity from his new book,' Olympia said. 'Drawing millions of humans to his website. I hope you realise how serious this is?'

'With respect, I disagree,' Alex said. 'Ignore it, and it'll soon be forgotten, along with all the fake footage of Yetis, ghosts and the Loch Ness monster. This is the *internet*, Supremo Angelopolis. It's already so full of shit that nobody will take this seriously.'

'We take it very seriously, Agent Bishop,' Donskoi said. 'We are not idiots. Within days, hours even, this footage will have spread virally across the entire web, and by then there will be nothing we can do to control the situation. We have technicians at work as we speak, attempting to hack and crash the site. That may buy us some time. But to avert this disaster fully, the footage must be destroyed at source.'

'You have forty-eight hours,' Olympia told her. 'Starting from now. Find and destroy all copies of this video, any hard drives on which it is stored, and anyone who tries to stand in your way. You will then track down the human who sent the footage to Knightly and erase his memory permanently. Are these orders understood?'

Alex nodded, avoiding Gibson's eye. She could feel delight radiating off him in warm waves.

'Forty-eight hours, Agent Bishop,' Olympia said. 'Fail this time, and you have my word that you will face immediate Nosferol termination.'

Chapter Forty-Two

Bal Mawr Manor

The day's anti-vampire weaponry training session with Knightly had been due to start five minutes ago. As he waited for him to show up, Dec wandered about the armoury room. It was a converted private chapel, partially demolished at some point in its history, but still retaining its original stained-glass windows through which the bright morning sun cast colourful reflections across the flagstones. Where the old walls had crumbled and been rebuilt – not so long ago, judging by the bits of scaffolding still propped up in one corner – a modern extension had been constructed to house an adjoining indoor archery range complete with big straw target bosses for crossbow practice. The weapons themselves were hung on the racks that took up two entire walls of the old chapel.

Dec paused to admire them and to gaze at the silver-tipped bolts in their quivers, before moving on down the line to examine some of the other devices intended for defence against the Undead. A huge spray gun with a butt like a rifle was attached by a pipe to a clear plastic canister marked 'HOLY WATER'; beside it, another canister was labelled 'CAUTION IRRITANT: CONCENTRATION OF GARLIC'.

There was a whole variety of crucifixes, mallets and stakes. Finally, a horizontal rack housed a collection of Samurai swords in ornate scabbards.

Dec liked the look of the crossbows best. He glanced back at the huge riveted iron door of the armoury to check nobody was coming, then reached up and took one down from the wall. Holding the bow end down with the foot stirrup, he grasped the thick, taut bowstring and heaved it back with a grunt until it clicked into place. He gingerly fitted one of the silver-tipped bolts, then carried the weapon over to the adjoining practice range, stood on the firing line, raised the stock to his shoulder and peered through the telescopic sight.

Twenty yards away, the circular straw archery target looked huge in the scope. Dec squeezed the trigger and the bow fired with a sharp *crack* and a satisfying kick to the shoulder. The deadly bolt whistled off downrange and embedded itself deep into the outer edge of the target, sending bits of straw flying.

Dec walked up to the target with a fire burning in his heart. In his mind's eye, the vampire now lay writhing helplessly on the floor with the bolt protruding from its shoulder. The next shot would be the *coup de grâce* – right through the heart. He yanked the bolt out of the target and returned to the firing line. He was just about to re-cock the bow when he heard the armoury door grate open on its massive iron hinges and turned, expecting to see Knightly.

It was Griffin. The bent old man shuffled into the range, threw a sour look at the bits of straw on the floor and another at Dec, and then disappeared and returned a moment later carrying a broom taller than he was. As Griffin muttered and cursed and began to sweep up the mess, Dec somewhat resentfully replaced the crossbow on the rack. 'Mr Knightly said I could practise here, so he did. I'm going to help him kill vampires,' he added.

'Said that, did he?' Griffin made a harsh crackling sound that Dec realised was laughter, ending with something that sounded like 'Bollocks.'

'Mr Knightly's a hero,' Dec said defensively, but the old man just went on chuckling to himself. Just a bit strange in his ways, Dec thought. Probably not such a bad old fucker once you get to know him. 'So you've been with the Knightly family a long time, yeah?' Dec said out loud, in an attempt at polite conversation.

Griffin shook his head and muttered something in Welsh.

'Say again?' Dec said.

'Knightly this, Knightly that. Knightly my arse,' Griffin muttered with an evil look as he finished gathering up the bits of straw.

Dec stared at him. 'But—'

'Dibble,' Griffin croaked.

'Beg your pardon?'

'Reg Dibble. That's his name. Had this draughty mouldy old place less than a year. Bought it with the money from that book.'

'Look, mister,' Dec protested. 'That can't be right. This house has been in the Knightly family for generations. Yer man in armour, on the horse there, he was his ancestor, so he was.'

Griffin leaned on the broom handle as his thin old shoulders quaked with mirth. 'Sir Useless Knightly. Aye. That pile of old tin came from a secondhand shop.'

Dec boggled. 'No, no! He was the first vampire hunter in the family, so he was. First in a long line.'

'Vampires!' Griffin wiped a tear of laughter from his wrinkly cheek. 'Never more killed a vampire than you or I have. Shit in his pants if he ever saw one, I reckon. *Duw, duw.*'

A bewildered Dec was lost for words when the armoury door opened again and Knightly strolled into the range. 'There you are, Declan. Good, good. Sorry I'm a bit late for our session. Been on the phone to my agent. Just the usual business matters I won't bore you with. A day in the life of a bestselling author, you know.' He sighed and gazed importantly out of the window at the view across the bay.

'Did you upload the video clip, then?' Dec asked, still reeling from what the old man had just told him.

'There for all to see,' Knightly replied. 'Did it this morning. Oh, Griffin, there you are. Go and make up one of the other bedrooms, will you, there's a good chap? We're expecting another guest shortly.'

'Aye, aye, aye.' The old man shot him a begrudging look as he shuffled off, carrying the enormous broom, and slammed the door behind him.

A visitor? Dec thought that was strange. He hadn't spoken to Joel an hour ago. Could he have got here so fast? Come to think of it, Dec hadn't even mentioned it to Knightly. 'Did he phone you, then?' he asked.

'*She,*' Knightly corrected him with a generous smile. 'Yes, she did, early this morning. A young lady who read my book and is desperate for my expert advice. It seems her father has been attacked by a vampire. I always look after my fans, Declan. And she sounded very nice. Well, she's certainly coming to the right place.' Knightly clapped his hands. 'Now, our training session. Today I'm going to instruct you on the mastery of one of the most vital weapons in our anti-vampire arsenal.'

'The crossbow?' Dec asked hopefully.

'The sword, Declan, the sword. Now these,' he said, walking

over to the rack and taking one down, 'are something really special. Japanese katanas, specially made for me by a venerable swordsmith in Kyoto. The blades are solid silver. Well, silver *plated*, in point of fact. Here, feel the balance.'

'Nice,' said Dec, who'd never held a sword before. 'Are you really Reg Dibble?' he wanted to ask – but kept his mouth shut.

'Formidable tool,' Knightly went on proudly. 'Available to order from my website. I offer a ten per cent discount to readers of my book. Of course, we're not going to fight with these. I wouldn't like to injure you by accident.' Opening a large drawer beneath the rack, he lifted out two flexible nylon training swords and tossed one to Dec. 'Now, let me show you the moves. You go and stand over there. Good. Now, imagine, Declan, that you are the vampire and I am the hunter. I'm going to attack you by surprise and slice off your head. Have no fear, my boy: I've done this many times. The blade will stop just short of your neck. Stand very still.'

Hefting the training sword, Knightly limbered up with a few awkward leg-bends and arm-swings. Then he took a couple of deep breaths, let out a sudden roar and rushed at Dec with the sword raised, pirouetted like an ungainly ballet dancer and whooshed the nylon blade through the air, missing Dec by several feet and smashing one of the overhead neons, which rained bits of glass down on his head.

'Of course,' he panted, red-faced from the exertion, brushing glass out of his hair and crunching fragments underfoot, 'that was deliberate. Just to give you an idea of the destructive range and power of this fearsome weapon.'

'You carry on like that with a real sword, you're going to slice your own head off,' said a voice behind them.

The training sword fell out of Knightly's hand. He and Dec whirled round simultaneously to see a young woman standing there. She was wearing a fleecy denim jacket, faded jeans, and there was a bag hanging off her shoulder. Her thick blond curls were tangled from the wind.

'W-Who are you?' Knightly stammered.

'Old guy let me in here,' she said, jerking her thumb back over her shoulder. 'I'm Chloe Dempsey.'

Chapter Forty-Three

London

Horns blared angrily and headlights flashed as Ash cut up the afternoon traffic. After years of drifting around the countryside on foot it had been a long time since he'd been at the wheel of a car, and the fast BMW Gabriel Stone had provided for him was a thrill to drive. He could get used to this, he thought as he carved aggressively through another narrow gap, forcing a bus to squeal its brakes.

He wasn't so sure he could get used to the suit and tie, though, or the false teeth he had to wear. He'd ditch them as soon as he could. Till then, they were all part of Stone's plan and Ash wasn't about to question the strict, detailed orders he'd been given.

Ash's blinded eye had stopped suppurating now, but the lids were badly swollen shut and the black bruise had spread from cheekbone to eyebrow. He didn't care about the pain, any more than he did about his lacerated right forearm. The pain just drove him on harder.

He smiled to himself as he glanced at the slim attaché case on the passenger seat. Inside, surrounded by a thick layer of lead lining, the cross nestled in a bed of soft velvet. He'd listened intently as Stone described exactly what he was to do with it. In order to become what he wanted to be, first he must destroy many of his future kind. Ash wasn't interested in the reason why. There was nothing he wouldn't destroy to win his reward. A whole undiscovered dreamworld had opened up in front of him and nothing could possibly stand in his way.

Which made it all the more frustrating when the traffic up ahead suddenly thickened and slowed to a standstill. More horns honked and blared impatiently all around him, but this time they were directed at the snarl-up that seemed to be caused by an accident a couple of hundred yards further up the street. An ambulance and a cop car were pulled up at the side of the road. In the flashing blue of their lights, Ash caught a glimpse of paramedics carting some old guy into the back of the ambulance.

He thought about the blood-encrusted sword that lay wrapped up in his old greatcoat in the BMW's boot. The old Ash, the one who hadn't given a fuck about anything except killing people, would have got out of the car right now, popped the boot open and taken the sword out. These people who dared block his progress would soon have got out of the way when he started chopping a path through them. Police? *Bring 'em on*, he'd have thought to himself. *Fuck 'em.*

But that had been then, and this was now. Now things were different. Now he had something to lose by being reckless. And something to gain – an unimaginably huge amount to gain – by being smart.

As he watched, he saw a policewoman threading her way back down the line of waiting traffic, pausing to speak to the drivers. He sat impassively with his hands resting on the wheel until she reached his BMW, then rolled his window down and gave her a smile. It had been years since Ash had been able to smile without scaring a fellow human being half to death.

'There's been an accident up ahead, sir,' the policewoman said, with a discreet glance at his bad eye. 'Afraid there's going to be a bit of a hold-up.'

'Rotten luck. I hope nobody was hurt.' Ash thought his put-on middle-class accent was pretty good. 'Problem is, I'm in a bit of a hurry, officer.' He reached across to the passenger seat and flipped open the catches of the attaché case to show her what was inside. 'I've been restoring this old cross for St Mary's. The bishop is attending a service there in just a few minutes' time, and was going to bless it. I've been working on it day and night.' He pointed at his eye. 'Which as you can see is hard for me to do, with my illness. Still, my faith keeps me going.'

He worried that he might have overdone it with that last part, but the policewoman cocked her head sympathetically and tutted. 'Oh, dear.'

'They're going to be so disappointed,' Ash said, shaking his head. 'I don't suppose there's another route I could take?'

The WPC thought for a moment. 'Tell you what we'll do,' she said.

Two minutes later, Ash was driving the wrong way up a one-way sidestreet guided by the kindly female officer, thinking about the blood-crusted sword he was carrying in the boot and how much he'd like to run its point through the bitch's throat. As he reached the end of the street, he paused to call out 'God bless you', waved and accelerated off on his new route. Taking out the phone he'd been given, he called up the only number in its memory and said, 'I'm almost there.'

The irritated voice on the other end was Gabriel Stone's. 'Drive quickly,' Gabriel commanded him. 'And remember above all to keep the cross inside the case until the very last minute. They must not sense its presence while they still have any possibility of escape.'

'Trust me,' Ash said, and ended the call. He pressed harder on the accelerator. The engine note climbed. Green lights all the way, and every rotation of his wheels was carrying him a little closer to his own personal heaven.

Less than a mile away across London, Gabriel Stone's double agent inside VIA was pacing nervously in the locked office, glancing every few seconds at the time. It was getting late. Soon, many of the VIA staff would be leaving for home. The man must surely be almost here by now. Carrying *it*. Just to think of *it* was enough to make any vampire shudder.

A growl of an engine from outside, and a squeal of tyres: far below, down in the car park, the headlights of Alex Bishop's black Jaguar were blazing into life. It roared out of its space and skidded off, leaving a twin trail of rubber.

Shit. That hadn't been supposed to happen. Where was she going?

The double agent burst out into the corridor and ran to Bishop's office. The door was slightly ajar, and there was nobody inside. At Bishop's desk were the telltale signs of someone leaving in a hurry: the laptop still whirring quietly, the swivel chair rolled back across the carpet, the desk lamp still lit, the polystyrene cup of VIA vending-machine blood still pleasingly lukewarm to the touch.

'Now then, Bishop, where are you running off to in such a rush?' Flicking a key on the laptop made its screen pop into life. It showed a Google Maps close-up satellite image. Green fields, white beach, rocky cliffs and, perched up high on top of them overlooking the sea, a big house that from overhead looked like a castle with its turrets and courtyard.

'Bal Mawr Manor,' the double agent read from the screen, then pressed the 'back' key to bring up the previous website that Bishop had been looking at: www.theylurkamongstus. com.

The double agent took out the mobile phone and hurriedly redialled the secret number. 'It's me again. We're too late. Bishop's gone. She just left in her car, heading for some place in west Wales called Bal Mawr Manor, Newgale, Pembrokeshire.'

'A minor setback,' Gabriel Stone said on the other end of the line. 'We will deal with her separately.' He seemed in much lighter spirits now, which only made his insider vampire more nervous. 'I was just on the verge of calling you myself,' he chuckled.

'What for?' the double agent asked worriedly, gripping the phone tightly.

'To suggest that you leave the building immediately, if you value your hide,' Gabriel said. 'Ash is downstairs.'

Chapter Forty-Four

Bal Mawr Manor

Errol Knightly wasn't a man to dwell long over an embarrassment. He was all welcoming smiles as he ushered Chloe through the plush corridors of Bal Mawr, Dec padding quietly along behind. In the library, the gracious host insisted that Chloe sit in the best Chesterfield armchair, and hollered for Griffin to bring refreshments.

Dec couldn't help thinking how pretty she was. She was around his age, maybe a year or so older. He kept his mouth shut and let Knightly do the talking.

'Now, Chrissie—' Knightly said, rubbing his hands together.

'It's Chloe.'

'Now, Chloe, I gather you've been having a spot of vampire trouble.'

'I don't believe in vampires,' Chloe said dryly.

Knightly raised his eyebrows and exchanged glances with Dec. 'Then why . . .?' Knightly began.

'Why am I here? Because there are plenty of people who *do* believe in them, and I'm not just talking about the saps who run out and buy your book. I'm talking about the kind of deranged freaks who'd kill an innocent man and drink his blood, so they could live out their twisted fantasies. I'm talking about the man who murdered my dad. I came here because I need you to help me find him.' Chloe's tone was hard, flat and unemotional. No more tears. Later, maybe, there would be again.

Knightly stared at her from the edge of his armchair, stunned into silence.

'That's what you do, isn't it?' she said. 'Find people who think they're vampires? His name's Ash. You might have heard of him. It was all over the news.'

Knightly let out a long whistling breath. 'Look, this isn't—' he began.

'I'll pay,' Chloe said quickly. 'I have money saved for my studies – none of that matters to me now. I can sell my car. Just tell me how much it's going to cost to hire you to help me find this "vampire".'

'My dear child,' Knightly said, looking genuinely pained. 'I'm so sorry to hear what happened to your father. But you must understand, I concern myself with the Undead. It's obvious that this lunatic is just a common criminal. That's a matter for the police, not for someone like me.'

'The cops? Oh, sure, the cops'll catch him. That is, when they're done harassing me because I shot the bastard's eye out with an air pistol, and *if* they can hold on to him for more than five minutes this time before he goes and does the same thing to someone else.'

'You . . . uh, shot him?'

Chloe frowned. 'Please, not you as well. I shot him, yeah. And next time I see him I'm going to do a lot more.'

'Hunting the Undead is not the same thing as going on a vigilante spree,' Knightly sniffed, as though the integrity of his profession were being brought into doubt. 'Nor am I some kind of bounty hunter.'

'I'm not asking you to drive a stake into the sonofabitch's

heart,' Chloe said. 'I'm asking you to use whatever contacts you must have with this whole wannabe vampire subculture. I think we can find him that way. You don't have to worry about what happens afterwards.'

'I'd be an accomplice to murder,' Knightly said doubtfully. 'You're talking about taking away a *life*.'

Chloe reached into the bag at her feet and took out the copy of *They Lurk Amongst Us* she'd bought early that morning. 'Says in here that you've killed hundreds of vampires. If that's true, you should have no problem with taking a life.'

'Vampires are already dead, young lady,' Knightly said emphatically.

'That's kind of convenient, huh? Or maybe they never existed in the first place.'

Knightly flushed. 'I hope you're not trying to suggest—'

'You know what, Knightly? You're an even bigger phoney than I thought you were.'

'I am not going to sit here and be insulted by some little twit in my own home,' Knightly said, getting up.

Chloe was on her feet faster. She grabbed her bag and started heading for the door. 'Keep the book. I won't tell you where you can shove it.'

'Don't go, Chloe,' Dec said.

'Can you get that old man to lower that stupid-ass drawbridge, please? Bye.' Then she was gone, marching off down the hallway.

'Of all the . . .' Knightly's face was purple as he struggled to find the words.

Dec jumped out of his armchair and went chasing after her. 'Chloe! Miss Dempsey!' She walked faster, heading through the grand entrance hall, shouldering through the heavy doors and stepping out into the evening cold. 'Chloe, please, stop and listen to me!'

He finally caught up with her in the floodlit archway that led to the courtyard. The drawbridge was lowering with a grinding of iron chains; beyond it, the last gasp of the sunset was fading on the sea horizon. Chloe paused in her stride and turned back towards Dec, brushing aside the blond curls that the rising wind was streaming across her face.

'All right, I'm listening,' she said.

'Don't go,' he pleaded. 'We can help you.'

'Him? Forget it.'

'*I* can help you,' he said. 'Honestly. I really want to.'

The ghost of a smile curled her lips, and the coldness left her blue eyes for a moment. 'Look – I don't know your name.'

'Dec,' he said. 'Dec Maddon.'

'Look, Dec, you seem like a nice kid.'

He flushed violently crimson. 'I'm almost eighteen,' he mumbled.

'You don't look stupid, either. Too smart to be hanging around this Knightly guy.'

'I've only been here a couple of days,' Dec said. 'And all right, maybe he's not all he cracks himself up to be. But there's nothing about vampires he doesn't know.'

'Oh, Dec. Vampires? Give me a break, huh? There's no such thing as vampires. Look, I have to go. There's so much I need to do, and I don't even know where to begin. I . . .' Her voice trailed off sadly. She turned to walk away, but Dec clasped her arm gently and stopped her.

'Chloe, there *are* vampires,' he said earnestly, looking deep into her eyes. 'Please listen to me, all right? I was just like you. I didn't believe in them. But now I know the truth, honest to God. I've seen the fuckers. Been *this* close to them. I almost became one myself.'

She stared at him.

'I'm not crazy,' he said desperately. 'Don't think that. I swear I'm telling the truth, so I am.'

Before he knew it, he was spilling out the whole story. She leaned against the wall, listening quietly as he let the words flow out of him. He could understand the way she was feeling, he told her, because someone had been taken from him, too, someone close. Nobody had believed him, no matter how many times he'd repeated it detail for detail, no matter how sincere he was. Everyone had laughed at his claims – the police, the doctors, even his own family.

'All except one guy,' Dec said. 'He was the one guy in all the world who listened to me and believed what I told him. And we were right, Chloe. Those things are out there and they're real and we've got to do something to stop them.'

The cold look in Chloe's eyes had returned again. 'So if there's this one guy in all the world who took you seriously and knows the truth, why aren't the two of you off destroying vampires and monsters together? Where the hell is he?'

Dec was about to reply when something caught his eye: a single headlight winding its way fast up the road towards the mouth of the open drawbridge. The sound of a motor-cycle engine drifted towards them on the sea breeze.

He strained to make out the rider. *Was it?*

It was!

As the bike crossed the drawbridge and rumbled under the stone archway into the floodlit courtyard, Dec's face split into a huge grin of recognition. 'You're about to meet him,' he told Chloe. 'Joel!' he yelled, and took off across the courtyard.

Chloe watched the rider dismount and take off his helmet. He was tallish, around six feet, dark-haired and clad from head to toe in black leather. Not bad-looking, either, she thought, though his face looked pale and hollow, as if he hadn't slept or eaten in a while.

'Hello, Dec,' Joel said.

Dec's grin faltered a little as he looked at his friend. It hadn't been so many days ago that Joel had gone off to Romania, but Dec had the odd sensation of meeting someone again for the first time in years, decades even – finding them changed, no longer quite the same person. He couldn't even begin to guess at the things Joel must have seen and done on his journey. He bit his lip. 'You all right, Joel?'

'I'm hungry,' Joel said. 'Feeling a little tired, that's all.'

'There's sausages in the fridge,' Dec said.

'Where's Knightly? I want to see that clip.'

'Inside. What do you think of the place, eh, Joel? Awesome, isn't it?'

'I told you to stay out of all this, Dec,' Joel said. 'You have no idea what's going on. It's dangerous. You're just a kid.'

'I am *not*,' Dec hissed, throwing a self-conscious glance back at Chloe, who was walking towards them.

Joel grabbed him by the scruff of the neck and was about to try and shake some sense into him, when he looked down and saw that he'd lifted Dec clear off the ground with one hand. Appalled, he quickly let him down again.

Dec stared at him. 'Jesus, man. Are you on frigging steroids or something?'

'Go home to your family, Dec. Stay safe.'

'But don't you see?' Dec protested. 'Look at this place. It's got everything. We can team up again, you and me.'

'You and me and your new pal.'

Chloe was getting bored watching them argue. She didn't need to be here. With a sigh, she started walking across the courtyard to where her little car was parked.

'Just like before, only better,' Dec said. 'You've got that cross, haven't you? Think of all the vampires we can take out.'

His face fell momentarily as he thought of Kate again. 'You've got to show it to Errol.'

Joel shook his head. 'The cross is gone, Dec. I lost it in Romania. On the battlements of Gabriel Stone's castle.'

Chloe froze with one foot inside her car.

'Never mind,' Dec said. 'Errol's got tons of crosses, so he has. We'll find another to replace it.'

'No. Other crosses don't work on vampires. They're immune to them. It's just this one that can destroy them.'

'Why would that be?' Dec said with a frown. 'Was it them funny symbols, like?'

'Excuse me,' Chloe butted in, and they both turned to look at her. 'Did you just say you lost the cross in a castle *in Romania*?'

Joel nodded.

'An old half-ruined castle right up in the mountains in the middle of nowhere?' Chloe said.

Joel stared at her in confusion. 'How could you know that?'

'Might it have fallen off the battlements?' she asked urgently. 'Maybe landed on the rocks at the bottom of the cliff? It would have got smashed, right?'

'I suppose so,' Joel said. 'I don't know what happened. I just know that I don't have it any more.' He turned to Dec. 'Who is she, anyway?'

'One more question.' Chloe dug in her jeans pocket and pulled out her father's sketch. 'Did it look like this?' she asked, unfolding it.

At the sight of the detailed drawing, Joel recoiled almost as if he'd been confronted with the real thing. He had to stop himself from shielding his face with his arms and letting out a cry.

'That's the one!' Dec exclaimed. 'Sure, I'd recognise it anywhere.'

'We need to talk,' Joel said.

Chapter Forty-Five

London

Ash slipped on a pair of designer shades as he crossed the dark car park and walked inside the brightly-lit foyer of the Schuessler & Schuessler legal firm. He kept a tight grip on the attaché case, feeling strangely naked without his sword.

It was well after five, but the place was showing no sign of slowing down. Ash had never before set foot in this kind of bustling professional environment: smartly-dressed people dashing back and forth clutching files and papers, receptionists busy on phones, fat business types sitting on plush sofas scouring the *Financial Times*. Another time, and he'd have walked over to the shits and snapped their necks just to watch them die. Maybe some other day. He had better things to do right now.

Nobody took the least bit notice of him as he crossed the spacious, shiny-floored lobby and headed for the lifts. In his sharp suit and with the expensive calf leather case in his hand, he could have passed for any one of the thousand high-rolling legal executives who swarmed in and out of the firm's offices every day. The worst anyone could have thought of him was that he was the kind of flash prick who thought it was cool to wear sunglasses indoors – but then, people at Schuessler & Schuessler were pretty used to those.

Ash pretended to consult his phone as he waited for a chattering crowd of executives and secretaries to exit the lift. When it was empty, he slipped quickly inside and prodded the button for the fourth floor. The lift whooshed quietly upwards. It was his first ever ride in one, and he disliked the sensation. He studied his strangely-attired reflection in the polished steel of the door and ran through in his mind the exacting instructions he'd been given.

With an electronic *ping*, the lift stopped at the fourth floor and the reflective steel slid aside to reveal a small, bare landing that contrasted noticeably with the plush décor of the legal firm downstairs. Ash made his way towards a sign that said 'KEILLER VYSE INVESTMENTS'. He didn't try to enter, knowing that the door would be locked. Beside it was a silver intercom with a little mesh speaker and a button. Security cameras watched him from above. He straightened his tie, pressed the intercom button, and calmly spoke the words he'd been told to say:

'Barry Renfield, from Northwood Estate Management. I have an appointment with a Mr Kelby.'

The woman's voice on the intercom sounded bemused, and for a few moments Ash was sure the ruse wouldn't work. He'd never liked the idea anyway. So much easier just to chop down the door with the sword and get to work.

But after a few seconds' waiting, a buzzer sounded and the door opened with a clunk. Ash found himself in a long windowless corridor, walls and floor gleaming white. At the far end was another door, which swung open as he approached. He was met by an austere-looking female in a dark suit, her hair scraped tightly back in a bun. The nameplate on her desk said simply 'QUECK'. Behind her was another set of closed doors that looked like they belonged in a bank vault. Ash realised that maybe the ruse was necessary after all.

'Mr—?'

'Renfield,' he repeated. 'Barry Renfield, Northwood Estate Management. As you know, my company represents the owners of the building.'

'Is there a problem?'

'I'd prefer to speak to Mr Kelby,' Ash said, noticing the way she kept glancing at his neck. She was flushing a little, pupils dilating. He smiled inwardly. *You want to drink my blood, bitch? You have no idea what's coming to you.*

'Mr Kelby is in a meeting right now,' she told him curtly. 'I can't find any record of an appointment.'

'I have a card.' He showed it to her, and she frowned at it. 'It is rather important,' he said. 'There's been an issue with the rent payments.' The irritation in his voice was genuine. Doing all this talking was making his mouth sore.

'Nobody notified us about this,' she said. With a sigh, she went back to her desk and pressed a button. 'This is Miss Queck. I have a gentleman here to see Mr Kelby. It seems important,' she added, glancing frostily up at Ash.

'Thank you, Miss Queck,' Ash said with a smile as they waited. He pointed to his case. 'May I?' She narrowed her eyes as he laid it down flat on her desk and turned the little wheels of the combination locks. The number was 666. He smiled and flipped open the catches, but left the lid shut. Queck was staring at him.

A moment later, the massive security door whooshed open and a tall, dark-haired man stepped out to greet Ash. 'I'm Cornelius Kelby,' he said, looking a little perplexed. 'Can I help you?'

'Nope,' Ash said. 'And nobody can help you either.'

Then he reached casually out and opened the lid of the case.

Twenty miles away to the south-west, Gabriel Stone was pacing up and down the length of The Ridings' wine cellar as Lillith lounged nearby in an antique velvet chair, sipping absently on a cup of blood and leafing through a fashion magazine.

She looked up and tutted irritably. 'Gabriel, you're making me all dizzy with your pacing.'

'Hmm?' he said, snapping out of his reverie.

'Relax, brother. You're wearing a trench in the middle of the floor.'

'Did Elspeth, Rolando and Petroc depart as I instructed?'

'The minute the sun went down,' Lillith said, and took another long, lazy swig. 'All taken care of. Though,' she added, 'I don't think Rolando's much of a pilot.'

'I believe I showed him all he needed to know in order to operate the machine,' Gabriel said testily. 'Where did you get that?' he asked, only now noticing the cup in her hand.

She clicked her tongue. 'Oh, Gabriel. From one of the humans we put in the basement, silly. Remember? It was your idea.'

'Lillith, those are not for helping yourself to whenever the whim takes you. How is one properly supposed to organise a celebration party if you persist in—'

'All right, all right, I'm sorry. It was just a little nip. I couldn't resist. Anyway, who's counting? One here, one there. There'll be plenty to go around. Zachary brought home another one last night. Some local girl, I think – on her way home from a discotheque, or whatever they call them nowadays.'

'I see. Splendid, splendid,' Gabriel muttered distractedly, his mind already moving on as he started pacing again, feeling for the phone in the pocket of the cream silk waistcoat he was wearing loose over his white shirt. Under normal circumstances, he disliked telephones and preferred to have as little to do with them as possible – but he kept toying with it, willing it to ring with the news he was expecting.

'It's not often I see you in such a taking,' Lillith said. 'Look at you. Grinning to yourself like a boy.'

'If all goes according to plan,' he told her, 'this should prove to be a historic day. Marking the destruction of the Federation, once and for all. Heralding the dawning of a new era for our kind. The age of the vampire is about to be reborn.'

'About time, too,' Lillith said, and returned to her magazine.

Chapter Forty-Six

Not even Ash had been prepared for what had happened when he opened the lid of the attaché case and revealed the cross nestling there against the rich red velvet.

For one moment of horrified utter disbelief, Queck and Kelby had stood there with their mouths hanging open, frozen like two rabbits caught in the beam of a hunter's lamp.

There had been no blinding flash of light, no cataclysmic explosion. The cross simply lay there inert in its soft bedding. But whatever power it contained was now suddenly released from inside the lead casing and radiated outwards with an invisible force that felt to Ash like a giant pulse of electrical energy. It hit the two speechless vampires and blew them apart, disintegrating and obliterating them before his eyes.

And through the open metal door from which Kelby had emerged, all Ash could hear now was a chaos of shrieking and screaming as the power of the cross made itself felt throughout the building. He grabbed it from the case and held it tight in his fist, the cold milky smooth stone suddenly filled with a crackling, thrumming energy that seemed to burn in his right hand. With the left, he reached back inside the attaché case, and from one of its zippered compartments he took the miniature digital camcorder Gabriel Stone had given him and switched it on.

With the cross raised high and the camcorder at chest height, Ash strode through the steel doorway and into the VIA office space – and the wholesale devastation began for real. If there had been anything left of them, he would have been scrambling over the bodies of the fallen in piles waist-high. All that remained instead was fine grey dust that lay strewn across the floor, over desks and computer terminals, and a few burnt tatters of clothing that floated gently through the air like cinders.

Now he could understand the significance of this thing, and the reason his new patrons had gone to such lengths to make sure that they acquired it. Very little had ever surprised him in his life, even less impressed him – but the sensation of omnipotence that coursed through his veins as he marched through the building, effortlessly destroying everything in his path, made him laugh out loud with sheer joy.

Beyond the range of the cross's power, dozens of screaming vampires were fleeing in desperation. A squat male in a grey suit was clawing frantically at a window catch, trying to open it and launch himself out, when Ash strode up within range of him and he burst apart with a scream that barely had time to make it out of his lips. Two others who were obviously guards of some kind were vaporised before the one with the pistol could draw it from its holster and the other could shoulder his semi-automatic shotgun. Their firearms clattered to the floor amid a cloud of dust.

Ash paused briefly to thrust the cross into his belt and pick up the fallen shotgun. Its short barrel was shrouded with a fat tubular silencer. Useful. He checked the breech, then pressed briskly on with his clear-out of the building.

Doors that weren't locked, he crashed open with a kick. Those that were, he blasted one-handed off their hinges with the shotgun. There was no need to use the gun on his quarry. Anything in his path that tried to crawl away into hiding was annihilated simply by his presence.

He had the whole layout of the upper two floors of the building clearly pictured in his mind from the diagram he'd been shown at The Ridings. As he reached the far side of the fourth floor, he swiftly made his way to the lift that led upwards to the fifth – home to the offices and conference rooms where, as Gabriel Stone had told him, the treacherous Federation intelligence chiefs planned and monitored their nefarious operation to degrade and oppress the vampire race.

Personally, Ash didn't give a shit about the politics. He was here for one thing only, and he set about his purpose the way a shark went after its prey. He stepped into the lift and pressed the button for the upper floor.

The top floor of the building was filled with a mayhem of screaming and panic as VIA personnel stampeded away from the source of the terrible power they could feel steadily approaching. There was no way out, nowhere to run.

Not without the proper authority. Behind locked door-ways marked 'AUTHORISED PERSONNEL ONLY', in the section of the VIA top floor to which few vampires had ever been allowed access, Olympia Angelopolis gathered up her trailing robes and fled wildly down the neon-lit corridor. The sensation that filled her body was horrific, making her gibber with terror. 'Out of my way!' she screamed at one of her bodyguards as he burst out of a doorway to her left and tried clumsily to shield her. Pressing both hands against his chest, she sent him crashing violently backwards against the wall and leaped over him. Before he was able to scramble back on his feet, his whole body spasmed into a massive convulsion and he let out a roar of agony.

The cross bearer was getting closer with every passing second.

More guards were emerging from doorways along the corridor, glancing about them in helpless, panic-stricken confusion. 'Stand your ground!' Olympia screeched at them, pointing back in the direction of the energy source. 'Your duty is to protect your Supremo!'

The guards shakily drew their weapons as Olympia stumbled away from them, almost tripping over her robes in her desperation to escape. She savagely ripped away the trailing material and ran on, crashing through another doorway that said 'NO UNAUTHORISED ENTRY'.

The place she was heading for was one of the VIA London Headquarters' most closely-guarded secrets, known only to the highest Federation elite. Leading from a secure doorway on the top floor all the way to ground level by means of the building's air-conditioning shafts, the escape hatch had been built in 1985 – the same year that the newly-formed agency had taken over the lease of the building. Great pains had been taken to keep it hidden from the owners and the legal firm downstairs. Its sole purpose: to protect its VIVs in the event of exactly this kind of contingency. The Federation rulers had never ruled out the possibility of an organised attack – though they hadn't anticipated one of such extreme lethal brutality. They'd been caught off guard, and all Olympia could think about as she raced towards the secret doorway was reaching the safety of her Federation main headquarters haven in Brussels. She *had* to get back there. She *must* survive, at all cost.

Her vision was punctured by the muffled report of a

silenced shotgun and the crash of a door bursting open, followed immediately afterwards by the screams of her body-guards echoing through the passageways. The Supremo was almost there now. The doorway just a few yards ahead was marked with the same fanged skull-and-crossbones symbols as the labels on Nosferol containers . . . but then the sound of lurching footsteps and a deep groan behind her made her spin round with a gasp.

It was one of the bodyguards. Half his body was blown away, the rest pitifully melted and blackened, one arm gone, a withered leg trailing behind him. 'He's coming!' he rasped through the unrecognisable ruin of his face, then collapsed at her feet.

Olympia felt the approaching energy of the cross wash over her and buckled up in pain. With a wail of effort she staggered the last couple of steps to the door and stumbled against it, reaching frantically to clap her splayed palm to the scanner panel on the wall. Her mind swam in a haze of rising darkness as the device seemed to take forever to scan and analyse the data. The agony was intensifying. Olympia screamed.

The cross was getting closer.

All Ash found at the foot of the locked door was a charred mess of vampire remains and some tatters of clothing. He poked about in the cinders with the shotgun muzzle, then raised the gun up and blasted a round of 00-buck into the electronic lock. Nothing. The door held. He shrugged, turned and started retracing his steps back through the corridors of the top floor.

Nothing stirred in what, just minutes earlier, had been the centre of VIA operations. All that remained of the destroyed vampires was a fine, chalky dust that billowed up in clouds at Ash's passing, hung drifting on the air and then slowly settled in his wake. The cross had cooled to the touch and now it was just an ordinary, inanimate lump of stone.

Ash turned off the camcorder. It had witnessed all there was to see. He rode the lift back down to the deserted fourth floor and returned to the security ante-room, where he dumped the shotgun on Queck's desk and replaced the cross and the camcorder inside the attaché case, shut the catches and rolled the combination locks.

On his way out of the Schuessler & Schuessler building, just another legal eagle on his way home after a long day at the office, Ash took out his phone.

'It's done,' he said quietly, walking back towards the BMW.

Gabriel Stone sounded pleased. 'Excellent. Proceed without delay to phase two, while the enemy is still off guard. The aircraft is waiting. Make haste.'

'Brussels,' Ash muttered to himself as he revved the BMW and went skidding out of the car park. He wondered what it was like in Brussels.

Chapter Forty-Seven

Bal Mawr Manor

'Spectro-what?' Dec interrupted.

Returning to the library to talk, the three of them had found the grandiose room empty – Knightly had disappeared somewhere to sulk, or to call his agent. The tall bay windows were growing steadily darker as the last rays of the sun sank into the sea. Slumped in one of the deep armchairs, Joel had closed his eyes as he listened to Chloe's account, but he'd been attentive to every word. So had Dec, perched on the arm of another chair with one foot hopping nervously, knitting his brows in concentration.

'Spectroscope,' Chloe repeated. 'This lab guy I was telling you about, Fred Lancaster – he used it to test what the cross was made of, and it turned out that it was some kind of rock that didn't come from here. Not from this planet, I mean.' Going back through it all had freshened the grief and she had to dab her eyes every so often with a tissue as she talked. 'So, he and Dad got excited that they'd found some-thing really amazing. It was Fred Lancaster's idea to call the local press about it. That's how it got in the news.'

The tears began to roll more freely as she described what had happened next. 'And it was really all my fault,' she sniffed.

'I wish I'd never brought that thing back. How was I supposed to know? How could I?' A sob burst from her throat. She covered her face with her hands.

While she broke off for a moment to collect herself and blow her nose, Dec got up and reached out an uncertain hand to touch her shoulder. 'You couldn't have known, Chloe,' he muttered softly. 'You can't blame yourself, so you can't.'

The memory of the murder scene was fresh in Joel's mind, but he chose not to mention it to Chloe – just as he preferred to keep to himself that his opinion of Thames Valley Police Inspector Murdo Williams, heading up the hunt for Matt Dempsey's killer, was even lower than hers. With a guy like 'Murder' Williams in charge, she was pretty much on her own.

'What *is* this thing?' Chloe asked Joel when she was able to talk again. 'This cross of – what did you call it?'

'Ardaich,' Joel said. 'It's called the cross of Ardaich. My grandfather spent years of his life hunting for it. He left a notebook when he . . . when he died. In it were a set of clues that helped me find the cross, in Venice. It had been hidden there, for centuries maybe, underneath an old church.'

'So your grandfather was a *vampire hunter*?'

Joel nodded. 'He wanted to destroy them all. It was his life's work.'

'And this cross of Ardaich. You're saying it's like some kind of ultra-special weapon against them?'

Even in the gloom of the darkened library, Joel's acute vision could read the hard look of disbelief in her eyes. 'That's exactly what it is,' he said seriously. 'I don't know why. But it seems to have some incredible power over . . . over them.' He'd almost said 'over us'. 'It's existed in their folklore for – well, I don't know for how long. They're very afraid of it. Even to go near it is lethal to them.'

'Vampires have *folklore*?' Chloe shook her head, then was silent for a few moments. 'Okay, let's imagine for a moment that this isn't just totally insane, but what you're telling me is actually true. It still doesn't make sense that some deranged psychopath who believes he's a vampire would want to steal this famous cross that apparently all vampires know is so harmful. It'd be like . . .' she searched for the right analogy '. . . like Superman looking for a lump of Kryptonite, even though he knew it could kill him. Or am I missing something?'

'It's a good question,' Joel said. 'I can't tell you the answer.'

A long silence fell over the three of them, so that the only sound in the room was the crash of the distant surf. Dec was watching Chloe with a look of deep concern as Joel sat very still and his mind raced to figure out the puzzle. He needed to know more about this Ash. Fishing out his police BlackBerry, in seconds he was looking up online news items about the killer. The whole internet seemed to be on fire with the story.

It was as he was speed-scanning a BBC article about the jailbreak that Joel drew in a sharp breath. 'I think I might have something here,' he said. Inwardly, he was cursing himself for not having noticed it before.

There had been no survivors among the prison staff, but prisoners who witnessed the massacre had given descriptions of the gang of three who had, incredibly, managed to break into one of the country's most secure prisons, spring an inmate from his solitary confinement cell and walk out free. One of the gang had been a woman. Dark and sexy, clad in red. Another a huge black guy.

Joel didn't need to read any more to know who the third one had been.

Thinking furiously, he remembered what Tommy had told

him back in Southampton: how millions of people out there would do just about anything for the rewards of eternal life and unlimited power. Rewards that only a vampire could give them.

And now it was suddenly all making horrible sense: the jailbreak, the attack on Chloe's father, the theft of the cross, the things Tommy had said about the vampire rebellion against the Federation. All of it.

'What?' Chloe said.

'Oh, shit,' he said out loud. 'I think I understand.'

'*What?*' asked Dec.

Joel turned to Chloe. 'Ash didn't steal the cross for himself,' he told her. 'He was hired to do it. By a vampire called Gabriel Stone.'

Chloe stared and said nothing.

'Stone!' Dec exclaimed.

Joel nodded. 'There are things going on that you don't know about, Dec. I don't have time to go into it all right now, but there's a war going on, a war between vampires. Stone wants to use the cross to destroy his enemies. Except he can't handle it himself, can't even go near it. He needed a human to get it for him. A killer, a raving maniac, someone obsessed with the idea of being a vampire. What wouldn't a man like that do to actually *become* one? Well, that's the deal that Stone offered him.'

'Let me get this right,' Chloe said slowly. 'My dad's killer *wanted* to be a vampire, so a *real* vampire hired him to steal the cross in return for making him one.'

'We say "turning",' Joel said. 'I mean, that's the term that's used.'

'Listen to him, Chloe,' Dec implored her, desperate to make her believe. A sudden flash of inspiration lit up his face. 'All right. Listen. I can *prove* to you that vampires exist.'

She raised an eyebrow.

'Don't move. Stay right there.' Dec jumped up, ran out of the room and came back a few moments later carrying one of the many laptops that Errol Knightly had lying around Bal Mawr. Flipping it open, he clicked on the desktop shortcut that took him straight to the home page of Knightly's website. A couple more clicks, and the video clip from Romania was starting to play. 'Wait till you see this,' he said with relish, setting the machine down on Chloe's lap. She was about to shove it away in protest, then relented with a sigh.

Joel hadn't forgotten the real reason he'd ridden all this way west. He rose from his chair and walked around behind Chloe to watch the laptop screen. Her neck was just a few inches away. He could hear the beating of her heart as though it were his own.

No, Joel. No. He cleared his throat and tried to focus on what Dec was showing them.

'This is the eighth time I've seen it,' Dec said excitedly, pointing at the screen. 'Can't wait to see the rest. Hold on. There, now. Look. Look. See the vampire? See the frigging teeth on the bastard? Watch, watch. Any minute now and that Federation woman's going to walk down them stairs and blow the fucker to hell.'

Neither Chloe nor Joel replied. They were both staring at the unfolding images with completely contrasting expressions: hers was one of undisguised contempt, his one of growing anticipation.

'Here she is,' Dec said, pointing. 'See?'

Joel barely heard him. He couldn't take his eyes off the screen as the unmistakable figure of Alex Bishop came walking down the cellar steps. 'I have to find her,' he whispered. 'I have to talk to Knightly.'

Chloe had seen enough. 'This is bullshit,' she muttered.

'Come on. Any third-rate media student with a Photoshop program could fake this, easy.'

'No way they could fake *that*,' Dec protested, pointing to the screen where the vampire was being cut down by the gunshot, his body peeling instantly, horribly, apart. 'Jesus, look at it.' Just then, hearing the door opening behind him, he looked up. 'Errol, I was just showing them the clip.'

Knightly strolled into the library, glancing out of habit at the mirrors behind the door before his gaze landed on Chloe. 'I'm so glad you decided to stay,' he said, beaming warmly; he was obviously prepared to forgive her earlier remarks to him. 'I've sent Griffin out to the local supermarket to fetch some extra goodies for dinner. Is it safe to say we'll have the pleasure of your company?'

From the glow in his face, Joel could tell that Dec had been hoping much the same thing. Chloe didn't seem to share their sentiments, however. 'I wouldn't be so sure about that,' she said.

'Errol, this is my friend Joel I was telling you about,' Dec said, working to cover his disappointment.

Knightly turned to Joel with wide eyes. 'The one with—'

'The one with the cross,' Dec said.

The glow in Knightly's face had suddenly drained away to nothing. 'You must tell me about it. You must show it to me.'

'He doesn't have it any more,' Dec said. 'He lost it in Romania.'

'You were in *Romania*?' Knightly marvelled, as if Romania were galaxies away. 'And you actually *destroyed* a—' He caught himself before he went any further. Flushing furiously, he said, 'Not being a professional at the job, I mean. You're lucky to be alive.'

Joel was searching for an answer when the faint sound his sharp senses had picked up a few seconds earlier distracted him and he glanced towards the library's bay windows. It was the rhythmic thump of rotor blades in the distance, growing steadily louder.

It wasn't long before the noise entered the range of human hearing and Dec followed Joel's gaze with a frown. Within a few seconds it had grown dramatically louder, and now it was filling the room. The window panes began to thrum in their frames. Dazzling white light shone through the bay windows and illuminated the bookcases at the far end of the library.

'Jesus,' Dec said, shading his eyes. 'He's a bit close, so he is.'

'Must be the coastguard helicopter,' Knightly said. 'They sometimes fly over.'

'It's not flying over,' Joel said. 'It's coming in to land.'

Chapter Forty-Eight

Moments later, the helicopter was hovering steadily over Bal Mawr's courtyard – then began to settle groundwards, the hurricane from the rotor blades tearing at the hawthorn bushes on the walls. The chopper's skids flexed under its weight as it touched down, and the deafening screech of the turbine instantly began to dwindle to a howl, then to a roar. The blazing white light suddenly faded to darkness.

Inside the library, Chloe looked at Dec. Dec looked at Chloe, and then at Knightly, whose jaw had dropped open.

And Joel was rushing towards the door before Dec could finish yelling 'Where are you g—?'

As Joel burst out of the library and into the hallway, he could hear the sound of footsteps outside. Three sets of feet, running, approaching fast. *Too* fast – the kind of speed that was beginning to feel uneasily familiar to him now. He braced himself for what was about to happen next.

And he wasn't surprised when the heavy front door crashed open with a violence that tore it half off its hinges.

Joel stood and stared as, one by one, the three black-clad figures stepped in through the wrecked doorway and returned his gaze. Of the two males, one was blond and handsome, the other short, ruddy and swarthy. The third was a female, fierce-looking and muscular, with a shaved head. Tribal tattoos ran down either side of her neck. Her eyes burned with hate.

They weren't from the coastguard. Joel knew what they were even before he noticed the swords dangling from their belts. He could smell it, taste their presence. Vampire sensing vampire.

The female was the first to draw back her lips to reveal her white fangs, fully extended for attack. Joel felt a twinge behind his lips as his own vampire teeth responded to the sudden threat. His hunger-weakness was completely forgotten.

'What do you want here?' he shouted.

'We want you,' the female spat, pointing at him. 'Federation traitor!' Before Joel could reply that he had nothing to do with the Federation, she'd whipped out the piratical cutlass from its scabbard and was advancing on him, swishing the short, curved blade through the air with a grin.

'Cut him, Elspeth,' laughed the blond male.

Joel backed away. The blade came slicing towards him; he bent his knees and launched his body into the air out of the path of the blow. Landing lightly on a sideboard he reached up lightning-fast and grabbed the antlers of the enormous stuffed moose head that was mounted on the wall above it. He tore it away and brought it crashing down on the heads of the three vampires. The one called Elspeth slashed wildly at him, but the antlers blocked her blade and chips of bone went flying.

With all the strength he could muster and a brutality he'd never known before, Joel bludgeoned her repeatedly, keeping up his frenzied counter-attack until he had all three pinned back against the wreckage of the door.

Behind him, Knightly and Dec had burst out of the library and were standing gaping in the middle of the hallway. Chloe was peeking around the door with a look of terror. Joel glanced back at them, waving frantically for them to get back – taking his attention off the three vampires for just a fraction of a second too long. Elspeth's cutlass hilt smashed into his face and he was sent sprawling on his back. He heard Chloe scream.

Then the blond vampire was leaping at him, fangs bared in a lunging bite. Not to drink his blood – Joel knew that – but to tear out his throat and then twist his head off.

Weakened and half-starved as he was, Joel knew there was no way he could take on another vampire in hand-to-hand combat – let alone three of them, armed and well-fed and plainly very angry. He lashed out with a wild punch, felt it connect, heard the grunt of pain and the snap of the vampire's teeth as they closed on empty air. He scrabbled to his feet, narrowly avoiding another furious swipe of Elspeth's cutlass.

Up the hallway, the three humans were still standing there as if paralysed. 'Run!' Joel screamed hoarsely as he sprinted towards them.

The first to break out of his trance, Dec grabbed Chloe's arm and hauled her bodily out of the library doorway.

'Go! Go!' he yelled, breaking into a mad dash and shoving Knightly on ahead of him. Joel raced after them. 'Faster!' Knightly let out a keening blubber as he ran, his face turning from ashen grey to purple.

The three vampires were right behind them and gaining with every leaping bound up the passageway. Joel picked up a little gilt ornamental side table and hurled it back over his shoulder. It smashed apart over the swarthy-looking vampire's head but barely slowed him down. All three had drawn their blades now, holding them out in front of them as they pursued their prey.

A few yards ahead, Dec skidded around the corner of the

salon doorway and emerged a second later with Knightly's flintlock pistol in his hand, still clutching Chloe's arm in the other. 'Joel, out of the way!' he yelled at the top of his voice.

What the hell was the kid doing? Instinctively Joel flattened himself against the wall. With a look on his face that Joel had never seen before, Dec aimed the heavy pistol at the pursuing vampires and pulled the trigger. The gun roared and a tongue of orange flame spat through the billowing white smoke that engulfed Dec from head to foot and filled the passage. Joel ran on blindly through it to where Dec was standing blinking and coughing with the discharged pistol in his hand.

'*Move!*'

They sprinted on, slipping on polished wooden floors and tripping over Knightly's antique Persian rugs. Through the dissipating smoke came the three vampires, all still very much animate, swishing their swords. Elspeth had a big round bleeding hole in the middle of her chest and her eyes burned with even more ferocious hatred than before.

Dec threw a disbelieving glance back over his shoulder. 'It didn't fucking *work*!' he screamed. Chloe grabbed his sleeve and tugged him onwards, pressing a hand into Knightly's back at the same time to make him move faster.

The vampire hunter's breath was coming in great wheezing gasps. 'It's not happening!' he panted. 'It's not happening!'

They went dashing round a corner, Knightly almost crashing headlong into a bookcase. Up ahead was the circular hallway dominated by his ancestor, Sir Eustace, astride his rearing charger. Urging the three humans to keep moving, Joel slowed his pace, grabbed the towering horse by one of its legs and jerked with all his strength.

Close on two tons of glittering steel plate came toppling down with a resounding crash. The horse went sprawling on its side; saddle and armour broke loose and cannoned off the wall. The knight fell apart as his mount collapsed under him. Shield, breastplate, pauldrons, codpiece, chainmail and the knight's great plumed helm all spilled clattering to the floor in a chaos of debris right in the path of the running vampires. The blond one tripped over a tumbling arm-guard and took Elspeth with him as he went down – but the swarthy-looking one made it over the heap of collapsed armour, scrambled over the side of the fallen horse and launched himself at Joel.

Joel twisted out of the way of the slashing blade and it embedded itself with a crunch in the wall. Spotting the fallen mace, he kicked away the knight's gauntlet that was still attached to it and snatched up the weapon. Only the strongest of medieval warriors could have swung the spiked iron ball on its thick chain, but to a vampire, even a vampire dangerously close to starvation, it felt like a pumpkin on the end of a rope.

Joel swung it at the swarthy vampire's head and caught him a massive blow in the shoulder as he tried to dodge out of the way. The vampire was sent spinning violently back into the debris, knocking Elspeth over again just as she'd been getting to her feet and reaching for her fallen cutlass. She let out a howl of rage, shoved her battered companion aside and came running, sword flailing.

By then, Joel had already dropped the mace and turned and bolted after the fleeing humans, just in time to see Dec haul Knightly through an archway up ahead and bundle him through a huge riveted iron door, closely followed by Chloe. He raced through the door after them and crashed it shut with his shoulder. Dec was instantly at his side, slamming home the sturdy deadbolts and wedging shut the door with a short length of scaffold pole.

'That'll hold the fuckers,' he said, dusting his hands.

'Not for very long,' Joel replied doubtfully. He looked around him. 'What is this place?'

'Armoury room,' Dec said.

Knightly was leaning heavily against the wall, bent double with his hands on his knees, wheezing loudly. Chloe's face was pallid.

'You all right?' Dec asked her softly. She nodded. He touched her arm tentatively, then turned and strode over to the rack of weapons. He reached for one of the crossbows, grabbed a handful of silver-tipped bolts and began to stuff them into his belt.

A heavy thump seemed to shake the walls. The vampires had reached the armoury door.

'We don't have a lot of time,' Joel warned.

'What *are* those things?' Chloe said in a whisper.

'What do you think they are?' Joel asked her sharply.

She couldn't say it.

'Vampires,' Dec grunted as he cocked his crossbow. 'That's what the fuckers are. And we're going to frigging murder them.'

Knightly hadn't spoken a word until now. His face had turned grey and he spoke in a quaver. 'Wha—wha . . . *real* vampires? But it's impossible . . . They weren't invited in . . . How could they cross running water . . . get past the hawthorn . . .?'

'You told me that silver ball would work, Errol,' Dec said, fitting a bolt to his bow. 'I got the bitch right in the heart. What's going on?'

'I . . . I don't know,' Knightly stammered. 'Perhaps the silver wasn't pure enough . . .'

Another crash, louder this time, brought a shower of plaster down from the ceiling. A long crack appeared between the blocks in the wall by the door. The scaffold pipe that Dec had wedged into place clanged noisily to the flagstones.

'Dec, there needs to be another way out of here, right now,' Joel said urgently.

'I say we stand and fight them,' Dec said, slinging the loaded crossbow over his shoulder and grabbing the spray gun with the holy water canister. 'We've got all this stuff.'

'Bad idea,' Joel said. 'And that stupid thing's not going to work, either.'

'What do you mean, it's not going to *work*?' Knightly roared indignantly, forgetting his fear for an instant.

'Trust me,' Joel said. 'I know.'

'I believe in it,' Dec insisted, clutching the spray gun. 'It's holy water, Joel. Blessed by a priest.'

Crash. They all turned. The armoury door had begun to buckle. An iron rivet fell to the floor. The cracks in the wall had widened a quarter of an inch.

'Suit yourself, kid.' Joel grabbed a pair of katanas from the sword rack and tossed one to Knightly, who fumbled and almost dropped it.

'What about me?' Chloe said. 'I know how to use a sword.'

'You need to take the head off,' Joel told her, tossing her another katana. 'Swing hard and hope the blade's sharp.'

'They're silver,' Knightly croaked.

'Fuck silver,' Joel said, but his words were drowned out by another crashing impact against the door, louder than before.

The vampires were using the medieval mace. One more blow like that, and they'd be inside.

Chapter Forty-Nine

The armoury door was battered off its top hinge and there was an eight-inch gap between its upper edge and the stonework. A hand darted through the gap, groping for the lock. Dec quickly aimed the crossbow and fired. The hand withdrew as the bolt whanged harmlessly into the wall. There was no time to reload.

'We have to go, Dec,' Joel said. He unsheathed his katana and tossed the scabbard away. He wouldn't be needing it.

Dec dropped the bow. 'Fuck it, I think you're right. This way! Through the archery range. There's another door.'

Joel grabbed Knightly's arm and yanked him away from the wall. '*Move! Move!*'

Seconds after they evacuated the armoury, Joel heard the final devastating crash as the iron door gave way to the power of the mace and the vampires came roaring inside.

Dec led the way. Nobody spoke as they hurried onwards. Through another door, along another passage, around another bend.

And suddenly they were facing a fork in the road. The passage divided between two flights of stone steps, one leading up and the other leading down.

'Where does that go?' Joel asked Knightly, pointing at the downward staircase.

'Cellars,' Knightly mumbled. His whole body was trembling. 'I think.'

'No good.' A cellar was a deathtrap, even if the door held. Down below ground, the vampires could happily besiege them for eternity while all four of them starved.

That was if Joel didn't find an alternative food source among his human companions that would enable him to outlast them. He couldn't let that happen.

'What about that one?' he asked, pointing at the other stairway. 'Quickly.'

'That leads up to the old servants' quarters,' Knightly blurted. 'Right at the top of the house.'

There wasn't a lot of choice. 'Okay, that'll do,' Joel said. Chloe bounded up the stairs, Dec behind, Knightly following. Running up behind them, Joel could hear the vampires giving chase.

The staircase curled into a tight spiral as it took them higher. It smelled of rats and mould. Plaster was falling off the walls and the only light came from the occasional dim bulb, crusted with dead moths and old spiders' webs.

The humans were getting tired. So was Joel.

But the vampires racing up behind them weren't slowing down.

'I've had enough of this,' Dec said suddenly. 'Get back, Joel.'

'What are you doing? Keep moving!'

'I want to give them a dose,' Dec said. The fierce look Joel had seen in his eyes before was back again. He turned on the stairs and brandished the holy water spray gun.

'Dec, I told you. That thing's not—'

But Dec wasn't listening. As the thundering footsteps of the vampires drew nearer and their shadows appeared on the spiral wall, he squeezed past Joel and trotted down two steps, ready to fire. Elspeth was the first to appear around the corner. She saw Dec standing there and her fangs parted in a grin.

'Ready to bleed?'

'You ready for this, bitch?' Dec let loose with the spray gun. '*Yaaaaa!* Die, you bastards!' he yelled triumphantly as the strong jet of water shot down the steps, splashing everywhere.

Elspeth screamed and started clawing wildly at her wet skin.

For an instant, even Joel began to think it was working.

Until Elspeth threw back her shaven head and began to laugh. 'Fooled you.' Moving faster than the human eye could track, she lashed out and tore the spray gun out of Dec's hands. Crushed it into pieces. Emptied the canister down her throat and tossed it away with a giggle. 'Refreshing. But that wasn't what I'm thirsty for.'

She lunged again to grab Dec, but this time Joel got there first. He chopped the blade of his katana through her arm – and this time her scream was for real. The severed limb flopped to the floor, its fingers clawing against the steps. Elspeth toppled backwards in shock, sending the blond vampire and his swarthy companion tumbling down a dozen steps.

'Go!' Joel roared, pushing Dec violently upwards. Chloe was screaming, 'Come on! Come *on*!'

'I don't believe it!' Dec yelled at Knightly as he ran. 'Errol! Fucking *dissolves* them, you said!'

Knightly made a helpless gesture. Chloe kicked him. 'Keep moving, asshole!'

Then, suddenly, they'd reached the top of the stairs. They found themselves on a narrow dingy landing with ancient creaky floorboards that stretched away into the shadows. A rat scuttled off at their approach. To their left and right were peeling old doors. Joel booted one open and flicked on a light switch, revealing a damp-streaked servant's bedroom that had obviously been unused for the past several decades.

'Great,' Chloe said. 'Where to now?'

'That way,' Knightly said, pointing to a rusty metal ladder leading to a cobwebbed hatchway in the ceiling. 'The roof. You three can jump into the moat.'

Joel pointed at Dec and Chloe. 'You're crazy, Knightly. There's no way a h—' He'd almost said 'human can jump that height'. 'There's no way a height like that can be jumped.'

He could hear the footsteps on the stairs. The vampires were approaching. Taking their time. They must have sensed that their victims were cornered.

Dec stared at Knightly. 'What do you mean, "you three"? What about you?'

Knightly seemed suddenly, strangely composed. 'I'm staying here,' he said quietly. 'I'll hold them off while you escape.' Reaching behind his neck, he slipped the chain of the big silver crucifix he wore over his head, gripping the stem of the cross with a determined set to his jaw.

'I'm going to make you suffer *soooo* badly,' Elspeth's voice echoed softly across the landing. The vampires had reached the top of the stairs and stood silhouetted in the dim light. Elspeth was still clutching her cutlass in her remaining hand.

Joel wearily raised his katana. He'd been lucky a moment ago. He knew he wouldn't be lucky again. This would be the final standoff.

'They'll kill you,' Dec said to Knightly, looking at the crucifix and understanding what the man intended to do.

'It doesn't matter any more.' Knightly gripped Dec's shoulder tightly. 'Listen to me. I have to tell you something. Jill – you saw her picture, Declan – Jill left me. Because . . .

because I can't have children. There. I said it. I've never told anyone else before.'

Chloe wasn't listening. She quietly unsheathed her katana and held her breath as she watched the three vampires step closer. She closed her eyes. Saw her dad's face in her mind. Thought one last time about the man who had murdered him.

'I so much wanted a child of my own,' Knightly went on, blurting it all out while he still had time. His eyes were filling with tears. 'A son, who could be everything I could have been. A real vampire hunter. Not a pathetic phoney like his father. Yes, yes, I admit it.'

The vampires were approaching slowly down the hallway. The scrape of a blade being dragged along the damp plaster. A low chuckle. A glimmer of fangs and the glint of a blade.

Chloe opened her eyes and tightened her grip on the katana's hilt. She was ready now.

'Take the money in the chest, Declan,' Knightly hissed. 'Everything. The house. It's yours. Use it. Be what I could never be. Now go, while you still can.'

'Don't talk crazy,' Dec said. 'Come on. We can all make it.'

'Take care of Griffin,' Knightly whispered. With a last wild stare at Dec, before Joel could stop him, he took off down the landing towards the three vampires with his crucifix raised.

'Errol, you stupid eejit!' Dec yelled. 'Get away from them!'

But Knightly was beyond recall. His voice echoed down the stairs as he cried out 'Get back, ye foul creatures of darkness! Back to the shadow whence ye came. Return to your coffins. Begone, I say!'

'Shut your stinking hole, human,' Elspeth said, and with a stroke of her cutlass Knightly's head toppled from his shoulders, went bouncing back across the landing and bumped into Chloe's feet. She screamed. Knightly's decapitated body staggered backwards a few steps, still clutching the crucifix; then his knees buckled under him and he collapsed twitching to the bare floorboards.

'That's shut him up,' the swarthy-looking vampire said.

'We haven't seen one like that for a long while,' said the blond one.

'Got to give him credit for trying,' Elspeth chuckled. She pointed the bloodied cutlass at Joel. 'Enough amusement. Now it's payback time.'

'Come and get us,' Dec said through gritted teeth.

'Let them go,' Joel said, stepping in front of him and Chloe. 'You can do what you want with me. You'll be doing me a favour.'

The three vampires burst out laughing.

'Not quite what we had in mind,' the blond one said.

'First the humans die,' said Elspeth. 'Then we deal with you. Then we wait for the other one. Gabriel's orders.'

Dec stared confusedly at Joel. 'What does she mean, "the humans, then you"?'

Joel ignored him. 'Which other one?' he asked Elspeth.

That was when a familiar voice spoke from the head of the stairs.

'*This* other one.'

Chapter Fifty

The three vampires barely had time to whirl around in surprise before the landing and stairway lit up with a bright muzzle flash and filled with the blast of gunfire. The blond vampire was lifted off his feet and slammed into the wall by the bullet that caught him in the chest. The second shot spun his swarthy companion like a top and he crunched down on his face. Elspeth froze as the big gun in the shooter's hand swivelled across to take aim at her.

The three of them had been around for enough centuries to have all been shot plenty of times before: arrow, matchlock, flintlock, cap and ball, every pathetic missile the human race could fling at them in vain over the years.

But even as the shots blasted out across the landing and the .50 calibre hollowpoint rounds punched deep into their flesh, their instincts told them this time was going to be different. And the last.

A terrible howl burst from the blond vampire's mouth when the Nosferol hit his bloodstream. His veins instantly began to distend and explode, his organs ruptured and his whole body was ravaged into a pulp. Within less than a second, the toxin had worked its effects on his companion and their gory remains lay spread across the landing at Elspeth's feet.

'Did I poop your party, Elspeth?' said Alex Bishop as she climbed the last step. 'It is Elspeth, isn't it? We ran into each other back in '87.'

Elspeth backed away with a snarl. She dropped her cutlass.

'So we're running around with Gabriel Stone now?' Alex said. 'I wouldn't have thought you were his style.'

Elspeth gave her the finger. 'Fuck . . . YOU!'

'Bye,' Alex said. The gun boomed. Alex stepped over her as the spatter hit the wall, and walked up the murky landing towards the figures she'd taken to be humans.

'Is everyone all right?' she was about to say. What would have happened next was the standard procedure. As witnesses to a vampire incident, the three humans would have had to be injected with a preventative 10cc dose of Vambloc. Alex would have taken the opportunity to snatch a quick feed or two while they were unconscious – what they'd never know couldn't hurt them – and then she'd have had to start the messy work of disposing of the evidence.

But as she approached them, holstering the pistol, already reaching for the little pouch on her belt that contained the Vambloc vial and syringe and wondering which of the three was most likely to bolt or put up a fight, she suddenly stopped in her tracks. What she sensed was more than just the instinctive recognition of one vampire by another.

'Joel?' she gasped.

He took an uncertain step forward and the dim light from the open bedroom door shone across his face. Alex swallowed hard. For a long moment, the two of them could only stare at one another, neither able to speak.

'It's good to see you,' she said hesitantly.

'Alex . . .' His voice was faint, barely more than a whisper. He staggered back and leaned against the wall, hidden by shadows. The blackness was rising. He could barely stand up straight any more. Feeling his foot splash down into something liquid, he looked down and saw that he was standing in the spreading dark pool of Knightly's blood.

Alex had been about to step closer to him when Chloe, pale-faced and fighting back the sickness that was churning her guts, blocked her way and challenged her. 'Who the hell *are* you, lady?'

Dec was crouched unhappily by the headless body of his former mentor. Straightening up, he looked at Alex with amazement and pointed. 'I know who she is. She's the agent from the Federation.'

Alex was stunned for a second, then remembered the video clip. *Great, just great.* Olympia Angelopolis would have relished this moment.

Dec stared at the gun in its holster. 'What *is* that thing?'

'It's nothing,' Alex said.

'Bollocks it's nothing. Silver doesn't work. Garlic and all that other smelly shite doesn't work. Holy water doesn't work. But that does.' He turned to Joel. 'Joel, did you see—'

That was as far as Dec got. Because while a moment before, Joel had been standing there right beside him, now he was down on his knees with his palms splayed out in the pool of Knightly's blood and his head lowered to the floor.

Bile shot up in Dec's throat at the sound of the wet lapping and slurping sounds. He couldn't believe what he was seeing. Joel was lapping frantically at the spilled blood before it all leaked away through the cracks between the floorboards.

'Joel! What the frig are you doing!?' Dec yelled, appalled.

'I'm sorry,' Joel gasped, tearing himself away and gazing up at his young friend. 'I didn't want you to find out – not this way,' he said. His voice was thick with the blood that bubbled from the corners of his mouth and trickled freely down his chin. 'But I couldn't wait any longer. I was fading, Dec.'

Chloe let out a gasp of revulsion. 'He's . . .'

'A vampire,' Dec finished for her. Tears welled in his eyes. 'No, Joel. Please. Not you. Tell me it's not true.'

'It's true,' Joel muttered.

Dec turned to Alex. 'Don't harm him, miss,' he pleaded. 'I know that's what you do, kill vampires. But he's my friend. You saw how he tried to save us. Didn't you see it?'

Alex didn't reply. She watched as the young lad visibly swallowed back his fear and disgust and rage, let out a groan of sorrow and went over to his friend to put a hand on his shoulder. 'Stone,' Dec whispered. 'Stone did this to you.'

'It wasn't Gabriel Stone who turned him,' Alex said. 'I know, because I was there when it happened.'

Dec stared at her. 'You were *there*—'

'It was me who turned Joel into a vampire.'

Chapter Fifty-One

Dec took Chloe's arm and the two of them backed away. 'I'm going crazy,' Chloe mumbled to herself. 'It's a nightmare, that's all it is. A nightmare. I'm going to wake up any second now.'

Smearing blood across his lips with the back of his hand, Joel rose slowly to his feet. Already he could feel the energising glow, that marvellous warmth that he loathed as much as he lusted for it, spreading through his whole being, tingling all the way to his fingertips. The dark mist was gone from his vision.

'How are you, Joel?' Alex said.

'That's one hell of a thing for you to ask me.'

'I know you hate me,' she said, stepping towards him. 'I know how you must be feeling right now.'

'Do you?' he laughed bitterly. 'Then you must know what I promised myself I'd do to you if we ever met again.'

'Yes,' she said. 'I do know. I'm sorry you feel that way.'

'Sorry? You think sorry makes it all okay again? That we can both just go back to the way things were?'

'I know we can't go back to the way it was between us,' she said. 'But I was hoping we could be friends again one day.'

He stared at her. 'Why did you do it? *Why?*'

'You'd have done the same for me.'

'No. Never. Not this. Why couldn't you just let me go?'

'I couldn't bear to,' she said. 'I did the only thing I could do to save you.'

'*Save* me?' He raised his bloody hands to show her. 'Look what you did to me, Alex,' he shouted. 'Look what you've turned me into. I didn't want to be *saved*! I didn't ask for it that day in Romania, and I didn't exactly ask for it tonight.'

'I didn't know you'd be here tonight,' Alex shouted back at him, taking another step closer. She pointed at the vampire corpses on the floor. 'But if I *had* known it, and known I could protect you from these, would I have still done it? Yes I would, Joel, yes I would. Because I . . . because I have to. Don't you understand?' She paused, looking deep into his eyes, seeing the agony there. What could she tell him? That she loved him? That even if he hated her now, she still could never regret what she'd done?

'Why are you here, Alex?'

'I was sent,' she said. 'For business.'

Dec blinked. Despite his terror he managed to croak out, '*Business?*'

'The video clip,' she told him, not taking her eyes off Joel. 'I need to destroy it before it gets out.'

'You're too late,' Chloe said.

'I'm only glad I didn't get here a moment later,' Alex said.

There was a long silence.

'You want your revenge on me, Joel?' Alex unholstered her pistol and tossed it to him. 'Then take it. Do it now.'

Joel looked down at the gun in his hand.

'Three rounds left,' she said. 'It's not a lot, but when you're shooting vampires with Nosferol tips it only takes one hit. Doesn't matter where. You can't miss.'

Joel thumbed back the hammer of the pistol with a sharp

click-click. He slowly raised it in one hand and pointed it at Alex, framing her in the sights.

'Shoot her,' Chloe said. 'Then shoot yourself.'

'No,' Dec blurted. 'He'll be all right.'

'I'll never be all right, Dec,' Joel said. He felt the smooth curve of the trigger against his fingertip. Alex was watching him steadily, waiting, not a flicker of expression on her face.

Just a tiny flick of a finger was all it would take for the hammer to drop. The firing pin slamming forward to punch the primer in the base of the cartridge lodged inside the breech. The charge igniting, gases welling up to propel the Nosferol-tipped bullet through the barrel and across the short distance between them and deep into Alex's body, carrying the toxin into her system and destroying her forever.

Revenge. The thought of it had sustained him all this time, and right now, right here, the moment had finally arrived.

Just a tiny flick of a finger . . . but the trigger felt like an immovable mountain. Joel's arm began to waver and the gun wobbled in his fist.

Dec and Chloe jumped at the sudden noise that rang out . . .

The shrill ringtone of Alex's phone in her pocket. It kept ringing persistently as they all stood there, silent and immobile.

'You going to shoot me, or should I answer that?' Alex said.

Joel let out a heavy sigh. The muzzle of the gun sank downwards, and his fingers loosened on the grip. The weapon fell from his hand, tumbled to the floor with a loud clunk.

Alex took out the phone to find that someone was making a video call to her from a laptop. The picture was grainy and badly-lit, but nonetheless she recognised the panic-stricken face that was filling the screen.

'Utz?'

'Bishop, is that you? I can't see you very well.' Utz McCarthy's voice was as distressed as his expression.

Alex stepped into the light that was shining from the bedroom. 'I'm here, Utz. What's wrong?'

'You made it out! Where are you?'

'What are you talking about? Made it out of what?'

'I only found out a few minutes ago. I've been calling every number in my database and hardly anyone's answering. Nobody's there, Bishop!' He broke into a gasping sob. 'I can't believe it's happened. I just can't believe it!'

'Calm down, Utz, you're not making any sense. What's going on?'

'Destroyed,' Utz wailed. 'They're all destroyed. Almost everyone we knew is gone.' He shook his head in anguish. 'It was a slaughter, Bishop. I've just spoken to Jen Minto. She's in shock. We all are.'

'Talk to me,' Alex said. 'Calm down.'

'They were attacked one right after the other,' Utz said, struggling to compose himself. 'London, then Brussels – bang, bang, one after the other. Agents reported into work to find nothing left but dust. Like they'd all just been mown down, vaporised where they stood. Everyone's saying that Supremo Angelopolis and all her staff were caught up in it. All gone.'

So much for having to destroy the video clip, Alex thought to herself.

'It was like the fucking H-bomb hit them, Bishop,' Utz went on. 'What could have done that?'

'It was the cross,' Joel told her. 'Nothing else has that power.'

'What was that?' Utz asked. 'Who else is there with you, Bishop?'

Alex ignored him. 'But how can that be?' she said to Joel. 'We got rid of the cross in Romania.'

'No, Alex, it's been found,' Joel said. 'A human called Ash has it.'

'Bishop? Talk to me!' Utz's voice was screaming from the phone.

'Utz, I'll talk to you another time. Take care.' She ended the call and looked hard at Joel. 'Ash? The sword killer? The massacre in Cornwall?'

'He murdered my father for the cross, and I'm going after him,' Chloe said.

Joel could see the stupefaction in Alex's eyes as she struggled to understand. 'Gabriel Stone found out that Chloe's father had the cross,' he said. 'Stone and his gang broke Ash out of prison, so he could get it for him. And now we know what Stone wanted the cross for. To wipe out your whole Federation once and for all.'

Alex's mind reeled as the implications began to hit home. 'Then we have to find him. We have to do something.'

'Why?' Joel said with a grim smile. 'For the protection of our fellow vampires?'

'For the protection of the human race, Joel. Without them, we can't exist, remember?'

'That's all we are, right? Your food source,' Chloe said, deeply sceptical.

Alex looked at her. 'That's all the reason I need to want to protect you. I know what Gabriel Stone and his lot have in mind.'

'We don't need protecting,' Dec said, defiantly jutting out his chin. 'We can handle a few vampires, so we can.'

'Yeah, you proved that tonight,' Alex said. 'But can you handle the Übervampyr? Because that's who's behind all this. They were backing Stone all along. And we're not talking about your regular blood-sucker here, folks.'

'The oober-what?' Dec said.

'You don't want to know,' Alex said. 'But you'll find out if we don't act fast. With Stone in control, it's not just the Federation that'll be wiped out. The whole world will change. Humans will be enslaved for blood, farmed like animals. And I'd be very surprised if the Übervampyr would be keen to share with the likes of us. We have to stop this from happening, Joel. We *have* to get that damned cross back. And there's only one way we can do that.' Alex turned to Dec and Chloe. 'You humans can't fight Gabriel Stone. And Joel and I can't touch the cross. But if we work together, the four of us, as a team . . . Then, maybe, just maybe, we have a chance.'

'You've got to be kidding,' Chloe burst out. 'I won't listen to this crazy talk.'

Alex gripped her arm tightly, willing her to believe. 'We have a common purpose, Chloe. You want to avenge your father? If we waste no time finding Stone, there's still a good chance Ash won't be far away.' She turned to Dec. 'And you, Dec, you want to destroy Stone for Kate, don't you?'

Dec looked down at his feet.

Lastly, Alex turned to Joel. 'What about you, Joel? You still want to shoot me?'

Joel let out a long sigh. He shook his head.

'Good. Because I can't do this without you.'

'All right,' Joel said softly. 'I'm in.'

'Fuck it, so am I,' Dec said, sticking out his chest.

Chloe stared at him as if he'd lost his mind.

'Can't you see she's right?' Dec said, seeing Chloe's expression. 'It's our only chance, so it is.' But as the look on her face only became more set, he sighed and added, 'But if you want to stay out of it, I'll understand.'

'I still don't buy a word of this,' Chloe said. 'But I won't be left out. Not if you think you can help me get to Ash.'

'Then we're all agreed,' Alex said. 'We're a team.'

'More like a motley crew,' Chloe muttered. 'Two crazy kids and a couple of blood-sucking lunatics.'

'So what happens now, like?' Dec asked. 'We go and get Stone?'

Joel shook his head. 'Not just like that, we won't. Stone doesn't leave a trail for anyone to follow.'

'I think I know how we can find him,' Alex said.

Chapter Fifty-Two

The Ridings

'He'll want to see you right away,' Zachary said to Ash when he stepped out into the night to greet the car on its return from the airfield. 'Follow me.'

Ash said nothing as Zachary led him through the manor house, but he noticed that the place had filled up noticeably with visitors since his departure. Vampire visitors: they eyed him curiously as he passed by, some hungrily, licking their lips and nudging their companions with a chuckle.

He wasn't afraid of them any more. When one of them got a touch too close and bared long white fangs at him, he held up the case and saw the sudden fear cloud the vampire's face. *That's right. You know what's in here, don't you?*

After that, nobody bothered Ash again. Even Zachary was nervous of the thing the human was carrying. He led Ash towards the sound of thundering piano music that was coming from the east wing. The playing ended abruptly in the middle of a crashing downward flurry of notes as Zachary knocked on the door and showed Ash inside the room.

Gabriel Stone was sitting at a gleaming black grand piano, glaring at the doorway, about to demand who could be so impertinent as to interrupt his virtuoso rendering of Franz

Liszt's *Revolutionary* étude (incorporating some of his own flourishes that the composer had been unable to get his fingers around) – then he saw Ash walk in, case in hand, and his expression changed.

'It is done, then?' he said.

Ash nodded. Gabriel leaped up from the piano stool and tentatively took the case from him. Grabbing a heavy chain from a nearby table, he triple-wrapped and padlocked it. Ash slipped the mini-camcorder from his pocket and offered it to him.

'Let me be the first to witness the deeds of this historic day,' Gabriel said, staring hungrily at the small, high-resolution screen. The annihilation of the VIA office, followed by Ash's equally devastating tour of the Federation Headquarters in Brussels: Gabriel watched it all unfolding with a rapt expression. When it was over, he looked at Ash and nodded solemnly. 'You have served me well, human. Come, now. Join our festivities. Everyone is waiting.'

With the hour of the party approaching, a hundred vampires assembled in the mansion's huge dining room and their excited chatter filled the air as the confirmation of Gabriel's victory spread. A glittering array of crystal decanters and carafes stood on the Chippendale sideboards, filled with blood: at last, and much to Lillith's delight, Gabriel had given his consent for the human prisoners to be used for the purpose for which they'd been stored in the basement. The two ghouls, Sharon and Geoffrey Hopley, were limping squalidly around the room serving glasses from silver trays (the consensus among the vampires was that, for all Gabriel's qualities, he was not the greatest judge of ghoul-flesh). Lillith had exchanged her favourite red leather jumpsuit for a beautiful black silk ball gown with a plunging neckline that drew dozens of admiring glances from around the room – but her glow of pride quickly turned to a scowl when Kali made her entrance wearing a shimmering white dress that wowed the crowd. Its magnificence upstaged Lillith's in every way, the effect crowned by a glittering ruby necklace that had been a gift from a powerful Afghan warlord nine centuries earlier.

A murmur spread through the dining room as Gabriel strode in. He was immediately surrounded by vampires wanting to shake his hand and pat him on the back. He waved them all away graciously, pressed through the crowd and leaped up on a table clutching a crystal flute of blood, calling for silence. The room instantly fell to a hush.

'My friends,' he began, 'words cannot express my joy in bringing you the news of this most momentous victory. The unspeakable filth that was the Federation need be spoken of no more, for it has been washed away. Save for a few scattered remnants, who will swiftly be rounded up and brought to justice, or persuaded to join us as we rebuild the glory that once was the vampire world, our enemy is finally . . . resoundingly . . . irreversibly . . . *eternally* obliterated: first the shameful spies and informants in London, swiftly followed by the tyrants in Brussels. Rejoice, one and all, and let us raise our glasses to this day when the shackles of oppression have at last been cast off!'

Wild applause ensued, a deafening chorus of cheers. Gabriel swallowed his blood in one gulp, dashed the empty glass in the fireplace and then waited for silence before continuing.

'How curious that we should owe a large part of our victory to one who is not of our kind – that is to say, not yet. A toast, my friends, to Ash, soon to be graced with the highest honour we can bestow and inducted into our family circle. To Ash, our new brother in blood.'

More riotous applause as all eyes turned towards Ash, who was standing quietly at the back of the room, gazing down at his feet. Glasses clinked and were drained.

'To Ash!' a hundred voices clamoured in unison.

Gabriel paused to pluck a long Havana from his breast pocket, snatch a candlestick from the mantelpiece and light the cigar with its flame. He smiled through a cloud of smoke. 'And now, my friends, as the modern saying goes . . . *let's party*.'

The wild celebrations rocked the mansion, quickly spilling beyond the dining room to the gardens. Gallon after gallon of blood and wine and iced champagne were consumed, together with dainty finger-food prepared by the ghouls. Crowds gathered around the giant television screen that had been brought down from the master bedroom and set up at one end of the room to play, over and over again, the scenes of delicious destruction in London and Brussels.

Meanwhile, two of the human captives were set loose outside in the grounds and chased for sport. Lillith was the first to catch one – hiding in the gazebo – and gleefully slash its throat, splashing the front of her dress. One of the severed heads was tossed away across the moonlit lawn, where Baxter Burnett, having already overturned Jeremy Lonsdale's golf buggy with a blood cocktail between his knees, was practising chipping balls into its open mouth.

'We need now only await the return of Rolando, Petroc and Elspeth,' Gabriel said to Zachary in the conservatory, 'telling us that our old friend Alex Bishop has finally been eliminated. Part of me will be sorry to hear it,' he sighed, 'but she was given a choice. She could have joined us. Instead, she saw fit to stand with the enemy.'

'Ash is coming,' Zachary said, nodding past Gabriel's shoulder. Gabriel turned as the human approached.

'Hero of the hour,' Gabriel said, placing a hand on his shoulder. 'What can I offer you?'

'My reward,' Ash said.

'Indeed, I made you a promise,' Gabriel smiled. 'And I am true to my word. You shall have it, the moment your mission is completed. For there is one more task you must perform before you may claim your prize.'

Lillith came bursting in from the garden, a blood-drunk Baxter Burnett staggering behind her. 'Gabriel, we're out of humans,' she said. 'Marcellus wants to know what to do with the icky bits?'

'Toss them to the dogs,' Gabriel said casually. 'Sister, I was just telling our friend about the final phase of our plan. Ash, you will take the cross to Siberia, to the domain of – how shall I put it – some extremely important distant relations of ours. Only you can perform the final ceremony that will see the weapon encased in liquid lead and embedded in the ice wall of the Grand Hall of their citadel, where it will remain as their trophy.'

Ash nodded slowly. 'And then?'

'And then you will return here so that I may personally fulfil my pledge to you. You will at last become the thing you have so long desired to be.'

'Siberia,' Ash said. He thought about it. 'I don't know where to go.'

'Lillith and Zachary shall escort you,' Gabriel told him. Something caught his eye and he glared at Baxter. 'What is that thing protruding from your pocket?' he asked sharply, pointing.

'Uh, this? Uh . . . just my vitamins,' Baxter said, shoving the tube of pills back out of sight.

'Vampires do not take vitamins,' Gabriel said. 'I know what they are. Give them to me at once, do you hear?'

Baxter handed them over sheepishly. Gabriel contemptuously tossed the Solazal packet to Zachary. 'Dispose of this garbage, would you, please?'

'*Siberia?*' Lillith said. She was about to explode in protest, but a glance from Gabriel silenced her.

'Back to the uglies,' Zachary sighed. 'I'd seen enough of those motherfuckers to last me a while. We taking Lonsdale's plane again?'

Gabriel shook his head. 'It would be pushing our good fortune beyond the bounds of sense to overuse it, as the human police are bound to track it down sooner or later. I suggest we leave it where it is, where the Romanian officials will be a long time finding it. Our Solazal-swallowing friend Baxter's mode of air transportation will be its replacement. No objections, I trust, Baxter?'

'Uh . . . none, no,' Baxter said hesitantly.

Gabriel rubbed his hands together. 'Excellent. For my own part, I have decided to take a vacation. My problem has been deciding where – after all these centuries, there is scarcely a corner of this world with which I am not already familiar to the point of utter tedium. I could have made use of the Tuscan villa vacated by our late ghoul Jeremy Lonsdale, but Italy bores me. Now, *Switzerland*, on the other hand . . . it has been a good eighty years since my last visit.' He flashed a knowing smile at Baxter.

'How did you know I had a place in Switzerland?' Baxter asked with a frown.

'Thank my Minister of Information,' Gabriel said, motioning to Zachary. 'The interweb may have its uses after all. Your amorous exploits at the hunting lodge, exactly nine and a half miles north-east of Zermatt, have been well documented in the human media. A most admirable location, Baxter. Fine views across the mountain valley; accessible only by its own private cable car; secluded, yet not too distant from the local villages where one can be assured of a ready meal.'

'I don't exactly let the place out,' Baxter said, reddening.

'Then I should be all the more honoured to make use of it for a while,' Gabriel told him. 'Naturally, I shall also require from you a certain quantity of spending money. What with all these bribes we have been compelled to pay to greedy customs officials and petty bureaucrats in order to pass unobserved from place to place, our coffers are rapidly running empty. And as you must know, Switzerland is not the least expensive of places for a personage of taste.'

Baxter was almost choking with outrage.

'I knew I could count on you,' Gabriel said, beaming. 'Shall we say, ten million euros in cash? To start with.'

Chapter Fifty-Three

A blood-red dawn was breaking as the Jag XKR crossed the Severn Bridge from Wales into England and blasted eastwards down the M4 motorway, speeding along the outside lane past lines of traffic that grew thicker with every passing mile towards London. Alex was silent at the wheel, eyes on the road, sucking on a fresh Solazal. The address she'd entered on the satnav was a street in Camden Town. She'd been evasive about the identity of the person she insisted might be able to help them find Gabriel Stone. Joel had given up asking even before they'd left Bal Mawr early that morning.

He threw her a glance every so often from the passenger seat. Even after the busy last few hours they'd spent together while the humans slept, disposing of Knightly's body and the remains of the three destroyed vampires, he still found it hard to believe this woman sitting next to him was the same Alex he'd known in what now seemed to him like another lifetime. The same Alex he'd been so consumed with hate for – or had believed he was. His mind was crowded with things he wanted to say, but his thoughts were too confused and contradictory to form them into coherent shape, and he was acutely aware of Dec and Chloe right behind them, crammed together in the tiny rear seats. He gazed at the road ahead and stayed quiet.

Dec was occupied with thoughts of his own as he leant against the window, staring numbly out at the zipping road. Whenever he pictured Errol, he felt a stab of sadness for what had happened to him. But his feelings quickly intensified to a confusion of disbelief and horror and black grief as his thoughts turned to Joel – his friend Joel, sitting within arm's length – now one of *them*. A vampire. Dec was facing the void now, with no way of knowing where all this would lead, no idea if he or Chloe would make it out alive.

Or human.

But somewhere behind all the horror and the traumatic shock of all that had happened over the last few hours, Dec's heart thumped at the thrill of the crazy adventure he was embarking on. He thought about Bal Mawr, about what Errol had said about him taking over his operation. He was resolved to go back there one day, if he could – and soon. For the first time in his life, he had a sense of who he really wanted to be, and that filled him with a glow that not even his grief could completely stifle. He found himself wondering, a little guiltily, how much money there was in that wooden chest Errol had shown him. Could it be five thousand pounds? Surely not as much as ten thousand? Dec found it hard to imagine being in possession of such wealth.

'Anybody notice anything?' Chloe said loudly next to him, cutting into his thoughts.

Alex's eyes flicked her a glance in the rearview mirror. 'Like?'

'Like it's, uh, *dawn*?'

'So?'

'Maybe I'm getting it all wrong,' Chloe said, 'but it seems to me that if you two were really vampires, we'd be looking at a couple of frazzled little green spots where you're sitting right now. Must be the twenty-million-factor sunblock you're wearing, I guess?'

Alex smiled. 'Spent the last few decades trying to pretend to humans I wasn't a vampire, now I have to persuade you that I am?'

'Some proof would be nice,' Chloe said with a shrug.

'Fact is, Chloe, Joel and I have something called Solazal that allows us to go out in daytime.'

'Sola-what?'

Alex showed her the tube. Chloe reached forward and snatched it from her fingers. 'Look like peppermints to me. Hmm. Smell like it too. Come on. These *are* peppermints.'

'Much as I would love to prove you wrong,' Alex said, 'the only way I could do that is to stop taking them. It wouldn't do much for my complexion, put it that way. Now give them back.'

Chloe grunted suspiciously.

'You saw the fangs on them friggers that attacked us last night, didn't you?' Dec said. 'How can you not believe in vampires when you've *seen* one?'

'Is my dad's killer a vampire?' Chloe retorted. 'No, he isn't. He's as human as you or me. Any wacko can go to work on his own teeth with a file. As for these two here, I haven't seen any evidence of anything. Do you people really think you're fooling anyone? It's pathetic. I actually feel sorry for you.'

'Give back the Solazal, Chloe,' Joel said. 'We don't have a lot left.'

'What if I don't? What if I just toss them out of the window?'

'Give them back, Chloe,' Dec implored.

Alex's fists tightened on the steering wheel as a junction came speeding up on the left. 'I've had enough of this crap,' she said suddenly, and swerved the Jaguar hard across two lanes of traffic. She took the exit at ninety, barely slowed for a roundabout and roared through an intersection in a chorus of honking horns. A few hundred yards further on was a little layby partly screened off from the road by trees, behind it a picnic area with tables and benches. Alex screeched to a halt in the layby, threw open her door and jumped out. 'Get out of the car,' she commanded Chloe.

Chloe got out, cheeks flushed, followed by Dec. Joel climbed out of the front passenger seat. Alex was already opening the boot of the Jaguar and taking out one of the katanas from the Bal Mawr armoury.

'Leave it alone, Alex,' Joel said.

'She's going to learn,' Alex replied. She slammed the boot and started marching towards the picnic area. 'Chloe, follow me.'

When they were out of sight of the traffic rolling past, Alex unsheathed the katana and handed it hilt-first to Chloe.

'What's this for?'

'Stick it in me.'

'Say again?'

'Stab me. Hard as you can. Right here in the stomach.' Alex untucked the hem of her blouse from her jeans and pulled it up to expose her toned midriff.

Chloe blanched. 'Are you nuts?'

'Do it,' Alex said, smiling. 'Don't be afraid.'

'I'm not doing it,' Chloe said with a nervous laugh. 'No way.'

Dec gently took the sword from her hand. 'I'll do it.'

'You're all insane!'

'I believe her,' Dec said. He got a good grip on the hilt, swallowed hard, took a deep breath and then rammed the point of the blade into Alex's stomach. A terrible, heart-stopping doubt seized him just as the tip speared into her

354

flesh – but it was too late to stop the katana driving itself all the way through her body and out the other side.

Alex let out a gasp. Chloe shrieked and covered her eyes. Dec let go of the sword and backed off, babbling, 'I'm sorry! Jesus, I'm sorry!'

Joel just stood and watched. During their short but eventful time together in Venice, he'd seen a paid gunman with a .45 automatic unload a full magazine on Alex and not leave a mark.

'It's been a while since I've been run through like that,' Alex said, wincing as she yanked out the blade. 'Forgotten how much it hurts.' She tossed it back to Dec. 'Nice stroke. Well done.'

'That was freaky,' Dec said, his heart still hammering like a road drill.

A very pale-faced Chloe peeked through her fingers at Alex's stomach, where the gaping wound was healing with unbelievable speed before her eyes.

'Believe me now?' Alex asked her, and tucked her blouse back into her jeans. 'Or do you want me to drain a pint or two of your blood as well?'

'I believe you,' Chloe said in a small voice. 'You're a vampire. Oh, my God, you really are a vampire.'

'You want to try it on him, too?' Alex asked, pointing at Joel.

'No thanks,' Joel said.

Chloe shook her head vigorously.

'Good,' Alex said. 'Now, please, give me back my fucking Solazal.'

Nobody said much for a long time as they got back in the car and rejoined the motorway. Chloe sat silent and pale, staring at Joel's head restraint in front of her, seeing nothing. Dec gently laid his hand on her arm and gave her a weak smile.

355

She didn't pull her arm away. He closed his eyes, and the next time he opened them the sun was higher in the clear sky and they were in heavy traffic that even Alex couldn't slice through. The massive city seemed to stretch out for endless miles ahead.

'So this is the Big Smoke,' Dec said, leaning forward to peer between the front seats.

'You've never been to London before?' Chloe asked him.

'Nearest I've been was Heathrow, when I went to Torremolinos with me ma and da in the summer,' Dec said. 'Jesus, look at the size of this frigging place!'

'Home sweet home to over a hundred thousand vampires,' Alex said.

'How is that possible?' Chloe said. 'How can all those vampires be out there drinking people's blood and nobody even seems to know about it?'

Alex glanced at her in the rearview mirror. 'We've been getting along just fine together, your kind and ours, since before you were born. Call it a symbiotic relationship. Nice and discreet – that's what the Federation was meant to be all about. You want to see some carnage and horror, just wait until Gabriel Stone's gang get started on the world now that the good guys aren't here to protect you any more.'

Alex was pretty handy in the London traffic, but even so it took a while before the satnav finally announced that they'd reached their destination and they rolled up in the quiet street in Camden Town. 'This is the place, folks,' she said, turning off the engine. 'Best if you wait here and I go in alone, okay?'

'So now are you going to tell me who lives here?' Joel asked.

'I already did. Someone who can help us.' Alex flipped open the glove compartment, took out the Desert Eagle and stuffed it in her handbag before opening the door.

'Someone you need a gun for?' he asked, but she just

slammed the door and he watched as she walked around the front of the Jaguar and trotted up to the front door of one of the neat little homes.

'Is she always like this?' Dec asked.

Joel nodded. 'She seems to know what she's doing, guys,' was all he could reply as he watched Alex disappear around the corner of the house and head round the back.

Chapter Fifty-Four

The back door was unlocked. Alex slipped quietly inside. The décor was pretty much what you might expect from a mid-pay-grade admin official at VIA, but Alex winced at the colour of the living room. *Ouch*. Last time she'd been here, for a hundred-and-fortieth birthday party (some vampires took longer than others to get bored of them), the walls hadn't been quite this shocking shade of pink.

Jen Minto was perched on the edge of an armchair staring intently at the TV news. Her short blond hair was unbrushed and she was wearing a T-shirt and tracksuit bottoms.

'I shouldn't imagine there'd be anything on there about us,' Alex said.

Minto jerked round in astonishment, her eyes opening wide. 'Alex! I . . . I wasn't expecting . . .'

Alex walked up to her. 'Door was open. Got to be careful. There are bad people around.'

'What are you doing here?'

'Utz McCarthy told me you made it out. I came to see how you were.'

'I wasn't there when it happened,' Minto said. 'I was one of the first ones to go in, after . . . oh, Alex, it's so awful. And the word is that Supremo Angelopolis . . .' She shook her head. 'I'm so glad that you didn't get caught up in it.'

'I would have been, if I hadn't been called away on urgent business,' Alex said. 'Not that any of it matters now.'

'What are we going to do?' Minto said. 'Everything's in ruins.'

'Too early to say. All I know is that right now, it's every vampire for herself.' Alex smiled, but it was a hard smile. 'You should know something about that, Jen.'

Minto gave a puzzled frown. 'What do you mean by that remark?'

Alex perched on the arm of the sofa opposite. 'Things have been kind of hectic for me lately,' she said. 'You might even say I've been a bit rushed off my feet, with one thing and another. Which is why certain little niggly details might have slipped my mind. Careless, I know.'

'That's normal enough,' Minto said, still frowning. 'Working for VIA takes its toll on the best of us.'

'Little niggly details like, for instance, something you said to me the day I got back from Romania,' Alex said.

The lines in Minto's brow had deepened to corrugated furrows. She kept glancing at the door and her breathing had quickened a fraction. 'I don't understand, Alex.'

'I think you do,' Alex said. 'I think you understand exactly what I'm saying. Remember what you told me? You said, "And Xavier Garrett? He was one of them?"'

'But he was.'

'Yes, he was. The whole time Gabriel Stone was mounting his uprising against the Federation, Xavier was his spy inside VIA, feeding him all the juicy little bits of information he needed. We lost a lot of good agents because of him. That's why I put a bullet in the bastard at the conference in Belgium. But the funny thing is, Jen, I never said a single word about any of it to you.'

Minto's face flushed. 'No . . . no, I know you didn't. It was Cornelius who told me about it.'

'Kelby?' Alex shook her head. 'Kelby couldn't have known about it either, because the one and only place I ever mentioned it was in the confidential field report I sent directly to Brussels HQ, and the one and only person who ever saw it was Olympia Angelopolis herself. Given some of the stuff I wrote about, I know for a fact she wouldn't have shown it to anyone else. So, any other ideas where you might have heard about Garrett, Jen?'

Minto said nothing.

'You know, Jen, it's less than twelve hours since our whole organisation got fucked sideways by something that's been hidden away for hundreds of years and hardly anyone could have seen coming – and you haven't even asked me what it was.' Alex smiled that hard smile again. 'That's because you already know all about it, don't you? Because Xavier Garrett wasn't Gabriel Stone's only mole inside VIA. He had an accomplice. Someone who knew all about the attack, exactly when it was coming, and was able to get out of the way just before Ash arrived there with the cross. Oh, and not to mention letting Stone know where I'd gone in Wales, so that he could send his goons to assassinate me. That made me feel so important.'

'You've got it all wrong,' Minto gasped.

'Really?' Alex stood up and whipped the Desert Eagle out of her bag. Minto's eyes bugged at the sight of the gun. Alex came a step closer. With a *snick-snack* of the Desert Eagle's slide she racked the top round from the magazine into the breech, then shoved the muzzle against Minto's right temple. 'You didn't give them a chance, Jen. But guess what. I'm giving you one, because that is what a nice vampire I am. Where's Stone?'

Minto opened her mouth to speak, but all that came out was a strangled croak. Her eyes strained sideways to stare at the gun muzzle pressed against her head.

361

'The Federation might be finished,' Alex said, 'but there's still some Nosferol left in this world. A nice fat hollowpoint full of it, about eight inches from your brain, to be precise. I'll ask you one more time: where's Stone?'

'They were all at Lonsdale's place in Surrey,' Minto blurted out. 'But Gabriel left there last night.'

'You're making progress. Where did he go?'

'Switzerland!' Minto said, her voice rising in pitch. 'Baxter Burnett's place in Switzerland. That's all know, I swear!'

'Good enough for me,' Alex said. 'See you in vampire hell, Jen. This will only hurt for a minute.'

Minto yelped in terror. 'But you said you'd give me a chance!'

'A chance to redeem yourself, sure. Not a chance to talk your way out of this. We're way past that.'

'No! Please!'

'And by the way, your buddy Gabriel would *really* disapprove of the décor in this place. Have to say I agree with him on that one.'

Alex didn't blink as she pulled the trigger. Even before Minto's throes of agony were over and the mess had spattered across the living room carpet, she was heading through the front door and walking back out into the street towards the parked Jaguar.

'Well?' Joel said as she climbed in behind the wheel.

'We're going on a trip,' she said, firing up the engine.

Chapter Fifty-Five

The Swiss Alps, north-east of Zermatt

Baxter Burnett had bought the luxurious, rambling three-floored chalet, perched high over the mountain valley, from an Austrian industrialist billionaire who'd used it as a hunting lodge. Taking pot-shots at curly-horned wild goats in a blizzard had never been Baxter's idea of fun; whereas entertaining two or three star-struck wannabe actresses at once by a crackling log fire was much more in his line, and with a little imagination and a lot of hard cash he'd transformed the place into a perfect haven of hedonism and debauchery. Gabriel Stone was unimpressed by the movie star's lamentable taste in art, and even more so by the tubes of Solazal he found in the bedside drawer and promptly tossed in the fire – but the chalet would do very nicely for a few weeks, as a base from which to celebrate the success of his mission.

It was eight thirty and the night was cold. Standing on the balcony overlooking the valley, Gabriel breathed in the crisp mountain air and looked out across the stillness at the twinkling lights of towns and villages in the distance. The heavy snow had come early that year, capping the tops of the pine forest. Stars were shining in their millions; the Milky Way laid a luminous wash across the whole white landscape.

Far below, a vehicle was tracking its way slowly along the winding valley road. Gabriel watched its progress like an eagle surveying its prey. He imagined the humans sitting inside, cradled in the warm blast of their heater, listening to their music, completely oblivious of the predator's eye on them from high above. Nobody out here in the snowy wilderness would have heard their cries for help. And they would never know how lucky they were to have reached their destination that night.

As Gabriel watched the vehicle disappear behind the trees, a pair of willowy arms encircled him from behind and Kali's tousled black hair nestled against his shoulder.

'Hmmmm,' she sighed happily. 'It's so good to be here, just the two of us. Like old times.' She kissed his ear. 'Do you remember the old days, Gabriel, sweet?'

'With as much fond pleasure as I look forward to the glorious times yet to come,' Gabriel said, stroking her hair. 'Get dressed, Kali. The hunting hour is here.'

Access to Baxter Burnett's top-of-the-range cable car was from a custom-designed boarding station on the ground floor of the chalet. Through its grand expanse of glass, the cable car offered a 360-degree view of the valley below and the stars above. Its smooth cable system glided it downwards, suspended high over the snow and the trees, to the landing station at the bottom, where a gated private lane led to the winding valley road. Waiting for them there, its black bodywork gleaming under the stars, was the brand-new Ferrari Enzo that Gabriel had had delivered earlier that day, the funds wired the night before to the dealership in Geneva from the numbered account in Zürich that his late, much-missed ghoul, Seymour Finch, had opened for him.

'This is a pretty little toy you've bought yourself,' Kali said as he held open the passenger door for her. Grinning boyishly,

Gabriel leaped behind the wheel and fired up the engine. The blast of the twin exhausts melted the snow, the tyres spun against the road and the Ferrari took off like a missile.

'Some aspects of the modern world suit you well, Gabriel,' Kali said, leaning back in her seat and noticing his obvious enjoyment as he threw the car into tight bends at 125 miles an hour.

'I will admit that it offers certain pleasurable distractions that we could once only have dreamed of.' He glanced at her and saw her broad smile. 'What amuses you?'

'I was remembering the look on that poor fool Baxter Burnett's face when you told him how much of his money you were going to take.'

'What of it?' he asked innocently.

She laughed. 'Oh come on. Don't you think it was just a tiny little bit mean of you, pretending that you were running low on funds? With all the gold and diamonds a vampire could wish for, and all those millions you have stored in the human banks?'

Gabriel powered the Ferrari hard out of a bend and the engine note soared like a racing car's as he accelerated down a long straight. 'You know as well as I do, Kali my dear, that a lifestyle such as ours requires a great deal of forward planning. I have no intention of spending all eternity as a pauper.'

Arriving at a small town twenty miles or so further on, the Ferrari prowled the streets in search of likely victims. 'There's a charming little Bierkeller,' Kali said, pointing. 'Let's scout it.'

Gabriel parked around the back of the place and showed Kali inside, down a spiral of metal steps leading down to a busy traditional Swiss beer cellar. Gabriel ordered a bottle of the best champagne, and at their little corner table they clinked a toast and sat surveying the humans in the place.

Discussing the *hors d'oeuvres* menu for the evening was almost as much fun as the actual feeding.

'What about those two?' Kali said, pointing with the rim of her glass at a hand-holding couple a few tables away.

'Possibly, possibly. The female is somewhat rachitic, of the unhealthy thin-blooded type. Most likely vegetarian. I would tend to favour the hale and hearty specimen over there,' he added, pointing at the fleshier of two men sitting near the bar.

One or two faces turned towards the stairs as a din of tramping footsteps announced the invasion of the beer cellar by a boorish troop of young males in their twenties. From the beery smell they brought with them, it was obvious this wasn't the first establishment they'd inflicted themselves on that night.

'British tourists,' Kali said, rolling her eyes. 'God help us.'

The seven young men piled around a table in the middle of the room and hollered for drinks. Within minutes their raucous laughter, crude banter and constant blaring of mobile ringtones made it all but impossible for anyone else around them to have a conversation. When the landlord went over to their table to ask them politely to keep the noise down, he was sent away with jeers and threats.

'Is there no escape from vulgarity?' Gabriel said. 'Come, let us pursue our activities elsewhere. I find this environment oppressive.' He and Kali finished their champagne and got up to leave. As they passed the rowdy table, one of the yobs twisted round in his chair to ogle Kali and lick his lips. His overfed pal next to him, sporting a roast-beef complexion and a neck like a bullock's, grinned up at Gabriel and called out, 'Hey, mate, what's the matter – couldn't you get a white one?' They all burst out laughing, elbowing each other and raising their beer glasses.

Gabriel stopped and peered down at him. 'This is Kali,' he said. 'Named after the Hindu goddess of death and destruction. I would advise caution. This Kali makes the original appear like Mother Teresa of Calcutta by comparison.'

'What the fuck's he on about?' the yob asked his pals.

'Woooo, I'm really scared,' another one said in a mock-frightened voice.

Kali tugged at Gabriel's sleeve. 'Let's go.'

It was twenty minutes later when the landlord finally managed to turf the rowdy crew out of his establishment. The street outside echoed with obscenities as the tourists staggered away in search of another bar. The large beefy member of the gang broke away from them for a moment to lurch a few steps up a dark alleyway near the Bierkeller and urinate against the wall. As he did up his flies, he let out a loud belch and was about to lumber off to rejoin his friends when a force that felt like a steel cable jerked him backwards off his feet and dragged him into the shadows of the alleyway.

By the time his companions missed him, his pallid, bloodless remains were already beginning to freeze at the bottom of three different rubbish bins and a recycling skip.

For Gabriel and Kali, the night had only just begun.

Chapter Fifty-Six

Siberia
3.44 a.m. local time

By the time the Citation Bravo touched down at the tiny airfield a few miles from the mining outpost of Norilsk, the night sky was turning white with snow and visibility was so poor that the landing lights were just yellowish blurs in the raging blizzard. Neither the pilots nor the ground crew would have ever contemplated being out in these conditions if it hadn't been for the handsome cash handouts promised by the mysterious Mr Stone.

Beyond the rusting hulk of an old Ilyushin jet liner was the little shack where the humans had strict orders to remain until the three travellers returned; they hurried over to it to warm themselves over the woodburning stove. Stepping out of the air-conditioned plane into a minus twenty degree gale, Ash might have taken refuge alongside them if he'd been willing to show human frailty in front of his two escorts.

He wasn't about to do that. Instead, he waited in the near-whiteout with Zachary and Lillith and shivered miserably under his fur-lined parka. Under his arm he was clutching the sackcloth-wrapped executioner's sword that he wouldn't be parted from. After a few minutes the lights of an approaching vehicle cut swathes through the blizzard and a snow-covered black Mercedes pulled up to collect them.

An hour later, when the car had cut as deep into the white wilderness as it could, they were picked up by a little convoy of snowmobiles.

The vampires were being careful. Even though he could see hardly anything out of his remaining eye but swirling snow, Ash was blindfolded for the remainder of the journey to the Übervampyr citadel. By the time it was removed, he was far below ground and the temperature had risen to something close to bearable. Ash looked around him at the fantastical ice caverns, like something from another world. His mouth twitched.

Zachary could see the faraway look of sadness on Lillith's face as the guards escorted them through the citadel. 'You're thinking about Gabriel and Kali?' he asked her softly.

She shrugged and said nothing.

'He'll come back to you,' Zachary told her gently. 'He always does.'

They were met by another squad of vampire guards. 'You have it?' their leader barked. Zachary took off the backpack he was wearing, unzipped it and took out the lead-lined case, still wrapped in the chain Gabriel had fastened around it. The guard went to snatch it, but Zachary jerked it up out of his reach.

'This is for Master Xenrai,' Lillith said. 'Nobody else touches it.'

'Is it just me, or are these guys more heavily tooled up than they were last time we were here?' Zachary rumbled as they were led through the ice corridors. Lillith had noticed it too: there were almost twice as many vampire guards in evidence, and they carried long, cruel halberds and pikes as well as swords.

'Only you two may enter,' the guard said, stopping at a doorway. 'The human comes with us.'

'Where are you taking him?'

'He will be kept safe. Your weapons, please. You cannot go before the Masters so armed.'

Lillith and Zachary reluctantly unstrapped their sidearms and were shown inside a high-walled chamber. Before long, the tall, bent figure of an Übervampyr appeared, followed by a second, their robes sweeping the floor as they seemed to glide along. Zachary looked away as the creatures drew back their hoods, and not just because it was impolite to make eye contact.

'I'd been expecting Master Xenrai,' Lillith said, recognising the face of the Übervampyr called Tarcz-kôi who had headed the prosecution at the trial.

Tarcz-kôi made a stiff little bow. 'Just as I had been expecting Krajzok – or, as you call him, Gabriel. I am afraid that Master Xenrai is . . . *indisposed*. You will deal with me and my esteemed comrade, Grak-shükh, from now on. Where is our prize?'

'Here,' Lillith said. She hesitated, then passed him the case. The Übervampyr took it eagerly from her and ran a clawed hand over its surface. 'That so small an object could cause such pain,' he murmured.

'Gabriel said you plan to encase the cross in liquid lead and bury it deep in the ice, where it can never do harm again and no human can ever find it,' Lillith said.

The Master's hideous face twisted into an expression that Lillith recognised as an enigmatic kind of smile. 'We shall dispose of the *Zcrokczak* as we see fit. Tell me, where is our beloved Young One? His absence here today is a disappointment to us.'

Lillith told him.

'A holiday,' the Master sneered, with a glance at his colleague.

Grak-shükh made a distorted creaking sound that Lillith supposed was laughter. 'What of your human companion?' he asked in a voice even deeper than Zachary's. 'Is it true what we hear?'

Lillith nodded. 'Ash got the cross for us. He was the one who carried it into the enemy's camp.'

'Then victory correctly belongs to this Ash, not to Gabriel,' Grak-shükh said, his mandibles contracting in a way that showed irritation. 'To a mere human we owe this?'

The rest of the conversation was short and strained. Tarcz-kôi and his colleague seemed desperate to take their prize away, and rapidly disappeared as guards came to escort Lillith and Zachary to the quarters where they were to rest a while before their long return journey. The swords they'd handed over seemed to have mysteriously vanished.

'What did the uglies say to you?' Zachary asked softly on the walk back down the icy passage.

'I'll tell you later,' Lillith muttered with a glance back at the guards.

'I didn't like the look in that thing's eye,' Zachary whispered, stooping closer to her ear. 'In fact I don't like any of this. You ask me, I'd say the motherfuckers are up to something.'

In another part of the vast citadel, the two Übervampyr observed unseen through a semi-opaque screen of ice as the human called Ash detachedly explored his new surroundings. They had observed many humans in captivity before, and this one didn't behave like any they'd ever seen. After pacing up and down his quarters a few times, Ash seemed to lose interest. He crouched down to unwrap the sackcloth from his sword. They watched as he lovingly caressed the blade, and then replaced it in its scabbard to drop down to the floor and begin a gruelling series of press-ups.

'This human is not like others of his kind,' Grak-shükh said in his deep, deep voice.

'You echo my sentiments, comrade Master,' Tarcz-kôi replied. 'And I sense that the same thoughts have formed in your mind as in my own.'

'Yes. This latest behaviour of that fool Xenrai's young protégé is further evidence of his growing decadence. Gabriel is weak, and he is untrustworthy. He celebrates a victory that is not his to claim, and he further insults us by sending mere servants in his stead. The Council should not have relented so easily to the Judge's wishes.'

'I did all in my power to influence the court,' Tarcz-kôi said. 'Xenrai held too much sway.'

'Xenrai no longer poses an obstacle to us,' said Grak-shükh. He rubbed his chin thoughtfully, watching as the human continued unrelentingly pumping out press-up after press-up. 'With our eminent Master eliminated, we are free to deal with his former protégé in whatever manner we deem appropriate. Gabriel may very well have outlived his useful-ness.' He tapped the tip of a black claw against the ice screen. 'This one, by contrast . . . Such a creature could serve our purpose far better.'

Tarcz-kôi nodded. 'We will put him to the test.'

The ice walls of Ash's quarters were streaming with conden-sation by the time guards opened his door and brought him an unexpected gift. The human female was one of the many hundreds kept in the dark caverns beneath the citadel. Born in darkness and deprived of sunlight for all of her seventeen years, she was as blind as she was naked. The vampire guards had scrubbed the filth off her body, brushed out her long hair and scented her with aromatic oils that glistened on her skin. Now they flung her down on the floor at Ash's feet by way of an offering, and left the two of them alone with shining golden platters heaped with meats, jugs of wine and spirits.

In return for the freedom she'd been promised – even if it meant being turned loose in the hostile frozen wilderness that some of the older captives said was all that existed up there on the surface – the girl was willing to do anything to pleasure this man. She undulated her body provocatively on the floor in front of him, crawled sightlessly on all fours like a dog, tried to touch him and press herself against him.

Ash just slapped her away as if she were an annoying insect, without the slightest glance at her nakedness. He sniffed at the wine, put down the jug untouched, pulled a face at the smell of the spirits. Grabbing a piece of half-raw meat from one of the heaped platters, he went and sat in a corner, tore off a hunk with his pointed teeth and chewed for a while, still ignoring the girl's best attempts to gain his attention.

When he'd eaten enough to take the edge off his hunger, disinterested by the piles of food that remained, he took a sharpening stone from his pocket and busied himself with total concentration whetting the edges of his sword with long, careful strokes up and down the blade. After half an hour, the girl had given up trying to gain his attention and lay curled, weeping, against the far wall.

The two Übervampyr had been watching the whole time. 'He resists admirably,' Tarcz-kôi said with a smile. 'Neither by his stomach nor his loins can he be tempted. Most unusual in so base a creature.'

'Never have I seen a human so pure of intent,' Grak-shükh agreed. 'He appears quite untainted by the moral degradation that corrupts his species as a whole, and to which our own Gabriel has too long been a willing party.'

Tarcz-kôi looked at him. 'Then it is decided?'

Grak-shükh nodded. 'It is decided. Gabriel's time is over. Ash's is about to begin. Is the cargo aircraft on standby?' He was referring to the old but serviceable Antonov An-124 transport jet that was kept in a hangar at a disused military air base a hundred miles away across the tundra.

'It is.'

'Good. He will need help. Gather fifty of our best *Zargôyuk.*'

'It shall be done.'

Grak-shükh drew up his hood and turned away from the screen. 'Send in the guards. Slaughter the female and have Ash brought to me, that we may commence his initiation.'

'What about the two servants of Gabriel who brought him here?' Tarcz-kôi asked.

'Destroy them. Immediately.'

Chapter Fifty-Seven

The door of Lillith and Zachary's chamber crashed open and armed guards rushed inside, swords drawn and the spikes of their halberds raised. They were taking no chances – no unarmed vampire could resist such force of weapons. But as they stormed into the chamber they met with even less resistance than they'd expected. The chamber was empty.

The guards glanced around them frantically, then stared in unison at their leader, whose face was filled with terror at the prospect of what the Masters would do to him now.

That was when a shower of little ice chips hit the floor at their feet, and they looked up at the ceiling.

'Whoops,' Zachary muttered, clinging to the crevice he and Lillith had been digging above them.

Instantly, a dozen halberd blades swung upwards. 'Get down,' the leader of the guards commanded. 'You are summoned.' It wasn't a suggestion.

Lillith and Zachary dropped to the floor, dusted the ice from their hands and let themselves be herded out at spear-point.

'I really have a bad feeling about this,' Zachary said.

The guards marched them through the echoing honeycomb of passageways until they reached the entrance to another grand chamber. They were prodded inside and the door was slammed shut and barred behind them.

'Now what?' Lillith whispered to Zachary.

A tinkling silvery curtain swished aside, and from behind it stepped out the ominous figure of Master Tarcz-kôi.

'We caught them trying to escape, Master,' the guard leader said.

'What's the idea of this?' Lillith demanded. 'Why are we being kept waiting for hours? This isn't what was agreed.'

The Übervampyr rubbed his claws. The vibration of his mandibles denoted pleasure. 'There has been a change of plan.'

'Hold on. We had an arrangement here. You've got the cross – now we want to go back with the human. Gabriel promised to turn him, and he will.'

Tarcz-kôi's smile widened hideously. 'He will, as you say, be "turned". But this shall be our doing, not Gabriel's, and not until Ash has served a further purpose. He will not be disappointed in the powers we bestow on him in the meantime, for they are far greater than those your bastard race can offer.' The black eyes twinkled. 'As for the Young One, by the time Ash has dealt with him, I can assure you that he will be in no position to "turn" anyone ever again.'

Zachary saw the look in Lillith's eyes, her mouth hanging open in horror. 'What's he saying?'

'The cross will go to Switzerland,' the Übervampyr went on, seeming to relish every word. 'When Gabriel is no more, Ash will continue his quest until the mongrel rabble the humans call "vampires" are all but extinct. Then, only then, shall we recreate the human after our own image. Not a vampire, but a *meta-vampire*. The first of a new race: an army that shall cover the face of this planet and bring us the global control that we have long sought.' Tarcz-kôi paused to wave his long middle claw at Lillith and Zachary. 'I tell you this, that you may go to your imminent doom in the knowledge of what is to become of all your kind, starting with your beloved Gabriel.'

'What do you mean, imminent doom?' Lillith burst out. 'You've used us and now you're going to *execute* us?'

'And rather than waste any more of the Council's time on foolish trials I will perform the task myself. Have you anything to say before sentence is carried out?'

'Just that you'd better do a damn good job of it,' Lillith said. 'Because if you don't, I promise you that Zachary and I will fuck every single one of you ugly pieces of shit and bury what's left of you inside this ice tomb.'

'I think not,' Tarcz-kôi said. For an instant, his mandibles quivered and the tendrils around them curled into slimy little hooks.

And then the horrible face split apart.

From between the fleshy folds of the parted mandibles snaked a tentacle-like tongue, grey and glistening. Its tip peeled open to reveal a set of sharp fangs. Sticky threads of ooze stretched and snapped as the fangs gaped wide open. The tentacle coiled back, gathering itself to strike – and then lashed out with blinding speed straight at Lillith's face.

Zachary grabbed the guard leader off his feet and thrust him in front of her as the tentacle struck. The fangs sank deep into the guard's chest and there was a crackling and splintering of bone. A scream filled the chamber as his heart and lungs and part of his spine were ripped out of his body. The tentacle hurled the guard's organs away and fired a powerful jet of black oily liquid that spattered over his face and into his screaming mouth. Instantly, he slumped to the floor, paralysed by the vampire nerve toxin stored in glands at the base of the Übervampyr tongue.

The tentacle flailed towards Zachary as he backed away. Lillith reached into the front of her jumpsuit and pulled out the concealed ice dagger she'd cut from the ceiling of their chamber earlier. The blade was as hard and sharp as glass. Faster than Tarcz-kôi could withdraw it, she slashed the knife at his tongue. Dark blood and venom spattered. The severed tentacle-tip fell writhing to the floor, the fangs snapping wildly. The Übervampyr recoiled with a wail of agony and fury and his tongue slithered back inside his mandibles.

'Get them!' he shrieked to the guards, pointing his claw at Lillith and Zachary.

The pair were already sprinting for the door. Zachary broke the neck of a guard who tried to block his way – it couldn't kill him, but it would slow him down – and grabbed his halberd, swinging it at another guard and slicing his head clean off. Then, with a blow that shattered the steel blade and shaft, Zachary used the weapon to crash open the door of the chamber. He and Lillith ran out into the maze of ice passages.

'This way!' she yelled, tugging his sleeve.

The screams of the enraged Tarcz-kôi echoed up the corridor as they ran. Zachary glanced back and saw the guards giving chase. He dipped his hand inside his jacket and came out with a disc of ice with glass-sharp teeth like a circular saw blade's. He spun it towards the guards. One managed to duck the flying disc, but two behind him weren't so fast and their heads hit the floor before their running legs crumpled and collapsed under them.

'Told you they were up to something,' Zachary said to Lillith as they ran. 'Didn't I?'

'They're going to murder Gabriel,' Lillith gasped. 'They're sending Ash after him with the cross.' She'd barely spoken before a jet of black venom spattered against a pillar just inches away. She jumped back with a cry of fear and saw the blobs of thick liquid clinging to the leather sleeve of her jumpsuit.

'Don't touch it,' Zachary yelled. 'It'll paralyse your ass.'

Lillith scraped her arm hard against the ice wall and glanced behind them to see five more Übervampyr bounding after them, moving horribly fast on their muscular legs, surrounded by sprinting guards with weapons raised. There was no time to be frightened. The two vampires ran faster than they'd ever run before, tearing down ice passages that they no longer recognised.

Suddenly, a fork up ahead.

'Which way?' Lillith gasped.

'No idea,' Zachary said. They took the left turn, dashing past entrances that could fly open at any moment and release hordes of pursuers to block them off. The twisting passage suddenly opened and they emerged into a huge, high, echoing space.

Then skidded to a halt as they caught sight of the ring of tall Übervampyr figures that surrounded them.

Chapter Fifty-Eight

Zachary grabbed Lillith's arm and was about to push in front of her to protect her from the flying venom, when he realised.

'They're statues,' Lillith said, staring at the terrifyingly realistic ice sculptures. And she remembered now – she'd seen them before.

'What is this place?' Zachary muttered, looking around him. 'Looks like some kind of a garden.'

Lillith suddenly knew just where she was. 'It is a garden.'

Craning her neck upwards, she spotted the window of Gabriel's chamber, from which the two of them had looked out. Fifty yards away beyond the ring of statues was the giant, tower-like shape of the astronomical telescope that Gabriel had pointed out to her – and above it, dizzyingly high up in the domed roof above the subterranean garden, the Ecliptic Portal.

The yells and footsteps of their pursuers weren't far behind.

'We can get out that way,' Lillith said excitedly. 'It's a window to the outside. There's a mechanism somewhere that can open the hatches. Look.' An ice gangway spiralled around the base of the enormous telescope. Midway up its height was what looked like an observation platform, and attached to a strange and complex arrangement of mechanical arms was a huge lever. 'Come on!' she shouted to Zachary, leading him towards it.

But as the Portal came into view, her face fell in despair.

They were too late. The Portal's dull mirrors were lightening with the glow of the rising sun.

'We're trapped!' she screamed.

A whooshing pike-blade tore through Zachary's shoulder and crashed into a pillar with a shower of splinters. He swore and clutched at the wound, turning to see the guards that were pouring into the garden, cutting off their exit. Five, six Übervampyr were bounding along behind them. Their cries echoed up to the vast ceiling.

Lillith knew how it felt to face certain destruction. She'd felt it that day on the castle battlements in Romania when it had seemed all was lost for her and Gabriel – and she could taste the same grim certainty now. They weren't getting out of here. She swallowed hard.

Zachary's eyes suddenly brightened. 'What are you doing?' Lillith said as he dug something out of his pocket and pressed it into her hand. 'What are these?' she asked, staring at the little white pill.

'Federation shit,' Zachary said. 'Solazal. Had them all along.'

'Do they work?'

'Only one way to find out,' he said, and tossed one in his mouth. Lillith hesitated, then did the same.

By this time the guards and their Masters were past the ring of statues and rapidly approaching. Another flying spear crashed against the base of the telescope.

'Let's move!' Zachary yelled, hauling Lillith up the ice gangway towards the observation platform. Lillith screamed as a jet of venom splashed off the hand rail right next to her.

Zachary reached the lever and gripped it with both hands. 'I sure hope that Solazal stuff works fast, 'cause here goes.'

He gave the lever a yank.

It didn't budge.

The Übervampyr and their guards had reached the bottom of the gangway. The tall creatures parted their mandibles. The extended tongues came slithering out, fangs bared, poised to squirt the paralysing venom. They were well within range now.

Zachary threw all his weight and muscle against the lever. His face contorted with the strain, teeth clenched, tendons sticking out from his neck.

And the lever rotated on its axis with a grinding clunk that echoed all the way up to the Ecliptic Portal.

The hatches began to slide open.

And then something happened that hadn't happened for more centuries than Lillith and Zachary could remember. Standing there on the observation platform, they were suddenly drenched in the golden rays of the early morning sunlight.

The shouts of rage from down below turned instantly to screams and then were silenced. Hit by the rays of light, the vampire guards disintegrated in flames. A terrified Übervampyr burst alight and became a cloud of cinders before it could scurry into shadow.

Lillith screwed her eyes shut in terror and clung tightly to Zachary as the silent scream filled every cell of her being. This was it. The horrific nightmare end that all vampires dreaded.

But it wasn't. Nothing happened. Lillith opened her eyes and held her trembling hands up in front of them. The sunlight shone brightly on her skin, and yet she wasn't on fire. She wasn't peeling or blackening or turning to cinders that floated away on the air.

'Looks like we're still here,' Zachary grinned.

It took less than a minute for the two vampires to swarm up the towering shape of the telescope, feeling the sunlight on them more intensely with every yard they climbed. From the rim of its giant ice lens to the edge of the hatch was a long leap. Lillith went first, then Zachary, and suddenly they were standing on the surface looking down at the burning remains of their enemies far below.

All around them was the vast white desert – flat snow-covered tundra to the south, craggy mountain ranges to the north.

'I never thought I could experience this again,' Lillith said, closing her eyes for a second and feeling the long-forgotten glow of the sun's warmth on her cheeks. It was an incredible sensation. 'But don't tell Gabriel I ever said that,' she added in a warning tone. 'And for the love of blood, whatever you do, don't *ever* mention to him we took those pills.'

'Believe me,' Zachary said, 'I'd be in a lot more trouble than you would. Say, how long you reckon the effects last?'

'No idea. Give me another one, just in case.' As she munched it and felt the strange fizzle on her tongue, she shielded her eyes from the sunlight and gauged their bearings.

'Now let's go and find that aeroplane,' she said. 'And pray that the humans are still there waiting for us.'

Chapter Fifty-Nine

It had taken far longer to get out of Britain than either Alex or Joel would have liked, but there was a price to pay for doing these things semi-legitimately. No matter how flagrantly Alex flouted the speed limits, the stop-offs at Wallingford, Oxford and Bedford to collect passports and personal effects had eaten a big chunk out of the day and it wasn't until two in the afternoon that the Jaguar was finally stowed on board the cross-Channel ferry en route for Calais.

'Alone at last,' Alex said to Joel as she joined him at the rail, looking out across the grey sea and the disappearing cliffs of Dover. 'Are you talking to me now?'

'Of course I'm talking to you,' he said glumly.

'I'm glad, Joel.'

He sighed.

'I really did miss you, you know. I'm not just saying that.'

'I came looking for you,' he said, staring down at the white foam that streamed alongside the hull of the boat. 'At your place in Canary Wharf.'

'I moved.'

'I gathered.'

'And if I hadn't?'

'I don't know what I'd have done,' he said. 'I thought I

did, at the time, but now . . .' He looked at her and saw she was smiling.

'And I meant it when I said I was sorry. I didn't mean to hurt you. I'd never willingly do that.'

'I know,' he sighed. She touched his hand. He gave her fingers a squeeze.

'Look at those two,' she laughed, pointing towards the porthole behind them, through which a sharp vampire eye could make out the figures of Dec and Chloe sitting together at the bar in the ferry's main lounge. 'They seem to be getting on well.'

'They have a lot in common,' Joel said. 'They've both lost someone thanks to a vampire. Thanks to things like us,' he added darkly.

'You can say "people like us", you know,' she said.

He looked at her. 'I thought we'd stopped being "people". Isn't that the whole idea?'

'Technically, yes. But I know I'd rather think of myself as a person than a *thing*, wouldn't you?'

'I'm sure your victims would be delighted to know that,' he said.

Her eyes scanned his face with concern. 'You're pale, Joel.'

'I'm all right,' he lied.

'You're not feeding, are you?'

'You saw me feeding last night.'

She shook her head. 'I saw you licking a puddle of dead man's blood off the floor, is what I saw. I'm talking about taking live blood straight from the vein. There's a difference. Do you know what'll happen to you if you don't start learning to feed properly, the vampire way? And it will, if you don't get the proper nutrition.'

'I have a pretty good idea what'll happen,' he said miserably. She was right about the nutrition part – drinking the corpse's blood hadn't sustained him half as well as he'd hoped and already he could feel the first hunger pains returning.

'Well, I'm not going to let it,' she said. 'I saved you so that I could have you near me, not to sit back and watch you wither into a wraith. That's worse than being dead.'

He almost smiled. 'For what it's worth, I'm touched.'

From the Pas de Calais they headed south-west down the *autoroute*, skirting the Belgian border. Alex was reminded of the Brussels Headquarters, and wondered whether Olympia Angelopolis had survived the London attack. As they drove on, the sky turned a solid grey and a heavy drumming sleet set in that didn't relent until they'd crossed half of France. They were still two hundred miles from the Swiss border when Alex had to pull over at a roadside fuel station. The Jaguar's tank was getting down towards the red line; and the car wasn't the only thing that needed replenishing.

The humans got out of the car and stretched their legs while Alex attended to the petrol pump. Dec borrowed a handful of euro coins that Joel had found in his jacket pocket – left over from his Venice trip with Alex – and, using a mixture of pidgin French and hand signals, somehow managed to communicate to the woman in the filling station shop that he wanted to buy chocolate bars and cans of Coke for himself and Chloe.

'Don't suppose you'll be wanting any of this,' he said tentatively to Joel as he tore the wrapper off his chocolate.

Joel gazed at it and shook his head. 'Not really, no.'

'Can't you – you know, eat? Regular food, like?'

'I can eat it, but it doesn't do me any good.'

'What does it feel like?' Dec said. 'Being, you know . . .'

'Look, Dec,' Joel snapped, 'I don't want to talk about it.' The thought of food, of feeding, was making his whole body cramp. Sorry that he'd spoken sharply to the kid, he said,

'All right, if you want to know, it feels terrible. It's not the best thing that ever happened to me. Let's just say I haven't come to terms with it yet. And I don't know that I ever will.'

'You wouldn't ever think about biting one of us, would you?' Dec said with a touch of nervousness.

Joel didn't reply.

'I'll take that as a no, then?'

'Where's she disappeared to?' Chloe said, looking around for Alex. Quarter of an hour had passed since she'd gone to pay for the fuel, and there was no sign of her anywhere. It was another ten minutes before she came back, looking just a little flushed.

'Where were you?' Chloe asked.

'Answering the call of nature,' Alex said, putting something away in the small pouch she wore on her belt. Joel had seen Vambloc before, but Chloe was understandably ignorant of the ways of a modern-day vampire. 'Vampires use the bathroom?'

'I wasn't talking about the bathroom,' Alex told her. Catching Chloe's look, she added, 'Listen, if I'm travelling with humans I'll understand if they need to stop off to go to a restaurant twice a day. You got a plate of something on the ferry, now it's my turn. You get my meaning?'

'You're sick.'

'We're vampires. Get used to it. Or get walking.' Alex turned to Joel. 'Are you all right?'

He said nothing. He was too busy staring at the tiny drop of fresh blood that was lodged in the corner of her lip. Realising, she dabbed it with her finger and offered it towards his mouth. When he turned his head away, she sighed and got into the car.

'Let's go. We still have a lot of miles to cover.'

* * *

The journey continued. By late afternoon they'd left the motorway for winding country roads that carried them onto higher ground, where the sleet had given way to snow and the red glint of the setting sun trickled down the white-capped mountains. They saw little other traffic. Dec was glued to the window, filling his eyes with the scenery before it faded into darkness.

The last glow was sinking below the horizon when they passed an unmanned border control and Alex said, 'Welcome to Switzerland.'

'Why are we stopping?' Joel asked her.

'To get our bearings,' she said, braking carefully on the slippery road and pulling the Jag over to the white verge. With the motor idling softly and the windscreen wipers batting away the snowflakes, she reached into the pouch behind her seat and pulled out a tiny notebook computer.

'Senior field agent privilege,' she said to Joel. 'This gives me mobile wi-fi access to the whole VIA database. I can pull up anything I like on any Federation subject in the world, *from* anywhere in the world. Specifically' – tapping keys – 'every single registered address for any given member. And they make them register them all, believe me, even if it's just a holiday home.'

'Sounds more like a dictatorship than a Federation to me,' Joel said.

'The thought's occurred to me more than once,' she replied with a sour smile. 'But right now, I'm not sorry. Being the pawn of a dictatorial regime can sometimes have its advantages.' When the search box she'd been waiting for popped up on the little screen, she typed in the name Baxter Burnett. In an instant, his whole profile had come up.

Joel's eyes opened wide. 'The actor?'

'I told you Jeremy Lonsdale wasn't the only VIP Gabriel Stone hooked up with,' Alex said.

'You never told me it was Baxter Burnett the movie star.'

'Who?' Dec asked, his face appearing in the gap between the front seats and peering at the laptop screen glowing in the darkness. 'Fuck me, that's Baxter Burnett! He was in that fillum *The Rat Pus*, so he was.'

'It was *The Raptus*,' Alex said. 'And you shouldn't really be seeing this.' Not that it really mattered any more, she thought, not if the Federation was history, and maybe it was this time.

'Jesus Christ,' Dec exclaimed, staring at the screen. 'Are you saying he's a frigging . . . I mean, he's one of you?'

'Managed to keep it secret from his adoring fans long enough,' Alex said. 'Looks like the cat's out of the bag now, though.' She scrolled down Baxter's list of registered addresses. He spent so much time at the Ritz that the Trafalgar Suite was one of them, along with his homes in LA, Bermuda and Antibes. Right at the bottom of the list was The Eagle's Nest, the name Baxter had chosen for his mountain retreat near Zermatt. Alex cocked an eyebrow. Maybe Baxter had never heard of Adolf Hitler. Or maybe he had, the little closet Nazi.

'Gotcha,' she said, flipping the computer screen down and typing the location into the satnav.

Seconds later, their route flashed up on the little screen.

'If all goes according to plan,' Alex told her passengers, 'exactly one hundred and thirty-seven kilometres from here is where we're going to find Gabriel Stone.' She replaced the computer in the pouch behind her seat and grabbed her pistol from its hiding place under the centre console. 'I hope he's having a hell of a good time right now,' she said. 'Because it's the last chance he'll ever get.'

Chapter Sixty

Gabriel was, in fact, having a very enjoyable time indeed. After another productive evening's hunting, he and Kali were nicely sated with the blood of five random victims – one middle-aged couple hijacked in their car, one fairly old but healthy male who'd put up an admirably spirited resistance before they'd run him down in the woods and ripped him open, and, as an unexpected bonus, two young females walking along the snowy roadside who'd made the mistake of trying to thumb a lift in the Ferrari. Foolish but tasty.

It had been such a productive evening that they'd decided to return home early to open some more of their absent host's vintage champagne and settle down to luxuriate a while in front of a roaring log fire. The night was still young as the vampires rode the cable car back up the steep valley and made their giggling, playful, light-hearted way back upstairs.

'My dear, I believe there is still a bottle left of the '76,' Gabriel said absently as he strolled into the dark living room and across the sheepskin rug towards the fireplace, where he struck a match and tossed it on the bed of dry kindling and logs he'd prepared earlier. Vampires had no warmth requirements, but an open fire was a pleasure he'd always relished and would relish again tonight: the spit and crackle of the flames, the dance of their glow against the honey smoothness of Kali's skin. He was distracted for a moment as he watched the fire leap up and take hold.

Then, suddenly alerted by his senses, he whirled round. To his amazement, Lillith and Zachary were standing at the far end of the room, the firelight flickering on their faces.

'My friends,' he began, walking towards them with open arms. 'What are you . . .' His voice trailed away and his eyes narrowed as he realised they weren't alone.

Alex stepped out from behind Zachary, the pistol aimed carefully at her prisoners but just as carefully out of their reach. She knew how fast they could move, especially Lillith. 'Look what we found at the bottom of the mountain,' she said.

Joel stepped out from the shadows, still slightly flushed from the little bit of exercise he'd done a few minutes earlier. While Alex and the humans had held the hostages in the chalet, it had been his job to ride the cable car back down to the boarding station below and return on foot, running back along the cable tracks with nothing but his sense of balance between him and a very long drop. In his hand was the katana he'd taken from Bal Mawr. He rested its razor-sharp edge against Zachary's neck.

'They caught us in the valley, Gabriel,' Lillith said.

'We were coming to warn you . . .' Zachary began, but Joel pressed the katana blade harder against his throat and he went quiet.

'I remember you,' Gabriel said, eyeing Joel. 'Solomon. The lawman. The intrepid detective. You have undergone a stage of evolution since we last met, it seems. I wish I could offer you a warmer welcome to the vampire race, but you appear to have chosen to stand alongside traitors.'

'I'm not here for the Federation's sake,' Joel said, mastering the tremor of anger and fear in his voice. 'I just want to see you sent to hell, you and all your evil kind.'

'Right,' Dec said in the bravest tone he could muster as he led Chloe out into the firelight and planted the tip of his sword against the floor, the way he'd seen the heroes do in movies.

Gabriel looked Dec up and down, and shook his head as he turned to Alex. 'I was sadly aware of how far you could stoop, Alexandra. But fraternising with humans – let alone these mere striplings with their toys?'

'Whatever gets the job done,' Alex said.

'If anyone would let us *speak*—' Lillith cut in angrily.

'Shut up,' Alex said, and shoved the gun hard into her side.

Without warning, the living room door swung open and Kali sauntered in, wearing relatively little and carrying a tray with two glasses and a bottle of champagne on ice. Two steps into the room, she let out a gasp and dropped the tray with a crash. At a nod from Joel, Dec stepped quickly over and pointed his sword at her.

'Over there next to lover boy,' Alex said.

Kali snarled at Dec, baring her fangs as he herded her across the rug towards Gabriel. His knees turned to jelly but he stood firm and raised the blade with both hands. 'Watch it, missus. Sure I can lop your head off quicker than you can say ...' Dec wasn't quite sure what she could say, and left it at that.

'I hope you realise the skill – not to mention the luck – it takes for a human swordsman to conquer a vampire?' Gabriel said coolly.

'Don't forget this one,' Alex said, stepping away from Lillith and pointing the Desert Eagle at him and Kali.

Gabriel gazed at the pistol. 'Loaded, I assume, with the vile poison concocted by your Federation thugs?'

'And you've seen what it can do, Gabriel,' Alex said. 'Anybody moves and Baxter's going to have a hell of a cleaning job with that rug.'

'Perhaps I have underestimated you. Yet you do appear to be somewhat at a disadvantage. If the weapon contained more than one or two bullets, I believe you would have treacherously gunned us all down by now. Instead your plan is to trick us into remaining your hostages until sunrise, whereupon I am guessing that you and Inspector Solomon here will enjoy the protective benefits of the filthy drug Solazal, allowing you to spectate while the four of us meet a fiery end.'

'Eloquent to the last, Gabriel,' Alex said. 'But the only reason I haven't pulled this trigger yet is that you're going to tell me where the cross is.'

'That's what we—' Lillith started, but Dec cut her off with a threatened strike.

Gabriel smiled. 'And if I reveal its whereabouts to you?'

'Nosferol's quicker and cleaner than frying. It's your choice.'

'Far less generous terms than those I offered you in Romania, as I recall,' Gabriel said.

'I'm all out of generosity.' Alex gazed at him steadily through the gunsights, while keeping Lillith in her peripheral vision. If things kicked off, it would all happen extremely fast. 'We know you have the cross, Gabriel. We know about Ash, too.'

'I'm afraid your information is somewhat out of date, Alexandra. The cross is now very far away, safely contained in a place where no human will ever lay their filthy hands on it again.'

'No, Gabriel!' Lillith cut in, backing out of the reach of Dec's katana. 'That's what Zachary and I have been trying to tell you. For blood's sake, let me speak! They didn't put the cross in the ice. Ash is coming, Gabriel. He's coming back here with it and he's going to destroy us.'

Gabriel stared at her.

'It's true,' Zachary said. 'The uglies betrayed you, boss.

They want you gone. They want all of us gone. And I mean *all* of us,' he added, nodding at Alex and Joel. 'They're gonna take the whole planet over for themselves. As for you blood-bags,' he said, motioning towards Dec and Chloe, 'we saw what they're doing to humans. Their asses stuffed inside giant icicles getting the blood slowly sucked out of them into a bunch of vats. Ain't no pretty sight.'

'Who the frig are the uglies?' Dec said, aghast.

'The Übervampyr,' Alex explained to him. 'The ones I told you about. Ever get the feeling you've been used, Gabriel?'

'Maybe if you'd been less preoccupied with your little playmate over there, you might have foreseen this,' Lillith raged. 'Face it, brother, you've been complacent. Your vanity won you over. You thought the Masters had chosen you, and you only, to help bring about their plans. You should never have trusted them. You delivered Ash to them on a plate and now they've superseded you just like that, as if you never really mattered to them.'

It was the first time in a millennium that Gabriel Stone had been completely at a loss for words. He slumped heavily into one of Baxter Burnett's designer armchairs with his chin on his chest and let out a long sigh. 'Evidently, I have made a grievous error,' he admitted after a silence. 'I always believed that our Masters would make room for us within their grand design.'

'Motherfuckers ain't no masters of mine,' Zachary said. 'Never were, never will be.'

'You are right, sister,' Gabriel went on. 'I should have seen this. I have always suspected that, in their hearts, the Übervampyr regarded us as nothing more than a bastard race. After all, they created us. Now it seems they plan to dispose of their inferior offspring, intending to become the exclusive dominant species.'

'Wait. You say they *created* us?' Lillith said, staring at him.

'Has none among you ever wondered where our kind originated?' Gabriel said. 'Who was the first vampire? How did we come to walk this earth? The result of some vulgar virus? A ridiculous notion.'

'Didn't the Devil create you, or something?' Dec asked meekly.

Gabriel chuckled. 'A devil, perhaps, but not one to be found within human myth and legend. Lillith, you asked me why the Masters loved to watch the stars. It is because they have always longed to return to the home that was once their Paradise, and which was destroyed. The Elder tales describe the meteoric cataclysm, first seen as a fireball streaking across the sky, that showered their world with a mineral substance so toxic to them that it wiped out virtually their entire population and forced them to embark on a desperate odyssey across millions of light-years of space in the search for a new home. Many of their craft were lost; others may have landed on planets unable to support them. Just one came down, in a state of near-destruction, on this world we call Earth. They remain there still. In Siberia.'

The room was suspended in an astonished silence; just the crackle of the fire in the background as Gabriel quietly continued:

'Finding themselves castaways on a hostile planet, they sought ways not only to survive but to gain control. It soon became clear to them that to reveal themselves to humankind would only cause mass panic and revolt. And so they created a hybridised form of themselves, incorporating some of their own capabilities into a more human shape that would allow them to take the world by stealth if not by force. The vampire, as we know it, was born.'

398

Chapter Sixty-One

'Brother, why have you never spoken of this before?' Lillith asked, stunned.

'Vampires are frigging *aliens*?' Dec burst out.

Chloe had understood. 'The cross,' she muttered, almost to herself. 'The cross wasn't from here. It was from somewhere else.'

Gabriel nodded. 'One can only surmise that the rock that fell to Earth, aeons ago, was a straggler from the same meteor shower that devastated their home planet. Its radiative properties remain mysterious to us: properties that your human ancestors must have discovered entirely by chance when they witnessed the destructive effect the rock could have on the feared beings they believed to be "supernatural". In an act of superstitious ignorance, attributing its powers to some divine intervention against evil, some foolish shaman then sculpted the rock into the shape of a Christian icon.'

'Lil and I didn't drag our asses across Siberia and half of Europe for a history lesson, Gabriel,' Zachary said. 'We came to tell you the motherfucking cross is on its way here, right now, while we're standing around talking.'

'We were delayed getting back on the aeroplane,' Lillith said. 'We wandered for hours in a blizzard, and when we finally got back to the airfield, the humans were passed out drunk. For all we know, Ash could have left not long after we did. He could be here any minute.'

'But how can he find this place?' Kali cut in.

'He knows where we are,' Gabriel replied. 'He was present when we discussed our coming here.'

'We need to get the fuck *out*. Right now,' Zachary insisted.

Lillith gave a shudder. 'He's right. I don't ever want to be near that thing again.'

'I'm with you on that one,' Alex said, exchanging glances with Joel.

'An interesting turn of events for you, Agent Bishop and Inspector Solomon,' Gabriel said. 'The two of you come here as my sworn enemy, ready to send me to hell, as you so charmingly put it; only to find that we are strangely allied to one another.'

'So are we leaving this minute or not, Gabriel?' Kali said anxiously.

'I fear that flight may not be the wisest choice,' Gabriel said. 'Ash will find us, wherever we go. He is a truly determined individual, and whatever motivation I was able to inspire in him will have been redoubled by the far greater powers the Masters can promise. He will not stop until he has destroyed us all.'

'Then we stay and fight,' Alex said. 'We won't get this chance again.'

Lillith shook her head. 'The chance to do what? There *is* no way to fight the cross.'

'There might be a way,' Joel said. Looking out of the window, the sight of the cable tracks stretching away down the valley had given him an idea. He glanced at the pistol in Alex's hand and said, 'Ash might have the cross but he's still human. Unless he's a champion climber, it'd be hard for him to scale the cliff. He'll come up the easy way, in the cable car.'

'Then we can prevent him crossing the valley,' Kali said. 'Simple. Destroy the cable car, right away.'

Joel shook his head. 'No, I think we should let him get on it.'

'That's madness,' Lillith exploded.

'Let him speak, sister,' Gabriel said. 'It may be worth hearing.'

'Is there any way we can slow it down before it gets here?' Joel asked. 'Better still, stop it halfway?'

'Isn't there a stop button or something?' said Kali, who never took notice of such things.

Gabriel shook his head. 'In all other respects the device works like a lift, able to be summoned from either end of the cable track. Once activated in either direction, however, there is no means of halting its progress.'

'Shouldn't be hard to cut the power to the motor,' Zachary said. 'Or else maybe jam the gears with something.'

Alex waggled her pistol. 'Sounds good to me. If we could stop the cable car over the valley, Ash would be a sitting target. I could take him out.'

'I thought that gun was just for shooting vampires,' Dec said.

'The Nosferol in the hollowpoints is pretty harmless to humans,' Alex told him. 'But I never met one yet who could withstand a 300-grain bullet moving past the speed of sound. Believe me, this'll kill the guy.'

'You would have to make the shot from a considerable range,' Gabriel said, 'if you wish to stay out of the cross's reach. Are you proficient enough with the weapon?'

'If you can stop the cable car fifty, sixty yards from the landing station, I can get him,' Alex said.

Lillith snorted. 'Don't kid yourself. Within forty yards of the cross's power you'll be in such agony you won't be able to hold the gun straight, let alone pull off a pistol shot like that in darkness.'

'I still have three rounds left,' Alex said. 'Two in the mag, one up the spout.'

'You couldn't do it with thirty.'

'Do you have any better ideas?' Alex snapped at her.

'You're forgetting us,' Chloe cut in. 'The cross can't hurt us, remember?'

'She's right,' Dec said. 'Let us do it. We can get closer to Ash than any of you.'

'Give me the gun,' Chloe said. 'I know how to shoot. I've shot Ash once before. I can do it again.'

Six pairs of vampire eyes stared at Chloe, opening wide at the implications of what she was asking them to do.

'We already have to deal with one human with the power to wipe us all out,' Lillith said. 'You think we're going to hand you over that gun? Not in a million years.'

'I'm sorry, Chloe,' Alex said.

'You don't trust me?'

'No vampire can trust a human. Not with something like that.'

There was a silence. Gabriel stood up. 'Let us take this one step at a time. I suggest we go downstairs and investigate the most effective means of halting the cable car.'

'Speaking of which . . .' said Kali, looking out of the window.

Everyone turned to stare.

While they'd been arguing, somebody down below in the boarding station had summoned the cable car. Whoever that somebody was, they were standing inside it as it glided silently back towards the chalet on its cables – and they weren't alone. Everyone in the chalet watched, breathless, straining to make out the faces of the half-dozen figures inside. Alex raised the pistol, but even her sharp vampire vision couldn't make out a clear target through the glass.

'Is it him?' Lillith asked tensely. 'I can't feel anything.'

'The cross may be still in its case,' Gabriel said.

The cable car loomed large; then its dark underside obscured its windows from view as it passed above the level of the chalet's living room and glided in to dock at the landing station.

And then they heard the sound of footsteps on the stairs.

Alex, Joel, Dec, Chloe, Gabriel, Lillith, Zachary and Kali: all eyes were on the door. Nobody breathed. Nobody spoke. Alex braced her feet apart and squared the sights of the Desert Eagle on the doorway. Joel, Dec and Chloe held their swords tightly.

The footsteps stopped outside. The handle turned.

And the door swung open.

Chapter Sixty-Two

An arm wearing a gold Rolex darted inside the door as it opened, and flipped on the light switch. Its owner took one step inside the room, staggered to a halt and stared at them all, colour rising instantly in his cheeks.

Not even Lillith could remember ever having seen Gabriel let out such a sigh of relief. 'Baxter, you infernal cretin, what do you mean by bursting in here unannounced?'

It was obvious that the infernal cretin had come ready for a fight. 'I've just about had it with all this bullshit, Gabe,' he launched straight in. 'Who the fuck are all these folks in my house? Who said you could have a goddamned party in here?'

As Baxter went on with his tirade, the rest of the group filed inside the room in his wake: a wearily resigned-looking Tiberius, then Yuri, followed by Albrecht shaking the snow from the brim of his fedora hat. They were accompanied by an extremely attractive pair of female vampire companions Gabriel recognised as Sonia and her inseparable Japanese friend, Makiko, both wearing outfits a human woman would have frozen to death in this time of year in the Alps. Sonia's white satin skirt was short enough to reveal the ornate little silver dagger tucked into her suspender belt. She flashed a hungry look at Dec, nudged Makiko, licked her lips and let out a burbling giggle.

'Oohh, *humans*,' they chorused. 'Gabriel, how thoughtful of you.'

Tiberius made an apologetic gesture to Gabriel as Baxter, sensing he was being ignored, redirected his ranting at Lillith and Zachary.

'He was going on so much, Gabriel,' Tiberius said. 'Announcing he was going to come over here and reckon things up with you. I thought we should accompany him, in case he did anything rash.'

'Rash?' Baxter yelled, interrupting his own stream of abuse. 'I'll give you rash, you buncha dipshits. Listen to me, Gabe, I want my fucking money back. That's all there is to it, okay? The deal's off. I don't wanna be part of this Trad thing any more. I mean, Jesus Christ, we were better off under the fucking Feds . . .'

'Enough,' Gabriel said.

But Baxter hadn't finished. 'And another thing. Where's my plane? What's the point of having my own goddamn plane if I've gotta charter another one just to fly to my own . . .'

'Enough!' Gabriel repeated more loudly.

Baxter's eyes bulged. He was about to add just one more tiny comment when he stopped suddenly and pointed at the window. 'Hey. Did you see that?'

'See what?' Gabriel said, turning.

'I saw it too,' Alex said. 'Something ran past the house. Down there in the snow, on the edge of the crag.' She'd only noticed it out of the corner of her eye – a flitting figure that had darted out of the shadows of the rocks and then vanished as quickly as it had appeared.

'What was it?' Joel asked. Alex shook her head, scanned the rocks intently for another sign of it.

'Extinguish the light,' Gabriel commanded, and Makiko flipped off the switch, the smile gone from her face.

406

'The back window,' Alex whispered. Joel and Dec followed as she trotted nimbly out of the living room and into the hallway behind it, where the rear balcony overlooked the face of the mountain behind the chalet. 'There,' she said, pointing. 'Two more of them.' She'd seen them better this time. As Joel followed the line of her finger he spotted a third: the hooded figure, no taller than a child, scampered out from behind a rock, darted across the snow and disappeared again.

'What *was* that?' he said again.

'God damn these local brats,' Baxter yelled, joining them at the back window.

'Kids couldn't make their way up here,' Joel said.

'Fucking gypsies,' Baxter growled. 'Last year they stripped out a whole ski hut for firewood, down the valley. Well they ain't robbing a solitary plank from this place, that's for damned sure.' He marched out onto the rear balcony, swung a leg over the sturdy wooden rail and dropped off the edge. It was only a twenty-foot leap to the snow below, nothing for a vampire, and Baxter prided himself on doing his own stunts.

There was nobody there. Baxter trudged around the corner of the chalet, wading through the thick snow, cupping his hands around his mouth as he shouted, 'Hey, you little rat-asses! Get away from here! You hear me? This is private property! So fuck off!'

A whistling sound, moving fast towards him. Baxter turned and felt something strike him in the chest. 'What in hell's name—?' he muttered, squinting down his nose at the peculiar object that had attached itself to him.

The shaft of an arrow.

'Those bastard gypsies,' Baxter said, outraged, but in a strangely slurred voice. He plucked the arrow out and was about to toss it away when he suddenly realised that his arm wasn't obeying the command of his brain. He tried to make his fingers open and release the arrow, but they wouldn't move. Panic began to surge through him. What was happening? He couldn't even turn his head. Gazing fixedly at the bloody point of the arrow, he could see its strange glass tip, like a vial, that had been shattered by the impact. Dripping from the broken glass was an odd kind of liquid that was too black and thick to be just his blood.

At that point, the paralysis took Baxter over entirely and he went down like a felled tree in the snow.

He didn't scream, didn't move, was completely unable to react as the horrible little hooded figures appeared as if out of nowhere and gathered around him in a circle. Something glinted in the moonlight. A razor-sharp blade gouged his flesh, and Baxter felt every bit of the pain.

Then the figures were all over him, hacking and chopping and slicing. The arm clutching the arrow rolled away across the bloody snow. The last thing Baxter saw was his body rolling away from him – no, it was *him* rolling away from his body. A glimpse at the stars above . . . then down at the snowy ground . . . and then nothing at all.

Chapter Sixty-Three

Alex was the first to leap down from the rear balcony and follow Baxter's tracks in the snow around the side of the chalet. She heard the meaty chopping sounds and the strange chittering, twittering noises before she rounded the corner and saw the strange little figures, no taller than children, that were crowded around what was left of the movie star. The crude, hooded robes they wore were like scaled-down versions of the habits worn by medieval monks, held in at the waist with broad leather belts or lengths of stout rope. But what drew Alex's eye was the cruel-looking assortment of bloodied butcher's knives, machetes and cleavers the creatures clutched in their grey, clawed, three-fingered little hands.

The twittering stopped abruptly. The creatures looked up from the bloody circle in the snow and stared at her from under their hoods. Alex counted eight of them as she backed away a couple of steps. Suddenly she was aware of Joel at her side. Lillith, Gabriel, Zachary and Tiberius had joined him. Glancing up, she glimpsed Dec and Chloe standing above on the balcony, leaning out over the rail with looks of horror.

'It seems to be curtains for our thespian friend,' Gabriel said, nudging Baxter's severed head with his toe.

'Never mind him,' Alex said. 'What about those?'

'Whatever they are,' Joel said, 'they're not afraid of us.'

As if to prove him right, the little hooded figures charged at them with uncanny speed and aggression. Alex shot the nearest one in the face and it somersaulted backwards in a dark mist of exploded skull and brain matter, the wicked machete flying from its hand.

Lillith snatched the weapon out of the air. As the creatures closed on them she windmilled it around her, splitting one from hip to shoulder and lopping off another's arm. Without a sound, the thing bounded away from her, blood spraying the snow from its stump. It would have knocked Joel off his feet if he hadn't thrust out his katana in time. Impaled through the middle, the creature fell back, its surprising weight almost tearing the sword from Joel's grip.

Tiberius stepped back out of the arc of a cleaver blow that would have halved a strong man, grabbed his attacker by the folds of its habit and dashed its brains out against one of the chalet's thick wooden support struts; meanwhile, Gabriel swept the feet out from under another and crushed its throat with a stamping kick. Zachary had scooped one up by the rope around its middle, knocked the knife out of its hands and was busy strangling it in his fists.

The remaining creature turned, chittering to itself, and went bounding away like a mountain goat over the rocks.

'One thing's for sure,' Alex said, using her foot to roll over one of the corpses. 'These things are no vampires.'

'Then what are they?' Joel said. He knelt down beside the dead creature and ripped away the hood, exposing its face to the moonlight. Its skin was grey and leprous. It had the wrinkles of a very, very old man. The large eyes of a cat. The jutting, muscular jaws of a barracuda, slick with slime and drool. Joel looked away in disgust.

'I've never seen anything like this before,' Alex said.

410

'Zachary and I have,' Lillith said. 'At the Über citadel in Siberia. Their answer to a ghoul, I thought.'

'This thing's never been a human. Look at it.'

'It is a *Zargôyuk*,' Gabriel said. 'The nearest translation of the ancient word would be "goblin".'

Lillith looked at him. 'You *knew* about these things?'

'They are drones, hunters, the slave workforce of the citadel, hatched deep in its bowels from mutated Übervampyr spawn. I told you before, sister, of the secrets and wisdom of the Masters.'

'I wouldn't say it was wise to create something like this,' Lillith said, pointing at the dead creature.

'The question is,' Alex cut in, 'how many more are there?'

Zachary gazed up the mountainside to where the goblin had disappeared among the rocks. 'She's right. There could be dozens of the little mothers hiding up there.'

'What do we do, Gabriel?' Tiberius said. 'Go up there and hunt for th—'

Before he could finish, something came whistling out of the darkness and thwacked into the wooden support next to them. A dark liquid spatter caught Tiberius across the face as he was speaking. He clapped his hand to his lips, spitting and choking. A second arrow whooshed out from somewhere in the rocks, narrowly missing Alex.

'Get inside,' Gabriel said. 'Quickly.'

Within instants of the strange black fluid spattering his face, Tiberius couldn't walk properly. He fell on his knees and would have collapsed on his face if Gabriel and Zachary hadn't caught his limp arms. As they dragged him across the snow to the chalet, more incoming fire came whistling in from the mountainside. A shaft juddered into the wall inches from Joel. Another plunged into Tiberius's calf and yet another embedded itself deep in his back.

Alex booted open a back door, shouting 'Everyone in!' It was a store-room filled with junk, tools, gas cylinders and old ski equipment. Gabriel and Zachary dragged Tiberius inside and laid him down on the floor. The remaining vampires piled in behind them and Alex slammed the door shut just as another arrow thunked into it.

By now, Tiberius was completely paralysed.

'We saw this too,' Lillith said, pointing at the black fluid that was dribbling from his arrow wounds.

'We sure did,' Zachary muttered. 'Some kinda ugly poison.'

'An Übervampyr neurotoxin,' Gabriel said grimly. 'Akin to the venom with which a spider paralyses its prey. It is less effective on our kind than on humans. But even for us, only in the tiniest quantities are the effects temporary. I fear that Tiberius has suffered far too great a dose.'

'You mean he'll be paralysed like this—'

Gabriel gave a solemn nod. 'For the rest of time. We must deliver him. Sister, hand me that blade.'

Lillith hesitated, aghast, then passed him the machete she'd taken from the dead goblin.

'My very old friend,' Gabriel said, bending over Tiberius's prone body. 'Forgive me.'

Joel had to look away as the blade came down.

'Poor Tiberius,' Lillith breathed.

'In such circumstances, I would expect any of my brethren to show me the same mercy,' Gabriel said, stepping up from the decapitated body and handing the machete back to her.

'I don't want it,' she was about to say – when they suddenly heard an urgent shout from upstairs.

Chapter Sixty-Four

The voice was Yuri's. They found him standing at the living room window, joined by Dec and Chloe. 'Look!' he shouted again as everyone raced into the room.

While they'd been distracted by the goblin attack, the cable car had started moving again. They watched, helpless, as the gleaming aluminium and glass cube glided smoothly back down towards the boarding station across the valley.

There was a woody *thunk* behind them as another arrow hit the chalet from the mountainside. Zachary grabbed hold of the living room door and ripped it off its hinges. 'Someone run down to that store-room and bring me up a hammer and nails, quick. We don't board up the windows and outside doors, those little fuckers're gonna be swarming all over this place.'

Joel left the room and crossed the hallway behind it to peer out of the rear window, across the balcony to the rocky slope behind the house. There was no sign of movement out there, no running figures flitting across the snow. No telling how many of these goblin things could be out there, either: and by now they should be pressing their attack, storming every weak point, swarming up the walls, jumping up on the roof, smashing windows. It would be tough to stop them getting inside.

So why wasn't it happening?

'I wouldn't bother boarding the place up,' he called through the open doorway to the vampires in the living room.

'Say *what*?' Zachary rumbled.

'This is no invasion,' Joel told him. 'It's a containment strategy. They've no intention of coming in; they only want to prevent us from leaving. Don't you see? They want to trap us in here.'

'Guys! The cable car!' Alex shouted from the living room window. 'It's coming back!'

Lillith turned to Gabriel. 'Can't we stop it?'

'I'm afraid it is too late for that,' Gabriel replied.

The solitary figure of Ash was unmistakable behind the glass front of the cable car. At one hip hung the executioner's sword in its scabbard; at the other, attached to a strap around his shoulders, was the lead-lined case. As in a trance of horror, the assembled vampires watched the man reach inside and slowly draw out the horribly familiar shape of the cross.

Standing by the window with Yuri and Makiko, Alex cried out at the jet of agony crackling through her body. All three recoiled violently away from the glass, their bodies spasming as the awful pain took hold. Alex's fingers loosened on the grip of the pistol and it dropped out of her hand and bounced away from her. To go back for it now would be suicide. She staggered away in the opposite direction, desperately trying to reach the door and widen the distance between herself and the approaching cross.

Makiko was attempting to do exactly the same. In her frenzied haste to escape she cannoned into Chloe, stumbled over the edge of the rug and sprawled on the floor. Makiko struggled to get to her feet, but the crippling power of the weapon was too much to overcome.

Chloe was standing just a few feet away as, with a final

414

shriek that rose up in a horrible tortured wail, Makiko turned black and then cracked and peeled apart and crumbled into a puff of cinders.

It wasn't the first time Dec had seen the effects of the cross, but even he gaped in appalled horror at the sight. Chloe covered her face with her hands.

Alex had reached the door, just inches ahead of the lethal energy field, and was racing across the hallway outside towards the back of the house along with Lillith, Kali, Gabriel and Zachary. Joel had no choice but to flee along with them. He could scarcely believe what was happening to him. Only days ago, wielding the cross himself, he'd been the predator. Now he was the prey, just one of the pressing mêlée of vampires all desperate to get beyond its reach.

Yuri hadn't been as fast as Alex to the door. A shockwave of agony arched his back to breaking point and slammed him down to the floorboards at Dec's feet.

'Help me!' Yuri croaked, reaching out a trembling hand.

For an instant that seemed to last minutes, Dec stood frozen. This was a vampire. It sucked the blood of humans. It deserved to fry.

Yet in that moment, all he could see was a man suffering horribly, screaming in pain, red-rimmed agonised eyes imploring him for help. Dec thought of Joel, and a powerful surge of pity made him reach out to grasp Yuri's wrist and drag him towards the door fractions of a second before the cross's power would have blown him apart.

'Thank you, human,' Yuri shouted as he went staggering off across the hallway.

'Any time,' Dec mumbled. *Dec Maddon, vampire hunter.* A great start to his career, this was.

The cable car was getting closer. And now the single figure inside could be clearly seen through the glass. Even from forty yards away, the triumphant jagged grin was visible on Ash's face.

Chloe spotted Alex's fallen pistol and scooped it up off the floor. The controls were different from the air gun she was used to, but the essentials were the same. She stuffed it into her waistband. 'Down the stairs, quick!' she yelled to Dec. 'We have to stop that thing so I can get a clear shot.'

They raced down to the chalet's ground floor, tore down the short passage and burst through the door of the boarding station to see the cable car just thirty yards away. Chloe ran to the landing platform and felt her knees turn to rubber at the sight of the dizzy drop to the valley below. The mountain wind blew her hair and whistled around the chalet.

She looked across at the approaching glass front of the cable car and her eyes met Ash's.

Both his eyes.

For a moment of bewilderment, Chloe wondered whether it could be the same man. Because Ash had changed. Something had happened to him. His features were sculpted, symmetrical, chillingly beautiful. The new clothes he was wearing clung to his leaner, taller and more powerful form.

But it was him, all right. Chloe could see the cross in his hands, clutched tightly against his chest – and, sticking up above his shoulder in a back-scabbard, the hilt of the great sword that had killed her father.

And now he was hers. All she had to do was halt the cable car, and there'd be nowhere he could run from her. She glanced around for the control box. Sure enough, there was no way to stop the cable car except by cutting the power. 'The wires, Dec!' she yelled.

Dec was no electrician, but the large transformer of the electric motor was easy to spot. There was just one thick cluster of wires running into it, wrapped up in a black shielded covering. He swung his katana at it with all his might, praying that the leather handle of the sword would protect his hands when the high voltage shot up the blade and the tang.

Crack. The blade missed its target and hacked a piece out of the transformer box. The cable car glided on another few feet.

Dec swore and hit the wires again, and this time the blade found its mark through the armoured covering. The jolt of electricity almost took the sword out of his hands. A loud bang, a flash and a shower of sparks, and the cable car motor drive suddenly ground to a halt.

'Got you now, asshole,' Chloe said, and raised the pistol.

Chapter Sixty-Five

On his way across the valley moments earlier, Ash clutched the cross tightly to his chest, smiled and his reflection in the glass front of the cable car smiled handsomely back at him. He liked this new Ash he'd become: he was stronger, more dangerous, and more determined than ever. So far, his new Masters had done everything they'd promised they'd do. And there was more to come, when he returned victorious to the citadel after this final mission. The new Ash would be renewed again, with capabilities far beyond anything a mere vampire could offer him. Tarcz-kôi had shown him things that even Gabriel Stone had no conception of.

The smile dropped from his lips as he felt the cable car's smooth forward momentum die away without warning and it juddered to a stop, swaying in the mountain breeze. He looked out of the window at the empty space all around him, the drop below. Then gazed back towards the girl he could see standing on the platform. He knew her face – where had he seen her before?

It didn't matter. What mattered was his plan. He mustn't fail.

And the powers that his Masters had given him would see to it that he didn't. They hadn't just restored his eye and made him prettier.

It was time for a change of tactics. Inside his head, Ash gave his soldiers the silent command to press forward the attack. Then, tossing the cross into the lead-lined case that hung from his shoulder, he drew out his executioner's sword. With a powerful upward thrust he punched the blade through the aluminium roof of the cable car. He yanked it out with a metallic shriek, punched it through again. In seconds he'd cut a ragged hole. He sheathed the sword, jumped up and hauled himself bodily through onto the swaying roof, between the parallel cable tracks.

The girl was still standing there, twenty-five yards away on the edge of the platform, nothing below her except the thick wooden support struts of the chalet and a snowy rock ledge. Clinging on to the steel cables with his right hand, Ash ripped the cross back out of its case with his left and thrust it out towards her. He frowned. Why didn't she fly into cinders? Everyone else did. Raising it higher, he hauled himself over the pulley apparatus towards her.

By the time he saw the gun in her hand, it was too late to react – but even as Ash tensed at the sight of the weapon, he knew that his soldiers had answered the call to attack.

Standing on the edge of the platform overlooking the dizzy drop to the valley below, Chloe squared the Desert Eagle's sights firmly on her target's chest. She saw her father's face in her mind. She nodded to herself and squeezed the trigger.

At the same instant that the pistol bucked wildly in her hands and its huge flat report filled the air, she heard a muffled cry from Dec and a staggering impact knocked the world sideways. For a dazed moment or two as she rolled across the platform, she thought that it was the gun's recoil that had sent her flying.

Then she saw the demonic-looking hooded goblin

creature coming in for another cut with the chopping blade in its fist. It was Dec who'd knocked her over as he leaped in between them. His face twisted in fear, he managed to parry the blow with his sword and knock the chopper out of the thing's clawed, muscular hand. It came on. He backed away, shielding Chloe with his body.

'Get away from her, you wee skitter!'

The goblin gazed at them for a second or two, making a strange twittering sound. Then, with terrifying speed, it pounced.

The force of the impact knocked the sword out of Dec's hand and cannoned him into Chloe. She staggered backwards towards the edge of the platform. Her arms flailed for something to grab—

And then she was falling into empty space, nothing but the black sky above her and the valley far, far below.

Chapter Sixty-Six

There was wild chaos as the remaining vampires crowded through the chalet, desperate to put as much distance between themselves and the fearful cross as they could. Gabriel, Kali, Lillith and Zachary pounded down the stairs towards the back exit on the ground floor. Alex and Joel were running down the passage towards the top of the stairs when Sonia, Albrecht and Yuri came crowding past in a panic.

'I'm not sticking around here to be cooked by that thing,' Albrecht brayed, suddenly breaking off from the rest of the group and turning towards a little window that overlooked the back yard. In his panic, he crashed into Alex, knocking the wind out of her and inadvertently dragging her along with him as he launched himself out of the window.

Alex landed heavily in the snow, hitting her head hard against a boulder. Dazed, she struggled up onto her hands and knees. She could hear Joel calling her name from somewhere inside the house.

Albrecht was sprinting madly away up the craggy slope. As she watched, an arrow flew towards him from behind a rock. Still running like crazy, he dodged it, and covered a few more paces before another pierced his throat. He'd barely hit the snow before a horde of little dark figures swarmed out from their hiding places among the rocks and descended on him. Knives and hackers rose and fell. Body parts were tossed up in the air.

Alex's legs were unsteady under her as she staggered to her feet. Even vampires could get mild concussion from a severe blow to the head. She inched away in the shadow of the house, terrified of being spotted by the goblins.

But in her dazed state she didn't notice the chopping block behind her, next to a stack of firewood logs and a precarious pile of old varnish cans. She bumped into the handle of the axe that was propped against the block and it fell and hit the varnish cans, which clattered noisily to the ground.

The nearest of the goblins started at the sound, whipped round and saw her standing there not twenty yards away. Suddenly they were all jumping up from what was left of Albrecht and charging towards her.

Alex broke into a run, heading for the cliff edge. One time, she'd jumped off the London Eye – and she was still around to tell the tale.

Shit, she thought as she neared the edge. It was a long way down. She didn't much fancy spending eternity as a smear of mincemeat spread across the rocks below, although even that was preferable to being paralysed and chopped into dog food by these things.

But then she realised that three of the goblins, darting around her flank with awful speed, were heading her off. One took out a slingshot as it bounded along, and fired something at her that smacked off a rock. It splintered into pieces and Alex saw what the missile was: a hollow glass ball filled with the black paralysing fluid.

Terrified, she veered away from the cliff edge, willing herself to run faster. She headed in the only direction she could – up the mountainside. Something whizzed past her ear and another poison ball shattered just a yard away. She felt the splash of poison hit her sleeve, tore it away in repulsion and kept running up the steepening slope, the goblins – maybe a dozen of them, maybe more – converging behind her in pursuit. The white peak of the mountain loomed high up above, as if threatening to topple over on top of her. She hauled herself over a ledge and found herself in a dip in the rocks. A glance back over her shoulder told her that the chalet was out of sight now.

She thought of Joel. *Run, Joel, run.*

Half a second's distraction was too long. Alex barely had time to react as the goblin launched itself from a hidden crevice up ahead and came lunging at her with a crooked black knife. She threw herself out of the path of the slicing blow and the blade struck sparks off the rock next to her. She grabbed the goblin's wrist and yanked it hard towards her, straight into the knee that she drove into its ribs. The foul-smelling breath burst out of its lungs and it doubled up in pain. She smashed its head against the rocks, once, twice, three times, grappling with its little muscular body with all her strength until the writhing death struggles had stopped and it lay still, oozing blood onto the trampled snow.

Then Alex heard a twittering sound behind her and turned.

Fifteen more of the creatures were gathering round her in a circle, and now there was nowhere to run at all.

Chapter Sixty-Seven

'*Chloe!*'

Dec's scream filled the boarding station as he saw her topple over the edge of the platform. The goblin's powerful little claws were around his throat. Its hood fell away; the hideous jaws opened wide and came snapping towards him. Before it could rip his face off, he headbutted it so hard that he saw stars. The thing chittered angrily and fell back. Dec twisted away towards the fallen sword. The goblin was back on its feet, muscles coiling for another pounce.

'Come on then, you fucker,' he said as he grasped the katana with both hands. The creature hurled itself at him, jaws distended . . .

And hit the floor in two pieces.

Dec spat goblin blood. 'Chloe!' he yelled, rushing to the edge of the platform and staring down in anguish at the sheer drop down the cliff. His heart almost burst with relief when he saw her just a few feet below him, crouching dazedly on a little rocky lip that protruded from the cliff face.

The crash of the pistol shot was still ringing in Chloe's ears. Her mind clearing suddenly, she looked up at the cable car and saw Ash. The shot she'd aimed at his chest had gone wide when Dec had knocked her clear of the goblin's attack – though not too wide.

Ash's left hand was still clutching the cross. But it was no longer attached to his arm. Blown away by the expanding hollowpoint bullet, the severed hand had bounced away over the cable car roof and entangled itself in the wire. Fingers curled around the cross's shaft like the legs of a dying spider, it slid down the cable tracks a distance, then stopped and hung precariously over the valley.

As Chloe watched, Ash crawled across the roof and tried desperately to work his way down the cable tracks to retrieve the cross – but the vibrations through the wire were only making it slide further away; too much movement risked shaking it free altogether.

The gun. Chloe scrabbled about the rocky ledge and for a terrible moment she thought it must have fallen off the cliff. *No!* There it was, half-covered in snow and dirt. Ash was suspended directly over the abyss now, his handless arm hooked over the cable, reaching out with the other towards the cross. Chloe grabbed the pistol to take another shot, but just as she got him in her sights another cloud passed over the moon and Ash was lost in shadows.

Dec was calling down to her. 'You okay?'

'I'm not hurt. Help me up.'

'Hang on,' Dec yelled back. 'I've had an idea.' If he could get the cable car to travel back downwards, he could scrape Ash off the wire and send him to his death, or else maybe mash him up in the pulleys. Seeing a big electrical switch lever that looked to him like a main fuse control, Dec yanked it. The lights went off.

'Dec, what's happening?' Chloe called out.

'Hold on, I'm coming.' Working frantically, Dec groped about in the dark for a handful of the electrical wires he'd cut earlier and started tearing at the insulation so that he could twist them back together and feed juice back to the control box.

He scarcely had time to think *Shit, wrong fusebox* before the electric shock jolted through him from head to toe, making him almost bite his tongue off and flinging him unconscious against the wall.

The wires fell in a heap and instantly began to smoulder and sparkle. A flame leaped up from the control box and quickly gained a purchase on the wooden panel it was mounted on. In just moments, the fire was spreading in a pool a few feet from where Dec lay inert.

'Dec!' Chloe called up. 'Dec, hurry!'

Ash had crawled down the swaying cable almost as far as the cross. One slip, one excessive movement, and it would fall, and so might he. He inched his way just a little further, gritting his teeth, the case dangling from the strap around his shoulders. He was almost there. He reached out. One more inch . . . and his fingers clamped tightly around the knuckles of his own severed hand.

He laughed in triumph. The cross was his once more.

Gripping Kali's arm, Gabriel led the way, Lillith and Zachary stumbling along behind as the four of them burst out of the chalet and into the night. Every running step took them further from the source of the terrible agony. For the moment it seemed to have stopped advancing on them, but Gabriel was intent on taking them as far from the cross's power as he could.

Dashing under cover of shadow as the gathering clouds obscured the moonlight, they found a twisting fissure in the rocks that led steeply away and up towards the eastern face of the mountain.

The only weapon they carried between them was the machete Lillith had taken from the goblin. The enemy were numerous and well-armed, and Gabriel knew he could ill afford to meet them head on. Cursing himself for having ever put his trust in the Masters, he considered the only strategy open to them: escape. Attempting the vertical cliff face to their right was perilous, even for a vampire – the risk of irreparable damage, whether dashed to pieces on the rocks or impaled on a tree far below in the valley, was enough to persuade Gabriel to skirt around the mountainside in the hope of finding a less risky descent.

'This way,' he called back over his shoulder. Kali had kicked off her shoes and was running barefoot over the snow. Lillith followed.

Zachary brought up the rear, glancing warily in all directions. A flitting movement caught his eye. Something scurrying behind a crevice above them. Then, almost immediately after, he heard the twang of the bowstring and the whistle of the flying arrow. 'Incoming!' he yelled. 'Ten o'clock!'

The arrow cracked on the rocks inches from Gabriel and stained the snow with venom.

'Everyone down!' Lillith shouted.

An instant later, a rain of arrows and glass missiles was showering down on them from a dozen hidden vantage points in the crags above. Gabriel hauled Kali behind the shelter of a snowy boulder to the right of the path, shielding her as best he could with his own body and steeling himself to feel the bite of a poisoned barb in his flesh. Zachary had hurled himself away to the right, rolling through the snow to press his bulk tightly into the angle of two big rocks.

Gabriel ducked as a glass missile whizzed overhead, then risked a glance around him. Something was wrong.

'Lillith?' he called out. 'Where are you?'

Chapter Sixty-Eight

Joel sprinted out of the chalet and hollered Alex's name. The only reply was the echo of his own voice ringing off the mountainside. To his right, he could see the distant figures of Gabriel Stone and his three companions winding their way up the slope.

'Alex!' he shouted again. He was sure he could smell burning. Glancing back at the chalet, he saw thick smoke drifting in the wind.

Then, out of the darkness, a running figure streaked towards him. Joel's first panicked thought was that it might be one of the goblins, and his grip tightened on his sword; but no, it was a tall female figure. With a mixture of extreme relief and bitter disappointment, he recognised her as one of the sexy she-vampires that had turned up with Baxter Burnett.

'Quick!' Sonia hissed, half-demented with terror. 'We have to run! The cross . . . the man . . . *he's coming!*' The fight-or-flight instinct had made her fangs extend – Joel could see them behind her lips as she spoke. He instinctively felt for his own, still holding on to some vain hope that they might not be there. They were. But there was no time for those kinds of concerns now.

'Have you seen Alex?' he asked as they ran.

'Who?'

'My friend who was with me before,' he explained frantically.

'I don't know,' Sonia babbled. 'I don't know. I think she was destroyed.'

Joel was still reeling from her words when the attack came out of nowhere. A leaping dark shape beat him down violently against the rocks, twisting the sword out of his grip, pinning him with its weight. He felt little clawed hands grasping at his ankles, stopping him from kicking out.

Sonia screamed as they took her down. For a moment she disappeared under a scrum of little bodies. When Joel caught sight of her again she was spread-eagled among the rocks, a goblin hanging tightly to each wrist and ankle. One reached into the folds of its habit and took out a little round glass ball, the size of a large marble. It jerked Sonia's head back by the hair, forcing her mouth open with its thumbs. She bit savagely. The goblins twittered in mirth.

These things are just playing with us, Joel thought. He twisted and fought, but the goblin sitting on his chest was holding him tightly down. All he could do was watch as the creature with the hollow glass marble forced it very deliberately between Sonia's fangs and shoved it down her throat with the handle of its knife. It watched intently as she swallowed it with a choking splutter, then lashed out with the knife handle, crushing the glass while it was still inside her throat.

Vampire blood and black poison bubbled out of her mouth and spilled down her cheeks. Sonia struggled wildly for a few seconds and then went limp as the paralysing agent took effect.

Then, tugging her in opposite directions, the goblins unhurriedly tore her apart. The left arm was first to rip from

432

its shoulder joint, trailing sinews and muscle. Then the right leg. The goblin clutching the ankle hurled the limb away and it flopped across the rocks and landed next to Joel. The most horrific thing wasn't seeing Sonia being torn apart – it was that she couldn't make a sound or lift a finger in resistance.

And now, from the way the little bastards were turning towards him, Joel got the feeling it was going to be his turn next.

As he twisted his head from side to side in desperation, something caught his eye: the little silver dagger that Sonia wore in her garter belt, still attached to her severed thigh.

Finally, with a desperate heave, Joel managed to dislodge the dead weight of the goblin from off his chest. He threw out his arm. Plucked the dagger from Sonia's garter belt. Slashing the throat of the nearest goblin, he brought the silver hilt down with a vicious skull-cracking blow on the head of another. Then he was free and springing up onto his feet, and his fallen katana was back in his hand, the long curved blade hissing through the air. Blood hit the snow. Five goblins were reduced to twitching body parts before the rest went fleeing over the rocks.

Joel stepped towards the dismembered trunk that had been the beautiful Sonia. He couldn't leave her like this, doomed to the worst possible fate a vampire could face.

He raised the sword. The last look in her eyes was one of profound gratitude.

When it was done, Joel bent double, retching and wheezing up the few drops of Errol Knightly's blood that were still in his system.

At that moment, he thought he heard a voice call his name.

Chapter Sixty-Nine

The smoke was pouring thickly out of the boarding station now and through it the flicker of flames was getting brighter. Chloe could feel the heat of the spreading fire and hear its crackle as she tried to gain a handhold on the slippery rocks and pull herself up to the platform.

'Dec! Where are you?'

No reply. As she called his name again, a gust of wind enveloped her in thick hot smoke and she fell into a fit of coughing. She couldn't see the cable car any more.

Suddenly there was a figure standing next to her on the ledge. Chloe backed away in dread, reaching for her pistol – but as the figure stepped towards her through the swirling smoke, she saw it wasn't Ash, but the vampire called Yuri.

'Come with me,' he croaked in his thick accent. 'Quickly!' Yuri let out a cry as pain racked his body. Chloe took his hand, and felt herself being lifted up towards the platform as though she weighed nothing. The smoke was blinding. The fire was everywhere, its heat unbearable. Then Yuri's hand was guiding her firmly through the middle of the leaping flames.

'Why are you doing this?' she gasped.

'Your friend save me. Now I save you. Move, move. There is no time.'

'Dec!' Chloe yelled. There he was, dragged free of the fire, sitting propped against the wall, groggy but alive, his face blackened by the smoke. His eyes widened as he saw Chloe. He swayed up to his feet, staggered towards her and held her by the arms. 'Where's Ash?' he coughed.

Yuri glanced back in terror in the direction of the cable car. His body suddenly twisted into a violent agonised convulsion. He screwed his eyes shut, opened his mouth to scream . . . and blackened and burst apart into charred nothingness.

'Ash is here,' Chloe breathed.

They turned to see him striding towards them through the fire. The flames flickered in his eyes and gleamed on his teeth. In his right hand he clutched the cross. The left arm hung limply, blood still dripping from the stump where his hand had been. His face twisted in hate as his eyes locked on Chloe and Dec.

Chloe wrenched the pistol from her jeans and took aim. She couldn't possibly miss him this time.

Ash took another step closer. He bared his teeth.

Chloe braced herself and squeezed the trigger.

Nothing happened. The trigger wouldn't move. *Safety catch!* Chloe feverishly felt for it, in case it had been accidentally switched to the safe position. But it hadn't. As if in a nightmare, she squeezed the trigger with all the strength in her hands. Still nothing happened.

Ash kept coming, the jagged smile on his face broadening as Chloe struggled with the gun. He dropped the cross into the case at his side and reached for the hilt of his sword.

But before the blade was clear of the scabbard, Dec was charging at him like a man possessed, yelling at the top of his voice. Dec was half Ash's weight but he hurled himself at him with such force that they both fell back into the fire.

All Chloe could see through the flames was a sprawling tangle of limbs, kicking and punching and gouging. One instant, Dec was on top, pummelling Ash's face with his fists – the next, Ash had flung Dec off him with a savage blow and was leaping back on his feet. His clothes were singed and the strap around his shoulders was on fire. He ran at Chloe, ripping the sword from its scabbard and raising it for a massive downward cut.

Then a loud meaty clang resounded off the back of Ash's skull and he fell forward, stunned. The sword spun away into the flames. The burning strap around his shoulders snapped, and the case slithered across the floor to Chloe's feet.

Dec emerged from the smoke, his face half-covered in blood from an ugly gash over his eye. He tossed away the large wrench he'd used as a club.

Not hard enough. Ash was already getting back up.

'Let's go!' Dec yelled to Chloe. Spotting the case on the floor, he snatched it up by its charred strap and they ran out of the burning room.

Ash roared with fury and raced after them.

Chapter Seventy

Joel hadn't imagined it – the sound of Alex's voice on the wind, calling his name. There it was again . . . It was coming from further up the mountainside.

He ran, leaping over rocks, stumbling through deep snow. As the slope steepened, he clamped the katana blade between his teeth and climbed like he'd never climbed before.

'Joel!' It came out as a scream this time, just the other side of a rocky overhang a few yards up the slope. He launched himself over it and saw her.

Alex was surrounded by a whole pack of goblins, desperately beating them off with a gnarled old tree root in one hand and a jagged lump of stone in the other as they attacked her from all sides.

In an instant he was there with her. One of the creatures that hurled itself at Alex fell back, headless. Joel's blade rose and fell. He killed another, then another, striking again and again with all the energy that was left in him, left and right, screaming with fury and hitting and slicing until he was standing knee-deep in the middle of a slaughterer's yard of dead or dying goblins.

Still they kept on coming. So many of them, swarming in from everywhere, their number growing faster than Alex and Joel could kill them.

And now the strength was beginning to ebb out of Joel's body, drained to such a low ebb that he could barely swing the sword or even stand upright. He dropped to his knees and looked at Alex. 'I'm sorry,' he groaned.

Alex shook her head. 'I'm not. At least this way, I don't have to lose you a second time. Better we go out together, Joel.'

He didn't know what to say.

'You know, I love you,' she whispered.

The goblins gathered around them.

'Where's Lillith?' Zachary shouted from behind the rocks.

'I don't see her,' Gabriel shouted back from the other side of the mountain path, where he and Kali had taken cover from the flying arrows. The shooting seemed to have abruptly died away. Gabriel craned his neck out a little further from behind the boulder. 'No,' he groaned. 'Oh, no, no.'

Lillith was still on the path, a few yards away. She was lying on her face in the snow, her arms outflung. Black against the snow, the shaft of a goblin arrow was sticking vertically from her shoulder. Gabriel shouted her name again. There was no movement.

And now the pause in the shooting was explained. Dark shapes came scurrying down the mountainside. As Gabriel stared in anguish, the first goblins reached her and began dragging her away by the wrists. Others stood by, their hooded little heads jerking this way and that as they scanned the rocks. The nearest of the creatures plucked a fresh arrow from the quiver at its side. Two others had their bows already at full draw, waiting for a target to appear. Lillith's body was out of sight now behind the rocks. There was the scrape of steel on stone, as if a blade was being sharpened.

Gabriel was fully aware of what was happening. The

Masters had trained their little hunters well. They were using her as bait to draw the rest of them out. 'I swear that if I survive this day,' he murmured through clenched teeth, 'I will strike back at the Übervampyr for what they have done to me.' He lashed out his fist in anger, and a rock next to him split in two.

'Let her go, Gabriel,' Kali said, clutching at his hand. 'She's only your sister.'

Gabriel turned to her with a terrible look. 'I have walked with Lillith since before you were born a human.' He sucked in a long breath. He couldn't stand it any longer. With a shout of rage, he tore away from Kali's grip and leaped out from behind the boulder, charging wildly at the goblins.

A twang of a bowstring; he felt something rip through his shirt and scrape his side. Zachary was right behind him, his roar of fury filling the air. They could fire a hundred arrows into that huge body and he'd still be on his feet long enough to rip every one of them limb from limb with his bare hands.

At the sight of him, the goblins threw down their bows and ran. Gabriel hurdled a rock to see five of them clustered around Lillith's prone body. A blade glinted in the dull moonlight as it rose and began to fall. Gabriel grabbed up a fist-sized rock and hurled it savagely. As the blade spun out of the goblin's little grey hand, he was already on the creature, ripping back its hood and pounding his fists into its face with a ferocious violence that crushed the skull in like a seashell. Zachary dodged a flying glass ball and dashed two goblin heads together, broke the neck of a third with a flying kick and sent a fourth tumbling to its death down the mountainside.

By the time Kali had joined them, the remaining goblins had fled and Gabriel and Zachary were kneeling by Lillith's side in the snow. Zachary was sobbing as he cradled her.

441

Kali stood over them with her fists on her hips, head cocked to one side, watching impassively.

'Let me attend to her, Zachary.' Gabriel gathered Lillith in his arms and rested her head on his knee. Her eyes seemed not to see him. Ripping the seam of her leather outfit at the shoulder, he grasped the base of the arrow shaft where it met the flesh and gave a hard tug. Black venom oozed from the wound as the arrow came out. Tossing it away, Gabriel pressed his mouth to the hole and sucked hard. He spat black on the snow, then sucked again; he kept on doing it until he tasted the sweet flavour of vampire blood on his lips.

'I have drawn what I could from the wound,' he said, laying her limp body back down on the snow. 'I can only hope that it was not too late.' He gazed down at her. 'I cannot envisage eternity without her at my side.'

Kali's eyes had narrowed and her lips were tight. Gabriel paid her no attention.

Lillith's hand was dwarfed in Zachary's great fists as he clenched it tight. 'Come on, Lil,' he pleaded. 'Wake up. Come on, Lil . . . Wake up . . .'

Chapter Seventy-One

The fire was gaining all through the lower floor of the chalet, timbers blazing everywhere and thick black smoke choking the stairway and passages so that Chloe and Dec were running almost blind.

'Which way's outside?' he yelled.

'Try that door,' she replied, her eyes streaming tears.

He crashed it open. 'Fuck it! Some kind of store-room.'

'Try another.'

But it was too late. Ash's footsteps were pounding towards them through the smoky corridors. Dec and Chloe ran into the store-room, clambering through the clutter of junk they could see in the dim moonlight from the window. Dec hid between an old Yamaha snowmobile and a stack of Butane gas cylinders. Chloe ducked behind a pile of packing cases.

Now they were trapped. They could only pray that Ash would run by the door so they could escape from the store-room and make their way outside before the whole place went up in flames. The acrid stench of burning was making it harder and harder to breathe.

In a tiny square of moonlight shining on the floor next to her, Chloe examined the pistol, trying to see what the hell had gone wrong with it. The answer came to her immediately. A piece of grit from the rocky ledge had got stuck in the crook of the gun's hammer, preventing it from snapping forward to hit the firing pin. She picked at it with her fingertip, breaking the nail – but the grit didn't move.

Ash's footsteps came storming down the passage. They stopped at the door.

Chloe held her breath as she scrabbled around for something to pick the blockage from the gun.

The door crashed open and Ash stood silhouetted against the smoke and the flickering orange fire-glow that was spreading through the chalet with every passing second.

'I know you're in there,' he said. 'I can smell you.'

Chloe's fingers clasped something in the shadows. It was an old nail, bent and rusty. As Ash burst into the room, she dug the point of the nail frantically into the crook of the pistol's hammer and felt the trapped piece of grit spring free.

'Give me back the cross,' Ash said, 'and I'll kill you quickly. You have my word.'

Chloe checked the Desert Eagle's magazine and her heart stalled for an instant as she saw it was empty. Then, in her panic, she remembered the breech: there might still be a round in the breech. That was how these weapons worked. She grasped the back of the slide, inched it back and the moonlight glimmered on shiny brass. Her heart began to race again. She still had one shot left.

She closed her eyes.

Make it count, Chloe.

'Give – me – the – CROSS!' Ash roared as he came charging through the smoke, kicking debris out of his way.

There was a rending screech from above as the ceiling gave way and a burning beam came crashing down into the store-room. The wall collapsed. Flames leaped through the broken planking and spread hungrily in all directions. An old armchair burst alight, setting fire to the heap of cardboard boxes next to it. The flames flew up the walls, hugging the contours of the room, spreading everywhere, flaring up into a raging inferno.

Chloe knew that if she and Dec didn't get out of here within the next few seconds, they'd be burned alive.

Or maybe it was already too late. Hot smoke seared her lungs. The taste of death: so this was what it felt like.

But then, through her streaming tears she saw the door at the far end of the room that had been hidden in the shadows before. She leaped to her feet. 'Dec!'

Together they raced for the door. Chloe wrenched it open and gasped as she burst out into the cold night air. The whole front of the chalet was ablaze now.

Ash marched through the burning room, ignoring the flames that licked up his trouser legs.

'Hey, Ash!'

He looked round. Chloe stood in the doorway, her face shining with sweat, her eyes glowing from the firelight. In her hands was the battered, singed case. She held it open for him to see the cross inside. 'You want this? Come and get it.'

Ash bellowed and came charging through the flames.

Chloe snapped the case shut. She tossed it to Dec and pulled out the pistol and fired off her last shot.

The bullet missed Ash by a good five feet. But that was only because she hadn't been aiming at him.

'Burn, fucker,' Chloe said. Then she ran.

Ash heard the impact of the bullet against the tall Butane gas cylinder. He had no time to do anything else but stare at the neat half-inch hole the jacketed hollow point had punched straight through the steel.

The gas hit the flames. And Ash was pulverised by a hot white blast that he never even saw.

Chapter Seventy-Two

The chalet exploded in a gigantic rolling fireball that lit up the night sky. Burning wreckage was catapulted hundreds of feet into the air.

Alex and Joel felt the heat on their faces from halfway up the mountain as the goblins closed in on them. A moment later, a great rumbling shook the ground under their feet. The whole mountain seemed to be trembling.

The goblins looked up in fright and then scattered as the entire face of the towering peak seemed to detach itself and came crashing towards them – millions of tons of snow and ice and rock dislodged by the sound vibrations of the explosion and hurtling downwards in a devastating wave. The fleeing goblins were crushed as if a giant fist had pounded down on top of them.

Alex and Joel ran to avoid the path of the avalanche, but not even a vampire could run that fast.

'Don't let go of my hand!' Alex shouted over the deafening roar.

Then it hit.

Hundreds of yards away across the mountain slope, Gabriel Stone was crouched forlornly by Lillith's prone body when the explosion lit up the sky.

At the same moment, Zachary let out a whoop of joy. Lillith was stirring. She blinked, once, twice, drew in a gasping breath. 'Gabriel, is that you? Zachary?'

'I thought I had lost you, my dearest love.' As Gabriel held her tightly, the ground began to shake and little landslides slithered down around them.

'Look,' Zachary said.

They watched as the avalanche flung its wrath down the mountainside, sweeping away everything before it. It bore down on the burning wreck of the chalet. Blazing timbers shattered and were driven over the edge of the abyss. The cable car went plummeting down the valley and smashed into a thousand pieces among the trees below.

Once the fury of the mountain was spent, all was silent. Just the whistle of the wind and the gentle patter as a fresh snow began to fall.

A large, flat rock suddenly overturned and Alex crawled out from under it, bloodied and bruised, her hair white with snow. She staggered to her feet.

'Joel!' she called out, anxiously scanning the new landscape that the avalanche had left in its wake.

There was no sign of him.

'Joel!' she called again. A healthy vampire could always dig its way out, even from under tons of rock and snow – but not one so close to starvation. She couldn't bear the thought of what could happen to him if he didn't feed very, very soon.

Her heart leaped as she saw a hand sticking up out of the snow. She ran over to it and clasped it. It was as cold as ice. She dropped to her knees and started digging. After a few moments, she was able to haul him out. He wasn't moving as she laid him down on the snow.

Joel opened his eyes. 'I'm starving, Alex,' he said, barely audible over the wind. 'I don't think I have much time left.'

Alex rolled up her sleeve, brought her wrist up to her mouth and bit deep into the veins. Dark blood trickled down her hand and onto the snow.

'Drink from me,' she said to him. 'It'll keep you going a while.'

Joel hesitated, then grasped her hand. She threw back her head in a strange mixture of pain and pleasure as he sucked greedily at the blood from her wrist.

'You'll stay with me now?' she said, and felt that rarest of all things trickle down her cheek: a vampire tear. 'Forever?'

He nodded. Blood on his mouth. 'Forever.'

They embraced, then turned to gaze at the spot where Baxter Burnett's majestic hunting lodge had once stood. Nothing remained except the few smouldering timbers that hadn't been buried in the avalanche.

But there was something else down there. Dark against the snow, two tiny figures, huddled close to one another, one limping, the other carrying a small rectangular object.

'What now?' Dec asked Chloe as they trudged along together. The snow was falling more heavily now, and after the heat of the fire he was shivering with cold. Like Chloe's, his hair was frizzed and scorched from where the explosion had rolled over them as they hurled themselves into the snow.

Chloe looked down at the case in her hand, her father's cross nestled inside. 'We're vampire hunters, aren't we?' she said.

'Sure, I don't know *what* we are exactly,' Dec replied.

Chloe nodded. She clicked the locks shut, rolled the combination wheels, then tossed the case down on the snow and walked away from it.

She and Dec were holding hands as Joel and Alex came down to meet them.

'Are you all right?' Joel asked Dec, noticing the blood that was caked over the kid's face.

'Ah, hardly a scratch, like. I'll do rightly.' Dec grinned through the pain.

'You did good, Dec,' Joel said. 'I'm proud of you.'

Chloe handed Alex the empty gun. 'Ash is dead. You can have this back now.' She jerked her thumb over her shoulder at the case lying on the snow. 'You can have the cross, too, if it's any use to you.'

'I'm sorry,' Alex said. 'I should have trusted you, shouldn't I?'

'It can't be easy.'

'I guess we all had some learning to do,' Alex said. She touched Chloe's arm.

Chloe smiled. 'Does this mean I have a new vampire friend now?'

'You know what?' Dec said. 'I'm beginning to wonder if there aren't worse things than frigging vampires.'

'You got that right,' Alex replied.

'Indeed he did,' said a familiar voice behind them. The four turned to see Gabriel standing there with Lillith and Zachary. Kali was skulking jealously in the background.

'The question is, Gabriel, what were you planning on doing about it?' Alex asked him.

Gabriel shrugged. 'I believe the time may have come to call a truce. Strictly on a temporary basis, you understand.'

'Depends on what you mean by a truce,' Joel said.

'We're gonna go back to Siberia and kick those Übers' asses,' Zachary grunted. 'Could do with some help from you guys.'

'I might not have put it quite that way myself,' Gabriel said. 'But he expresses my intentions accurately enough. Well? What do you say to the notion of our joining forces?'

'We need the humans, Gabriel,' Alex said.

'Why, naturally. Who else can wield the cross for us?'

'Which means you'd have to swear not to lay a finger on them.'

Gabriel looked hurt. 'Was ever a vampire so cruelly misjudged? What do you take me for, Alexandra? A monster?'

'I won't answer that.' Alex turned to Chloe. 'You don't have to do this, you know.'

'We've come this far,' Chloe said.

'Dec?'

Dec shrugged. 'Like I said. There are worse things than vampires.'

Alex looked at Joel. 'What about you?'

'I don't think I have a choice,' Joel said.

'Then we're a unit,' Lillith said.

'A veritable alliance,' Gabriel said with a smile.

The snow was falling more heavily now, rapidly turning into a blizzard.

'So . . . which way is Siberia again?' Dec asked.

Read on for an extract from the first book in the Vampire Federation series, *Uprising*

Prologue

The Scottish Highlands
November 1992

Outside the cottage, the storm had reached its peak. Rain was lashing out of the starless sky, the wind was screaming, the branches of the forest whipped and scraped violently at the windows.

The lights had gone out, and the old place was filled with shadows from flickering candles. The twelve-year-old boy had been cowering at the top of the creaky stairs, listening to the argument between his parents and his grandfather and wishing they'd stop. Wanting to run downstairs and yell at them to quit fighting. Especially as he knew they were fighting about him—

. . . When the thing had come. A creature that looked like a man – but could not have been a man.

The boy had seen it all take place. Watched in speechless horror, peering through the banister rails as the intruder crashed in the door and strode through the hallway. The argument had stopped suddenly. His parents and his grandfather turned and stared. Then the sound of his mother's scream had torn through the roar of the storm.

The creature never even slowed down. It caught his father and his mother by the arms, whipping them off their feet as though they weighed nothing. Like dead leaves. It dashed their heads together with a sound that the boy would never forget. Candles hissed, snuffed out by the blood spray.

Then the thing had dropped the bodies and stepped over them where they lay. Smiling now. Taking its time. And approached his grandfather.

The old man backed away, quaking in fear. Spoke words that the boy could not understand.

The thing laughed. Then it bit. Its teeth closed on the old man's throat and the boy could hear the terrible gurgle as it gorged on his blood.

It was just like the stories. The stories his parents hadn't wanted his grandfather to tell him. The boy shrank away and closed his eyes and wept silently and trembled and prayed.

And then it was over. When he opened his eyes, the killer had gone. The boy ran down the stairs. He gaped at the twisted bodies of his mother and father, then heard the groan from across the room.

The old man was lying on his back, his arms outflung. The boy ran to him, kneeled by his side. Saw the wound in his grandfather's neck. There was no blood. All gone.

Claimed by the creature.

'I'm dying,' his grandfather gasped.

'No!' the boy shouted.

'I'll turn.' The old man's face was deathly pale and he gripped the boy's arms so tightly it hurt. 'You know what to do.'

'No—'

'It has to be done,' the old man whispered. He pointed weakly at the sabre that hung over the fireplace. 'Do it. Do it now, before it's too late.'

The boy was convulsed with tears as he staggered over to the fireplace. His fingers closed on the scabbard of the sabre, and he unhooked the weapon from its mounting. The blade gave a soft zing as he drew it out.

'Hurry,' his grandfather croaked.

The boy pushed the sword back into the scabbard. 'I can't,' he sobbed. 'Please, Granddad. I don't want to.'

His grandfather looked up at him. 'You must, Joel. And when it's done, you have to remember the things I told you.' His life energy was fading fast, and he was struggling to talk. 'You have to find it. Find the cross. It's the only thing they truly fear.'

The cross of Ardaich. The boy remembered. Tears flooded down his face. He closed his eyes.

Then opened them. And saw that his grandfather was dead.

The storm was still raging outside. The boy stood over his grandfather's body and wept.

And then his grandfather's eyes snapped open and looked deep into his. He sat upright. Slowly, his lips rolled back and he snarled.

For a second the boy stood as if mesmerised. Then he started back in alarm as his grandfather began to climb to his feet. Except it wasn't his grandfather any more. The boy knew what he'd become.

Candlelight flashed on the blade as he drew the sabre. He raised it high and sliced with all his strength – the way the old man had taught him. Felt the horrible impact all the way to the hilt as it chopped through his grandfather's neck and took the head clean off.

When it was done, the boy staggered out into the storm. He began to walk through the hammering rain. He walked for miles, numb with shock.

And when the villagers found him the next morning, he couldn't even speak.

Chapter One

Eighteen years later
October 27

Pockets of thick autumnal mist drifted over the waters of the Thames as the big cargo ship cut upriver from the estuary, heading for the wharfs of the Port of London. Smaller vessels seemed to shy out of its way. With its lights poking beams through the gloom, the ship carved its way westwards into the heart of the city.

On the approach to the docks, the beat of a helicopter thudded through the chill evening air.

Eight sailors of mixed Romanian and Czech origin were assembled around the helipad on the forward deck, craning their necks skywards at the approaching aircraft. At their feet lay a row of five steel-reinforced crates, seven feet long, all identical, unmarked, that had been wheeled up from the hold. Most of the crew preferred to keep their distance from them. The strong downdraught from the chopper's rotors tore at the men's clothing and hair as its pilot brought it down to land on the pad.

'Okay, boys, let's get these bastard things off our ship,' the senior crewman yelled over the noise as the chopper's cargo hatch slid open.

'I'd love to know what the hell's inside them,' said one of the Romanians.

'I don't fucking want to know,' someone else replied. 'All I can say is I'm glad to be shot of them.'

There wasn't a man aboard who hadn't felt the sense of unease that had been hanging like a pall over the vessel since they'd left the Romanian port of Constantza. It hadn't been a happy voyage. Five of the hands were sick below decks, suffering from some kind of fever that the ship's medic couldn't identify. The radio kept talking about the major flu pandemic that had much of Europe in its grip – maybe that was it. But some of the guys were sceptical. Flu didn't wake you up in the middle of the night screaming in terror.

The crewmen heaved each crate onto the chopper and then stepped back from the blast as the cargo was strapped into place. The hatch slammed shut, the rotors accelerated to a deafening roar, and the chopper took off.

A handful of the ship's crew remained on deck and watched the aircraft's twinkling lights disappear into the mist that overhung the city skyline. One quickly made the sign of the cross over his chest, and muttered a prayer under his breath. He was a devout Catholic, and his faith was normally the butt of many jokes on board.

Today, though, nobody laughed.

Crowmoor Hall
Near Henley-on-Thames, Oxfordshire

Forty miles away, the gnarled figure of Seymour Finch stepped out of the grand entrance of the manor house. He raised his bald head and peered up at the sky. The stars were out, seeming dead and flat through the ragged holes in

457

the mist that curled around the mansion's gables and clung to the lawns.

Finch couldn't stop grinning to himself, though his big hands were quaking in fear as he nervously, impatiently awaited the arrival of the helicopter. He glanced at his watch.

Soon. Soon.

Eventually he heard the distant beat of approaching rotor blades. He rubbed his hands together. Took out a small radio handset and spoke into it.

'He's coming. He's here.'

Printed by RR Donnelley at Glasgow, UK